The Language
of Good-bye

A Novel by

Maribeth Fischer

PIATKUS

Visit the Piatkus website!

Piatkus publishes a wide range of exciting fiction and non-fiction, including books on health, mind body & spirit, sex, self-help, cookery, biography and the paranormal.

If you want to:
- read descriptions of our popular titles
- buy our books over the internet
- take advantage of our special offers
- enter our monthly competition
- learn more about your favourite Piatkus authors

visit our website at:

www.piatkus.co.uk

Copyright © 2001 by Maribeth Fischer

First published in Great Britain in 2001 by
Judy Piatkus (Publishers) Ltd
5 Windmill Street, London W1T 2JA
email: info@piatkus.co.uk

First published in the United States in 2001
by Penguin Putnam Inc.

The moral right of the author has been asserted

A catalogue record for this book is available from the British Library

ISBN 0 7499 3276 7

Printed and bound in Great Britain by
Mackays of Chatham Ltd, Chatham, Kent

After the difficult birth of her first child, my sister commented to me, "I can't imagine having another child without Mom to help me." I think of that now because I feel similarly when I imagine trying to write another novel without Elsa Hurley. Her generosity with her time, her unfailing encouragement of me, and her belief in this book truly sustained me. I am also indebted to my agent, Candice Fuhrman, not only for introducing me to Elsa, but also for taking a chance on me, and for continuing to believe in *The Language of Good-bye* throughout the arduous process of revision. I feel incredibly lucky to have found an agent so dedicated to her writers. Consequently, I am grateful to Sheri Reynolds for recommending me to Candice to begin with.

I also owe an enormous debt to Laurie Chittenden, my editor at Dutton, who helped me to reimagine the book yet again and whose skillful editing has taught me, in a short time, more than I could have imagined. Thanks, too, to my friends and gifted readers, whose comments were invaluable: Linda Bensen, Robin Farabaugh, Joan Timberlake, and Lisa and Doug Wilson. Thanks, as well, to Marriott Nielsen for always listening; to Rebecca Childers for all of our "writing dates" at City Café, during which I wrote the first draft of *The Language of Good-bye;* to Colin Ives for being my margarita-drinking soul mate; Louis Juhlmann and Frank Balistreri for roofing advice; and to my student Karan Lee, who cooked me countless meals during the last month of working on the revision, when I was too tired to cook for myself.

I want to thank my entire family who has always been supportive, but especially my mother, Mary Jo Balistreri, who taught me long ago to take risks, and who believed that when it came to art, it was okay to "put all my eggs into one basket." My father, John Fischer, has also been wonderfully supportive. I can't begin to count all the newspaper and magazine articles and books about writing that he's sent me over the years. My aunt Jane Glaser has been a huge promoter of my work, and Bob Cieri never once gave up on me even when I had given up on myself. His presence in my life is truly a gift for which I will always feel grateful.

Finally, Murray Carter: you recognized something in me that I didn't know was there; you saw the story before I knew it existed. In many ways, *The Language of Good-bye* is for you and for all you have taught me through your enduring friendship,

And, Sean: in a little over a week from the day I write this, you will become my husband. Your unfailing support and understanding, and your willingness to allow me "my space" are immeasurable. Thank you.

The Language
of Good-bye

"You have betrayed me, Eros.
You have sent me
My true love."
> from "The Reproach,"
> in *The Triumph of Achilles,*
> Louise Gluck

Chapter One

Annie set the phone back into its cradle, the side of her face warm from holding the receiver to her ear. She loved his voice: *Have a great day. Everything will be fine.* She believed him.

The phone rang again and she laughed, assuming it was Will, who'd forgotten to tell her *I love you. I adore you.* But it was a student trying to reach the registrar's office. She transferred the call and felt her mood transfer, too, shifting toward work. Already she was anxious.

She paced slowly back and forth in the narrow office, reviewing the list of student names to make sure she pronounced each one correctly: *Sungae, Shin-pin, Farshad.* For a moment, she faltered and lost track of the name she was reading. What if this were her last semester here? she wondered. What if they didn't hire her back? She couldn't imagine not teaching in a university, or what autumn would be like if she weren't in a classroom. She suspected that it would be similar to the autumn four years ago when she had been told that she would never have children. As the leaves in the Blue Ridge Mountains changed from green to yellow to brown, everything had hurt: TV commercials for the back-to-school sales at Sears, Halloween costumes, the sight of a yellow school bus. Like wanting to have children, teaching had always been a part of who Annie was—only with teaching, it would be the feel of chalk on her fingertips she would miss, the burnt-nut aroma of the vending-machine coffee her students drank, the silence in a classroom just before she returned a graded essay. Annie closed her eyes, ordered herself to stop thinking this way, then returned to the list of student names: *Ahmad, Sacide, Ba.* They *had* to like her, she thought. So much of the next four months hinged on today. The way she walked into the classroom and said *good morning* (Did her voice shake? Did she look her students in the eye when she called the roll?) made a difference. Her clothing mattered: black skirt, white T-shirt and sandals, a bright red scarf looped around her ponytail. Understated without being serious; artistic without being flashy. Nothing too young, nothing too old, nothing pastel—which would make her look too vulnerable.

Outside, the sky was the smudged gray of an empty chalkboard. Burgundy and gold flags—the university's colors—fluttered from the porches of the stone and brick houses across the street, where various administrative offices were located. The banners read, 100 YEARS: AN HONORS UNIVERSITY.

Annie found herself thinking that if she lost her job, grief would fill her like water flooding a boat. There would be nowhere to go; she would capsize and drown.

Annie taught English as a second language to international students. Many of them, sponsored by local churches and charity organizations, had arrived in Richmond from war-devastated countries; others, having emigrated to the United States in hopes of receiving a better education, had settled in Richmond because of the city's renowned Medical College of Virginia, one of the oldest and largest medical schools in the country. They came to Richmond because they had relatives living here—a lot of Koreans, a growing population of Ukrainians—and they came because Richmond was close to Washington, D.C., only a two-hour bus ride if they ever needed to get to their foreign embassies. Annie stood at her desk, holding her coffee mug to her cheek for warmth. Perhaps, she mused, they also came to Richmond because in this city of Civil War battlefields and monuments to Confederate war heroes, her students somehow sensed, as she had lately, that this was a place where people understood better than most how to relinquish loss and rebuild their lives.

She hadn't always known this. How could she have, when she hadn't been marked by her own losses yet, when she couldn't fathom that loss—like so much that mattered—was a choice? Many of her students had chosen to leave their children behind, promising to send for them as soon as possible; they had chosen to fake cheerful good-byes to aging parents knowing that "as soon as possible" would not be soon enough. And now, a word at a time, they were struggling to translate both their histories and their futures into a new language, as if words were all it took to create a new life.

Years ago, when she'd had more confidence, when she hadn't yet received the third set of below-average teaching evaluations and a probationary letter from the dean, Annie, too, had believed that starting over could be this easy: a matter of determination and desire. On the first day of class, when she would ask her students to fill out an index card with their major, their native country, and their hobbies, she used to also ask for a nickname, telling them, "You can be anyone you want here. You can write *Superman* or *Beautiful Woman,* and that's who you'll be." They smiled when she said this, some of them playfully heeding her advice. *Brilliant and Handsome Scholar,* a Chinese student wrote a few autumns ago, and the first time Annie called him this, he stood and bowed as the students laughed.

She smiled, remembering. She had been so comfortable, so sure of herself. "How do you do it?" a colleague once asked. "Your students have some of the highest improvement scores, and yet every time I pass your class room, all I hear is laughter!" The students had trusted her, Annie knew, in part because she had trusted herself.

Abruptly, she turned from the window, another wave of grief pushing against her chest. *Nina, Keyuri, On-Aree.* The foreign names were like exotic foods she tasted only tentatively. *Korkut. Yukihiko . . .*

Please, she whispered silently. *Please let this semester be better.* Not like the last one when the Russians and Turks had argued with her all spring, one young man arrogantly tossing his notebook at her feet and storming out of the room. "You think we have time for games?" he shouted. Or the semester before that when the Asian women had sat with their heads bowed, giggling into their cupped palms whenever she asked them a question; and the boy from Kenya had sat apart, his eyes dark with accusation. An impossible, segregated group and, in the midst of her own separation from her husband of nine years, Annie hadn't had the heart or the energy to salvage either—the marriage or the class.

She glanced at her left hand, at the pale band of skin where for nine years she had worn a wedding ring. She missed wearing it, which surprised her because there were more important things it seemed she *should* miss—the condominium on Grace Street she and Carter had begun to refurbish, their monthly trips to New Jersey to visit their families. She should have missed trying new restaurants with him, ordering too much of everything—even the waitresses laughed as they set plate after plate in front of them. She should have missed *him*. But it was her wedding band. In idle moments she often found herself holding out her hand and staring at her fingers as if seeing them for the first time. She felt like a toddler discovering herself in the mirror and finally making the connection: *This is me.*

But what Annie felt when she stared at her bare ring finger was the opposite: *This isn't me.* Perhaps because she remembered too easily lounging with Carter on the balcony of their hotel in Saint Augustine the second day of their honeymoon. He'd slipped off his ring, shown her where the absence of sun had created its own pale band on his skin. "Like we've been married for years," he said.

"Years? So you'll give me a blender instead of lingerie for our anniversary?" She'd lit a cigarette and squinted into the sun, one hand shading her eyes.

He traced his finger around her tanned kneecap. "I'll never give you a blender if you promise never to give me socks." He traced higher.

She had shivered despite the midsummer heat. Already she wanted him again. "No toaster ovens, either," she laughed, trailing her hand along his leg. "Or gardening books . . ." The kind of gifts their parents gave each other. How easy to joke about these things then: At twenty-three, neither could imagine a time when their love would be any less passionate, when one of them wasn't waking at two a.m. and drowsily rolling toward the other, rising out of sleep into the gentle rhythm of lovemaking before they were fully conscious.

Nine years later, her wedding ring sat in an envelope in a filing cabinet. What had happened? It seemed impossible that love could simply disappear. It should have been something huge that killed love, something cataclysmic. Not the subtle erosion that it had been. Now only fragments remained: the silly cards Carter used to hide in her book bag or under her pillow on her birthday and on Valentine's Day; a snippet of song—"Please come to Boston for the springtime"; that afternoon in Saint Augustine when she glanced at Carter in the fading beach light. She had known Carter since she was four years old, and when she looked at him something quieted in her, like the settling of an old house at night, things shifting, falling into their right place. *My husband,* she had thought, wanting to say that phrase over and over: *my husband, my husband, my husband.*

No wonder then, that when Annie left him last April, Carter had believed (as had her mother and her in-laws and, at times, her closest friend, Lois) that Annie was having some kind of a breakdown, a delayed reaction to the news that she couldn't have children—as if by leaving Carter, she could leave behind her inability to conceive. Some days Annie herself longed to believe that it was this simple. Sobbing in the bathroom before class one morning because of a run in her stockings, crying inconsolably when she spilled coffee on a new blouse or got a speeding ticket or misplaced a paper, she had willed herself to fall apart. A breakdown was so much easier than the truth: She loved someone else, and her love for Will Sullivan called into question whether she'd ever really loved Carter at all. And she didn't know what terrified her more—the possibility that she *hadn't* loved him all these years or the probability that she had loved him and, in the end, it wasn't enough.

Is it worth it to give up so much? she had wanted to ask her foreign students last semester as she watched them struggle over basic grammar exercises. *And for what? A second chance? A hope?* The questions had seemed flimsy and insubstantial to her then—like bright paper kites that would be torn apart with the first strong wind.

The street below her office was filled with the sounds of traffic now: the drone of a bus, the slamming of car doors. The sky was lighter. She'd stood here every morning these past two years, at this same hour, sipping coffee from this same mug. Staring across Franklin Street toward Carter's bookstore, she'd sent memories like smoke flares as if they could save her marriage: circling a roller-skating rink with Carter beneath strobe lights at Matt Wittstock's eighth-grade boy-girl party; standing on Carter's front porch and sobbing the afternoon her older brother died in a car accident; falling into sleep on the narrow bed in Carter's dorm at Boston U. And yet for those last two years, she was also thinking of Will and counting the minutes until eight when finally he would be at work and could phone her.

She had asked Will for the seasons once, meaning simply that she wanted to spend one of each with him—a winter and a spring, a summer, one more autumn. They had met in the fall, and it was winter when she asked—a bright Sunday morning, the air so cold it hurt to breathe. She had told Carter she was going grocery shopping; Will told his wife he would be at the gym. Instead, they were sitting in his car in the deserted parking lot of an Italian restaurant, the heater set to high. She leaned forward, cupping her hands to the vent as if the warmth were a liquid she could capture and drink. He watched her with amusement, and she laughed easily.

"I'm being greedy, aren't I?" she said. "It's only February, and already I'm talking about April. . . ." It was her way of asking, Will you still be here two months from now? In six months? A year? She tested him, began phrases with "in the summer . . ." or "when it gets warmer . . ." or "next Christmas we'll have to . . ." and then she'd scrutinize his face, watch his eyes to see if he glanced away before answering. They both knew that no matter what he said, there were no guarantees.

She set the class roster on her desk and paced again to the window, still holding the names in her mind. *Sacide. Ba. Ahmad.* Already they were becoming familiar. Behind Founders Hall, the sun had risen over the rooftop. Orange light reflected in the windows of the high-rise apartments across the street so that the building seemed on fire.

Keyuri. Shin-pin. It was going to be a gorgeous day. She smiled despite the nervous ache in her stomach. She loved autumn. She always had. Autumn with its new class rosters and syllabi brought order to her life, the hope of a new beginning. She needed that more than ever right now.

Yesterday—Labor Day—from this same window on the third floor of Founders Hall she had watched as the freshmen arrived, their parents' vans and station wagons loaded with computers and stuffed animals, duffel bags crammed with clothes, stereo speakers as large as footlockers. Annie knew the dorms would buzz with talk that first night. Scared that someone would discover they were still virgins, the guys would brag about sexual exploits as they scissored holes into the knees of their new Levi's. They'd share the beer someone's dad had sneaked in, and they'd try not to think about the fact that they already missed their moms' cooking—had they been home, they would have taken out the trash in a minute without being asked. On the next floor, the girls would lie on new pastel-colored sheets, and they'd reinvent themselves for these new friends, changing their names from Beth to Liz, from Kathy to Kate. Annie knew now that leaving behind who you are was not that simple—though sometimes when Will called her Anne instead of Annie she felt like he was speaking to a woman she barely knew.

Again, that sense of loss. She had learned after her second miscarriage that even emptiness has its own weight. She shook her head, as though the sadness were a stray hair fallen across her eyes.

Will had been in the shower when she left for work this morning. When she'd called good-bye from the hallway, he yanked back the shower curtain. "This is what we've come to after three months?" he teased. "No kiss good-bye? No I'll-think-of-you-every-minute-while-I'm-gone? No How-can-I-bear-to-go-eight-hours-without-you?"

"You're wet," she had laughed. "Don't come near me." But already, she was leaning forward to kiss him. Not the quick perfunctory kisses she and Carter had shared the past five or six years, but a kiss that made Annie feel as if a taut rope were pulling through her insides. A kiss she felt in her stomach, in her knees.

Despite her happiness with Will, what she often felt—in the midst of making love with him or teaching a class or standing in line at the supermarket blankly reading the headlines of the *National Enquirer*—was grief. A word whose root meant *heavy* or *burden*. Grief. Annie felt as if she were pushing it around in front of her like the shopping carts the homeless wheeled. All the bundles and rags and scraps of her life, her past.

Until this autumn, she hadn't truly understood that who you are is a matter of who you have been. Her students knew it, though, even the seventeen- and eighteen-year-olds. Learning verb tenses, they would become confused, unable to distinguish past from present. When she wrote an example on the board, "I *knew* him a long time ago," past tense, someone always asked, "But don't you still know him now? How is it possible to *stop knowing* someone once you have met?"

She glanced once more at the class roster, at the names of people from Turkey and Korea, Vietnam, Iran, Russia, Palestine, the Philippines. Annie knew that if a student posed that same question this autumn, she would think of Carter and she would understand her student's confusion. Even if she didn't see Carter for ten or twenty years, she would never say she had stopped knowing him. She would always use the present tense.

Chapter Two

From the second floor of his bookstore, Carter gazed down Franklin Street toward Founders Hall, toward the third floor. He imagined she was in the office already, pacing around in her stocking feet, shoes beneath her desk, practicing her students' names and pausing every few minutes for a sip of coffee. She never slept well before the first day of school, was too unsettled to eat.

He watched the traffic light at Franklin and Harrison change to yellow, then red, then back to green. He hadn't slept last night either. With the start of classes, she'd be nearby, he'd kept thinking. *A block away. One block. Not even a tenth of a mile.* It seemed incomprehensible that she could be so close and that he wouldn't talk to her. Except for the four years they'd attended separate colleges, she had never begun a semester without him. Not even in elementary school at Our Lady of Good Counsel where they were in Sister Michael Steven's first-grade class together.

From the radio he'd turned on below, the faint hiss of a rock song: "Did I tell you I was okay? I lied. I lied." He shut his eyes and took a sip of tea from the inscribed mug Annie had given him a few birthdays ago: WITH BOOKS ONE IS NEVER ALONE. Did anyone really believe this? Did she? He had never been more alone in his life. Thirty-four years old and he didn't have friends or hobbies because he'd never needed them—he'd had the store; he'd had Annie.

And she had had him, and for all these years, it had been enough. And it wasn't that they didn't have their own lives. She kept her maiden name after they married. She had her own career, had gone to her first choice of colleges, no matter that it was three hundred miles from his. He had never asked her to quit smoking—that was something *she* chose to do—and even when he became a vegetarian and stopped eating food containing fat or chemicals, he never cared that she wasn't into it. In fact, he loved taking her out for dessert and watching as she ate something completely decadent. It had made him happy because it made her happy.

They had loved being together, and even now he couldn't believe, *refused* to believe, that he had been wrong about this. They'd still held hands in the grocery store or when they took walks around the neighborhood at night. They liked the same books, the same movies, and they both thought it silly when other couples talked about a "guys' night out" or a "girls' night." Why? they used to wonder, because the times they did go out separately they always felt incomplete: He couldn't catch her eye across a room and know by the look she gave him what she was thinking. He couldn't laugh with her later in bed or the next morning over coffee about something someone had said or done. He couldn't glance up in the midst of a discussion and find her eyes on his and know that no matter who else disagreed with what he was saying, she understood.

At a party once, Annie mentioned that Carter had gone clothes shopping with her, and the women she was talking to acted shocked, as if Annie had told them that Carter liked to dress up in her clothing.

"You're kidding me?"

"Are you serious?"

"I didn't know men like you even existed," one woman teased.

"You're a better man than I am, Carter," one of the husbands said.

"You mean you really don't get bored?" someone else had asked.

"Watching her try on clothes? Hell, no." Annie blushed, but Carter meant it. Always it surprised him that other men didn't enjoy being with their wives as much as he loved being with his.

Even now, if Carter closed his eyes, he could see Annie reaching across the booth at Uncle Lee's, feeding him a cashew with her chopsticks. He could see her turning to him in the shower, her hair a shiny dark rope down her back. Or crawling into bed in the mornings and lifting the pillows, which he'd placed over his head against the assault of sunlight streaming through the east windows. "Good morning, my vampire," she would coo, kissing him on the neck. Later, standing barefoot in the kitchen, drinking coffee and making plans for the day, she'd sometimes interrupt herself midsentence to tell him, "I love you, Carter," then go back to whatever she'd been saying. All of this during those two years with Will. How? he wanted to know. How could she have told Carter she loved him, how could she have *made love* to him while she was loving someone else?

He moved about the room, turning a book so that its spine faced outward, pulling out misarranged novels and replacing them. Light slanted across the shelves, yellowing the wood, highlighting only parts of titles. He played a guessing game as he worked, trying to fill in the blanks of the fractured titles. A book half in and half out of sunlight: *Trying to . . .* He couldn't read the rest. *Trying to survive? Forget? Love?* If he guessed correctly, he told himself, she'd stop by.

He played these games often now: counting cars (fifteen and she'd walk into the store), grocery shopping in alphabetical order (broccoli first, then cereal, eggs, lettuce, yogurt). Passing time, stalling, thinking that if he simply followed some order, his world would make sense again. Like a novel. He wanted a plot he could follow.

He crouched down and pulled out the book, illuminating the hidden word—*smile. Trying to Smile.*

Five before nine. Annie would be walking to class. It was a gorgeous day, an Annie day—chilly and clear, bright sunlight. Carter's eyes burned with tears. He had hoped she would stop by. *I can't start a semester without at least talking to you,* he'd imagined her saying. He'd even dressed for her. The khakis she liked, a shirt she had given him. But she was in class now, calling roll, the names she had practiced.

Starting the semester without him.

He stood at the window, blaming his tears on the harsh morning light. *Maybe she'll stop by after class,* he reassured himself, *or on her way home.* Another game he played so that he could keep moving, working, talking to customers, breathing. *Trying to Smile.* And if she didn't stop by? He'd phone her tonight, as he did most nights. Not to talk—they hadn't spoken since the afternoon he signed the divorce papers in her lawyer's office—but to hear her voice, to reassure himself that she hadn't vanished, that he wasn't going crazy. After everything she had done to him, he loved her.

Chapter Three

Sungae Oh sat alone at her kitchen table, glancing now and then at the clock on the wall near the door. From outside came the whoops and shouts of kids at the bus stop. A group of mothers, some in sweatshirts and jeans, others in suits and heels, congregated in front of the Fitzpatricks' house across the street. Sipping coffee, jostling toddlers on their hips, they shook their heads in dismay: Where had the summer gone? It seemed a silly question to Sungae, another example of why words were unnecessary in this country. Why ask a question that had no answer? Time wasn't like the 747 that had brought her from Korea to America. Time didn't go anywhere. Only people did.

She had lived in the United States for seventeen years without learning to speak English. She shopped at the Korean grocery every Wednesday, attended the Korean Baptist church on Sundays, and spent the afternoons painting memory into oil. She covered huge canvases with Korean landscapes: the *chinhae* cherry blossoms in Seoul Grand Park—a blur of pink, or Pongun temple submerged in early morning mist, or *Changgyong,* the Palace of Bright Rejoicing. The zoo was housed there, an amusement park. Beneath the layers of paint, she'd penciled the outlines of schoolchildren, families, and young couples. And in the top corner of the canvas, the thin charcoal strokes so light they were nearly invisible, she drew a man and a little girl.

Her husband had injured his back four years ago and could only work part-time for the roofing company. Since then Sungae had also worked—at Kayla's Espresso Shop, baking olive bread and French baguettes, too-sweet carrot cake with cream cheese frosting, cappuccino brownies flavored with coffee and Grand Marnier. At fifty-three, she had panicked at the prospect of working, of having to talk to Americans.

She had asked Mrs. Jung from church to teach her some important sentences: "I need a job. I'm very good cook. Many years experience." She'd had her husband visit every bakery and coffee shop in town, then come home and report to her: What kind of breads did they make? What kind of cakes? How big were the cookies? Sometimes she sent him back a second time to buy what she wasn't familiar with, so she could taste it herself: maple walnut scones, tiramisu, Bourbon Street bread pudding. She and Mrs. Jung spent hours translating American recipes into Korean—two middle-aged women paging through a Korean-English dictionary, giggling like schoolgirls when Sungae wrote down two tablespoons of soap, for they knew it wasn't possible to put soap in a recipe for chocolate eclairs. They laughed, too, at the words whose definitions they could not find—*ladyfinger* or *zest*—which meant "excitement," Mrs. Jung said. But how do you add the teaspoon of excitement into the batter for a chocolate cake? There was no *mousse* in her pocket dictionary either, so Sungae read the definition of *mouse* and the two women laughed until they cried. The kitchen smelled of chocolate and nutmeg and buttery breads, and they listened over and over to the same cassette of So-wal Kim's famous love poems sung by Eun Hye Park. Sometimes they sang along: "If you have to leave me, then I will put the beautiful flowers in your way. . . ." Never had Sungae felt as full of confidence as she did those afternoons when, for the first time in her life, she could laugh at her mistakes.

Only at night, when she fell asleep, did these errors return to haunt her. A tablespoon of baking powder instead of a teaspoon became an angel food cake swelling into an enormous woman, pregnant with emptiness. It terrified her how easy it was to ruin the sweetest things: a birthday cake, a marriage, a love.

Her interview at Kayla's had been her eighth. Sungae was convinced that Kayla would treat her as the others had, talking with baby-talk words, their voices pitched high as if she were deaf, refusing to eat the desserts she'd brought as proof of her talent. But Kayla was different. She ate two cookies, a brownie, three bites of a croissant and said, "I'll have to run six miles for this, but you're hired."

Sungae glanced again at the clock on the kitchen wall—7:24. Her throat was dry. It hurt to swallow. Maybe she had the flu. Maybe she should stay home. She touched the back of her hand to her forehead to see if she was warm, but her hands were clammy and freezing. "Keehwan," she called to her husband. *"O-ji-rop-sum-ni-da."* I feel dizzy.

But he only called back from the living room where he was doing his back exercises and watching the *Today* show, "You going to school!"

School. She whispered the word in Korean. *Hak-gyo.* The syllables caught in her throat. What if she got lost and couldn't find her classroom? What if she hadn't heard the dean correctly and she wasn't supposed to be there? But Keehwan had already sent in the tuition, and she had her class schedule here in her pocket: English Composition, Advanced Landscape Painting, Graduate Art Studio.

She stood and set her teacup in the sink. In the glass door of the microwave, she stared at her reflection. *A too-round face,* she thought, *old-woman haircut*—despite the Miss Clairol Auburn Brown Mrs. Kim has rinsed in for her three days earlier. She glanced again at the clock. Seven–twenty-six. The hollering of the kids outside, the mothers' laughing, seemed louder. Where was the bus? she wondered anxiously. She hoped it would come soon; she hoped the mothers would leave. She didn't want Mrs. Fitzpatrick to call hello when she saw Sungae slip out of her house with her canvas shopping bag full of books and painting supplies and a portfolio the size of a screen door.

"Where are you off to so early?" Mrs. Fitzpatrick might say. And what would she think if Sungae answered, somehow pulled from this language she barely knew the words *university* and *going*? What if Mrs.

Fitzpatrick laughed? What if she smiled and asked, "Why? What for?" Even if she said the words kindly, Sungae knew that she would just turn around, throw the new notebooks and pencils and the Korean-English dictionary into the metal trash cans out front, and forget she had ever believed she could be an American, beginning her life over again just because she wanted to. Americans have an average of three spouses and five jobs, and they move seven times in one life, her husband had told her last week, translating what Peter Jennings was saying on *World News Tonight*. Sungae could not imagine it. Moving once had nearly cost her her life.

Which was why she was going to school, to steal this life back like the infant daughter she had left behind in Korea seventeen years ago. For the last two years, whenever Sungae wasn't working at Kayla's or attending church, she had sequestered herself in the garage, which Keehwan had converted into a studio, but she had been unable to paint more than a few strokes. For hours, she would stare at the unfinished canvases stacked three and four deep along the walls, trying to recall what she'd had in mind when she had started, but her memory refused to comply.

Until this past summer, Sungae had believed that she could not finish her paintings because the story she was trying to tell was incomplete. Just like the daytime operas she had been watching for seventeen years. Even when someone died in those stories, the possibility of return remained, a miracle two or five or ten years later. In the soaps, Sungae knew, death was not about the loss of life but about the loss of memory. Forgetting was crucial to plot.

Lately, though, Sungae had begun to wonder if it wasn't the endings that were the problem in her paintings, but the beginnings—for who could say when any story truly began? She had always believed that her own love story with the man who was not her husband started on the day she met Hwang Yi, but maybe the true beginning had occurred years before when she was still a girl accompanying her mother to the tiny shop in *Namdae-mun* market where Hwang would one day work. Perhaps it was the memory of shopping with her mother in his store that had allowed Sungae to feel so comfortable with Hwang that first afternoon when he smiled shyly at her and added an extra handful of rice to her order without charging her. If this was true, no wonder Sungae could not finish her paintings. How do you reach your destination if you do not begin on the right path?

Years ago, Sungae had started watching the daytime operas because the ladies in church told her this was the best way to learn English. She could never concentrate on the words, though. You did not need words to understand who was in love with whom, who would cheat on his wife, who was the adopted daughter given away at birth and come back to find her mother. Words were not necessary in the United States, Sungae had decided. In this country, all you had to do was look at someone to know that he was falling apart inside, that she was scared of losing her job. Americans might smile all the time, just like Erica Kane did on *All My Children* when her mother died, but everyone knew she was going to explode at the funeral. It was the same way Americans always asked, "How are you?" even to a stranger, but never wanted to hear the truth. What was the point of learning a language only to lie?

Because she didn't rely on words, Sungae saw what others did not. And so she wasn't surprised when she heard that Kayla's husband had fallen in love with another woman and moved out. All spring Kayla had been quieter than usual, coming to work in her running clothes and disappearing midmorning for ten- or eleven-mile runs. She came back exhausted, her skin dewy with sweat, her red hair curlier than usual from the humidity.

Months earlier, when Will, Kayla's husband, had come into the shop and Kayla brought him a hazelnut coffee without asking if he would rather have amaretto decaf, Sungae noticed that he started to protest, but then didn't, setting the coffee aside after only a few sips and letting it grow cold. As he stared out the window at the winter sky, Sungae saw in his face a longing to be elsewhere—and for a moment, her heart had lurched in her chest, and it was not December but early August, and she was forty years old, standing outside of Hwang Yi's Market, laughing shyly as he clumsily hung ducks in the shop window. When Will looked up and smiled at her, Sungae glared, then abruptly stormed into the kitchen, slamming cookie sheets onto the metal counters and banging shut the oven door, as if memories, like evil spirits, could be frightened away by noise.

Other times, late at night while she was icing a cooled carrot cake or cleaning a tray of wounded gingerbread men, Sungae would hear Kayla talking on the phone to her husband, her voice bitter, and she would recall that look on Will's face. She felt as if she were watching a suspense movie—the audience knows something horrible is going to happen, and there is nothing they can do to stop it. She had gone with Keehwan to one of those movies only once. Driving home, she had raged at him in Korean, half sobbing, half shouting: "Why? Why would you watch such a thing? Why would you pay the money to see pain and sorrow?"

Another time, in mid-January or February, Will stopped by the cafe to surprise Kayla on his way to work, and Kayla teased him because his tie didn't match his shirt. "Dressing in the dark again?" Kayla said as she moved around the counter to give him a breezy kiss. The next day she went out after lunch and bought him two new ties, both silk, but Sungae knew that Kayla was treating her husband too much like she treated her business, as something that had to be managed instead of loved. Not that this was a reason for Will to have done to Kayla what he did. Sungae knew that the hurt was deeper than anyone could imagine because Kayla didn't cry. Her face looked gray and she lost weight slowly like someone dying, but she never shed a tear.

Sungae wanted to tell Kayla that duty is more powerful than love and that because of this, her husband would return. But she didn't know Kayla well enough. Even after four years, Kayla had never bothered to ask Sungae's real name, still calling her Sarah, the name Sungae used with Americans. Sungae had chosen the name because in the Bible, Sarah was the dutiful wife of Abraham, so loyal that she had allowed him to offer their only son, Isaac, to God as a sacrifice. In her heart, Sungae felt that she had done the same thing with her daughter.

Still, Sungae missed Will. Waiting for Kayla, he used to chat with the waiters and waitresses about their classes and what books they were reading instead of talking about nonsense things like the weather or spring break. And he didn't ask Sungae foolish questions, questions without answers: Where has the time gone? Or, Do you miss Korea?

All summer Sungae wondered where Will had gone when he left Kayla, and if he was happy now, and if he understood yet the truth about happiness—that it was like a beautiful dragon, so enormous and powerful that it could exist only in a legend or a dream. Was this what she had been thinking of last month when she decided to paint *Kyongbokkung,* the Palace of Shining Happiness? She had visited it only once with Hwang, whose name—even after all these years—filled her heart with shame.

She had been unable to paint even a single stroke that afternoon, and she realized then that she was in trouble, trouble just as bad as it had been seventeen years earlier when she'd had the breakdown and found herself—still bleeding and in pain, her breasts swollen with milk—gazing blankly from the window of a 747 while her husband, Keehwan, someone she no longer knew, patted her hand and promised her she would be all right.

Only two things had allowed Sungae to survive once she reached America. The first was Erica Kane on *All My Children,* who had lost her child and her business and the man she had loved and who refused to give up. The second thing was the oil paintings, layer upon layer of color, as if she could bury the whiteness of grief. Canvases as big as refrigerators and colors so bright the paintings looked wet years after Sungae had lugged them to the attic or out to the shed where she kept her unfinished pieces. Not being able to paint again was a warning for Sungae. And so, without thinking twice, she pulled her Korean-English dictionary from the drawer near the phone, called the university, and made an appointment to see someone in the painting department. She chose ten of her best works and slid them carefully into the unused fake-leather portfolio her husband had bought her years before. Two hours later, when she had propped the canvases against the walls of the chairman's office, he drew in his breath sharply, his eyes suddenly moist, and without a word signed the permission slip enabling her to take two graduate painting classes. The only condition he gave was that she learn English as well.

Chapter Four

Annie had once compared walking into her class on the first day of the semester to entering a shopping mall during a sale. Half of the students (at least) would be wearing stiff new Levi's or Guess jeans, Nike running shoes, and JUST DO IT or VIRGINIA IS FOR LOVERS T-shirts. On their desks would be Coke-bottle-shaped pencil cases, notebooks with pictures of Mickey Mouse or Michael Jordan on their glossy covers, Garfield erasers, neon-colored pens. L.L. Bean or Eddie Bauer backpacks lay on the floor beside them; packs of Marlboros protruded from shirt pockets. Iranian and Indian women wore Reeboks beneath their black chadors or gold-threaded saris, and one semester, a turbaned eighteen-year-old Sikh from Bengal wore a Chicago Bulls windbreaker every day to class.

"I'm horrible with names," Annie apologized as she began calling roll, "so *please* tell me if I say yours incorrectly." A few of the students smiled; most just watched her nervously. In some of their countries, for students to correct a teacher about anything, even their own names, would have been considered an insult.

She was sitting on the desk instead of "hiding behind it," which a former professor had once accused her of doing. As she called each name, the students relaxed, gratitude washing over the tense lines of their faces. The Korean woman, Sungae, beamed when Annie said her name. "Really?" she asked. "I am here?" The others laughed in relief, and for a moment, Annie felt her own anxiety lifting away from her like a bright helium-filled balloon. Sungae had spoken the words they were all thinking, Annie included. *I am here?* How many times in these past two months had Annie glanced at Will and thought something similar? She smiled, thinking of his voice on the phone this morning, *Everything will be fine.*

He had been right.

She began the class with an ice breaker. ASK THREE STUDENTS FROM DIFFERENT COUNTRIES TO TELL YOU AN INTERESTING FACT ABOUT THEIR COUNTRY, she wrote on the board. ASK THREE MORE PEOPLE TO NAME THE ONE THING THAT MOST SURPRISED THEM ABOUT THE UNITED STATES.

They moved warily about the room, still wearing their coats, glancing uncertainly at Annie. She remained sitting on the desk, holding the class roster in one hand, her travel mug of coffee in the other, trying to attach the names to faces now. Korkut and Sacide were husband and wife, doctors from Turkey. They had left their seven-year-old son in Ankara with his grandparents for the year. Shin-pin, a tall round-faced girl from China in tight Gap jeans, needed to score well enough on the TOEFL—Test of English as a Foreign Language—to be accepted into a nursing program. If she wasn't accepted, she had already explained to Annie outside the classroom that morning, she would lose her F-1 student visa and be sent home.

The Iranian man, Farshad, had also been waiting for Annie when she arrived. "*You* are the professor?" he had asked. She nodded, and disappointment seeped into his eyes. She had encountered this before: She was too young, they thought. How could she understand—even *begin* to understand—what they had endured? Hurriedly Farshad had tried to tell her that he had just begun his first year of residency as an audiologist in Shīrāz when the war with Iraq began. When he refused to fight, the Jihad had put out the execution order on his life. He and his wife and his then-infant daughter had walked for seven months across the Dasht-e-Kavīr, the Great Salt Desert. "We lived in Greece for one year, and then we moved to Germany for three years," he said. "We saved all of our money to come here." He now delivered pizzas at night and dreamed of becoming a doctor again. "Learning English is like crossing the desert," he told her. "I will learn one grain of sand at a time."

As the students gained confidence, their voices grew louder. Annie moved around the perimeter of the room, eavesdropping on their halting conversations.

"What country you are come from?"

"How long you arrive here?"

Outside, the quad was empty but for a few students lingering outside of the University Commons. She used to meet Will there after classes. A breeze fluttered the row of colored flyers taped to the back wall: an announcement for the Campus Ministry, Corporate Visibility day, ads for part-time jobs.

"Korea is called land of morning calm," she heard Sungae say.

"In my country, Vietnam, if you pass a funeral on the street, you will have good luck."

"Did you know more than twenty kind of roses grow in Iran?"

She smiled and moved on. The Japanese boy was asking, "You do not know who is Astroboy? How about Pokémon?" This was what she loved about teaching English as a Second Language: In a new country, even ordinary details became almost magical. Roses—in Iran! It had probably never occurred to most Americans. They associated Iran with the Iran-Iraq war, the hostage crisis, the shah, Ayatollah Khomeini. By the same token, most Americans probably wouldn't have guessed that Annie's students were surprised not by the freedom in the United States or the opportunities or the technology—but by squirrels, and interstates "so big that some of them have the garden right in middle!"

"Squirrels?" Will asked when she first told him this. *"Squirrels?"*

"They've never seen them before," Annie laughed.

She circled back to the front of the classroom, the students no longer paying attention to her as they chatted with each other. She sat again on the desk, watching them and remembering the afternoon, not long after she met Will, when he phoned her at work to tell her he had just read an article she'd published.

*   *   *

"Oh, God"—she pretended to cringe—"which one? *Why?*" He wasn't an academic; this wasn't his field.

"I was blown away," he had said, ignoring her. "Honestly, I'm not a reader, Anne, but I couldn't put your article down; it's the one about *han tan*. . . . Is that how you say it?"

She nodded, though he couldn't see her. *Han tan* was a Korean term that meant "unrequited resentment." It referred to the accumulation of bitterness and sorrow, passed down from one generation to the next, which social scientists attributed to the Korean people's long history of being oppressed by other nations. Learning a new language, Annie had suggested in her article, seemed to ignite her students' *han tan*: "No matter how great their desire to learn English, a part of them resists, and every new word becomes a betrayal."

"You might as well have been writing about the kids I teach. . . ." Will said. He counseled delinquent teens in the Richmond Boys' Home, an in-house facility outside of the city. "I understand resentment, of course, but that it would be unrequited, like *love* . . . I'm not even sure yet what that means." He laughed at himself. "I probably sound like a babbling idiot. It's just that reading your article, I felt as if all these buzzers and bells and warning lights were going off inside of me and I needed to slow way down, just *think* about this." He paused. "I haven't felt this energized by something I've read in ages."

She remembered setting down her pen and leaning back, her face and neck suddenly warm. "I'm glad," she said quietly. "And flattered."

"You sound surprised."

"I guess I am."

"Why?" Before she could answer, he said, "It's funny: I assumed that you published—you almost have to if you teach in the university, don't you? But you never mentioned anything, so I figured it wasn't a big deal."

I didn't think it was, she had wanted to tell him, *until right now,* and for some unexplainable reason, she had been dangerously close to tears. She thought of the first time she published: she'd been ecstatic, and Carter had taken her out to dinner to celebrate. He even ordered extra copies of the journal for the store and had sent copies to her parents and his parents and his sister, Molly. . . . And yet for all of that, his enthusiasm, even then, hadn't really been enough, maybe because with Carter, her successes somehow always became *his* or *theirs*—never solely *hers*. It made sense, of course: He read all the drafts of her articles and had been proofreading her writing since high school. He had always been proud of her, had always encouraged her. It seemed unfair to blame him, then, if he was no longer surprised, *blown away,* by Annie's writing the way Will had been and still was.

"Anyway, I just finished reading it," Will was saying. "I had to call."

She had taken the article home with her that night and reread it in bed, trying to see what he had seen. *I had to call.*

"What are you reading that for?" Carter had asked.

"Someone mentioned it," she told him. "I was curious to see what I'd said." She glanced at him uncertainly. "It's actually pretty good. It makes me want to write again."

"Of course, it's good," Carter told her. "How many times have I said that?"

Sitting in the classroom, the students mingling easily now, Annie also remembered the first birthday she had celebrated with Will—her thirtieth—when they'd been together for nearly six months.

He gave her silk lounging pajamas from Victoria's Secret. They were pale green, her favorite color. "I thought maybe you could say you bought them for yourself," he said.

A skein of sadness unfurled inside of her. "I sleep in sweats and T-shirts," she said quietly. "I don't—I've never had anything like these . . ." She glanced at him shyly. "I've never even been in Victoria's Secret. . . . They're beautiful."

"But?" He raised his brows. "You want me return them and buy you a pair of sweats, don't you?"

"No! Absolutely not." She clutched the silky fabric against her chest as if he might try to take it from her, and they both laughed. "It's just . . . I won't be able to wear these with you," she said. "And I don't want to wear them with Carter."

"You know what I pictured when I saw them? You, in the mornings when you didn't have an early class, wearing these, drinking your tenth cup of coffee, and working on an article or grading your students' essays. I wanted to give you something totally frivolous and luxurious. I wanted you to feel special even when I wasn't there to tell you."

She had felt special. He made her feel beautiful, and for the first time in her life, she found herself buying expensive moisturizers and lipsticks, and shopping for clothes. Waiting in the checkout line at the Safeway, feeling giddy and girlish, she perused articles in *Marie Claire* or *Glamour* with titles like WHAT'S SEXY? MEN TELL ALL! or WHAT REALLY MAKES A MAN FALL IN LOVE—AND STAY THAT WAY! She started walking up the three flights of stairs to her office instead of taking the elevator: She wanted to stay in shape for him.

Even arguing with Will was novel. The first time they fought was the night he told her he'd voted Republican in the last election. "I've never been friends with one of you," she had teased. "I'm afraid this might be the end for us." Her friends and colleagues, like most people who had gravitated to universities, were mostly liberal Democrats.

Will hadn't been amused. "So you're prejudiced about something you haven't tried to understand?" he said, and she laughed.

"I haven't tried to understand the Ku Klux Klan either, but—"

"Whoa. You're *not* suggesting they're comparable?"

"I don't know," she pretended to muse. "Do you own a gun?"

"Oh, that's right; *all* Republicans own guns, don't they?" His voice deepened with anger. "No, I don't own a gun, Anne, but does everyone have the right? You bet." They'd been in the Stonewall Café, a bar near campus.

"I hope you're joking," Annie said. It was no longer funny. "You, of all people—you *see* what guns are doing to kids."

"Come on. That 'you of all people' crap isn't an argument, Anne." He took a sip of his Guinness. "And even if it was, this isn't about *my* beliefs or even what *I* see. It's about our Constitution."

"It's a piece of paper. It can be changed."

"Oh, like a marriage license." He shrugged. "You get tired of the rules and just alter them, right?"

She jerked away from him, more surprised than hurt. A group of women in ragged jeans and pierced eyebrows a few bar stools away were smoking cigarettes, and for the first time in years Annie wanted one. She tried to recall the last time she'd argued with Carter about anything beyond books—and couldn't. Was that really what people wanted? she wondered, remembering how she and Carter had bragged—to each other mostly, but to others as well—that they were "soul mates," and they had actually believed this, when in truth, they had no idea whether it was true or not because *no one,* themselves included, had ever challenged this belief or any others.

Will nudged her shoulder lightly. "I'm sorry," he said. "That last remark was uncalled for."

She nodded. "But you were right."

Still, it wasn't the arguments or the passion or his appreciation of her writing that made her fall in love with Will. It was their car rides, something so ordinary, which that first winter was how they often spent their one night a week together. Driving back roads Annie hadn't even known about, places he'd cycled, the route the Tour du Pont took through the city when the race still existed. He'd point out local landmarks to her on the way out of town: the Tredegar Ironworks, or the Third Street diner—Did she know the building was originally a Confederate hospital? Away from the city, the silhouettes of leafless trees and wood-rail fences stood out against the moonlit sky. He'd slow the car suddenly, point to the pair of glittering eyes watching from the side of the road. "A fox. They're beautiful animals."

"How could you tell it was one?" she'd ask, and he would explain that foxes had longer legs than most animals their size, that they didn't gallop so much as they pranced. He knew about things she'd never noticed, never cared about.

The first time they kissed was along one of those roads. He pulled over onto a bluff overlooking Richmond. "Do you want to get out for a minute? The stars are incredible." He left the car running, music thrumming through the closed doors, and leaned against the passenger window, she leaning back against him, his arm crossed over her neck.

With his free arm, he traced the constellations against the sky. Orion the Hunter. The Big Dipper. "Do you see the North Star?" he asked.

"People used to believe that it was the opening in the sky that linked different worlds; it was how heroes moved from one world to another." His breath was warm against the side of her face. She shivered against him. The last time she had stargazed was on a camping trip years before with her dad. Her brother had still been alive.

And then Will's hand was on her neck, his fingers cold, as he gently turned her face toward his and kissed her. The thump of the bass from inside the car pulsed in her legs and breasts as she swiveled in his arms. And then she felt his hands tugging at her hair, his tongue in her mouth, on her neck, back to her mouth. He groaned softly and pulled away finally, still holding her against his chest, his heart beating so hard it seemed to be hammering inside her.

The students were clustered into groups, talking about supermarkets now, laughing. "Entire aisle, whole block long, just for the pet food!" someone said.

"Even American dogs have special diet food," Yukihiko laughed.

"What about whole aisle just for the toilet paper?" Korkut asked. "Why Americans think it is so important?" Shin-pin giggled. Korkut's wife said something to him in Turkish—a scolding maybe. He blushed and shrugged his shoulders.

Farshad grinned and glanced at Annie. Sungae, who had already returned to her desk, nodded. "Good job," she said.

They took a short break halfway through the class. When they returned, Annie had written the phrase TELLING LINES in white chalk on the dark blackboard. The first lesson of the semester. In any story, the "telling line" was the single sentence forecasting what the rest of the narrative would be about. Annie had asked the students to write one for their lives.

Sungae sighed and glanced at the other students to see if they understood what Annie had just said. Most of them were bent over their desks, already writing. Inside Sungae, plates and glasses shattered; a bowl of *manduguk* was smashed against the wall; broth splattered the nearby windowpane, then the floor. Sungae felt her stomach heave with nausea and sorrow. *Why?* she wondered. Why did Annie want Sungae to remember what had been buried in her heart all those years ago? Why was she encouraging the students to write about their pasts?

"No understand," Sungae said to herself. She raised her hand, feeling like a fool. Maybe she was too old to learn English, after all. How could such a young teacher understand this, though? "We foreign students," she blurted out nervously before Annie called on her. "We make many mistake."

"Mistakes are okay," Annie said. "I'm not grading this."

Grade? Sungae wondered. How could this woman believe that something as inconsequential as a grade would matter? What difference could a grade make to someone who had lost her life seventeen years ago as she sat in a tiny kitchen overlooking the Han River on the southern side of Seoul? *Shik-mo-gil,* Arbor Day: *Whatever you plant, will flourish.* That night, April 5, Sungae watched her husband argue with Hwang, the man for whom she had shamed herself and her family. She no longer recalled the words Keehwan used that night, but she never forgot their sound, her husband's voice like shattering glass, the jagged shards of grief and rage exploding into her skin.

After that, how could a grade mean anything? Especially a grade given by a woman too young to know that it was not her right to dismiss another's mistakes, no matter how inconsequential. Mistakes were like the ghosts of long-dead ancestors. They always needed to be appeased. They always needed to be remembered. Always. If you forgot, they lingered forlornly in your dreams and haunted your afternoons.

What Sungae wanted wasn't permission to make mistakes—she wanted rules to avoid them. Rules for which verb tense to use when you speak of a future that is already over; rules about when to put *a* before a noun, when to put *the;* rules about how to use commas in such a way that you never have to end the sentence you are writing, the sentence that sums up your life. But this skinny woman, this American with her white teeth and eager eyes, wanted Sungae to believe that mistakes were okay. Sungae shook her head. If mistakes were okay she wouldn't be in this country, in this class, in this life that had been thrust over her head like a dress that didn't fit.

Twenty more minutes of class, Annie thought as she glanced again at the index cards she had asked the students to fill out. Light spilled on the blue-black hair of the Asian women: Shin-pin, On-Aree, Keyuri. The three of them sat in the second row, backs straight, heads bowed forward over their desks. In front of them, Sungae was writing, bent close to the paper, a woman so tiny her feet didn't reach the floor. Annie wondered what her story was, but suspected she'd never know—unlike eighteen-year-old Ahmad, who sat in the back of the room wearing a suit and tie, and who had seen his best friend killed by Israeli soldiers and had already stated this fact three times on his index card in three different sentences—once when he was supposed to be writing what his major was: "I am premed because I want to be a doctor because I saw my best friend killed by Israeli soldiers and could not help"; once when he was supposed to be jotting down how long he'd been in the United States: "I come here after I see my friend shot down by Israeli soldiers"; and once when he was supposed to name his home country: "I live in Palestine until Israeli soldier kill . . ." as if he yearned to write the memory out of himself. As if by translating it to another language he could empty it of its pain. Unlike him, Sungae Oh had listed only the most basic facts of her life—address, date of birth, height and weight, as if there were nothing more to her than this.

"You think Vietnam a war, you forget it is my country," Ba had written on his card. A sallow-skinned man in his late twenties, a dark scar along one side of his face. He was staring defiantly out the window and seeing, most likely, not a sunlit university courtyard in Richmond, Virginia, but a grass-roofed house in a tiny village in the Mekong Delta. Rice paddies everywhere so that the narrow dirt roads seemed more like floating piers. Pale green. Americans did not know that this was the color of the new rice in the spring, Ba was thinking, that everything seemed to reflect that green, even the sky, even his mother's skin as she stood at the stove in the early mornings stirring a pot of *xoi dau phong*.

Farshad was paging through his Persian-English dictionary again. For most of the second half of the class, he'd sat with his well-muscled arms folded across his chest like a bouncer in an after-hours club, nodding solemnly when Annie spoke, smiling at her jokes, scowling at anyone who dared to rustle a paper or whisper while she was talking. "My protector," she thought now as he began writing again. Already she was imagining how she would characterize him to Will.

On Farshad's desk lay an assortment of pencils and erasers, a ruler, a bottle of correction fluid. Every few seconds he would pause to cover over with Wite-Out what he had just written. Annie wondered what his telling line was and why he was having so much trouble with it. She imagined he was remembering the desert: white sand indistinguishable from white sky as if the world had lost its dimension. She imagined, too, that when he finally handed her his paper, it would be so textured with the tiny blobs of Wite-Out that it would be like reading Braille, the truth of what he wanted to say not in the actual words but in the raised pattern of his mistakes.

Carter had taught Annie about "telling lines" thirteen years ago, when he was an English major at Boston University. She was an education major at Rutgers and was visiting him for the weekend. All afternoon, they made love in his single bed, drinking White Russians, she chain-smoking, the two of them drunkenly trying to cite the telling lines of their favorite books—*The Razor's Edge, The Odyssey, Sophie's Choice*. The day had dismantled into laughter as they argued playfully, listing telling lines for TV shows, cartoons, then people they knew: their parents, former high school teachers, his best friend. Finally, each other. Twelve years later, when Annie walked out on their marriage, she had remembered that afternoon, remembered the taste of Kahlúa and Virginia Slims cigarettes, the Irish Spring soap and beer smell of his flannel sheets, Peter Frampton singing on the radio, "Whatever will be will be, the future's not ours to see," and she was stricken with grief because back then neither of them could have imagined a "telling line" for their own stories that didn't include each other. If she chose one now, though, it would be, "I fell in love with Will." The plot of her life irrevocably altered in six words.

Outside the high classroom windows, the campus filled with students let out early from their first classes or lingering in the sunshine. Annie watched them for a moment, listening to the ticking of the clock in the classroom, the shuffle of paper, the scratch of pencils.

When she glanced back at the students, Sungae was gazing at her unhappily.

"This not teaching," Sungae said mournfully. "You not teaching us rules. Foreign student need rules."

A few of the students looked up anxiously from their papers.

"Writing isn't only grammar rules, Sungae."

Sungae. Not Sarah. Not even Sun-gay, which was how most Americans incorrectly pronounced her name. Sungae felt something tear inside her. She wished she could like this woman, this Annie, who pronounced her name as it was meant to be said. *Sungae.* Like *Soongee.* Instead she asked, "Why? Why not only the grammar rules?"

Before Annie could answer, Farshad jumped in, telling Sungae, "It is not our right to question teacher, we are mere students."

But in exasperation, her dark eyes brimming, Sungae told him, "Sentences belong to *me.* They not for others!" This was why she had not wanted to come to school; this was why, for seventeen years, she had never attempted to learn English. She did not need it, had been fine without it, could not bear the thought that after all this time, the memories she had fought to leave behind in that apartment overlooking the Han River would suddenly show up here, in America.

Why are you doing this to us? She wanted to say to Annie. All these years she had been protected. All these years she had believed—hoped—that if she never learned the English words for what had happened, it could not haunt her in America as it had in Korea. If she never knew the words, she would not be pained when she overheard another woman say the word *daughter,* she would not feel her heart fall from her chest like a bird falling from the sky every time she heard a man tell a woman she was beautiful. If she never learned those words, she would not be reminded that Hwang Yi had once said them to her, had once stood in the entranceway of his store and confessed that his hands shook whenever Sungae came into his shop, that he wanted to talk to her and know her name, that he thought she was beautiful. Sungae was forty years old then; she was married to a good man. But no one had ever spoken such words to her and so she had revealed to the store owner her name. Her voice shook when she whispered it. Already she sensed that she would one day give this man so much more than words.

Now, Sungae was starting to hate Annie. Two hours with this American who had her own secrets and Sungae not only had the words for what had happened to her all those years ago in Korea, but she had somehow linked those words into a chain and now her story, her "telling line," was here in front of her, plain as day, right on the first page of her English Composition notebook.

"Why?" Sungae asked her. "Why you teach us sorrowful sentence today? So beautiful outside. Why you want us remember our life?"

As if it were something you could forget, Annie thought. And yet wasn't this what she had tried to do the first time she met Will in secret, the first time she lied to Carter in order to be with him?

She and Will had been meeting for coffee for nearly two months by then, always in the Student Commons—as if to convince themselves that this was no big deal. The first time she met him at night, they went to a bar on the north side of Richmond, a bar neither of them would have ventured into had they not needed to hide. Cheap mirrors surrounded by red chili pepper Christmas lights, and thirty-year-old sports trophies on dusty glass shelves. Staring at herself and Will in the mirror over the bar, she had felt she was watching two strangers, actors on a movie screen. She had laughed a lot that night, her cheeks flushed, and at one point when he leaned close, she caught a glimpse of her eyes and saw in them a desire that hadn't been there for a long time.

Abruptly, she had shifted away from him. Already she felt like a fool. "I can't do this," she said softly.

"*This?*"

She glanced at him, angry suddenly, though she wasn't sure why. At herself for being here to begin with? Or for being here and then backing out? Or at him, for being so cavalier? "You seem so comfortable with this," she accused him, "and maybe you are, but . . ." She fiddled with the straw in her Diet Coke. "I lied to be here, and I'm not good at it, and I'm not sure I want to be." She wanted to smile, to be as nonchalant as he was, but the corners of her mouth gave her away.

"You're suggesting I am good at it?"

She shook her head. "I didn't mean that. Or maybe I did, I don't know. I'm not sure what I think right now."

"Anne, I like you," he said, "and I *am* comfortable with you. You're fun and smart and easy to talk to." He paused. "It sounds like you're blaming me, though."

She nodded, afraid that if she said anything, she'd start crying.

He stared into his beer, his fingertips circling the rim of the glass. "I don't know what to say. Do you want to leave?"

She shook her head. The word *no* reverberated in her chest.

"Look," he said, "Whatever you need or want out of this is fine, okay? I'm dead serious. I like talking to you and spending time with you, and if that's as far as *this* goes, so be it."

"But what do *you* want? Is this something you just *do*?"

Hurt flashed across his eyes, and for a moment he didn't answer.

"I didn't mean that," she apologized.

"Maybe you did, Anne; maybe we're both trying to push each other away a little bit." He glanced around the bar. "I didn't exactly bring you to the classiest place for our first date." He attempted to smile, though his eyes remained sad. "Isn't that what *this* was supposed to be?"

"It's not the bar, Will. I guess I'm just trying to understand . . ."

"What? That I'm attracted to you? That I think about you constantly? That meeting you for coffee has been the highlight of my week for the past two months? Yes, okay? But I'm not a kid, Anne—" His voice broke. "If all I wanted was a casual affair . . ." He glanced at her. "It's not, okay? I'm risking my marriage and my daughter's happiness and I'm not proud of that, Anne, and I'm not sure I understand what I'm doing here any more than you do. I only know that it's where I wanted to be."

Her eyes puddled with tears. "I'm sorry," she said again.

"Don't be." He handed her a bar napkin to wipe her eyes. "This whole thing is terrifying. Just the fact that we're here."

The students were still watching Annie expectantly, waiting for her to reassure Sungae. Patiently, Annie said, "If you don't want to write a sentence about yourself, it's okay, Sungae. You can write about any-thing."

"Anything?"

"Maybe a telling line about Korea?"

Korea? Her country split in half like her life? Sungae closed her eyes and shook her head. *A-ni-yo.* No.

"What about someone you know?" Annie coaxed. "A friend?" A tiny wave of fear rose in her chest. *Not already,* she thought, *not on the first day. Please don't let this woman be a problem.* But Sungae seemed so frightened, still wearing her coat and sitting as close as possible to the door.

Who did she know? Sungae was wondering. Who were her friends? The women at the church? She shook her head again. Those women didn't know her any more than she knew them. Her husband, Kee-hwan? He didn't realize that when she rubbed his shoulders at night or fixed him *miyuk kuk,* the special birthday soup made of seaweed to represent the long life she hoped he would have, her actions weren't born of love but gratitude. Not because he had stayed when she be-trayed him, but because when Keehwan pushed her gently up the steps of the 747 that warm February morning seventeen years ago, he had helped her *kibun,* her spirit, to die, which was all she wanted once Hwang had dropped her off at the maternity hospital, saying only, "I will phone your husband, Sungae, like we promised."

Ever since that time, Keehwan had never asked her if she still thought of Hwang. He never spoke of that final year in Korea, he never regarded January 31, her daughter's birthday, any differently than he did any other day of the year; he hadn't even raised his eye-brows the first time she made *manduguk,* the spicy meatball soup he had flung across her lover's kitchen that April evening in Seoul. So how could she say she knew him, this man she had lived with for nearly forty years?

But Annie was waiting.

"Okay," Sungae relented. "I write about somebody. Good job." She would write a telling line for Erica Kane on *All My Children.* As she began, trying to explain in one sentence how a woman could be so hurt that she would give up her daughter for adoption and try to stab the one man who loved her, Sungae watched Annie from the corner of her eye. Annie was sitting on her desk and gazing forlornly out the window, and it occurred to Sungae then that Annie's telling line—whatever it was—was just as sorrowful as Sungae's.

Chapter Five

Will understood, as he hadn't until meeting Anne, that nothing disappears. Lies, like water, can evaporate, but both eventually return in another form. In the punishment of rain; in the silence of snow.

He had never intended to lie to Anne about his past infidelities. But that first night in the seedy deserted bar when she asked him, "Is this something you just *do*, Will?" he had panicked at the possibility of losing her. It shocked him, how cold his hands were, how his heart faltered, how he didn't want to say or do anything that might scare her away. How he wished he had never been unfaithful before, and how he was willing to lie if that would keep Anne in his life for half an hour longer.

A few weeks after that night in the bar, driving through the early rush-hour traffic on the way back from the Holiday Inn, where they had made love for the first time, she told him, "I've never checked into a hotel without Carter."

"I know," he answered. "Me either—without Kayla."

She glanced at him, and for the first time in an hour, he saw her relax. "Really?" she asked.

"Really." And for a second, it had almost seemed true. The words shook him, though. With the others he had been honest. What did it mean that he couldn't be truthful with Anne?

As with the others, he never hinted that he would leave Kayla, because he had never imagined a day when he actually would. Always, he spoke well of his wife: her great taste in clothing, her knowledge of antiques. He bragged about how she ran six, seven miles a day; how she had a fantastic voice—pale and southern, but strong, too, so that you knew she didn't take shit from anyone. Talking to her on the phone late one night during his sophomore year in college, he realized he wanted to hear that voice for the rest of his life. Sometimes he thought he still did.

His cat, Ethan, gazed at him from the kitchen windowsill. "Don't look at me like that," Will said out loud. "You miss her, too." His wife of twelve years. His best friend for twenty. Ethan only squinted and yawned, and despite himself, Will smiled. He turned up the CD he'd put on earlier, Van Morrison singing Irish ballads with the Chieftains: "But the sea is wide and I can't swim over . . . and neither have I wings to fly . . ." Home early, making pizza dough, wailing along with the music, Will felt like a college kid again.

He could no longer imagine his life without Anne—her students' papers scattered across the kitchen table, her white cotton underpants lying on the floor by the side of the bed where she'd tossed them, her books everywhere (a row of them on top of the TV, on the windowsill in the den, and in the two full-length bookcases in the oversize kitchen). When they made love, her eyes turned from hazel to green and her hair, dark as oil, splashed over his eyes and nose and mouth. He felt as if he were drowning in her, and he didn't fight it.

But other times, finding a smudge of her lipstick on a coffee mug or watching from the bedroom window as she walked toward the university, he would regard her almost as he would a stranger, wondering who she was and how she had ended up in his life. It terrified him, the sense that beneath his love for her, beneath the passion, he was angry— angrier than he'd been since the afternoon twenty-four years earlier when his mother died after a yearlong fight with ovarian cancer. *Her life wasn't supposed to turn out this way,* he had railed then to the God he barely believed in. Everyone probably said this, he had realized, except sometimes, goddamn it, it was supposed to be true. His mother had been determined and positive, and they had caught the cancer early, and even the doctors had believed that she would be one of the lucky ones. So what the hell happened? Twenty-four years after she died and still, whenever he mentioned his mother's death—even to strangers— he always told people, "It didn't make sense."

And now, loving Anne. It seemed incomprehensible in a similar way. Again, it made no sense to Will, only now it was his own life that hadn't turned out as he had always imagined it would. Who was he? At forty-one, all his notions of who he was, of what he believed, were called into question. And what was he doing here, living in a graduate student apartment without his daughter?

Countless times, he had tried to retrace his and Anne's relationship, to find that single moment where, rather than thinking of saying good-bye to Anne, he had started thinking instead about leaving Kayla. But if there had been any such point, it was at the very beginning. That first night, sitting in the Angel's Grotto beneath the chili pepper Christmas lights, when she glanced up from her soda, her eyes glittery with tears, and asked him, "But what do *you* want?" and he panicked at the thought of losing her.

How, then, could he have admitted the truth to her? The truth that there had been others? *It's different with you,* he might have said. *I'm falling in love with you.* It was true that night in the Angel's Grotto. He had been in love with her ever since the first time they met for coffee; for days afterward, he couldn't stop imagining all the conversations he wanted to have with her. Still, to have said even this would have been yet another lie because he had loved and at times, had been *in love,* with the others as well.

Why, then, had he uprooted his life for Anne? he wondered as he moved about the kitchen of the second-floor apartment they now shared, retrieving flour, sugar, and olive oil from the cabinets over the stove. He yanked open the refrigerator, grabbed a packet of yeast, then shut the door firmly so that he was face-to-face with his daughter's drawings. "I miss you, Dad." A stick figure with tears. Another picture of him on his bike. "Love Brooke." Her *r*s and *e*s backwards. It was how his life felt lately. Sometimes he thought that if he could just cry, he'd be okay with all of this, but he hadn't been able to, not once. *You don't have the right to cry,* he told himself furiously.

He glanced about the Matisse-bright kitchen—red and white checked linoleum, blue table, yellow-green bananas in a white bowl—as if the answer to his leaving Kayla were here, hidden beneath the clutter of newspapers and old magazines on the table, or packed in one of Anne's boxes lining the far wall, each one neatly labeled with black marker: DISHES, SWEATERS, PHOTOS/KNICKKNACKS, GLASSWARE. Her handwriting was usually so messy even she couldn't decipher it. The too-careful script on the boxes touched him.

His own packing had been a guilty tossing of possessions into boxes. Cycling gear, CDs, a quilt his mother had made, coffee mugs—all jumbled together, and when one box was done, he'd start another, packing till it was full. He hadn't wanted to think about what he should or shouldn't take, or to consider what he was abandoning. He had tried to pack only what he knew Kayla would never want, but even in this he had failed. A few days after he picked up the last of his things, she had phoned, her voice skidding out of control with sadness: "You didn't want the portrait?" she asked. It was of Brooke. She'd commissioned it for Father's Day the year before, and he'd wanted it more than anything, had reached to lift it from its nail half a dozen times. But he couldn't bear the idea of Kayla coming home to the empty space on the bedroom wall.

The Chieftains CD clicked off, and the room stretched into silence. He added yeast to the lukewarm water, leaned over the bowl to inhale the rich odor. The huge west-facing windows were yellow with sunlight. Streamers of it trailed to the floor and transformed Ethan's white fur into blond. He left the yeast, giving it a chance to ferment before he would add the flour, and moved across the room to Anne's bookshelves. A habit now. He often found himself here, reading the titles of novels while waiting for coffee to brew or pasta to cook. Each title a line of poetry: *Fugitive Pieces, The Age of Grief, Skating in the Dark, The Book of Laughter and Forgetting.* He believed that every book held a fragment of her life, specific pages, paragraphs, sentences she had lingered over. He imagined her reading *The Age of Grief* during the inconsolable weeks following her miscarriage; or reading *Roadsong,* about a family who moves to Alaska, during her second summer in Richmond, the year they'd had the heat wave. Her and Carter's apartment had had no air conditioner. She said she had drifted from one café to the next, reading, drinking too many iced teas, eating too many croissants. "We probably passed each other in Kayla's shop a dozen times," she said, though neither really believed this because how could they have looked at each other and *not* recognized their own future?

Sometimes he retrieved a book from the shelf, found sentences she had underlined: "Time is a blind guide." "A heart is something that can't be saved for very long." Other books held inscriptions: "Happy 26th, Annie Roonie. Love, Dad." He tried to picture her at twenty-six and saw the pale Alice-in-Wonderland headband she'd once worn in a photo, a sleeveless blouse, the thin brown line of her arms.

There were other books: dictionaries in French and Russian, *The Encyclopedia of Scientific Facts, A Natural History of the Senses.* He learned that humans breathe twenty-three thousand times a day, that jazz music makes plants grow more quickly, that rock music causes them to die, that patients in hospital rooms that are painted yellow require more painkillers.

Despite everything, he was looking forward to tonight. Anne loved his pizza, was like a kid about junk food, maybe because Carter had been such a health nut. She was easy to love, he thought and, for a second, despite all of his self-doubt and self-hate and worry, he felt unexplainably, inappropriately happy—happy for no reason at all, happy the way he'd been at sixteen riding around in his '65 MG.

This, *this* was the reason he'd left Kayla, he told himself, *this* was why he couldn't imagine being without Anne anymore. She had brought *this* into his life—this pure uncomplicated happiness and sudden giddiness, this joy for no reason. He added cornmeal to the pizza dough with a dramatic flourish. When he and Anne were first lovers, it had seemed so harmless to want to give each other these simple pleasures: He'd bring her a slice of pizza at work, a bowl of homemade spaghetti; at night, she'd drive a half hour out of her way to meet him for five or ten minutes in the parking lot of the Dunkin' Donuts near his school. They'd hold hands, tell each other about their day, kiss like teenagers. If he was late, he'd see her car from the rise on Papermill Road, the interior light illuminating her as she propped a book on the steering wheel or balanced a student paper on a folder, pen in hand.

He added more flour to the yeast and stirred with a long wooden spoon until it was easier to use his hands. Brooke's favorite part, he thought, as he dug his fingers into the spongy mess and began kneading. Ethan was asleep now, sunlight shimmering through the leaves of the maple and casting dappled shadows on the checked linoleum. A breeze riffled one of the drawings on the fridge, and he remembered Kayla standing in the spill of kitchen light the night he left her. A breeze then, too. Papers rustling on the fridge. Or last New Year's, staring at the paper cup blowing across the empty parking lot of the Burger King near campus where he'd met Anne for half an hour, desperate to see her. He hadn't had a good excuse to get out, and Kayla had seemed suspicious, and he'd practically bitten her head off. *Jesus, Kayla, can I take goddamn breath without giving you a reason why?*

Anne asked if he'd made any resolutions, and he'd told her that he didn't believe in resolutions so much as he believed in trying to be a better person. He'd meant it and always had, but that afternoon, saying it to her, he'd wanted to weep because it sounded so false. He was lying to everyone in his life who mattered—*including Anne*. Before the new year was out he would leave Kayla, would walk out while she stood at the sink scrubbing an already-clean cookie sheet, her curly hair defying a ponytail, her back so straight with pride it hurt to look at her.

"I hope your little affair is worth it," Kayla had sobbed. "I hope it's worth all the pain you're causing, all the damage."

That night he had believed it was, but sometimes he wasn't so sure.

Earlier he'd bought wine, flowers, and a box of cherry Pop-Tarts because as he and Anne lay in bed last night talking about her classes and the kids he was working with at the Richmond Boys' Home and *squir-*

rels, for God's sake, Anne had told him that whenever she was sick or upset, her mom would bring her hot tea and warm Pop-Tarts.

He punched the dough a few times, watched with satisfaction as it rose back up. She'd thrown up that morning—he had heard her in the bathroom—though half an hour later, she was sitting calmly at the kitchen table, glancing over her syllabus, her dark hair still damp from the shower.

"You okay?" he said, pouring hot coffee into her mug. She had smiled and nodded, seemingly at peace, but he saw how haunted her eyes were. He remembered that look from the first time they had made love in the ninth-floor suite of the Holiday Inn on a shimmering March afternoon. Though there was plenty of passion that first time, there wasn't much joy. They had clung to each other like survivors of a catastrophe, and he had asked her then, too, "Are you okay?" She had nodded, but she didn't say a word, and he understood that she couldn't, that if she said yes it would be a lie and if she told the truth it would hurt him.

He put the pizza in the oven and checked the clock. Almost five. She should have been home by now. He knew her schedule, knew what rooms her classes were in. He used to watch her from the Student Commons as she hurried across the courtyard from the Business Building where she taught an afternoon class. Her arms loaded with folders, a leather book satchel hanging from her shoulder, her hair held back from her face with a silk scarf. Now and then one of her students had walked with her, sometimes a group of them. It pained him to remember this and then to think of her as she'd been this morning, scrutinizing herself in the mirror, worrying over that syllabus. Last night, he took her car to fill it with gas and found it reeking of cigarette smoke, though she said she had quit years ago.

He shook his head, tired of his own thoughts, and checked the clock again, anxious for her to come home. *I love her,* he thought, running a sponge over the countertop, brushing the flour into the sink. *I love her.*

Chapter Six

On Monument Avenue a woman in Nike running shorts and curly auburn hair sprinted with the rush-hour traffic, racing with cars from one intersection to the next, slowing only when she passed whichever one she'd determined to beat. At the corner of Harrison, she slowed finally to a jog, then a walk. She'd run six miles already and needed to return home, but her legs felt strong. The orange sun was smeared across the sky like a color in her daughter's finger paintings, and the scent of burning charcoal from backyard grills and fire escape hibachis wafted through the streets. Rock music drifted out of open windows and passing cars. Songs from twenty years ago, when she and Will were in college. For the first time since he had confessed that he was in love with Anne Helverson, the pungent smell of late summer chrysanthemums growing along the avenue wasn't making Kayla nauseated. All summer she had grown pregnant with grief. She couldn't eat or sleep, though constantly she was exhausted, her moods erratic. Two nights ago, she was so angry she'd had to force herself to sit in the bathroom for five minutes so that she wouldn't tear up the photocopied flyer Brooke had brought home from day camp announcing a father-daughter picnic.

An hour later, though, some idiotic line from a sitcom had reminded her of the affair and, though she wouldn't allow herself to cry, the sadness spiraled through her. What hurt most was remembering all those nights, two years' worth, when Will would give Brooke a bath or read *101 Dalmatians* to her, then come sit with Kayla on the couch, one hand on her knee, or lean against the kitchen counter and offer to dry while she did the dishes. They'd talk about their days, laugh at something silly Brooke had said. He would casually mention going out with one of his cycling friends, and she would encourage him, glad that he was getting out and relaxing more.

After he told her of the affair, she recalled those nights and knew that nothing about them had been casual, except for maybe the sex with Anne, which Will insisted on calling love. She'd laughed at him when he told her this. "And you call yourself a psychologist?" she spat. "Get a clue, Will. What you *think* you feel for that woman has nothing to do with love." But it hurt now to recall how he'd sometimes pretended to waver about going out—"I don't know, Kay, I'm kind of beat"—and how she, like some dumb wife from a fifties' TV show, would urge him, saying, "Oh, go on, sweetie. Once you get out, you'll be fine." How all along it must have been rehearsed and planned—maybe days before—the where and when of meeting *her,* how the two of them would fuck for hours in some cheap cliché of a hotel room, how he'd come home, *reeking* of that woman and then dare to touch Kayla's arm or her shoulder, dare to ask how *her* night had gone. And how all this time, Kayla had loved him.

"Did you have fun?" she would ask when he came home, her voice groggy with sleep. Propping herself up on one elbow in the bed, watching as he undressed in the diagonal sliver of light from the hallway. He removed his watch and set it on the dresser, emptied his pockets, always in the same order: wallet, car keys, loose change. "Where did you go? What did you talk about?" But she couldn't remember his answer. That bothered her now. He had accused her for years of never listening to him, and now she wondered what else Will had told her that she'd never heard.

Some nights, though, after Will moved out, there was neither anger nor grief, which was odd. It reminded Kayla of how she felt when they traveled to Vermont, where Will's father lived. The first few days there, one of them would inevitably stop talking midsentence, hold up a finger, and say "Listen" or "Wait—do you hear that?" And there would be nothing. No traffic or music or people laughing. No slamming car doors or roar of airplanes overhead. No sound at all. Just a silence so rare you held your breath, afraid you might scare it away.

On nights like those, curled on the couch reading the classifieds—people selling antique bookcases and credenzas, Depression-era glass, Art Deco reading lamps—Kayla would glance around the living room and she would imagine redecorating the house, and something would bloom tentatively inside of her. She hadn't lived alone since she was twenty-two, the year she moved in with Will. She thought about finding some antique frames for the black-and-white photos she'd taken years ago of the Boston Marathon and hanging them over the sink; she thought about replacing the kitchen table with something round, smaller—maybe a wrought-iron porch set from the 1920s. She would paint it white and ask Sarah if one of the women in her church could sew some cushions for her. She thought about living alone and she would take a deep breath and think maybe, just maybe, she could be happy again, not like she was all those years with Will, but like she was in the years before him.

Chapter Seven

Anne was sitting Indian-style on the couch, student papers on one knee, a mug of cappuccino balanced on the sofa arm. She had come home after her first day of classes triumphant, had tossed her satchel on the couch, peeled off her sandals, unhooked her earrings with her free hand, and said quietly, "It was a good day." Five simple words, and suddenly she was the Anne of two autumns ago—fierce and beautiful, refusing to let anything get her down.

Will wanted to remember this moment—her pacing around the apartment in his oversize polo shirt, describing her classes: the frightened Korean woman, the Iranian doctor, the young boy from Palestine. Another habit now, this stashing away of memories inside himself the way people had once hidden away emergency supplies, saving them for a time of need, the time he still sometimes foresaw when she would return to Carter and he would return to Kayla, and they'd realize it had all been a mistake.

He was most afraid of losing the details: the precise enunciation of her words, consonants held like notes in music—not *Richmon', Virginia,* as most said it, but *Rich-mond.* The way, in the midst of grading a paper, she would pause, pen poised midair, to gaze outside. He wondered what she thought of in those moments. Once he stood just beyond the window of the Commons and waved to her, but she stared through him. It both scared and angered him, all the things Anne saw and thought that he would never be a part of.

Tonight, it was the sound of her students' names he wanted to hold on to, the syllables foreign and poetic, the pink flush on her face and neck as she spoke about her day.

The autumn he'd first met her, he had bought a small marbled-cover notebook to record these thoughts. It made him feel silly, almost ashamed, like some furtive high school kid keeping a diary about a girl he had a crush on. He'd bought it after meeting her for coffee one day and watching her walk into Founders Hall. She wore a short gray skirt, and he saw she had a beautiful walk and he wanted to freeze that moment when something so goddamned simple could make him happy. The campus bookstore was right there, and without thinking about what he was doing or why, he'd bought the book and a pen and was abruptly back in the Student Commons, sipping from a cup of coffee and staring at the blank white paper, wanting to write pages and pages—how he felt, how she looked, the way she smiled, the smell of autumn in the air—but he didn't know how to begin.

After twenty minutes, he scribbled the date, then a single sentence: "She wore a gray skirt today." It was enough. Two years later, he could read those words and see again the protest of orange leaves against blue sky, the mournful bleat of traffic on Franklin Avenue, the pleats of her skirt brushing the backs of her knees as she walked. How she turned at the entrance to Founders Hall. A quick pivot left, hair splashing sky. She waved to him, and something in him had soared.

There were other entries: "Drowning," he scrawled the afternoon they first made love. On another page, "Leaves in her hair." The words evoked the Saturday afternoon last fall when they met in Pocahontas State Park and hiked the trails, dry leaves crunching underfoot. If he turned to that page in his notebook, he would feel the scratchy wool of the picnic blanket on his arms as he lay on his back, staring up at her as she sat beside him. A pair of bald eagles had soared over the tree line, and he followed them with his eyes, telling her, "Richmond's the only city in the U.S. that has a pair of bald eagles nesting in the city limits."

He loved the way she looked at him and said, "You better never stop telling me these things." When she kissed him, he could smell the suntan lotion on her arms, taste the sandwich she had eaten for lunch. Yellow leaves still clung to the uppermost branches of the hickory trees, and every time the wind gusted, they spiraled downward, flashing in the bright light. Later, as they were packing up their things to go, Anne had stood and shyly pulled her cable-knit sweater over her head to shake it free of leaves. Her hair was wild with static electricity, her arms prickled with goose bumps in her thin T-shirt. As he tried to untangle the leaves from her thick dark hair, she bowed her head forward patiently like a little girl at the hairdresser's.

"You look like one of my students," she said now. She didn't look up from the paper she was reading. He was stretched out on the floor across the room as if on a picnic blanket. Legs crossed, drinking a beer, surfing through the TV channels.

He smiled. She could read him so well, picking up signals he wasn't even aware of sending. "What? I look like I'm head over heels in love with my beautiful English teacher?"

"No, homesick." She continued to focus on the paper, though she wasn't reading it and hadn't been for the past twenty minutes. As soon as he'd paused on that sitcom about the three little girls living with their single father, something crashed inside her like a kite nose-diving into the ground. But she continued to stare at the words in front of her, though none of them made sense, and she continued to sip her coffee calmly. The affair had taught her this: how to lie. And it hadn't simply been a matter of lying to Carter: lying about where she was; lying about what she was doing and feeling and thinking; lying when she couldn't make love to him; lying when she could and thought instead of Will.

She had lied to Will, too, because she never let him know what the lying had cost her. Weeks of not sleeping and barely eating, weeks of being unable to concentrate on her classes, weeks of working late simply because it was easier than going home and living another kind of lie. For weeks, and then months, she didn't tell Will about her unsatisfactory student evaluations, about the warning letter from the dean.

She didn't tell him that his love had splintered open her life, that if she had never met him, she would have gone on as she always had, and she would have been okay.

The window was pale green with twilight and pollen. Will's reading glasses on the coffee table, the August *Velo News,* the tie he'd worn to work draped over the back of his leather reading chair. She had lied to him again, not in what she said—*It was a good day. The students seemed enthusiastic*—but in all that she hadn't said. Already, the students were expecting too much. She couldn't guarantee that Shin-pin would improve her TOEFL score enough, that the sentences Sungae had to write wouldn't be just as sorrowful as the one she'd written today, that Farshad would find what he wanted in this new life. But she didn't want Will to worry, didn't want him to stay with her out of pity or misguided guilt.

Every night, she listened as he talked to his daughter on the phone. The conversations were stilted, awkward. Will asked questions—about Brooke's kindergarten teacher and her best friend and her dolls, about what she had eaten for lunch and if she'd brushed her teeth and what was ten plus five and how did you spell *stop* and did she know how much he missed her? After he hung up, he never wanted to talk about her with Annie, never wanted to talk, period. He'd sit in his desk chair, rocking gently, the springs creaking. Except once. Once, when he walked down the long hallway to the kitchen, where Annie was finishing up the dishes. He hugged her from behind and whispered into her neck, "She's always been shy on the phone. She sounds so scared." Annie had thought that Will was the one who sounded frightened.

He was watching a cereal commercial now, two people falling in love over oat bran. Two years ago, she would have scoffed at this, but now she knew better. She knew that sometimes love truly did happen this simply—you walked across a gravel parking lot with a man you'd only just met, your husband and his wife a few steps ahead, and suddenly, you don't want to go home to the eleven o'clock news and the new novel you started reading that morning. Instead, you want to linger in the humid air with this man who is not your husband. You want to talk to him and smile and make him laugh. And all because of something as innocuous as oat bran, or a shared preference for white wine instead of red. One link and then a chain.

She glanced up. He was grinning at her. Despite herself, she grinned in return. "Now what?"

"You haven't read one word on that paper, Anne."

"How do you know?"

"You haven't made a mark or turned a page in—" he glanced at his watch, "twenty-two minutes."

She laughed and set down the paper. "Call your daughter, Will, and then let's go for a walk."

"A walk is not quite what I had in mind." He pushed himself up from the floor, groaning because his legs ached from bicycling earlier. It had been a good ride, twenty-two miles with hills. As always he thought of her when he rode, in part, because when he was still with Kayla, he and Anne often met on weekends for a quick cappuccino at the end of one of his rides. Two years from now, or ten, would he be able to ride without conjuring images of her, of how when he rounded the curve at Lake Avenue she would be sitting at one of the window tables? Her head bowed over a cup of coffee and a book at the Daily Grind. She would be reading *The English Patient*. She had read it three times, saving lines to quote to him: "If I gave you my life you would drop it wouldn't you?" "How does this happen? To fall in love and be disassembled?" "There is a whirlwind in Southern Morocco, the aajej, against which the fellahin defend themselves with knives."

He massaged the back of his neck with one hand; he really was sore today. The hills. Anne cocked one eyebrow and half smiled. "A walk may be all you can handle, my love."

"Is that a challenge?" He leaned over her, his hands on the couch-back behind her, his forehead resting against hers. She felt something give way inside her. Not a day went by that she didn't want to wrap her arms around his neck and tell him, "Don't leave me, Will," but she never had. She had taught international students long enough to know that sometimes leaving what you loved most—your home, your family, your country—wasn't always the best choice or even the right choice;

it was simply the only choice you were capable of making . . . or maybe the only one you could live with.

"Are you going to call her?" Annie cupped her hand to the side of Will's face, his jaw scratchy with stubble. She touched the tiny scar on his chin where he'd cut himself as a child. For a moment, he rested his head in her palm, eyes closed as if too weary to answer. When she and Carter were still in high school, they had learned in health class that an average human head weighs eleven pounds. That afternoon, they took turns lying on the fluffy white mat in his parents' bathroom as they tried to gauge the weight of their skulls on the bathroom scale. She teased him for years that she was smarter: her head weighed eleven pounds, his ten and a half. He insisted it was her hair that had made the difference.

"Hey," Will said. He was staring at her, his eyes dark with the questions she knew he wouldn't ask.

"Sorry." She smiled, combing his graying hair from his face.

"I'll phone her in a little while," he said. "I'm not up for another battle with Kayla right now." He pulled away, trying unsuccessfully to conceal a yawn.

"You really are tired," she said. They both were, neither of them sleeping well, still trying to accustom themselves to sharing the same bed for an entire night, to how sleeping with someone—just sleep—was more intimate than sex.

The phone rang and, yawning again, Will answered it. She watched him, this man for whom she'd turned her life upside-down. "Hello?" he said for a second time. The crank caller again. Sometimes they'd go a week without a call and then get one every night, sometimes more than once. "Hello?"

He hung up without saying another word. He stared at the unused fireplace, filled with crumpled newspaper to keep Ethan out. In his refusal to look at her, Annie saw the accusation he no longer needed to put into words: The caller was Carter. She didn't understand why he believed this, why it was the first conclusion he had jumped to, when she, who knew Carter better than anyone, couldn't fathom it. Carter with his morals and his rules.

She glanced at Will, resisting the urge to tease him out of his funk. "Whoever it is hangs up on me, too," she'd told him a dozen times. "Why would Carter bother?"

He didn't look at her. "People do things all the time that make no sense."

She cocked one eyebrow at him. "People, yes, but not Carter." Carter saved all of his bills and bank statements in individual files; he removed the dust jackets from the books he read so as not to ruin them; he only ate apples or pears that were peeled because of all the insecticides farmers used.

Annie knew Carter as well as she knew herself, their histories so inextricably entangled that at times she and Carter had seemed like the same person. She had no memory of a life without him. His family had moved into the house behind hers the summer she turned four. He became her playmate and later her best friend; he was the first boy she hated and the first boy she kissed. In high school, they were each other's confidants, sitting on Annie's front porch for hours, talking about their respective boyfriends or girlfriends or sometimes saying nothing as they stared off across the neighborhood, at its well-manicured lawns and tract houses. It wasn't until their junior year, when both of them were dateless and decided to go to their prom together, that they found themselves kissing on the dance floor halfway through the evening while Bob Seger sang "We've Got Tonight."

Annie took a too-big gulp of cappuccino. Her hand shook as she returned the mug to its saucer. Will glanced up. "Believe me," she said, "Carter has better things to do with his nights than phone us and hang up."

"Does he, Anne?" Will spoke quietly, no anger, no irritation. It unsettled her, the suggestion in his tone that he understood something about Carter that she didn't. As if Carter were one of his teens, confused and desperate and scared.

She sighed. "Don't pity him, okay, Will?"

"Come on, Anne." He stroked Ethan's belly with his foot as he leaned against the mantel, his empty beer bottle in one hand. "You were married to him for nine years, and he lets go just like that?" He snapped his fingers. "That anger's got to go somewhere." He'd seen it day in, day out for twenty-some years, what happened when you tried to bury your rage.

She got up from the sofa, balancing her empty coffee mug on her pizza plate. She flashed him a look of disgust. "Of course, it would never occur to you that maybe it's Kayla, would it? What about her anger?"

He shook his head. "Believe me, I wish it was Kayla, but her anger's detonating all over the place. She doesn't need to make crank calls."

"Neither does Carter, Will, and your pity is condescending."

She disappeared down the hallway, Ethan waddling after her, thinking he was going to get some food. "Let's just change the subject," she called, and he smiled again, loving even this, her fierce loyalty to Carter.

He swallowed the last of his beer, picked up his pizza plate and followed her to the kitchen. He wanted her to understand, but he didn't know how to say it so that the words wouldn't sound trite or corny: He imagined that he could understand Carter, could understand that being connected to where Anne was—even if only by phone for half a minute or fifteen seconds—was somehow reassuring to him. Will wanted to explain that it wasn't pity he felt for her ex-husband, but guilt, and that sometimes when he looked into the eyes of the boys he worked with, he thought of Carter. Not when the boys were angry or defiant or wanted revenge, but when, standing in his office after a reprimand, they didn't say anything at all. He wanted to tell her that when someone is suffering the greatest pain, he often responds not with yelling or with tears but with silence. And sometimes all he needs is just a response. One word. A hello, so that he knows he's not alone. He wanted to tell her that if the time ever came when she was not in his life, he would do the same thing. He'd call just to hear her voice.

He set his plate on the counter next to the sink and traced his index finger along the curve of her forearm. She glared at him and kept washing, but he didn't move—just stood there, touching her skin, inhaling her, reluctant to let her go.

Chapter Eight

Carter paced about the spotless two-bedroom condominium he and Annie had shared for six of their nine years of marriage, the pizza he had ordered untouched, still in its box on the kitchen table. He wondered how the day had gone for her and hoped that it had gone well, that the students had loved her, that she'd been relaxed and easy with them. She was a teacher at heart, had always been a teacher. Even when they were four years old and he was drawing a picture of a tree, she had calmly placed her hand over his green crayon and told him, "No, Carter, like this," and showed him how to make a weeping willow weep.

Each time an international student had entered his bookstore this morning, he had wanted to ask, Who is your teacher? But if they told him it was Annie, what could he have done except ask how she had looked, if she still had dark circles beneath her eyes, if her voice had been shaky when she read their names? So he didn't ask at all. He helped them find the books they needed, and he wished them luck. Then he watched with a sinking heart as they walked back along Harrison Street toward the university. Later, though, when the guy who delivered his pizza spoke with a foreign accent, Carter couldn't help but ask, "Are you a student at the university?"

"First day today," the guy said. "I am learning the English."

Carter had wanted to weep. Annie was the only one who taught beginning-level English. So this guy was probably her student. He'd been in the same room with her that morning. "Is Ms. Helverson your instructor?" he asked.

"You know her?"

I know her well, Carter had thought. *I know that she loves the ocean in the winter and that the afternoon she found out she couldn't have a child, she drove to the beach alone and walked in the wind until she was numb. I know how beautiful she looked at her sophomore Homecoming dance, and I know that she's scared of losing her job right now, and that no matter what her evaluations say, she doesn't deserve for that to happen because, during all those years she was struggling with hormone injections and surgeries, she never once missed a class.*

"She's an excellent instructor," he told the guy. "She'll teach you a lot." He had glanced again at the student, who was close to his own age, and wondered what he'd done before coming to the United States—a lawyer? Doctor? Annie used to tell him stories about her students all the time. He imagined this man had survived something devastating. He would understand, Carter thought, and for a moment, he had been tempted to confide in him: *She was my wife.*

All night, he'd tried to read, tried to watch TV, tried to sleep, but he couldn't do any of it. She was always there—in a song on the radio, Sarah McLachlan singing, "I will remember you"; in the pale stain on the arm of the sofa where she'd once spilled tea; in a commercial for Lady Schick razors; in anything and everything. It didn't matter that the day she left, he'd taken the photographs of her from the bedroom, bought a new shower curtain and towels—navy—grilled himself a Harvest Burger and heated a no-cholesterol apple pie for dessert, vowing as he swallowed the last bite that he wouldn't become one of those ex-husbands who refused to let go. But despite his good intentions, he had been noticing these past few weeks as he walked home from work how the sky was growing steadily darker and the air chillier; he had seen a line of geese stitched across the purple clouds, and he had sensed that his resolve was taking flight, abandoning him, just as, six months ago, Annie had.

After dinner then, he would clean the house as if expecting a guest, he would pace the hardwood floors and listen to old Peter Frampton albums, he would pick up a volume of Thoreau, wanting more than anything to learn how to live alone. When none of these things helped, though, when despair and grief settled over him completely, he'd walk to the phone and dial the number where she lived now, hoping that she would answer. He could tell by the tone of her *hello*—a single word, two syllables—if she was okay or not. And that's all he wanted, to know that she was fine so that he could believe that he, too, would one day be all right.

There were days when he didn't know who he was without her. In fact, on the nights when Will answered the phone, Carter would lie in bed, wide-awake, and it would occur to him that when she left, he'd gone with her. And the person who remained behind, staring at the ceiling and watching the play of shadows on the wall and listening to the leaky faucet dripping into the tub—that person was just an outline, like the chalk silhouette policemen draw around the bodies of people who have been killed.

Chapter Nine

Animals can detect people's moods through their smells, the odor of happiness distinct from contentment, from grief, from fear. As she stood in the kitchen, drying the last of the pizza dishes, Annie wondered if Ethan sensed her sadness. What is the odor of sorrow? It frightened her to think that maybe Carter was making those phone calls, that her betrayal had hurt him *that* much. And if it wasn't him? Sometimes she feared this, too. It seemed impossible that Carter could be completely gone from her life.

But what had she expected? That they would remain friends? That it was even possible? *Yes.* The word stung. She told herself that she didn't want Carter in her life, that there was no place for him—or maybe it was that there *should* have been no place for him and still there was. She stood for a moment, eyes closed against the tears that threatened so often lately. Was it wrong to miss him, selfish to hope that he might one day be a part of her life again?

Will was in the bathroom. She paused, listening for the sound of the running faucet. Bowed over the sink, brushing his teeth or lifting warm water to his face in the bowl of his hands or maybe simply staring into the mirror and wishing he were with Kayla and Brooke. "I love you," she'd said to him a minute ago, standing in the bathroom doorway like a scared little girl. She wanted the words to compensate for all that he had lost.

Wearily Annie wiped down the counter. She folded the dishcloth over the sink's edge. Her bureau was shoved next to the refrigerator; plants were everywhere. A stack of clay pots sat on the newspaper-covered table, a ten-pound bag of potting soil leaning against one chair. Beneath the ironing board were Will's cycling shoes and a bowl of water for Ethan. In front of the single window that overlooked the narrow yard, Will's bike. A Cannondale. She knew nothing of bikes, only that this was a good one. She remembered the first time he'd challenged her to lift it.

"Why?" she had laughed. "I can't lift your bike!"

"No, go ahead, one hand."

She had been stunned by its weightlessness. Lighter than her book bag. No more than twenty pounds.

"You know what we need?" Will now stood in the doorway. He was wearing boxers patterned with sunflowers, a white T-shirt.

I need you, she thought. *I need you to need me.* But she smiled quizzically and cocked her head toward the clutter and said, "Closets?"

"Well, that, too, but I was thinking candles. Do we have any?"

She turned to him, eyebrows raised in question. He held her for a minute, kissed her forehead.

I love this woman, he thought with the sudden fierceness he'd often felt watching Brooke as she struggled to tie her shoes, or as she played alone in her room, making her animals talk to one another. In those moments, Will's love for his daughter was so strong it catapulted into fear. When she was born he understood for the first time that he was capable of murder, that he would kill anyone who tried to harm her.

"Will?" Annie pulled back so that she could search his eyes.

He glanced away, unwilling to answer her silent questions. He wanted to tell her that no, he wasn't okay. No, things might not be all right. But no—*God, no*—his feelings for her hadn't changed, hadn't lessened, not one bit. And yes, sometimes he did regret leaving Kayla. Sometimes he *was* homesick and not only for Brooke. He missed Kayla's damp running shorts and sports bra and T-shirt hanging over the side of the tub when he awoke each morning, her runner's log open on the kitchen table, her neat girlish handwriting: "6.4 miles—felt strong!" He missed her throaty laugh when she got drunk, and he missed the twenty-dollar wrought-iron couches and Mission-style rocking chairs that she'd drag home from a flea market or garage sale and leave sitting in the driveway. These were stupid, inconsequential things, he knew, that meant nothing next to the fact that Anne made him laugh, Anne made him want to get out and cycle even when he was dead tired, Anne made him feel that what he did mattered—his work, his cycling, his phone calls to Brooke each night. "You're a good father." Constantly she reminded him of this. "When she's older, she'll remember. How you called her every night, how you never missed a single day."

"You know what I'd love?" he said to her now.

"I'm afraid to ask."

"No, not that."

"Since when?"

They were both smiling.

"Really," he said. "I just want to light some candles and lie in bed, and maybe put the radio on and talk to you, touch that beautiful face of yours. Can we do that or do you have a lot of work?"

She did, but she'd do it later or she'd get up early. All she wanted was to be with him.

Ten minutes later, leaning against the extra pillows he had stolen from the couch, she watched the reddish-orange glow from the candles flicker unevenly over his face. The dimly lit room, the whisper of traffic from the street out front, reminded her of the nights she had sat in his car after work or he had sat in her car during lunch—a car, because it was the only place they could safely be alone.

Will held one finger to his lips. "Listen."

Outside their open window, the leaves of the enormous maple rustled in the breeze like silk dresses. On the stereo Frank Sinatra was singing "Fly Me to the Moon."

"What?" Annie said. "You want to fly to the moon with me? On this bed?" She pictured the three of them, she and Will, with Ethan curled at their feet, sailing over Richmond like visitors from another world, like a scene from *Bedknobs and Broomsticks,* the black sky sequined with stars and the tiny neighborhood with its dark row of houses.

"Oh, I want to fly to the moon all right." He leaned over and kissed her collarbone. She smelled the toothpaste he'd used, his shampoo. Like a high school boy on a date. She scooted down on the pillow, looped her arm around his neck, pulled him closer.

Will nuzzled her throat. "We'll have to make jack-o'-lanterns soon," he whispered, working his arm underneath her T-shirt, lightly circling her breasts with his hand. He loved that he could make her come some nights just by caressing her nipples; he loved her hunger for him, the way she shouted into the pillow during orgasm and, later, hid behind her hair, embarrassed to have been so loud.

Jack-o'-lanterns. It was only September. Was this his way of asking for the seasons? she wondered, and felt a tug of fear. What had made him unsure tonight?

She stared at the wavering shadows, which made the walls seem to billow like the sides of a tent. When he touched her like this, she felt as if she were disappearing. There was only sensation—his fingers, her breast. "I've never made a jack-o'-lantern," she said.

"You're kidding!"

In the orange light, he looked younger than his forty-one years and, for a second, Annie imagined she had known him at nineteen when he was a sophomore at the University of Colorado, or at twenty-nine, the year he married Kayla. They'd gone camping on their honeymoon, somewhere in the Rocky Mountains, a place she had never been. She imagined that in the dim glow of a fire, lying close, Kayla had watched him as Annie did now, believing they would always be together. Annie closed her eyes, returned to Will's fingers, her breast. "We always painted our pumpkins," she said.

"Paint?" His fingers stopped moving, though he kept his hand on her skin, his warmth seeping through her. "How'd you make pumpkin pie?"

Annie laughed and pulled him forward for a kiss. Another thing she loved about him: She loved the fact that, like her, he had a sweet tooth, something she and Carter had never shared. She loved that sometimes when she came home, the kitchen would be a shambles of baking utensils and mixing bowls as he scanned a recipe book, making pineapple upside-down cake or oatmeal raisin cookies, or once, tiramisu, a runny, goopy disaster which they poured into glasses and drank like milkshakes, ladyfingers and all. Even as she was thinking this, though, another part of her ached. None of this was a reason to have left a marriage.

He was watching her, his tongue darting back and forth in his mouth. He didn't know that he did this whenever he was teasing or playing a trick on her. "So was it canned? Your pumpkin pie?"

"This matters?" She laughed again. Of course, it did. It was details that created a life.

He furrowed his brows. "If we don't sort these issues out right from the beginning . . ."

"Ah, so pie is an *issue* now?"

He started to protest, but she held her hand over his lips. "No, don't say a word. It's one of the reasons I love you."

"What?" He laughed, the sound escaping through her fingers.

"Somewhere in the wonderful, cholesterol-laden heart of yours, you really believe pie is worth arguing over."

He pulled her hand from his mouth. "Absolutely."

Annie shook her head, watching him. If only, she thought. If only it were this simple. If only we were kids in our twenties and this was our first love. If only we could believe that the biggest problems we'd encounter would be as easily solved as this.

Will was lying on his side now. Annie liked to look at him and always had, each time discovering something new: that tongue thing when he was teasing; a new expression—surprise, delight, worry; how his eyes were never the exact blue she remembered, always changing. Even the first night she met him with Carter and Kayla in the Tobacco Company, an historic brick warehouse converted into a restaurant, even then, she thought: He's handsome. She had noticed how he smiled without opening his mouth, how he blushed when Kayla complimented him, how he touched Kayla lightly on the wrist when Kayla began chatting blithely about Brooke.

Will was shorter than Carter, and in the low heels Annie wore that first night, she had been as tall as he. Walking with him across the cobblestoned parking lot of the restaurant, Kayla and Carter just ahead, commiserating about the hassles of running their own businesses, Kayla's voice floating back to them like the scent of a perfume, Annie had felt disconcerted and uneasy each time she met Will's gaze. She blamed his height, unaccustomed to anyone regarding her so directly; she blamed the cobblestones, which made walking difficult, she even blamed her discomfort on indigestion—the food had been southern Creole, spicy and fried, never mind that Annie loved hot peppers and salsa and could bite into a raw onion as if it were an apple. She blamed everything imaginable for the sudden imbalance she felt walking to the car with Will, her equilibrium disintegrating, as if she were walking along a cliff's edge, as if she were afraid of falling. She didn't want to confront the truth: She was attracted to him, enough so that by the time she got into the car with Carter, she felt guilty, as if already she had betrayed him—and hadn't she? Don't all lies begin in silence? A hundred times she had wondered what would have happened had she simply told Carter: *He's good looking. I think I have a crush. . . .* They could have laughed about it. He might have teased her, and the words, the feelings out in the open would have dissipated, as insubstantial as smoke.

Instead she'd been quiet, staring pensively out the dark window. "You okay?" Carter had asked.

"Just tired," she told him.

At the foot of the bed, Ethan purred, eyes narrowed to slits.

A breeze drifted in the open window and leaves swooshed lightly along the sidewalk like the muffled sound of applause. It felt like October or November. Not the first week of September. She pictured herself and Carter as kids, racing through the darkened streets of their subdivision on Halloween night, dashing from house to house, cutting across lawns to get to the next one. He was a cowboy; she was a gypsy. Or he was an astronaut; she was a fireman. He was a Blues Brother; she was Olivia Newton John in *Grease*. Pumpkins glowed on porches, ghosts made of sheets dangled from trees, orange spotlights shimmered across the cement driveways. She thought of the year he was a die, wearing a huge painted box with pips on all sides. She was a pirate, furious because he couldn't run very fast. . . .

"You're avoiding my question," Will teased.

"Which was?"

"Canned pumpkin, right?"

"Nope." She moved her hand to his waist, ran her fingers beneath the band of his boxers.

"Was it a mix?"

She moved her hand down further—he let out a soft groan. "I hate pumpkin pie." Seductively, she whispered into his ear, "I despise it."

"*You.*" He grinned, eyes closed. "You're one of *them.*"

"Pumpkin-pie haters?"

He lay on his back, arms crossed behind his head, inhaling the citrusy smell of her skin, enjoying her touch, her fingers in his shorts teasing, light, like their conversation. Most of the time these past two years they had been so serious, so afraid. Stealing hours here and there in the middle of the afternoon or their one night a week—Thursdays, running a gauntlet of lies, then trying to cover them over with a thin layer of truth. She'd rush to meet Will, applying makeup as she drove, adding jewelry, changing her shoes at a red light, arriving out of breath and anxious. He was the same way, scarfing down a hurried meal with Brooke and Kayla, maybe reading Brooke a story as if he were auctioning it off, eliminating a page and racing to the next. By the time they got to their room in the Holiday Inn, they were both wired, and though the sex was incredible, it was also fierce and exhausting, his hamstrings aching the following day. Their conversations had been no different. Trying to reassure each other, trying to figure out what to do, trying to say the right thing, to not say the wrong thing—which was anything having to do with Kayla, sometimes Brooke, and anything connected to Carter.

"So, do you also go out to dinner on Halloween just so you won't have to answer the door?" he asked, squinting at her in the orange darkness.

She smiled playfully, trying to keep her voice light, despite the sudden tightness in her throat. She and Carter *had* gone out to dinner on

Halloween. *Not* because they didn't like the holiday, though, *not* because they didn't enjoy the trick-or-treaters. It startled her to realize that she hadn't told Will this. How could she not have? But Halloween had been on a Sunday last year; they wouldn't have talked that day. She stared at the ceiling, her hand trailing back to Will's stomach, his arms. A metallic taste in her mouth.

He knew that she couldn't have children. He knew there had been years spent in and out of doctor's offices, years of hormone therapy, laporoscopies, laser surgeries. But did he know how many years? Four and a half. *Brooke's age,* she thought bitterly. And he knew about the miscarriages, three of them in two years. But he didn't know about the weekly blood tests, her arms black and blue for months at a time, or the daily injections of Lupron, and Metrodin and Pergonal, which gave her hot flashes and insomnia, and terrible bouts of sobbing. *It's the details that create a life.* He didn't know about the night Carter gave her a hormone injection in the back of one of her thighs and hit a blood vessel by accident, blood spraying everywhere, scaring Carter so badly that he'd begun to cry and later rage: "I can't do this, Annie. Goddamn it, it's not worth it!" He didn't know that after her first attempt at in vitro fertilization, they'd bought a book of baby names. She still had it: *From Jennifer to Jason.* They had sat on their back porch drinking lemonade and laughing at some of the possibilities: Loyce, Twila, Willodene.

She shifted away from Will, as if needing to emphasize the distance between them. She felt his eyes on her face and knew he didn't understand what had just happened, knew it was up to her to explain, but it seemed hopeless. The difference between reading about a foreign country and actually living in it. Was this how her students felt when she asked them to write about themselves? How impossible it must seem to them, how frustrating. Because though they might tell her that they had escaped Vietnam when they were ten or eleven, she could never truly know the details.

The first Halloween after Annie was told that she would never be able to have a child, she had filled the wooden salad bowl with Reese's Peanut Butter Cups, donned a plastic witch's mask and pointed black hat, and went out to greet the kids. She saw a Pilgrim and a vampire race down the walk to where their father was waiting, and a woman with long dark hair like her own who was kneeling at the curb tying the sneakers of a little boy dressed as a rabbit. From up the street, she heard the echoes of "Trick or treat," the slamming of screen doors, a child's high-pitched giggle, and it had struck her that always she would be this woman, standing alone on her porch, watching children from a distance. She would be like Mrs. Roccuiti, the older woman who had lived across the street from her family, who on Halloween would sit in a lawn chair on her porch and hand out three or four expensive candy bars to each child and fuss over the children's costumes in the too-loud voice of someone who did not have a child of her own.

Crying, Annie had phoned Carter at work and asked him to come home early and take her out to dinner—somewhere downtown, somewhere surrounded by high-rises, too much traffic—somewhere with no children. She waited for him in the kitchen, the front door closed, the lights off. Early evening, the light brownish yellow, like the inside of an old woman's apartment. The doorbell would ring, reverberating through the silent rooms two, three times, then she'd hear a child's disappointed voice saying, "Nobody's home."

"Come back here." Will was staring at her, tiny laugh lines etched around his eyes. "You disappeared on me."

"I'm sorry."

He pushed himself up on one elbow to look at her. "Where were you?"

"Halloween. A couple of years ago."

He skimmed his eyes over her face, lights searching the darkness. "Are you okay?"

From the den, adjacent to the bedroom, the phone rang.

"Saved by the bell," she said, but he didn't respond. Already his body was tensed.

"Come on, Will." She waited for it to ring again, for the answering machine to click on. "You don't even know who it is."

"If it's another hangup, I do."

It was Kayla. Her voice stumbled into the room. Muted, southern, edged with anger. As soon as Will heard her speak, he sat up. "Brooke and I just got off the phone with your dad," she was saying. "It's his birthday today, Will. I can't believe you forgot."

"Shit."

Kayla paused. He heard the sound of her breathing. She was probably enjoying this, he thought, yet another fuckup on his part. Softly, she added, "Actually, I guess I can believe it. You seem to have forgotten a lot of things lately."

She still spoke to him like a wife, Annie thought miserably. Which she was—the divorce not final until December, another three months. And Annie was just the girlfriend. She hated how inconsequential and naïve Kayla made her feel. Kayla. Even her name was exotic and beautiful.

As soon as the machine beeped, Will walked across the room, Ethan behind him, meowing. "My dad's going to see this the same way Kayla does," Will said, punching his father's number into the phone. "Irresponsible, selfish, too wrapped up in my own world. All of which is probably true."

"You're not allowed a simple mistake?" Annie asked.

"Was that all it was?" He glared. Blaming her. Unreasonably, he knew, and unfairly. It wasn't her responsibility to remember his father's birthday. She had never even met his father.

"No answer." He hung up. "He's in bed, too pissed to answer because he knows it's me or he's out drinking. Shit."

"It's not even ten, Will. Try him again in a little bit."

"I know." He climbed back into bed, gestured for her to rest her head on his chest. For a while they didn't say anything. He combed her hair with his fingers. Rubbed her back. Stared at the mosaic of light on the ceiling. *I'm going to end up hurting her,* he thought. And, *She's the best thing in my life.*

She listened to his heartbeat, faster than usual. The candles flickered eerily on the walls. *It's not my fault. I cannot replace Kayla.*

Quietly, still stroking her hair, still staring at the ceiling, he asked, "So what *did* you and Carter do on Halloween?"

"We really did go out."

"Why?"

"What do you mean *why*? *Why* does it matter?"

He sighed. *Jesus, what now?* What else had he forgotten? "That wasn't the day your brother—" She didn't talk about him much. He knew only that Patrick had been three years older than Annie, that he had died in a car accident when he was seventeen. He'd been on his way home from a Saturday afternoon football game.

"No, it's not that," she said. Patrick had died on November 20. Carter always sent Annie flowers that day to brighten her office and they always sent Annie's mom a plant for her garden. She wondered what day Will's mom had died and what he did on that day. "Maybe we should get little date books for each other," she said. She meant to tease, but neither of them laughed. She thought of her students paging through their second-language dictionaries for a word or a phrase only to find that some things are untranslatable.

Will was watching her patiently, something else she loved about him, his ability to wait, to trust in silences. She imagined this was how he was with the boys he counseled.

"Halloween is a children's holiday," she said finally. She held up her hand when he started to apologize. "Don't, Will." She sounded exhausted. "It's not your fault that you don't know these things." Wearily, she pushed her head up. "I'm going to make a cup of tea and sit on the porch for a minute. Why don't you try your dad again?"

She wanted a cigarette probably. He wondered when she'd tell him she'd started again.

She sat on the wooden steps, a long T-shirt tucked around her legs, and inhaled slowly, staring up at the starless sky as she blew out a long stream of smoke. A car drove soundlessly past, lights gliding over the asphalt. Through the upstairs window, she could hear the murmur of Will's voice and from the apartment next door, the sound of a radio, a talk show. She thought of what a Vietnamese student had written in one of his essays last semester. Describing his escape from the communists in an open fishing boat, he wrote that the strongest memory was the sound of people talking and whispering all night long. Husbands and wives had told childhood stories to each other; fathers had given their young sons stern instructions about becoming men; mothers had whispered beauty secrets to their infant daughters. Afraid they wouldn't survive the journey, they had tried to teach each other everything the others might need to know in order to go on without them.

From upstairs, she heard Will say Kayla's name, his voice agitated. Please, she thought, not another argument. "My dad loved Kayla as much, maybe more, than me," Will had told Annie once. Kayla had known Will's mother, had flown up from Georgia for her funeral. Annie was only nine that year, still playing dodgeball and jail break with Carter in the field between their houses.

Her tea had grown cold, though the ceramic mug was still warm. Quietly, Annie walked upstairs. "Jesus, Dad, do we need to do this right now?" Will said as she was closing the door behind her. "What? You want me to say it?" he asked. "You need me to spell it out?"

Say what? Annie wondered anxiously. Ethan rubbed his back against her calf as if to offer comfort. Will was standing at the window, staring out at the dark moonless night. He didn't turn when she stepped into the room. Almost inaudibly he said, "I don't love her anymore, okay? I don't."

Numbly, Annie sat on the bed with Ethan. One of the candles had blown out, and the other one seemed sad, like a flare for help that no one sees.

"How can you question that?" Will asked quietly into the phone. "Of course, I did." His voice trembled with anger and grief. "I loved her more than I thought it was possible to love anyone, but it didn't work, Dad. It didn't goddamn work."

Later, Annie would replay those words in her mind—as she lay in bed, Will snoring lightly beside her; as she sat in her office the following morning before it was light out and looked over the student papers, their "telling lines," which she hadn't finished reading; as she stood in front of her class and talked about verb tenses. She thought of how, in the Vietnamese language, the meaning of a word is dependent on the inflection used when it is uttered and how, if this were true in English, *loved* would mean many things. Said in such a way that the *ed* ending was emphasized, the *d* sounding hard and terminal, the word would mean something very different than when it was said softly, the way Will said it to his father, with a small break in his voice between the root and the suffix as if the final *d* didn't really belong, as if *love* was a word that never should have been used in the past tense to begin with.

I loved her more than I thought it was possible to love anyone. Annie would hear these words as she stood in the kitchen, cooking bacon for a spinach salad, as she lay in bed the next night and the night after that and the next one after that.

But that first night, after Will hung up the phone, that night when he crawled into bed with her and held her more tightly than he ever had, that night was the worst. The words were loudest then. Annie lay awake, her heart swollen in her chest, and listened to the squeak of tree branches against the side of the house, stared blankly at the gauzy curtains that fluttered in the breeze like sails. She wondered what Carter was doing and imagined him as he always used to be, sitting in his blue armchair, reading one of the history books he loved, the stereo tuned to something classical. And Kayla? Alone in her house on Grove Avenue, sipping hot chocolate as she watched the local news, light from the hallway slanting into her bedroom. Annie wondered what she and Will were supposed to do with these people whom they had once loved *more than they ever thought possible.* She wondered what had happened to that love, and she wondered how she and Will had so easily let it go.

Or had they?

Annie no longer knew. Sometimes, she felt as if Kayla and Carter were sleeping between them like children afraid of the dark. Other times, though, like that night, it seemed Will and Annie were the frightened children, refugees adrift in an open boat with no idea, in the end, where they would land.

Chapter Ten

By October the mornings were chilly enough that men put on their suit jackets before leaving for work, and parents insisted that children wear sweatshirts or windbreakers outside. The leaves changed colors, and in the autumn sunlight they glowed neon in their brilliance: chartreuse, magenta, gold. At the farmers' market in Shockoe Bottom, the wooden stalls were piled high with red peppers, squash and pumpkins, and farmers' wives from Henrico County offered samples of sweet potato pie and sold gallon jugs of homemade apple cider. NASCAR fans flocked to the Richmond International Raceway for the Winston Cup races, and residents of the historic fan district lined Monument Avenue to cheer on the runners of the annual Richmond Newspaper Marathon.

In town, Kayla's Espresso Shop was selling fewer iced coffees. Customers ordered cappuccinos or double lattes and asked that the milk be steamed extra hot. And instead of ordering a light strawberry tart or a peach Rugulach as they might have only a month earlier, they now ordered the double-fudge brownies and Bourbon Street bread pudding. Stores decorated their window fronts with the colors of Halloween. Three-pound bags of individually wrapped Butterfingers or Milky Ways went on sale in the Safeway, and an entire aisle of the Rite-Aid was now devoted to plastic masks, fake blood capsules, and vampire teeth.

Nights were chilly and clear and achingly beautiful. Rectangles of yellow light shimmered from kitchen and bedroom windows into blurry pools of blackness. Leaves blanketed sidewalks and front lawns, the statue of Robert E. Lee and Stonewall Jackson, the tombstones of the eighteen thousand Confederate soldiers in Hollywood Cemetery.

Inside the houses, exhausted parents made spaghetti for the second time in four days because it was the quickest and easiest thing they could think of; they questioned their children about homework and teachers, soccer matches, cross-country meets, and cheerleading practice. They remembered also to ask what their children wanted to be for Halloween. And sometimes, as they lounged at the table, sopping up the last of the spaghetti sauce with a heel of garlic bread even after they were full—because as long as they lingered in the kitchen they didn't have to confront dishes and the laundry, reports to edit, bills to pay, school lunches to pack—they would remember instead Halloweens from when they were children, how they had once believed that they could be anything they wanted to be—a world-class figure skater or a pitcher for the Red Sox, a dark-eyed gypsy or a movie director. Later that evening, as they nursed a Jameson on the rocks or downed the last of a beer or took a sip of ginseng tea, they would stare out their kitchen or office or bedroom windows at the bright quarter moon, and they would recall how they used to count and recount their Halloween candy, organizing and arranging it in stacks and piles, and how it was okay to be greedy then, to want more than they could ever possibly need.

"You just don't get it, do you?" Kayla asked Will. He had phoned to ask if Brooke could spend Halloween night with him and Anne. Kayla placed the soles of her feet together and pulled herself forward, wincing as she stretched her muscles. Light undulated forward on the newly waxed floor as the gauzy curtains billowed outward, then back, pulling the light with it. She'd refinished the floor a few days earlier, and now the pale oak emerged from beneath layers of dark stain. She'd left it bare but for a handwoven rug—white and light blue, and replaced the heavy blinds with sheer curtains. The room was light and airy now, and each time she stepped into it, she felt the urge to pause, to gather in a deep breath, to exhale slowly. Like a girl in her first apartment.

Her quads had still been tight from the workout she'd done at the university track the previous night, she and Brooke making a game of it, Brooke holding the stopwatch and timing Kayla on her sprints, then jogging with her on the cooldowns, her curly brown hair falling from its ponytail as she chattered breathlessly about her kindergarten teacher, Miss Turner, and her new best friend, and how she and Aisha were going to write a book all about two girls and Miss Turner said they could read it to the class during show and tell, and in art they were making junk sculptures. . . . *I wouldn't have had this with her if Will hadn't left,* Kayla kept thinking. *I would have been out here alone; it would have been the two of them.* Kayla had felt as she used to when Brooke was first born, never wanting to leave her, not to go to the Safeway or out to dinner. How she had sobbed the afternoon Will made her leave the house to take a walk, had told her she had to start doing things by herself again. Having a child made her distrust everyone: How could anyone else possibly care for her daughter as she did?

The track had been well lit, surprisingly crowded for a Saturday night. The sky was more indigo than black, and the air smelled strongly of wood smoke, a scent Kayla associated with the autumn holidays. She still couldn't imagine what Thanksgiving or Christmas would be like without Will. Like trying to imagine running a marathon. *26.1 miles.* She couldn't do it now, but she would, she promised herself, just like she *would* cook her usual Thanksgiving meal and she *would* decorate the house to the hilt and she *would* get a fantastic Christmas tree and a sexy New Year's Eve dress and she *would* be okay. For now, though, she dealt with it as she dealt with fatigue when running—she took it a mile at a time and when she was tired, she fractured the distance into smaller increments, coaching herself. *Just make it to the third telephone pole, run until you reach the traffic light.* And then she'd get there and she'd search for the next object on the horizon, promising herself that as soon as she reached it, she could stop, though she never did. This autumn was similar, a distance she needed to conquer in increments—a month or a week at a time, sometimes a day. An hour.

"You think you can simply say the word *love* and it justifies what you've done, absolves you of all culpability," Kayla told Will over the phone. "Poor thing. You just couldn't help yourself, could you?" The bitterness in her voice still surprised her, sometimes scared her. She wanted to blame it all on Will—*he* had made her this way—but she sensed that she had been hardening herself against him, against everyone in her life, for a long time. There was no one she was truly close to, no one who understood how fallible and scared she felt that she'd mess up the business, that she wasn't a good enough mother to Brooke, that if she didn't run every single day, no matter how exhausted she was, she might just quit altogether.

"None of this is *okay,* Will," she heard herself saying now. "You're an adulterer. You committed a crime against me and against my daughter. So, no, she will *not* be spending Halloween night in your home."

"*Your* daughter?" he laughed. "A *crime*? Would you listen to yourself, Kayla?"

"Yeah, *my* daughter, Will. You walked out, remember?"

"Not on her. Don't you dare—"

"Don't *you* dare, Will. You can see Brooke anytime you want, as much as you want, but I don't want her around that woman—"

"Anne."

"Whatever." And she hung up, too furious to speak.

She was still furious. Fourteen miles and she was below an eight-minute pace. Did he really think that he and Anne could just play "happy family" with Brooke and that she, Kayla, was going to step aside and make it easy? Poor Anne, who couldn't have a child and wanted to borrow Kayla's—and hey, why not borrow the husband, too, while she was at it? Kayla had barely glanced at Will when, a half hour after the phone call, he arrived to take Brooke out for waffles. She and Brooke waited on the porch, and as soon as Will pulled into the drive, she kissed Brooke on the forehead, coldly informed Will she'd be back by noon, then clicked on the Walkman and jogged away, hating Will more than she could have ever imagined hating anyone. But she also loved him, loved that he fought back, that he called her on her bullshit, that he *knew* her. Little things—that she liked to eat her soup out of a mug not a bowl, she didn't like her top sheet tucked in on the bed; she needed the TV on to fall asleep, that her mind raced at night with worries and details to take care of at the café. She was scared of getting old, was dreading her fortieth birthday, had once dropped, by accident, Brooke's stroller, with her in it, down the escalator at the mall. This was knowledge only they had shared, unimportant trivia that wouldn't have mattered to anyone else. She knew that Will hated wearing socks, he had never smoked a cigarette, he always shaved *before* he showered. He had never believed he was smart. What did people do with these details once they no longer needed them? she wondered.

She was worried about Will—he looked awful lately—and she was angry, so goddamn angry at him for ruining everything that she sometimes thought if she didn't vent her anger by running she could easily become filled with rage. She had a redhead's temper, lashing out at nothing, saying things she didn't mean and didn't know how to retract, saying things she did mean and never knew until she heard herself say them, the words hurled like rocks at her victim, causing damage that was often irreparable. "My whirlwind, my tornado, my Hurricane Kayla," Will used to say. He had learned to seek shelter from her rage, had learned, too, that once it passed, she was often more devastated than anyone, frightened by her ability to wreak damage and consumed with guilt.

She forced herself to slow her pace. She wasn't sure what neighborhood she was in. Tiny single-story brick houses, enormous oak trees. She exhaled a long breath, glanced at her watch. She had wanted to do twenty miles today, something she'd never done. It looked like she'd be able to. Maybe she should thank him for getting her so angry—the first hour had been fueled by pure adrenaline. Maybe she should invite him to the marathon she was planning to run for her fortieth birthday in April. Tell him to bring Anne and she could probably win the race, set a record. She started to laugh, but it wasn't funny. She would have loved to have him there. A marathon. He would have been proud of her, would have stood along the course with Brooke on his shoulders and cheered.

She slowed to a walk, incredulous to realize how close to tears she was. *No*, she told herself furiously. *No way. He doesn't deserve your tears, Kayla.* She started to walk faster, her throat tight, her breathing uneven, started to jog again and then run, refusing to give in, telling herself over and over, *No. Not when he hurt you like he did, not when he lied, for God's sake, night after night, out with her, screwing her, no.*

By the time she stopped thirty-eight minutes later, she had only a vague idea of where she was. Residential streets without sidewalks, the houses old 1950s' ranchers. Street names she didn't recognize. Coneview. Rockwood. Sunlight fell in splotches through the bright leaves onto the asphalt. Except for the rush of traffic on the interstate a block away, the street was quiet, an older person's street, everyone at church. A plastic skeleton dangled from the basketball net of one home, but the rest were unadorned, the lawns well-groomed and raked of leaves. No scarecrows made of stuffed clothing sat in lawn chairs on front porches, no jack-o'-lanterns in the windows.

Jack-o'-lanterns. She tripped over the thought, ordered herself to keep moving. She and Brooke would carve their own this year. No Picasso-esque faces, half one thing, half another, no elaborate swirling eyes or Mohawk tops, but they would make do. Her chest ached. She tried to convince herself it was from running. She remembered how after Brooke was in bed, she and Will would snuggle on the couch, maybe split a beer, the room reeking of burnt pumpkin and glowing with the grinning, leering faces. And then a week or so later, his pumpkin pies, which Kayla had finally, reluctantly confessed were better than Sarah's.

She glanced up, the sky broken by clouds, tiny islands. Her throat tightened. Why couldn't she have given him even this much, a compliment—*This is wonderful, Will, the best pumpkin pie ever*—without making him work for it? No doubt, Anne would rave about the pies, telling him what a great cook he was, swoon over every damn forkful. Is that what he needed? Kayla wondered sadly. Ego-boosting? God, it seemed so pathetic—not only that he'd needed something so childish and clichéd, but that she hadn't been able to give it to him.

She didn't notice Sarah's husband until he was directly in front of her, tugging the Sunday paper from its rubber-band wrapper. He wore a back brace over his white undershirt and flimsy hospital-like slippers. Kayla had spoken to him only a few times in the four years of employing his wife. She wasn't sure he would recognize her, but when she called "Good morning!" he glanced up and broke into a smile.

"Ahhh, you visit Sungae!" he said, nodding eagerly. "She very happy to see good friend like you. Big surprise."

"Actually, I . . ." Her voice trailed off. Was he merely being polite? It embarrassed her to think that Sarah . . . or Sun-gay—was that her name?—considered Kayla a friend. She'd never even seen their house before, this aluminum-sided rancher with plain utility shades sealing every window. She'd never wondered about Sarah's life, why she and her husband had moved here, why they never went back to visit Korea, what they did in their free time. Kayla glanced at the husband—Kien, or Keenan, something that began with a *K*. A thin, hobbling man with a full head of dark hair. Handsome by Korean standards, she imagined, and wondered if Sarah loved him. She'd always assumed it didn't matter, that marriages in Korea were based on other things: respect and family connections. She'd never asked Sarah about her life, never thought to, never cared, really.

"She's in the studio, hours and hours, so happy again, finally painting," the husband was saying. "You go, I make you tea." He gestured to the detached garage behind the house, its automatic door pulled three-quarters of the way down. Stretched and gessoed canvases— huge, six feet by six feet at least—lay scattered about the driveway like white sails drying in the sunlight.

Kayla tried to protest, but Sarah's husband insisted: "Just surprise her, walk in."

Already it was noon and she was late returning to Brooke, but it seemed the easiest thing to do: visit Sarah, admire her paintings or whatever, call a cab. Will would do his superior act, of course, make a big show of looking at his watch; ask in that tight, falsely magnanimous headmaster's voice of his if she'd enjoyed her run.

Kayla ducked beneath the partially closed garage door into semi-darkness. Two artist's lamps illuminated Sarah, her short, rounded shadow huge against the concrete walls and across the canvas she was painting. As soon as Kayla entered, Sarah whirled around, speaking rapidly in Korean, splaying her arms as if to shield the canvas from Kayla's view. Then, Sarah's own eyes must have adjusted. "Kayla?" she asked in a puzzled voice, "You Kayla? Not Keehwan?"

Kayla glanced at the painting, the canvas as large as a mini-movie screen, and immediately felt ashamed—thoroughly, deeply, ashamed—by her own stupidity, that she'd never talked to Sarah, never asked about her life, didn't even know her real name. To have painted something like this. *This. My God.* Four years of referring to Sarah as "the Korean woman who baked the pastries." How arrogant. *You must despise me,* she thought, turning her eyes toward Sarah again. She wanted to cry. Is this how she'd acted with Will? *But I was running a business,* she reasoned, remembering how, for the first few years, she'd been at the café seventeen, eighteen hours a day, how Will would bring Brooke by before dinner so that Kayla could at least see her baby daughter for a little while, and how driving home at night with the windows down even in the winter because she was scared of falling asleep at the wheel, all she could think about was how much money they'd borrowed to do this, and how much she wanted to quit, and how afraid she was to tell Will that it wasn't anything like she'd dreamed it would be.

At first glance, the painting seemed to be of the front of a Korean market, everything rendered in excruciating detail—the bloody chickens and tiny pigs hanging in the window, the jars of pickled peppers and spices below, the women with their straw baskets picking over piles of cabbage and onion, long ropes of seaweed drying on wooden racks. But when she continued to look, Kayla saw the enormous painted-over outlines of a man and a pregnant woman. In the woman's belly was a window front splashed with light—HAN MARKET—and a little girl flying a kite; in the woman's hands hung the dead chickens. Broken dishes shattered the man's eyes and the same little girl with the kite now stood at a window. It overlooked a dark green river which flowed into the hanging seaweed of the storefront.

"It's beautiful," Kayla said quietly.

"Beautiful?" Sarah gazed at the painting. She repeated the word. "Beautiful?"

"I don't know what to say. You should have a show somewhere, maybe the café or . . . People should see these, Sarah." Kayla glanced at her. "Is there a story behind this?"

But the minute she asked, Sarah—Sun-gay? Soon-gee?—turned from the painting and started clearing her brushes away, putting them into a bucket of turpentine. "You Americans always want story," she sighed. "Stories for childrens." She climbed a ladder to switch off one of the lamps mounted atop the canvas, climbed down, hefted up the garage door.

Kayla watched her, this tiny woman not five feet tall squinting into the sudden burst of light that streamed into the garage. She knew that Sarah had not answered her. She wondered if the pregnant woman was Sarah, if she and her husband had lost a child, the little girl with the kite. No wonder they had never returned to Korea.

Whatever Sarah's story was, it wasn't finished, Kayla thought as she followed her outside. No story ever is, not even hers and Will's, no matter how angry she was with him, no matter how firmly she swore it was over, promising him the night he left that she would never take him back once he walked out that door. Never. She glanced back at the painting, a 747 reflected in the woman's earring, and remembered, too, what she'd known since the night Will left and what she had wanted to forget: Every story was entwined with another story, and another after that.

There was Will's story, of course, the one everyone knew. He met Anne, had an affair and fell in love—or fell in love and had an affair. He left Kayla for her. But there was also Kayla's story: She hadn't yelled or railed at him the night he confessed he was in love with Anne, but spoke so coldly he flinched. "You walk out that door and I will not take you back." And then she stood at the sink and stared through the window at Brooke swinging on the swing set until Kayla thought she would be sick. She listened to Will opening the hall closet, the front door, then the screen door, the squeak of the hinges so loud she thought she'd explode—and then he was gone. Twenty years. Just like that.

She had finished the dishes, her hands trembling uncontrollably like those of an old woman, wiped down the table, called Brooke inside, gave her a bath, read a Berenstain Bears story, tucked her in. She lay awake all night and into the morning, her senses so alert to every noise—every car passing, the humming sounds as the dishwasher two floors below switched through its cycles. She didn't cry. Her eyes ached with dryness, the skin around them tight as if she'd lain in the sun all day. She got up twice in the night to rub moisturizer into her face and hands, refusing to acknowledge the emptiness in the bed beside her. Sirens wailed from another part of the city; the Lavertis' dog three doors down barked continuously. She watched the sky grow light, got up to run, but then remembered as she was tugging on her shoes that she couldn't go because she was alone. There was no one to stay with Brooke.

It wasn't until a week later, trying to close a window when a thunderstorm began, and slamming it down on her finger, that she began to cry uncontrollably, as she hadn't cried in years, enormous gulping sobs. Sitting on the floor in her bedroom, she cradled her hand in her lap as if it were a doll or a stray kitten, not even a part of her. She wasn't only crying because Will had left her, but because the moment the door shut behind him, a part of her had shut down, accepted the fact that her marriage was over. Just like that. *Twenty years.* It terrified her. She knew that in a way, she, too, had walked out, said good-bye and let him go without a fight or a reason. At least he'd had that—a reason. What did she have?

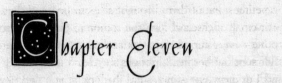

Chapter Eleven

The graduate students in Sungae's painting classes treated her like a ghost, an invisible presence without a name. When she dragged the broken wooden easel that no one was using across the studio to prop up her canvases, which were too large for one easel, none of the boys offered to help her, though she had seen them fly across the room to open the door for the younger girls. And midafternoon when one of the students would offer to make a "supply run" to the Sweet Shop, no one ever asked Sungae if she wanted anything. She worked alone—even during the breaks—a specter outside of their circle, her easel in the back of the room near the high leaded-glass windows where no one wanted to be because the autumn light was too harsh.

It was the professor's fault, always praising Sungae's work and making the other students study it, and never praising theirs, even though the fat girl with the gold earring in her nose had done a beautiful abstract of a sugar refinery last week, and the boy from Jamaica painted the best trees, the moonlit leaves on a magnolia like shallow bowls filled with watery light, or the wrinkled leaves of a maple—ancient yellowed maps.

The studio classes lasted four hours, one to five. The students wore ragged coveralls and listened to Walkmans, ate bagels one-handed as they squinted at their canvases or walked about barefoot over the dirty wooden floors, scrutinizing each other's work, offering comments. Sometimes one of them brought a boom box and they argued across their circle of easels about what station to play. At night as she worked on her composition homework at the kitchen table, Sungae still heard their songs in her head, phrases she didn't understand: "She's a brick and I'm drowning slowly" or "To look at you and never speak is so good for me tonight."

"Silly fool," she scolded herself now as she sat at the table studying. She smiled because *silly* was an adjective, the very thing she was learning. "Silly, old fool," she said out loud, and then "silly old Korean woman fool." She laughed, happy for the first time all day. *Psshh,* she thought, getting up from the table to reheat her tea in the microwave. *Why I need friends?* She chuckled. If she didn't watch out, she would become just like the English teacher, trying so hard to be everybody's friend, she was forgetting how to be a teacher. Big smile all the time, asking students "Was the homework difficult? Did it take you a long time?" *Learning is supposed to be difficult,* Sungae would think. In Korea, all students knew the famous saying: "Learning is like a ray. There is a beginning point but never an end."

"Always studying," Keehwan teased as he passed by the kitchen on the way out of the house to take his before-bed walk. She pretended not to hear, knowing he did not really mind. In fact, Keehwan was a little bit jealous, she thought. Twice she had caught him reading her grammar book during *World News Tonight* or looking at her flash cards for irregular verbs when he thought she was busy cooking vegetables for *kujolpan* or folding towels. "You want me to test you?" she had teased last night. He acted angry, asked how long was she going to make him wait for dinner.

But the week before last when she showed him the A– on her pronoun quiz, he told her, "My wife is a scholar now. Perhaps *I* will cook dinner for her?" And he had, making *polgogi*—"fire beef." They had shared the bottle of *kukhwja,* chrysanthemum wine, the two of them getting silly and making a mess of the dishes—she brushing her soapy forearm against his sleeve, he bumping her hip playfully as he reached over her to put away the rice bowls. They were laughing, speaking to each other in English, which sounded silly, and then, without warning, she was sinking. Her chest ached as if she had been pushed underwater, and the room blurred so that the orange light falling through the windows turned brown. Happiness had destroyed her life once. She could not bear it again.

Now, as soon as the door shut behind Keehwan, Sungae counted to ten, then rose from the table, from her opened grammar book, from the mug of black tea, and hurried to the window. She tugged the shade down, then let it snap back up. All she could see were the florescent stripes on his Nikes. There were no streetlamps along their road, and though the houses were close together, most of them were dark. Here and there, a porch light glimmered through the leaves of the oak, magnolia, and maple trees, and from the picture window of the Fitzpatricks' shone the bluish flicker of a TV. Sungae loved this time of night, everybody tucked into his or her own pocket of darkness. No need to hide from the neighbors, or to smile and pretend to understand the mailman's conversation. She wished Keehwan wouldn't insist on going out, though. An old man in a dark sweater. Some drunken driver might hit him and keep going just like that evil doctor did when he ran into Maria on *All My Children* a few years ago. She thought that maybe she would buy Keehwan a reflector vest like the one Kayla wore when she ran at night. They reminded her of life jackets, as if darkness, like water, was something you could drown in.

She sighed and pushed her face to the cold glass, the window a compress. A car crept by, lights pulling at the blackness. It wasn't really a drunk driver that frightened Sungae. It was the paintings, especially her newest one, "The Telling Line," which Kayla had seen when she barged into the studio last week. The moment Sungae realized that someone was in the garage, her mind went blank, as if a fuse had blown inside of her. She sensed that if Keehwan saw the painting something terrible would happen to them both, worse than seventeen years ago when she had lost her mind and her memory, and his eyes had turned so dark with pain that they looked like open wounds in his face.

The silhouettes in the background, the man and the pregnant

woman, were supposed to have been Erica and Jack from *All My Children,* never mind that Erica had married Dimitri or that Jack had fallen in love with Laurel. Didn't Sungae know better than anyone that what survives isn't always what is best or right or true? Still, she wished she could tell Keehwan that she hadn't meant to paint her own telling line, that even *she* had been surprised when she stepped back from her canvas and saw that the man in the painting was shorter and heavier than Jack, that his shoulder slumped from years of hefting bags of rice and butchering pigs, that the woman wore a white *han-bok.*

Sungae lifted the window a crack, straining to hear. From the end of the block came the scatter of dry leaves as her husband shuffled slowly through them. He was headed back. Sungae lowered the shade and moved from the window. Spying, she thought. Just like the months before her baby was born, the months when Sungae lived with Hwang in the three cement-walled rooms above his store. Each Thursday afternoon Keehwan had arrived at the shop and handed Hwang an envelope containing half his week's salary. Hwang always accepted the envelope with both hands, the left guiding the right, his eyes focused to the floor—an offering of respect to the man he had cuckolded. My husband is a proud man, Sungae would think, watching him from the office in the rear of Hwang's store, where she kept the books in the afternoons, trying to help, trying to keep busy, trying to speed the time up and slow it down all at once.

Each week, watching Keehwan through the latticed paper screen, Sungae would understand anew that she was still Keehwan's wife, his *uiri,* his duty. And Keehwan was hers. It wasn't something Americans could understand, Sungae had long ago realized, for in Korea, unlike in the United States, to refuse your *uiri*—to your parents, ancestors, spouse—was like refusing to breathe. This was why, although Keehwan could not bear to see Sungae grow large with Hwang's child, he refused to allow Hwang to support her, either. It was also why Sungae understood that once her child was born, she would return to her husband; she would allow him *chae-myun* "to save face," thus, fulfilling her *uiri* not only as a wife, but as a daughter, who must undo the knot of shame she had woven into her family's history.

Often on those Thursday afternoons when Keehwan came to Hwang's store, he left a formal note for Sungae. The paper was wrinkled, as if he had opened it and read it a hundred times. Trying to decide whether to send it. The characters were labored, each word like a struggling fish reeled in and forced into polite formalities. "I hope you are eating well," or "I send you my regards." She kept the notes in the red lacquer chest Hwang had bought for her, and when she unpacked it years later when she arrived in America, she found in another envelope the money Keehwan had paid Hwang each week. She understood then that Hwang had been a proud man, too, and that it must have cost him as much to take that money with *both* hands as it had cost Keehwan to walk into the shop and hand it to him.

It still hurt to remember. She closed her eyes, her head in her palms. She smelled of turpentine and the gluelike scent of gesso. She tried to force her brain to think of adjectives. *"Mushik,"* she said out loud. Stupid. The assignment was to write fifteen adjectives describing herself. "Why?" she had asked when Annie explained the homework.

Annie had smiled and told Sungae to just try, as if were a matter of effort, as if nothing would be lost in the attempt. Didn't she see, though, that Sungae had already lost too much? Why didn't Americans know that feelings, memories, emotions belonged *inside* a person? Not outside, not on a composition paper.

Wearily, she got up, went to check on Keehwan now sitting in his recliner, watching Jay Leno. Sungae had only watched this show once, when Erica from *All My Children* was on, only it wasn't really Erica but the actress who played her, Susan somebody. Tonight it was some skinny girl with a mole on her cheek.

Skinny. That was an adjective. But it didn't describe Sungae. *Fat* wasn't right either, and she wasn't sure which word meant "in between fat and skinny." She paged through her Korean-English dictionary and saw *haeng-bok-han,* happy. The word pressed down on her heart, and she kept going. The wind moved in the trees, sighing like an old woman. Sungae listed to the rise and fall of the comedian's voice in the next room, laughter, applause. She wrote *unrequited* in her notebook. Could a person be this? The dictionary definition said "not returned."

Wasn't that what had happened to her when she gave herself away all those years ago? She thought of how Koreans believed that dreams were really memories that the soul had experienced while the person was asleep, and if you moved a person or covered her face, the soul would not recognize its home upon return. Sometimes it seemed this had happened to her. Her life with Hwang had been a dream, and when she woke up, her soul could not find her.

And yet lately, Sungae sensed that maybe her soul had returned, that it was there in the pale outline of herself that she had sketched on the canvas, then hurriedly painted over, not to hide her soul, but to protect it. From the next room, she heard the clink of china as Keehwan set his teacup onto the saucer. She remembered how she used to lie on her side next to Hwang at night, the baby kicking inside of her, pale moonlight flickering through the leaves of the bamboo tree outside the window. Hwang's face in sleep was rounded and boyish, though he was in his forties. Sometimes he'd half wake and reach for her, place his callused palm on her belly, mumble, *An nyung hasae yoo?* How are you? She would whisper, "Happy," the word like a silk scarf pulled from a magician's sleeve. It had surprised Sungae each time she said it out loud and realized it was true, for how could the happiest time in her life have also been the saddest?

She paced across the cold linoleum to the window and lifted the shade, trying to distract herself. The street was completely cast in darkness now. No flicker of blue light from the Fitzpatricks' window, no shimmer of orange. Her own reflection stared back at her in the dark glass. Who was this old woman with the sagging jowls and deep lines across her face and the too-short hair? she wondered. *Where did I go?* But then she smiled because she was thinking like an American, asking the nonsense questions. Again that word, *happy*—an adjective—flickered tentatively inside her.

At the table, she wrote *tired,* and when her stomach growled she wrote *hungry,* then *thirsty,* though this wasn't true; she had a cup of *Hong Ch'a,* black tea, sitting on the table next to her notebook. Still only seven adjectives. She stared at the pattern of yellow teapots repeating themselves endlessly across the wallpaper she had always hated, the dirty floor, the ugly brown magnets from the roofing company where Keehwan still worked. Brown roof with the words, DON'T WORRY, WE'VE GOT YOU COVERED. Worry. Was that an adjective? If only she could paint a description of herself, it would be so much easier, she thought.

Five minutes later, she was in her studio, wearing flip-flops, gray sweatpants, and an old jacket of Keehwan's over her sweater. Her artist's lamps cast eerie shadows on the cinder-block walls. Cicadas chirped outside, and the small space heater Keehwan had bought her clicked loudly as it warmed up, the coils glowing dull brown, orange, then red. She reached for a tube of mars white, added a dollop of cobalt blue. She wanted the purple-white of distance, of the moon; and then the yellow-white of memories, of the Korean sky in the winter; the pink-white of happiness, of daughters.

She adjusted one of her lamps so that she could rest her free hand on its dome, using it like a hot potato to warm herself. She felt chilled and tired. Her memories had been haunting her lately, entering her sleep like ancestors who hadn't been properly buried and so wander endlessly like frightened children, searching for what they have lost. She knew how to appease a restless spirit: Leave some *ttokkuk,* rice dumpling soup, and a glass of *paekhwaju,* hundred-flower wine, on the mantel to give the soul energy to find its rightful destination, and burn paper cars, paper money, paper houses, paper clothes, paper servants—all the things the soul would need in the next life. But memories, these memories of happiness—how could she make them go away?

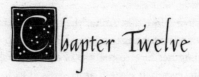

Chapter Twelve

"You give us quiz today?" Sungae asked the moment Annie walked into the classroom. Rain streaked the windows, and the room seemed like an exotic fish tank: Yukihiko with his mohawk, a spike-tailed paradise fish; Sungae a gray angelfish, intent on remaining un-noticed; the young Russian girl, Nina, a moonlight gourami, elegant and shy, so pale it was nearly see-through; Farshad, a lionhead carp, peaceful despite its name.

"No quiz," Annie told Sungae. "Not today." She sipped from the Styrofoam cup of vending-machine coffee, all she'd had time for this morning. Watery. Bitter. Like the day. Like her thoughts. She glanced at Shin-pin, who'd folded her arms across her desk, her head buried in the sleeves of her bright turquoise sweatshirt, and felt a rush of empa-thy. Outside the rain continued. Rivulets of dull light, a pattern made by the water, streamed down the classroom walls.

She had overslept that morning, the silvery light and muffled hiss of traffic fooling her into believing it was earlier than it actually was. She drifted in and out of sleep, waiting for the alarm to go off, listening to the rain pouring from the gutter just outside their window. And then suddenly it was nearly eight—the alarm still hadn't gone off—and she was scrambling to get dressed, no time to make coffee, and Will was leaving without having taken a shower, yelling up the stairs on his way out for Annie to put a pot in the stairwell because the roof was leaking again.

"I'm tired of living like this, Anne," he told her before he left.

Shin-pin was sleeping. Sungae poured herself a cup of dark tea from a thermos, holding her face to the rise of steam. Farshad was leaning back in his chair, eyes half closed, arms crossed in front of his chest. How weary they seemed.

She glanced at the clock. One minute before nine. Everyone was here but Ahmad.

She returned Sungae's homework, the paper nearly transparent, torn in places, from having been erased repeatedly. And yet it remained so full of errors that it had taken Annie nearly an hour the previous night to struggle through the page and a half of unintelligible phrases, ran-dom punctuation marks, and Korean characters. Not wanting to make her feel bad, Annie had circled only her incorrect verbs and adjectives. Nevertheless, as soon as Sungae took it, her eyes filled with tears. "I make many mistake," she uttered in a low voice. "I try very hard."

"I know you do." Annie touched her shoulder, the gesture more honest than whatever words she could muster. What she really wanted to say was that sometimes trying isn't all that matters, and sometimes you have to do more. Each time she and Will argued, as they had this morning; each time he made reference to something from his past that she didn't understand; each time she heard him talking to Kayla on the phone, his voice so altered that he might have been speaking his own language; each time, she sensed that it didn't matter how hard she tried because she couldn't learn all she needed to quickly enough. The mis-takes were a constant reminder.

She'd forgotten to bring a dry pair of shoes, and her sneakers—worn for the walk to campus—squeaked loudly as she moved up and down the aisles, returning the homework. Outside the sky was dark, the color of wet sand, and blue campus-security lights shone eerily along the paths. Students in sweats and jeans and flannel shirts ran for cover, books shielding their heads as they darted across the quad. Annie watched them, these worried, anxious twenty-year-olds. Worried about their grades and their girlfriends, about student loans and jobs. The theories she'd learned years before in graduate school about mistakes "representing patterns of growth" seemed vague and unreal. Had she actually said this to her students less than a month ago? Told Sungae that her mistakes didn't matter? No wonder Sungae didn't trust her.

She glanced at Korkut, the doctor from Turkey. He was reading the *Washington Post,* tracing his finger beneath the words and mouthing them silently to himself. Three afternoons ago she sat in on the genetics class he was teaching and watched as the students pretended not to understand him. They laughed each time he was forced to repeat himself or said, "shit" of paper instead of "sheet."

She thought, too, of Will, standing in front of the bathroom mirror as he had that morning, knotting his tie, eating a leftover taco for breakfast, his eyes scanning Annie's coldly. "I'm tired of living like this, Anne," he had said quietly, stepping aside as she reached in front of him for her hairbrush.

"Living like what?" She followed him into the bedroom, which remained dark, lighted only by the small bedside lamp. The bed was unmade and clothes and books were strewn about the floor.

"This." He gestured at the mess.

"You're upset because the apartment isn't clean?" She was sitting on the bed, pulling on a pair of dark tights, watching him as he rummaged angrily through the papers littering his desk.

"I'm upset," he said, "because I've been sleeping in crumbs for a week, I don't know where my keys are, I'm already—" he glanced at his watch, "—almost an hour late, Anne." He searched the pocket of a suit jacket draped over a chair.

"And you're blaming *me*?" She began to pet Ethan, who was meowing plaintively, the way he always did when Will raised his voice. The last few days they had been squabbling a lot—over how strong to make the coffee, over Annie's habit of not closing the refrigerator door firmly enough, over his taking pens from her desk and not returning them, over his Halloween plans to trick-or-treat with Brooke and Kayla. Annie understood his wanting to be with Brooke—she wouldn't have loved him nearly as much had he not. But she also resented him leaving her alone on a night that was painful for her. And she resented him—unfairly, of course, but she resented him nonetheless—because he had the one thing she would never have. He had a child.

She had stared at Will pawing through a desk drawer, his white shirt iridescent in the dark bedroom.

Angrily, he glanced over his shoulder. "Do you think you could help me look, Anne? And no, I don't blame you, all right? I blame myself."

Because you overslept? She wanted to laugh. *Because we haven't been too diligent about housework? It's not a big deal, Will, forgive us both for God's sake.* But forgiveness wasn't the problem, because his frustration had nothing to do with lost keys or crumbs in the bed or anything else they'd been bickering about lately. It had to do with Kayla. Kayla, who woke every morning at five-thirty to run, he once told Annie, without an alarm. Annie imagined she smelled of sweat and antiperspirant and tasted salty when she kissed Will awake. Kayla in her nylon running shorts and damp T-shirt would never have let him oversleep.

Annie handed Shin-pin her homework. Outside the rain smashed against the ground and exploded in tiny bursts. Will had left without his umbrella this morning. Would he blame her for this, too?

Sungae was still staring unhappily at her homework. "We can go over that after class," Annie told her. Sungae looked old this morning. Her short henna-colored hair was disheveled, and she hadn't bothered with her usual bright lipstick and earrings.

No help, Sungae said to herself. She couldn't imagine sitting alone in the classroom with Annie. What if Annie started asking her questions? Made her write another sentence for her life, fifteen more adjectives? *No.*

"Don't you guys ever sleep?" Annie joked as she handed Farshad his homework. He was unshaven, his blue-and-red Pizza King shirt wrinkled. She imagined he must have slept in it. He had been staring morosely out the window at the dark sky and the rain drumming against the glass.

Farshad scanned the paper Annie had given him. She hated this moment, the quick slide of disappointment across her students' features as they scanned their returned work. They rarely noticed the underlined sentences with a "Good!" scrawled next to them in the margin. They saw only the circled or highlighted errors. Everything they'd done wrong.

Immediately, Farshad placed the paper in his knapsack. Tomorrow he would hand her a manila folder with his homework retyped and painstakingly corrected. She didn't require this, but he did it anyway. Is this why he looked so exhausted? She thought of the night a few weeks before she left Carter, when she woke to find him sitting at the computer in their living room, typing her a letter.

"Let's just talk. I'm right here," she told him.

"Just go back to bed, Annie, please?" He had been in tears.

"But why? I don't understand—"

"I'm not asking you to understand! I'm asking you to leave me alone!"

She lay in the next room, listening to the clicking of the keyboard, unable to fall asleep. Twice more she got up and begged him to come to bed, to talk to her.

The second time, nearly weeping with exhaustion, he shouted, "Goddamn you, I can't! Don't you get it? I can't!"

The next morning, when she read the letter, nearly seven single-spaced pages documenting all the reasons why she shouldn't leave, she understood how desperate he had been to somehow correct all the mistakes of their marriage, and how frightened he had been of failing. The letter had been like the closing argument in a trial, she thought sadly, where a single error might lose the case.

Annie nudged Ba gently as she passed his desk, and he started. "What's the past tense form of sleep?" she teased.

Yukihiko laughed. "In Japan we have saying: 'If you sleep two hours a night, you pass exam. If you sleep three, you fail.' "

Farshad nodded. "We can not endure failure. This life, it is our last chance." He continued to stare out the window. His hair was thinning in the back, though he'd carefully combed it to try to hide his baldness. On his desk, as usual, he had placed a yellow legal tablet turned to a fresh page, his number-two pencils, a pink eraser, the bottle of correction fluid, a ruler. Like Will on Sunday mornings, Annie thought, waiting for Kayla to drop off Brooke while Annie disappeared for a few hours. She went to her office at school or the grocery store—once to a church, though it had been years since she'd believed in God. She wasn't sure what she had been looking for, only that she didn't find it. In the apartment, Will would have the ingredients for chocolate chip pancakes arranged on the counter in the order they'd be needed: Bisquik, milk, an egg, Hershey's semi-sweet morsels. He would be wearing jeans, his NUMBER ONE DAD T-shirt, the silly baseball cap shaped like a dog's head that Brooke had given him for Christmas. Drinking coffee from the I LOVE YOU mug she'd made for Father's Day. Evidence that he loved her. His preparations made Annie sad. As did Farshad's. *It shouldn't be this hard,* she thought.

She wrote the words *late, later, latest* on the blackboard—a quick review of the comparative and superlative forms of adjectives before they moved on to the next lesson. As she did this, Ahmad, walking as if on a tightrope, tried to sneak into the room, balancing two extra-large 7-Eleven coffees and holding a bag of Twinkies between his teeth. Annie whirled around, feigning anger, and the class burst into laughter.

Yukihiko pointed at Ahmad and said, "He is later than us."

"Latest," Farshad corrected.

Shin-pin clapped her hands with delight. "Funny guy, Ahmad, very funny."

Ahmad grinned at Annie and blushed. A shy twenty-year-old, he still described in every assignment how he had seen his best friend shot in front of his house by Israeli soldiers. Studying adverbs, he found new ways to describe how the soldiers had acted: *cruelly, viciously, unfairly, suddenly.* He made long lists of verbs: *shot, killed, murdered, executed,* then conjugated each into all twelve tenses, his friend's death unable to be contained by the past alone. But there was no grammar Annie could teach that would help him to answer *why.* Why had it happened? Why his best friend?

"You think my tardiness, it is good idea today?" he asked shyly, trying not to grin at Yukihiko.

"And why would I think that?" Annie furrowed her eyebrows in mock anger, elated at how quickly the mood of the class had changed. It takes so little, she thought. She felt her throat tighten. She wished she'd stopped Will on his way out this morning for two seconds simply to tell him she loved him, to make him smile, to agree with him even— *Of course everything is a mess, we've been having way too much fun, but we'll work on it.*

"You forgive me today because I help you," Ahmad teased. "I am example." He nodded to the words chalked on the board. "I am late, later, latest!"

Yukihiko asked, "How about laterest?"

"Wise guy," Annie retorted.

Again, laughter. They had just learned this expression, *wise guy,* in their conversation class, and for two days had besieged Annie with questions: "Can woman be wise guy?" "Is wise guy smart?" "Why you call foolish man wise guy?"

Yukihiko raised his hand, a grin on his face. Annie sat on the edge of her desk and eyed him suspiciously. The raised hand was much too polite. Not in character. Rain clinked noisily on the metal bike rack three floors below. "What," she said, "you're going to be a wise guy now, too?"

He nodded.

"All students can be wise guys today." Sungae spoke so softly that she was barely audible, her eyes downcast, her skin flushed with embarrassment. It was the first time she had voluntarily entered a conversation where she was not complaining, not asking, "Why?"

"Sarah suggests very important idea," Yukihiko was saying. "Even our teacher be wise guy today. She teach us very important American tradition. It is called cutting the class."

"One hundred percent I agree!" Ahmad called out. "This concept, it is necessary ingredient in foreign students' education!"

Annie felt as if she were on a swing, sailing higher and higher into the sky. She didn't want to slow down, to stop the momentum of this morning. "Yukihiko is absolutely right," she laughed. "Cutting class *is* an American tradition."

Ahmad grinned and slammed shut his book. "Ye ha!"

"But . . ." Annie glared playfully, pointing to the three adjectives on the board. "These are an even more important tradition. A tradition on which you will be quizzed tomorrow."

Collectively, the students groaned, shaking their heads in disappointment. Annie began writing additional adjectives on the board. The classroom quieted. She pulled in a deep breath, inhaling the odor of bricks and chalk, the metallic scent of rain and wet plastic. She held the breath inside her, her lungs expanding as if to make room for this single moment of joy. Behind her, the murmur of rain, the scratching of pencils as the students copied the adjectives she wrote, the scrape of a chair as someone shifted forward. She stopped after twenty words and sat at her desk and began glancing through the homework from the previous night. Fifteen adjectives to describe yourself. Ahmad, of course, had described his friend instead: *courageous, best, brave, fearless . . .*

Now and then a student glanced up and grinned at Annie. She smiled in return, feeling as she had years before, when she first started teaching, when every small victory in the classroom was a cause for celebration.

That first year, she phoned Carter every day after class to tell him how it had gone. She could still see herself sitting in a phone booth in the lobby of the library, her voice trembling as she tried to analyze what had gone wrong. Or, giddy with excitement on the days when everything clicked, she'd replay the class for him, and he'd ask questions, laughing as she recounted in exaggerated detail what she had said and how the students had responded. "You're a great teacher, Annie," he would tell her, no matter what kind of day she'd had.

Annie missed him. When class was over today, she wouldn't go to her office and phone him; she wouldn't tell him about Ahmad's arriving late or Sungae's attempt at a joke, about the way the students had laughed when she sat on her desk and called Ba a wise guy. She sipped her coffee. The students were still writing, copying the adjectives from the board, changing them to comparative or superlative forms and using them in sentences.

At the back of the room Shin-pin coughed. Farshad dropped a pencil on the floor, then leaned down to pick it up. Outside the wet trees glimmered in the phosphorescent grayness and in the distance, the rumble of thunder was like a heavy truck going over a pothole. It wasn't that she couldn't have phoned Will, she thought, staring at the lines of water trickling down the windowpanes. He would have been thrilled that her class had gone so well, but he wouldn't have really understood why it was such a big deal.

But Carter . . . Carter had been there for her first year when she hated herself—for being twenty-three and nervous and too pretty to be taken seriously. Yawning, Carter had stood with Annie in the bathroom in the early mornings, awkwardly helping her pin up her long hair so that she would look older. He helped her plan lessons at night, was good at thinking up games and exercises. The adjective assignment had been his idea, she remembered now, feeling guilty because she'd ended up resenting this, too—his involvement in her classes. She remembered shouting at him after a bad day once, "Why don't you just teach the class yourself, Carter? Take over my job the way you take over everything!"

He had glanced up from the exercise he was sketching out for her, his face reddened with shame. "I thought you wanted my help," he said.

She had. It pained her to recall how she'd made him feel bad for this, and his apologizing to her. Why, she wondered now, did it always seem that people ended up resenting the very thing they'd once loved? Or was it that they resented only what they had come to depend on?

When she used to fall asleep reading grammar texts, Carter would gently take them from her hands without waking her and stack them in her book bag, sticking Post-it notes on the pages to mark her place. The next morning, standing at the blackboard in one of the conservative brown skirts and flat shoes they'd bought to make her look more mature, her hair stiff with bobby pins and hair spray, she'd find his note—*You look gorgeous, Annie. I love you.—Carter.*

Annie.

That's who she had been to Carter; that was the difference. So much history in a syllable, and so much lost without it. To Will she was only Anne.

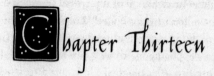

Chapter Thirteen

As a kid Carter had loved Mary Janes—those peanut-buttery rot-your-teeth taffies, but he wasn't sure they made Mary Janes anymore; some fifteen or twenty years ago, he'd stopped eating sugar. He couldn't recall anymore exactly why he'd decided to give it up—it had started over his losing some silly bet with Annie. If she were here, she could tell him of course, pinpoint the exact date, describe where they were and what he was wearing and what they had been betting upon. His reminiscences were silent black-and-white stills, grainy and out of focus. Hers had always been full-color.

As he pushed his grocery cart down the candy aisle, he wondered if his refusal to eat sugar was one of the reasons she had left him. It sounded crazy, but the night Annie met Will, the one and only night the four of them ever went out together, Will had ordered a chocolate espresso dessert that Annie helped him finish. *What if I had been the one splitting dessert with her?* he thought. *What if we had joked about sugar highs and chocolate ecstasy?* The thought made him mad because it shouldn't have mattered. She was his wife. They had a marriage. A friendship. But it *did* matter, and he knew now what he'd been too naïve to understand then—the big words like *love, trust, fidelity* didn't count. It was the little things—sharing a decadent dessert; Will's laugh as he gestured with his napkin, indicating the smear of chocolate on her chin; Annie's blush. Acts almost more intimate than sex.

So this was what he dreamed of now, what he wanted: to take her to Captain D's for a greasy cheese steak even though he didn't eat red meat; to sit with her in a café and read the *New York Times* and drink a grande mocha cappuccino with whipped cream; to eat Oreos in bed the way they used to as teenagers. He wanted to have fun with her again.

Outside the rain fell relentlessly, seeming to wash the color from everything. He thought of something Kandinsky said about how colors directly influence the soul, and he understood it for the first time. Without Annie, nothing seemed to touch or affect him anymore. All morning he'd wanted to smash something—a coffee mug, a window, his hand against the wall—wanted to break this unrelenting grayness even if only to see the red color of blood.

Halloween and she was gone.

It was the worst, worse than Christmas or New Year's could possibly be. She was the only person in his life who knew what Halloween did to him. "I wanted a child, too," he had sobbed the night she told him about Will. "I lost my son, I lost my daughter as much as you did when we found out we couldn't have kids."

"It's not about that," she had cried. They were in the car. She hugged herself tightly, as if to hold herself intact. He remembered reading that very few marriages survive the loss of a child.

The radio had been on, news of a Northwest flight that had plowed into an Illinois cornfield minutes after takeoff. No survivors, debris scattered for miles. He imagined the dread in his stomach was similar to what those passengers felt in the minutes before the crash, when they knew, really knew, that they were going to die, that there would be no miracle.

Just as it was today, it had been raining the night she told him about Will, and he could barely see, the windows fogged, the wipers clicking furiously, making him dizzy, Annie hunched over in the seat as if she were about to be sick, as if preparing for a crash, begging him to understand her foreign words, *I'm in love with Will.* He kept wanting to say, *Wait, wait, tell me again,* as if hearing the words enough times would somehow straighten them out so they would make sense to him. But they never did. They still didn't.

As he tossed a couple of packages of Nestlé crunch bars into his grocery cart, he could hear Annie telling him to get the good stuff: no lollipops or imitation M&Ms. He'd once committed the unforgivable sin of buying butterscotch suckers to hand out for Halloween. Annie had held up the bag of candy by one end as if it were a dead rat, fixed her disappointed teacher-stare on him, and teased, "Carter, Carter, Carter. Every window in our house will be egged if we hand these out." She was laughing, wearing a pair of his jeans which had been splotched with furniture stain. She was beautiful. He would have handed out Godiva chocolate to the trick-or-treaters if it would have made her happy.

Now he wondered how she could have cared about something so unimportant. He pushed the cart down the freezer aisle: broccoli florets, creamed spinach, mixed vegetables in alfredo sauce. He wanted to hate her, to be angry with her, but his chest ached. The real question was: How could she *not* have cared about their marriage. How could she *not* have cared about him?

He piled his food on the conveyor belt, surprised, as he was each time he food-shopped now, by how little he bought: a bag of oranges, frozen vegetables, pasta, potatoes every now and then, spaghetti sauce, toilet paper, maybe a couple of cans of soup. And today the candy, something he hadn't bought since the autumn their baby died, which is how she had always referred to the news that she would never have a child. Lately, he found himself noticing kids more, wondering what a child of theirs would have been like. He pictured Annie reading Thomas-the-train stories to their son or making airplane noises, zooming a spoonful of cereal into a little girl's mouth. *Twila. Willodene.* He heard her laughing the night they picked out those names. Her laugh was as comforting as a hand-knit scarf. He wanted to wrap the sound of it around his neck; he wanted to bury his face in it.

The ghost of her voice was a constant now, asking about his day as he sat alone in the kitchen eating a microwaved potato for dinner, or complimenting him as he stood before the bathroom mirror. At night, he still brought home new books from the store to peruse, and she told him, "This, my love, is absolute heaven." Climbing into bed with the electric blanket on high, the books surrounding her like the walls of a fortress. He loved to read, but Annie was the critic. She never read without a pen in hand, underlining words she liked or an idea she wanted to remember.

Now, even when Carter woke in the morning, it was still Annie he saw on the empty side of the bed, fully awake, the day already planned. "You know what I want for dinner tonight . . ." It had annoyed the hell out of him, her constant scheduling, every hour like a complicated class plan, but now he was the one lying there in the four-thirty darkness, trying to figure out how to get through the day, trying to imagine dinner, which more and more was pizza because then he could talk to that Iranian student who usually delivered it, ask him how his English class was going, what Annie was teaching. They had just finished adjectives—the assignment *he'd* created; she'd given them a test on Friday.

Not until later that night as he was sitting on the steps of the condominium, watching for Farshad's Chevette and the Pizza King sign which hung from the passenger window, did it occur to Carter that he didn't need to keep ordering pizza in order to find out about Annie. Why not hire Farshad for the bookstore?

But if Annie found out, she would hate him. She would accuse him of being duplicitous, would tell him he needed a shrink. And she would be right. He'd already considered this, knew he wasn't handling things well, but he sensed that a psychologist would suggest exactly what his mother, his older sister, his assistant at the store already had— get on with your life, go on a date, put an ad in the personals, join a gym, find a hobby. It was all he could do not to cry out in protest: "But I love *her*!"

Through a blur of tears, he stared at the white-sheeted ghosts and pudgy dragons and Princess Esmeraldas who raced across the dark lawns still damp from the earlier rain. Parents stood in clusters at the ends of driveways, beer or sodas in hand as they watched their kids. He swiped his hand across his eyes. "No, no, honey, leave the man alone," he heard a woman say in a southern accent, and realized after they'd hurried on to the next house that she'd been talking about him. As if he were someone to be afraid of, someone capable of damage. *I'm the victim, I'm the one who was hurt!* he wanted to call after them, but as the family passed beneath a street lamp, he saw the woman's curly red hair. Kayla. And then he looked at the man, at his University of Colorado sweatshirt. *No way,* he thought. Will wouldn't do that to Annie—leave her alone to go trick-or-treating with his wife and child. But the *no* dissolved in his throat, changed colors, became a *yes.*

Before he knew what he was doing, he was up and striding toward them. Kayla shook her head in disgust at Will, then at Carter as she hurried over to the girls, ushering them forward. Will simply stood there, hands in his pockets. "My daughter's right over there, Carter," he said calmly. "You want to have it out with me, it's not going to be in front of a five-year-old little girl."

"You left Annie alone tonight?"

"Anne's a big girl."

Anne. Carter blinked away his tears. "You have no idea about her!"

Will opened his arms with an I've-got-nothing-to-hide gesture. "I don't want to argue with you, Carter. I'm sure there's a lot about Anne that you could tell me, but this isn't the time or the place."

She probably loved his calmness, how confident he was, his even voice. And she would hate this, what Carter was doing, but he couldn't stop himself. "You have no clue what kind of damage you've done tonight," he said. "Did she tell you that she wouldn't love you as much if you *didn't* go out with your child?"

She had. He saw it in Will's face. "And you believed her?" He laughed bitterly. His eyes spilled tears, but he didn't give a damn. "She probably said you were a great father, and she never wanted to interfere in your relationship with her—" He nodded toward where Kayla was standing with the daughter. "You're a fool."

Will didn't answer for a moment. He was looking at his daughter, a cute little girl with his dark hair and eyes, and Kayla's curls. The muscles in Will's jaw were clenched, and in the light from the streetlamp, his hair looked silver. He had great hair, no receding hairline for him, no using Head and Shoulders because it helped prevent hair loss; Annie probably loved his goddamn hair.

Will glanced at Carter. "I appreciate your concern, but this isn't your business anymore." He started to walk away, then stopped, his face fractured by shadows. "You phone my house one more goddamned time and hang up, and I'm calling the cops."

"I don't know what you're talking about," Carter said coldly. "And don't threaten me again." He didn't care if Will knew. He would call every night if that's what it took to know she was okay.

"I'm sorry if I'm wrong," Will said calmly. Casually, he slid his hands into the pocket of his sweatshirt. Where had he learned that self-assurance, the ease with who he was? Carter could imagine Will comforting Annie when she was upset—not trying to analyze things or come up with solutions as Carter had always done, but just holding her, whispering into her hair that everything would be all right. And she would believe him.

"You're wrong if you think Annie's okay," he said quietly as Will turned to leave. "The one thing she wanted more than anything in the world, including you, was a child she could be out trick-or-treating with right now."

Will stopped.

"You'll go home," Carter continued, "and she'll tell you she got tons of papers graded, and your apartment will be clean and she'll have made banana bread or apple pie or some crap like that, and it'll all be a lie because if you look in her satchel the papers won't have a goddamned mark on them, and the only reason she'll have cleaned or baked is that if she didn't keep moving she would have exploded inside."

Carter walked away then, shaking, his eyes burning with tears. "Fuck you," he said quietly, but he wasn't sure anymore who it was directed at: Will or Annie. It scared him. He hadn't thought it could be possible to feel worse than he'd felt when she moved out, but right now he did, and though he promised himself that this was a good thing—the *real* beginning of falling out of love with Annie, it didn't feel good at all.

All this time—five months, twenty-eight days, nine hours—he had been beating himself up. *He* hadn't done enough, he thought. He hadn't taken her out enough, hadn't told her often enough that she was beautiful and sexy and smart. He hadn't appreciated it enough when she surprised him at work between her classes or woke before he did on Saturday mornings and made the sugar-free blueberry muffins he could eat six of in a single sitting. All this time he thought he hadn't loved her enough; he thought he had failed. Not once had it occurred to him that maybe she was the one who had fucked it up, made a mistake. How could she have chosen someone who didn't understand her, didn't love her as much as Carter had, as much as he still did? And how could he ever forgive her?

He glanced down the street, idly wondering where his pizza was—Pizza King had a thirty-minute-or-get-your-pizza-free policy. He unwrapped one of the Nestlé Crunch bars, broke off a tiny piece, and let the unfamiliar flavor dissolve on his tongue. For a moment, he was twenty-three again. It was their first Halloween as a married couple. He had finished work late at the mall bookstore; trick-or-treating was over by the time he got home. But Elvis was sitting on the steps of their apartment building, sideburns taped to her face. She was eating a Nestlé Crunch, and when he sat next to her on the cool cement, she leaned into him and fed him a tiny taste of chocolate. "I had so much fun tonight," she said dreamily. "You should have seen some of the kids." And then she was describing them, and he didn't really listen so much as just watch the images she drew: the toddler in the bright orange cowboy hat and six-shooters that hung to his knees; the little girl in her older brother's football uniform, black grease painted beneath her eyes; the teenage boys dressed as Charlie's Angels. And then she paused, and in that serious soft Annie-voice she used whenever she was happy, really happy, she said, "We are going to be the best parents, Carter. Our kids are going to be so lucky . . ."

He had given up on the pizza. His stomach was growling, but he felt drained, too tired to move. Across the street, a family went inside and turned off their porch light; a few houses away, someone's lighted living room windows went dark. It was colder now, yet he remained out-side in his flimsy jacket, wanting to call up more good memories of her. Each time another house went dark, though, another light flickering out—from a porch, a driveway, an upper window—he felt something shut off inside him, too. He remembered the times she'd been in a lousy mood, had taken it out on him, shrugging when he tried to ask questions, flinching when he touched her. If he did the food shopping, she complained that he'd bought the wrong kind of detergent or yo-gurt; if he cleaned the windows, she commented on the streaks. And now this. Will.

He thought again of the night when she finally told him what the hell was going on. For weeks he had thought maybe she was ill and he kept urging her to go to the doctor, had fought with her about it when she kept refusing. "I'm *fine,* Carter, okay?"

"Fine? You barely eat, and every time you come home you look like you've been crying. Talk to me, Annie." He had been terrified. What wasn't she telling him? And he had imagined the worst—that she was having a nervous breakdown, that she had cancer and was trying to protect him. When she finally said the word *affair* instead, he under-stood that this news was far worse than any he had imagined. By the time they got home—they'd been in the car, picking up Chinese take-out and a video—he didn't know what to think or do anymore. She was sick to her stomach, and when she came out of the bathroom, sobbing, her nose running, he'd actually felt sorry for her, had rocked her in his arms and whispered into her hair that he'd be okay, that if she needed to go, he would understand.

"I don't," he said out loud, staring up at the stars. "I don't under-stand." He pulled himself up and trudged to his third-floor condo, put a potato into the microwave, went to the phone, dialed her number. She answered on the first ring, her quick hello straining to sound cheerful. He knew she'd been hoping it would be Will, and he felt his stomach tighten. Ten-thirty and the bastard wasn't home yet. Quietly he set the receiver back into place. In the kitchen, he opened the re-frigerator to get out the margarine and fat-free sour cream. What rea-son could Will possibly have for not being home by ten, and Jesus, was she so desperate that she'd wait by the phone, willing to accept whatever excuse he called to deliver?

Carter slammed the refrigerator door shut, opened it again, slammed it again so hard the whole refrigerator shook, bottles rattling, falling against one another. He pictured Will and Kayla sitting on their front porch—slammed the door again—eating candy together and laughing about him—slammed it again—pictured Will and Annie sharing that godawful dessert the first night they met. He heard jars falling over inside the refrigerator, saw Will with his hands in his pockets telling Carter to mind his own business, heard Annie's voice on the phone just now, pathetically hopeful.

The microwave was finished, beeping incessantly, but he didn't stop. He kept opening and slamming the door until he heard something shatter and saw the broken glass and the Italian dressing seeping across the floor.

Chapter Fourteen

The campus was quiet as students prepared to celebrate Halloween. Earlier Annie had bought a sandwich and coffee from the University Commons, and now she sat, shoes off, feet tucked under her, at her computer, searching the Internet for information about trauma and writing in the ESL classroom. YOUR SEARCH RETURNED NO MATCHES, the computer informed her. She typed in GRIEF + WRITING. No matches. GRAMMAR + EMOTION. Again nothing.

Her mind had been racing with ideas for articles she wanted to write. Something about the connection between emotional loss and grammatical errors. How else could Annie explain why lately, whenever Ahmad wrote of his friend who had been shot, he slipped into present tense? Why Ba did the same when he wrote of Vietnam; Farshad when he described his life in Iran? Did they write in present tense because the losses *were* so present still? Annie wondered. Or was it that the further away they moved from their experiences in chronological time, the greater their need to hold on to them? That foreign students would struggle with verb tenses wasn't a surprise, of course, but never before had Annie been so aware of the implications behind their mistakes—if they even were mistakes.

She typed in the words LOSS + VERB TENSES, but again, there were no matches. SORROWFUL + SENTENCES, she wrote. Sungae's term. She thought of how Sungae wrote everything in the past tense, even when talking about the present—*I was a painter; I was married to a good husband*—as if the life she lived now had already ended. Was this how she felt? Annie wondered.

The building was quiet. Everyone had gone home hours ago, though it was only a little past six. Will was probably on his way to Kayla's for trick-or-treating right now. The thought depressed Annie, and though she tried to push it away, she couldn't.

"Did you ever talk to the baby when Kayla was still carrying her?" she had asked Will a few nights ago as they were finishing up the dishes.

"Constantly," he laughed. "Why?"

"What did you tell her?"

He turned and leaned against the counter, still drying. "Well, first of all, I had no idea *it* was a *her*." He shook his head. "I don't really remember. I probably told her we couldn't wait until she—or he—arrived, and I know I mentioned the Denver Broncos." He grinned. "I had my priorities, you know."

She smiled. "With Carter it was the Red Sox."

He glanced at her. "I didn't realize—"

She kept washing. "Nobody does. *Miscarriage* sounds so benign, like *mistake*. Everybody believes all those platitudes about how its nature's way of getting rid of a child that would have been too sick to survive anyway."

"That's not true?" His voice was careful. His psychologist voice. She tried not to feel irritated.

"It's irrelevant," she said. "You've lost a child and all the dreams invested in that child. Who cares why?" She felt Will's eyes on her, felt how he held her with his gaze. "The first time, we were going to name her Erin Kathleen, if it was a girl," she told him. "Patrick John for a boy." Her voice caught. She told him how she'd seen the baby's heartbeat on the sonograms, and how with the second one, the boy that she carried for nineteen weeks—

"Nineteen weeks, Anne?"

She nodded, tears stinging her eyes. *Now do you understand?* She told him how they were going to name him Danny, how she'd felt him kick.

"Nineteen weeks is a *miscarriage?*"

"Anything under twenty-two, I think."

"Why didn't you ever tell me this?" Gently, he touched her arm, but she shifted away from him. She didn't want to be comforted or pitied. "I assumed you understood," she said bitterly. "It wasn't some abstract *idea* of a child that I lost." She was crying. "And I know it's not your fault, Will, but sometimes I hate you for not understanding that they're real to me."

Not they *were,* she thought now, staring at the computer. They *are.* It occurred to her that maybe her students were right: Maybe grief *is* always present tense, and translating it into the past tense was the real mistake.

She found a ton of information on poetry and healing, poetry therapists, journal writing for cancer patients, therapeutic writing in psychiatric hospitals and prisons, an article from the *Journal of the American Medical Association* about how writing helped reduce symptoms of asthma in patients. But nothing about grammar and healing. Grammar, connected to the lower Latin *gramme,* meaning "a small weight" and the Greek *gramein,* to write. It made sense, she thought, words a measure of who you are.

For a while Annie lost track of time. She had forgotten how much she loved this part of any project, the research, the figuring out what the topic would be, the ideas. She scribbled down random notes, titles of books she wanted to read. *Because trauma does not occur within the boundaries of what is "normal," it does not fit into the structure of chronological time.* Her coffee grew cold; her sandwich remained untouched. *The origin of language is the desire to express emotion.* She thought of the infertility message boards she used to read on the Internet, and of the women, who always wrote the abbreviation *ttc* after their name: trying to conceive.

When she glanced away from the screen finally, she saw that it was already after nine. Halloween was over, she thought as she stood, suddenly tired. She threw the uneaten sandwich in the trash. Will would be home by the time she got there, she promised herself. He'd arrive bearing gifts of candy bars and M&M's and try to woo her back with sweets, and it would work. She smiled. It had been a long day and she missed him; she couldn't wait to tell him about her ideas for an article. "I won't be late," was the last thing he'd said when he had called earlier that afternoon.

The night had turned cold enough that she could see her breath against the air. The streets were wet from the rain earlier that day. At a few houses, votive candles still flickered along sidewalks, but for the most part, the streets were dark and quiet, even Annie's footsteps muffled by the rain-soaked leaves. At the corner of the street where Annie lived with Will, someone had smashed a pumpkin in the middle of the street and the air was filled with the smell. She walked quickly, chilled and hungry and eager to be home.

But Will's car wasn't parked out front, and whatever momentary euphoria Annie had felt drained away from her. Where was he? It was nine-thirty. Brooke would have been in bed half an hour ago—at least.

There was no message on the answering machine. She heated a can of soup, but poured it down the drain after a few spoonfuls. She lay in bed with the lights out and listened for his car. Her heart slowed each time one approached, accelerated as it sped away. What if he'd been in an accident? Nobody would even know to call Annie. They'd phone his *wife*. They'd go to the address on his driver's license. Annie was invisible. Her name wasn't even on the answering machine yet—Kayla still had to phone Will about Brooke, and he didn't want to upset her.

Annie wished she could sleep, but she was too angry, too hurt, too alert to every sound from outside that might be him. *How could you do this to me?* she thought, and almost wished he had been in an accident—nothing serious—but enough so that his not being here, not even phoning, would somehow make sense. He was supposed to love her more than anything; she was the most important thing in his life; she was the love *of* his life. What did any of that mean anymore?

Twice, she got out of bed and stood by the phone, holding the receiver against her chest, trying to talk herself into calling Kayla. But Annie had no right to phone Kayla asking where *her* husband was. She heard a car door slam and hurried to the window, but it was the downstairs tenant. She lay on the bed again and tried to close her eyes, but her mind was awake with possibilities she couldn't bear to think about. He was with her, they were getting back together, and he was afraid to call, afraid to come home because he didn't know how to tell Annie. It was almost ten-thirty now. She felt sick, realizing that she had somehow become the wife, and Kayla was the girlfriend.

"Where are you?" she said out loud, crying now. Ethan meowed back. Another car door slammed from outside, and still hugging the pillow, she walked again to the window.

When the phone finally rang, she grabbed it on the first ring. "Hello?" she said, but whoever it was didn't say anything. "Carter?" she asked quietly, "Is that you?" But the caller had already hung up.

When Will got home, Anne was asleep—or pretending to be asleep, he wasn't sure, though he stood in the doorway for nearly ten minutes staring at her shapeless form beneath the blankets. He wanted to cry—no, not cry, *cry* was the wrong word. He wanted to scream, though he didn't know exactly why. A cone of light from the moon or the streetlamp out front washed in through the windows and spilled over his side of the bed, illuminating his absence, which is how he felt, utterly absent from his own life. Like some guy who'd dressed up as Will Sullivan for Halloween, but had no clue who Will Sullivan was or what he wanted.

In the kitchen, a soup bowl was sitting unwashed in the sink. The minute he saw this his heart lifted, because it meant that pompous asshole of an ex-husband had been wrong. She hadn't baked, she hadn't cleaned, she hadn't spent the night in some sort of grief-driven mania because he'd left her alone. She'd probably stayed at school late and gotten started on one of those articles she'd been excited about. She was strong and capable, he thought, and so few people really understood that.

And yet, as he stood in their bedroom doorway, he felt only the same spiral of rage and confusion that he had felt ever since he'd left Kayla's. *I love you,* and *I'm sorry for not getting home sooner,* he thought, staring at Anne, but the words felt hollow. A part of him wished she were awake: He needed to hold her, talk to her, hear her voice, to make love to her. She more than anyone in his life could make him feel alive. *Tell me it's okay to feel this empty,* he silently willed across the darkness. But another part of him was grateful that she was asleep. There was no reason to upset her, he told himself. It had been an emotional night; that was all.

Kayla had sucked the energy out of him, told him he had been the love of her life, and she could hardly bear to look at him—he made her sick—all in one breath. She wanted to know if he had cried *even once* over the whole breakup, if he'd ever loved her at all or if it had all been a lie, on and on, and then the end of the night, tucking Brooke in, he'd remembered how kissing her *and* Mr. Boo Bear good night, leaving her door slightly open, these ten or fifteen minutes spent ensuring that his daughter's world was safe, had once been the scaffolding of his entire night. He missed her, and he missed being a full-time dad in the same way he'd missed his mom after she died, and he wanted it back.

He had stood outside of his daughter's bedroom, and in the half darkness, illuminated only by the orange smiling-faced night light in the corner, he stared at the framed photos of her that lined the walls in the hallway. Neither Will nor Kayla had been prepared for the enormous and terrifying love they felt immediately for their daughter. He stared at the photo of Brooke at six months asleep on his chest, thumb in her mouth. He remembered trying to match the rhythm of his breathing to hers so that her tiny chest would rise and fall in sync with his, as if they shared one heart.

From outside had come the echoes of "Trick or treat!" then the murmur of Kayla's voice from the porch. How could he have left this house where his daughter lived? The question tumbled through him like a stone through dark water. When he left last April, it had seemed crucial to be clear on the *why. Why* was he doing this? He wanted to be sure that it wasn't some kind of midlife crisis; he wanted to be sure that he truly loved Anne. And the night he left, he had been sure, and most days, he still was. But the actual leaving—opening the screen door, the sound of water running in the kitchen sink, walking outside, getting into the car, turning the key in the ignition, sliding the gear into reverse—this was the part that now seemed unfathomable.

In the bathroom he turned on the light, saw the plastic bath toys in a beach bucket near the toilet, the Little Mermaid shampoo on the edge of the tub, a dirty towel on the floor. He thought of the Christmas after his mom died, how he'd still found things of hers in the bathroom cabinets and he'd had the eerie feeling that she was still alive, and that he was the one who had actually died. He felt this way again now.

Kayla must have seen the grief on his face. Sitting on the porch swing, sipping hot chocolate, her own face saddened, all she said was, "You were the one who wanted this, Will. Not me."

"It wasn't quite that simple," he snapped.

"Just go."

"Don't you think we need to talk?" he asked helplessly.

She shrugged. "What's there to say? We screwed it all up, and she misses you—" She glanced to Brooke's window overhead. Five years ago they wallpapered it together. Kayla was pregnant then, and in love with being pregnant, amazed by her body, silly and hormonal and happy. Never a complaint about how much weight she was gaining or how tired she was. She used to tell him that she wanted to have another child by her fortieth birthday, which was only a couple of months away. He wondered if she still thought about this, if she still wanted another child, if she would find someone else to love and to have that with. And if she didn't? Was it his fault? *You* were the one who wanted to wait to have kids, he silently accused her. *You* were the one who wasn't sure.

He stared down their street, her street now, the houses mostly dark, the trees black against an even blacker sky. An acorn fell from the oak tree near the driveway and pinged against the roof of his car. He thought of the story he used to read Brooke in which an acorn falls and Henny Penny thinks it is a piece of the sky falling down.

"Brooke isn't the only one who misses you, Will." Kayla spoke so softly that he wasn't sure he'd heard right. She was leaning back, her head resting against the brick, eyes closed. The porch light cast dark shadows along her face, accentuating her high cheekbones and the taut line of her neck. She looked empty—or was he just projecting what he felt onto her?

"I—" He shook his head, ran a hand through his hair. *I what?* he thought. *I miss you, too?* He did, desperately sometimes, but he also didn't. He finished work some days, and he was so goddamn glad he was going home to Anne. And yeah, he missed *them,* meaning the three of them; he missed them a lot. He missed the reward wheel on the refrigerator that Kayla had made for Brooke whenever Brooke did something well without having to be asked. He missed lunch at McDonald's on Saturday afternoons, Kayla insisting she only wanted a diet soda, then scarfing down half his fries. He missed *them,* but he didn't know anymore if he missed *her.* "Jesus, Kayla," he said, finally, "I—"

"Don't bother," she snapped, pushing herself up from the swing. It creaked as she lifted her weight.

"Hold on a minute," he said. "You can't—"

"Can't what? Watch you squirm, trying to think up something to say? Bravo. For once, you're right, Will. I can't."

"Kayla, come on." He touched her arm, but she jerked away. "You can't just throw stuff like that at me," he said, "and then get pissed when I don't respond the way you want."

She sat back down. Again, the moan of the swing. He needed to oil the chains, he thought.

She hugged herself against the chill. "I'm sorry," she said. "It's just hard, you know? No matter what happened or how lousy we treated each other, and I didn't treat you well, I know that—it hurts to think that you wouldn't miss me or that after twenty years we'd so easily go our own ways—"

"It's not easy, Kayla."

"But you just go on, Will. You show up here and you take her out or you go trick-or-treating with us, and it's like nothing really affects you, nothing's really changed."

He felt as if she'd dumped icy water down his back. He stared at her, fighting the urge to just get up and leave. The wind rustled and blew a strand of curly hair across her face, and she reached up and tugged it away. He closed his eyes, unable to look at her.

"What? What did I say?"

"*I'm* the one who just goes on?" he laughed, glancing away from her. "For the record, I am hurting, okay? Is that what you want to hear?" His voice wavered. For a moment he hated her, hated himself, for allowing her to manipulate him still. "I hurt every time I walk out of her room or drop her off here—"

"*Her!*" Kayla cried. "*Her!* I know you miss *her*, Will. But what about me? *I* was your wife."

"I do miss you," he said softly. "Are you happy now?" He didn't know what she wanted from him. Of course, he missed her, but what did it mean other than that she was absent now from his life? Did it prove that he loved her? That he was meant to be with her?

She shook her head. "You really don't feel anything do you? It's like we were just buddies or pals or housemates all these years."

"Weren't we?"

She glanced across the street. A SOLD sign had been planted in their neighbor's yard. "Sometimes I try to tell myself that maybe it's inevitable that this happens, that lovers, I don't know, dissolve, become just friends, partners in the same job of raising a family. Maybe it happens to everyone, but no one's really honest about it. And maybe if they just said, 'Look, this is the way it goes,' we wouldn't end up so devastated when it happens. We wouldn't keep looking for someone else, for more than what we already have." She glanced at him, then continued. "But then I look at her." She gestured to Brooke's window again. "And I am so furious at both of us for forgetting, because we *were* more, Will, we still *are*, because we created her and she's so incredible and . . ." She shook her head, sort of half waved him away. "I'm sorry. And I know you don't want to hear this, but I thought I should tell you this before everything's final. I don't want our marriage to be over. I don't think it has to be."

She was staring off down the street, curly hair tumbling across her face. He noticed the lines around her eyes. She was the age his mother had been when she died. Thirty-nine. He gazed up at the sky, searching for stars, a constellation, something.

He didn't know what to say to Kayla or what he felt. Panic, maybe. Fear. *I don't want to come back. Please don't give me this choice.* "I'm glad you told me," he said finally. But he wasn't, he wasn't at all. *What the hell happened to "You walk out that door and I will never take you back"?*

She glanced at him, her eyes like silver fishhooks, reeling him in with her pain. She pushed slowly back and forth on the swing, the chains squeaking.

"Don't you think it's natural that we'd miss each other?" he began. "At least at first, Kayla?"

She stared at him it seemed, daring him to continue. He shook his head. He didn't know how to explain himself without hurting her even more. He thought of how every time something important had happened in his life—getting accepted into grad school, marrying Kayla, getting his first real job, buying the house in Richmond, Brooke, meeting Anne—how he'd missed his mother. She'd been dead for twenty-four years. He had no idea what kind of woman she would have been, what kind of grandmother, or if, as an adult, he would have liked her, even. But it didn't matter. You don't only miss what you love or need or even *want*. Anne had told him that when she asked her students what they missed from their native countries, they often mentioned the most trivial, ordinary things imaginable: a certain kind of bread or the weather. "I'm not convinced that missing each other is enough of a reason to rethink this, Kayla." He spoke softly. "I mean, even people who don't like each other will miss one another after they've been together a long time and one of them leaves. . . ."

She had closed her eyes and nodded. "Please just go."

Anne rolled over, her hair catching the light on his side of the bed. What was it like to lose a child, he wondered, to lose the hope of having a child in your life? What would his own life be like without the word *daughter*? He had no idea what Anne's night had been like, if she had grieved for those children she had lost—*Erin Kathleen for a girl, Patrick John for a boy*—and if she had missed Carter because at least he knew how she felt. He wanted to tell her that he understood, that lately he felt as if he were losing his child, her day-in, day-out presence in his life. But it wasn't the same, was it? And she would resent him for suggesting that it was.

He rested his head against the door frame, watching her, the anger he'd been trying to douse all night flaring inside him now. "I love you," he said, this time out loud. The words felt certain, weights momentarily anchoring him. His love for her was the one thing, besides his love for Brooke, that he felt sure of. But he knew, too, that he was using these words in a desperate attempt to quench the truth he didn't want to face: His love for Anne *wasn't* everything in his life no matter how much he wanted it to be. Nothing and no one could replace what he felt for his daughter. And the truth was that as much as Anne wanted to believe that Will was everything to her, he wasn't. Listening to her talk about those babies she had lost the other night, he'd understood that she would not have left her child for him. And right now, he hated her for this, hated her for imagining that he was somehow more capable than she.

"You okay?" she mumbled groggily. Her voice sounded sad and far away.

"I'm fine. I'll be in in a little bit," he lied. Why couldn't they have just continued having an affair? *Why* had they thought that this would be better? It was too hard. He closed the bedroom door slowly, quietly, the way he used to close Brooke's.

In the living room he put in a bike tape, the *Paris-Roubaix 1996*, which he'd watched a half dozen times, Johan Museeuw making an early breakaway from the Peloton with two of his teammates, but Will didn't care that he could practically recite verbatim every word out of Phil Liggit's mouth. He wanted a distraction, something to knock him out, something that didn't require anything from him. All he knew was that he and Kayla weren't right and hadn't been in a very long time. But his dad, Brooke, twenty years of memories, and now Kayla—they were all tugging at him to go back, to make it work.

He closed his eyes, hugging one of the couch pillows to his chest. Ethan crawled into his lap, and gratefully he reached to pet him. Kayla was right, he thought numbly. Brooke was incredible, a reminder of everything good and kind and honest that he and Kayla had once been. And maybe the marriage hadn't been great, but it hadn't been lousy, either. They had been friends, at least, and he owed her something for that, didn't he?

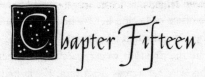

Chapter Fifteen

Kayla stayed outside on the porch swing, though it was after midnight. Light filtered from streetlamps onto the autumn sidewalk. The swing creaked slightly as she nudged herself back and forth with the toe of her running shoe. *I don't want it to be over.* Her words were like stones thrown against glass, shattering its smooth surface. It wasn't that she'd been fool enough to imagine Will would be happy when she told him that she wasn't ready to let go. She'd expected surprise or confusion, even anger: *Why are you doing this, Kayla. Why now? Weren't you the one who said that once I walked out that door, you would never take me back?* But she hadn't expected to see his fear. *Was our marriage really so horrible?* she'd wanted to shout. *Was I?*

She glanced up to see dark clouds pushing east, toward his apartment and the bed where he slept now with her. Wind rolled through the tree branches. *I don't want you back,* she said out loud, but she was crying. She wanted to mean it, wanted to feel again the surge of anger that had surrounded her these past six months like a magnetic field. She had felt protected by that rage. The night he left, she had assumed that any woman who would tolerate her husband's cheating was pathetic at worst, weak at best, and she'd prided herself on being neither. She hadn't changed in an effort to win him back, begging for another chance. She hadn't used Brooke as ammunition against him, hadn't crawled into bed and given up, hadn't stopped running or working, hadn't sat at home bingeing on cookies or spending her time weeping in a counselor's office or boring her friends with details of how much Will had hurt her. No, she had flourished.

But in the café the previous week, watching a father hold his new-born baby as his wife sat across from him, Kayla had felt that anger slide precariously inside her. She thought of Brooke's birth, of how proud Will had looked the first time he held their daughter.

And then tonight, Brooke's hand in his. Stopping to talk to old Mrs. Peterson two doors down. "Now there's a sight for sore eyes," Will had called to her across the tree-shadowed lawn.

"Dad . . ." Brooke whined, tugging on his arm, and he shook his fin-ger furiously at her, and whispered, "Don't *dad* me; this is a nice lady. You can't stop and say hello for two minutes?"

Kayla loved him right then. Loved him for caring about older peo-ple, for teaching their daughter this. She listened to him as he spoke to Mrs. Peterson and thought of how Will always cut her grass, shoveled her walk or cleaned off her car in the snow. And she thought of all the times these past few months when she had seen Mrs. Peterson out wa-tering her dogwood or picking up the paper and had pretended to be immersed in carrying in the groceries or listening to Brooke so she wouldn't have to stop and talk.

Kayla leaned her head against the porch wall and closed her eyes, the brick cold against her skull. She couldn't recall the last time she had felt a tiredness this deep, as if she could sit here all night, not moving, not sleeping, just rocking herself slowly, the wooden arms of the swing holding her intact. She still wore Will's University of Colorado sweat-shirt. He'd handed it to her wordlessly on the walk home and she had smiled when she took it from him. Now, she tugged the shirt over her left knee and cried.

Later, she paused to look in on Brooke. Her bride costume was tan-gled on the floor near her trick-or-treat basket. Again the rise of sad-ness. *A bride.* At almost five, was this really what she most wanted to be? Or was she trying to win her dad back? Had she somehow sensed

Kayla's wish to be a wife again? Kayla leaned her head against the door frame and watched her daughter sleep. Perhaps what you want most in your life is always what you've lost. Why then, didn't Will want her?

Her own bedroom no longer felt spacious, but empty—and she wondered what the difference really was. She lay atop the bed, turned the TV on. The darkness took on the different hues of the pictures on the screen, the walls yellow black, then red black, purple. Light circled the blades of the fan she hadn't yet moved to storage.

"I liked who I was," she said out loud. She no longer sounded like the woman she'd been a week ago, she thought. Where had her strength gone? It was that strength that allowed her to succeed at long-distance running, at owning her own business—that strength that helped her to put herself through college.

Through the gauzy curtains, she stared at the dark fringe of trees, at the milky sky, empty of stars. The room stripped of color but for the strobe of the TV. "She lets me do things for her, Kayla," he'd told her over the phone a few weeks ago when Kayla asked him for the nth time what the hell he had wanted. "And she appreciates it. I buy her a cup of coffee, fill the car with gas—"

"You want some little woman who can't—"

"I want to be needed! Is that so foreign to you, Kayla? So despicable? What are you so frightened of that you can't let anyone do anything for you?"

"This!" she had screamed at him. "This! That as soon as I trust or love or need someone they'll do to me exactly what you already have!"

She flicked on the light and reached for one of the library books stacked near her bed. *After the Affair. Marriage and the Temptation of Infidelity. Men Who Cheat.* Will would have laughed at her had he known. One of his favorite diatribes every time they went into a bookstore: *"Ten Steps to a Better You.* Jesus. Can you believe people actually read this stuff?" A traditional psychologist, he'd never believed in solutions or even cures. He believed that wounds were simply stories that needed to be remembered, protected, and then understood. Not erased or revised or *fixed.*

"Easy Answers to Life's Toughest Questions," she could hear him

scoff. "What'll it be next? *Overcoming Depression for Dummies?*" And she would have laughed with him, so sure that *she* would never be desperate enough to seek this kind of help.

One of the books suggested making a list of pros and cons for saving the marriage. Another listed fill-in-the-blank sentences to use as conversation cues with the estranged spouse in order to rebuild the "marriage narrative":

Remember the time we_____

What surprised me the most about you was_____

The best gift you gave me was_____

And Kayla could—and did—fill in the blanks so easily as she lay in this darkened room trying to sleep, as she was running her six miles, or standing in the kitchen in the early morning, microwaving Cream of Wheat for Brooke. *The thing about you that surprised me the most was how much you always wanted kids. A daughter. Even more than me, remember? And the best gift you ever gave me? Besides Brooke? My Christmas stocking.* She'd told him this before and it always surprised him. He'd given her the stocking their first Christmas in Boulder. Plain red felt with white cotton across the top and her name in silver glitter. He'd tacked it next to his on the wall, and at night their names sparkled in the darkness.

She wondered if these exercises had worked for other women, but she couldn't fathom it, humiliation rising in her throat like acid at the thought. She'd seen Will and Annie at a gas station yesterday on her way home from the café. Will pumping gas and Annie standing there next to him, hands moving in conversation. All Kayla could think as she drove by was that whatever they were discussing was so important that neither could bear to pause even for a few minutes. Conversations as intense as sex. She felt old. When was the last time she and Will had talked like that? "She asks me about my cycling; she knows the names of the kids I'm counseling right now."

Kayla lay in the darkness, the room cold, the TV on. He used to page through his cycling catalogs at night, or read a few pages from a mystery—as if there were none in his own life.

She kicked off her shoes and, still wearing his sweatshirt, climbed beneath the sheet, then turned off the reading lamp. Moonlight puddled on the glossy cover of the library book lying next to her. "If he comes back," the book said, "it may take months, years even, before he stops grieving the end of the affair; it may take you just as long to trust him again. You may become obsessed, always looking for signs." She felt doubly betrayed tonight. First by him, now by herself. *I thought you loved my independence.* She was crying softly, again. She didn't want to become a jealous, nagging wife, competing with the ghost of Annie—or whoever else it would be after her—checking his pockets, scrutinizing his bank statements, smelling him like a police dog when he came back from a bike ride, an errand. Always wondering, *Who were you with? Where were you? Why were you gone so long?*

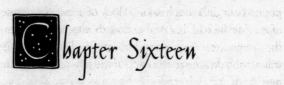
Chapter Sixteen

Last night was the first time Will and Annie had slept apart since she had moved in. He had fallen asleep on the couch in front of one of his bike tapes. Annie had awoken later, her heart pounding with dread. She closed her eyes, willing herself back to sleep. She didn't want to think about why he had come home so late, why he wasn't in bed now. *Had he slept with Kayla?* The Irish announcer's voice slid under the door as he said the cyclists' names—Italian names, Belgian, Russian, French—like a teacher of English as a Second Language calling roll. When the bike tape ended, she heard Will's quiet snoring, the movement of the second hand in the old-fashioned clock on his desk. She'd thought, for the first time in months, of her friend Claire, a native of France, who had taught in the States for three years. On Claire's last night, Carter and Annie had thrown her a going-away party. Claire had gotten drunk on sake and sobbed most of the evening, grief-stricken over all she had wanted to do and never had: drive to New England in the autumn, visit Martha's Vineyard, Disney, the Grand Canyon. Last night Annie had understood.

Now, it was nearing lunchtime and the University Commons smelled of stir-fry and pizza. A rock video blared from the large screen TV, a song from the Cranberries' *No Need to Argue* CD. She had given it to

Will the first Christmas she knew him. They listened to it in his car when they stole an hour at lunch or after work to take a drive while he pointed out deer and hawks, a flock of geese. The geese reminded him of cyclists, he said, because of how they took turns flying at the head of the formation, like a pace-line, one cyclist pulling the others in his wake, then drifting to the back of the line and letting the next one take over.

She glanced up from Ba's list of adjectives and scanned the Commons. Her closest friend, Lois, who was also the English department secretary, was supposed to have met her ten minutes ago. Each time the outer doors opened, orange and black helium balloons from the previous night's party shuffled along the ceiling. Clusters of students were starting to file inside, their hair shiny and windblown, their faces pink.

Two years ago, it had been she and Will stumbling in from the cold, laughing and blowing into their cupped hands. Every Thursday. The same table in the corner near the window. She'd have coffee; he'd get a Coke. She smiled at the thought of him, wired on caffeine, boyishly good-looking in khakis and a V-neck sweater, or a white T-shirt and a casual cotton vest, sometimes a tie. "You're such a clotheshorse," she would tease. "It's a great sweater." Or shirt or tie.

"Birthday present." He'd blush. Or Christmas, anniversary.

"I'll have to tag along next time Kayla shops. I'd love to find something like that for Carter."

That was the beginning, of course, the beginning when they were still trying to convince themselves that they were simply friends—the beginning, when they dutifully included their spouses' names in every conversation. The beginning, when he would ask after Carter, and she would casually mention the new Thai restaurant on Fifth Street they'd tried the previous weekend or a movie they'd rented. In return, she would pretend to smile at his stories about Kayla and Brooke.

That was the beginning. When they brandished those names like shields, as if to protect themselves: Carter and Kayla. Kayla and Carter. Now she hated that name—*Kayla*—because it was beautiful, and because it still softened his voice when he spoke it, and because it was unique and strong and interesting and seemed to represent all the things that Kayla was and that Annie never would be. She wondered if it was one more thing Will had come to miss. Even her name.

Two years ago, the mention of their spouses' names had gradually become less and less frequent, until after a while, the names were replaced with pronouns—*she* was out shopping; *he* was at the bookstore. Eventually, even the pronouns changed, the possessive *our* becoming the definite article *the*: *the* bedroom rather than *our* bedroom; *the* house, *the* Christmas tree, *the* marriage. And *we* became *I*: *I* was eating dinner last night; *I* was watching TV. *I*. Singular. They tried it on like an item of clothing to see if it would fit.

The balloons picked up their pace with the lunchtime bustle, shuffling right when the doors opened, drifting left when they closed, then right again. Annie spotted Yukihiko in a leather bomber jacket and Discman weaving through the salad-bar line, bobbing his head ostrichlike to whatever beat he was listening to. He caught Annie's eye, gave her a thumbs-up, and she laughed gratefully, shaking her head as if to say, What am I going to do with you?

"My, my, aren't we in a good mood today," Lois said, sinking into the plastic chair opposite Annie, cup of coffee in hand. Tall with model-thin legs and cropped blond hair, she looked twenty-eight instead of thirty-eight. Her husband had left her for another woman over a year ago and only recently had she started dating again. *She looks fantastic,* Anne thought, *the way I did that first autumn with Will.* Constantly he had told her, "You're a beautiful woman, Anne." Beautiful. Her throat ached. She thought of her students' homework: fifteen adjectives to describe yourself. Not even Carter had ever chosen that description in connection to Annie. Attractive, pretty at times, sexy. But beautiful? Never.

Will still said it. Just the other day he'd watched her pulling grocery bags from the backseat of the car, and the sunlight had struck her face and hair in a certain way, he said. It had caught him by surprise, how beautiful she looked. He had been lying in bed when he told her this, arms clasped behind his neck, watching unabashedly as she blow-dried her hair, then knotted the still-damp ends haphazardly into a scrunchy.

"You're only saying nice things because you had your way with me."

She tilted her head sideways in the mirror, as if trying to see herself from a different angle. He smiled at her reflection, the kind of easy smile she sometimes saw him give Brooke. An I-like-you smile, you're-a-neat-person smile. After a moment, she said, "Beautiful's the wrong word. Try happy." *I am,* she thought.

She felt the memory slip and struggled to hold on to it as proof: He couldn't have decided to go back to Kayla again, not when they had been so happy. It didn't make sense; things didn't just change that quickly, not without reason.

She had turned from the mirror last weekend, naked except for her blouse—white silk. He was giving her his "come hither" look as she called it, and she had laughed, shaking her head, her damp hair cold on her neck. "No way am I getting back into that bed with you—at least not until after sundown." But already the sky was tiger-striped black and orange, and church bells echoed from Saint Anthony's a few blocks east, announcing the start of five o'clock mass. "Besides," she had pleaded, "You need a shower, and I'm hungry."

"And beautiful."

She shook her head. "Happy."

"They aren't interchangeable. And besides, Anne-I-am, you're beautiful even when you're sad, and you're beautiful when you're bad—"

"Stop—"

"You're beautiful when you tell me to stop—"

Laughing, still wearing nothing but the blouse, she had crawled over him, pushing him back into the pillows, clapping her hand over his mouth.

"And you're beautiful when you're on top," he had mumbled into her palm, his hands sliding up her naked thighs.

"Yoo-hoo, earth to Annie," Lois said. "Or do you want to beam me up to wherever you are?"

"Sorry." She flicked her eyes over Ba's still-untouched adjective list, unable to look at her friend. "I don't suppose you'd buy it if I said I was thinking about work?"

"And I'm late because the dog ate my lunch pass." She sat in the chair across from Annie's. "What's the expression? The cat that swallowed the canary?"

"Are you implying I looked guilty?"

"Guilty? No. Satiated? Definitely."

"Oooh, *satiated*. Good word."

The Commons was full now, a cacophony of sounds: clattering dishes and silverware, the too-loud music videos, the *thu-thunk* of sodas falling to the bottom of vending machines, chairs scraping back, the squeak of a wheelchair, voices, laughter, different languages. Annie loved the chaos and always had, preferring to meet students here rather than in her office.

"I don't think it's going to work with Joe," Lois said after a moment.

Joe. The man she had started dating a month ago. "Why?" Annie asked. One of the helium balloons suddenly popped, and a girl shrieked, then broke into laughter. "I thought everything was going so well." Saturday night dates, a wine festival one Sunday, dinner at her house with her daughters. Lois had seemed energetic lately, and happy, shopping for new clothes like a teenager. "Is it because of Eric?" Her ex-husband.

"I just wonder why, you know?"

"Why what? Why Joe's interested in you? Because you're smarter than half these Ph.D.s around here, and you're gorgeous—"

"And screwed up. I really am, Annie. I don't know what I want, except to run away, maybe go live in Germany for a summer, or France, ride my bike everywhere, eat lots of baguettes." She grinned. "Want to come?"

Annie thought of the previous night, Will on the couch. "I'd love to."

"No men." Lois cocked an eyebrow at her. "Think you could bear it?"

Annie smiled, distracted by an amorous couple sitting a few tables away. PDA, the students called it. Public Display of Affection. The two of them looked ridiculous acting like that in the midst of a crowded cafeteria, and yet only the summer before last Annie had made love with Will at the James River Beach, underwater so no one could see, and awkwardly with their bathing suits half on, but still, with people, families, cavorting around them, playing water polo, sun tanning on the huge rocks which protruded along the river's center like a spine. She had leaned against Will in a shallow tide pool away from most of the crowd, the water too murky for anyone to have been able to tell what they were doing. Later, though, it scared her, how uninhibited and unafraid she had been.

Lois turned to see what had caught Annie's attention. "If my kids ever acted like that in public, I'd lock them in their rooms for a month," Lois said. "Hell, if Jilly even kisses a boy before she's twenty-five, I'm sending her to a convent."

"Does she know this yet?" Annie laughed. "The last time I was over I heard a certain boy's name mentioned an awful lot."

"Keith." Lois rolled her eyes. "Don't remind me. Can you believe she'll be a teenager soon? God, we'll probably be getting ready for dates together, trading clothes, showing up on *Oprah*. 'Mothers and Daughters Who Double-date.'" She started to laugh, but stopped abruptly, her eyes full. "I didn't want this, you know. I loved my life with Eric. Maybe I'm naïve, but I'd take it back in a heartbeat. Whoever said 'the unexamined life is not worth living' was full of it. I was happy."

Annie reached across the table and squeezed Lois's arm. "And you will be again."

Lois waved her hand dismissively. "Oh, I know. I am now, I guess. I'm just not in the same place as Joe, Annie, and I'm not sure I ever will be. And then I start thinking how it's always like this in a relationship. One person loves the other just a little bit more, and that's the person who's going to get hurt. This time it's Joe, last time it was me. Next time? Hopefully, Eric."

Or me, Annie thought.

"The worst is that maybe all these years Eric felt for me what I do for Joe," Lois said quietly. "You know what I mean. You love the person, of course, but it's not quite there, not a hundred percent . . ." She paused, stared outside again, her face glossy in the silvery light, like an airbrushed photo. "Did it happen right away with Will? The sparks, the fireworks, the—I don't know what to call it." She shook her head in frustration. "I just know I don't feel it with Joe, and then I think maybe it's stupid to even expect: I mean, I'm *not* seventeen anymore. Maybe it is different at thirty-eight, maybe it should be."

The University Commons was emptying now, student-workers busing tables, pushing in chairs. Students crowded the quad outside, moving along the various paths which crisscrossed the lawn. A man in a warm-up suit jogged toward Founders Hall. Anne followed him with her gaze, stopping at the pewter-colored statue of William Byrd, Richmond's founder. She used to meet Will at that statue. "Don't you look preppie today," she teased him once, the second or third time he had come to the campus. He had looked like one of the students. She'd been in the Fine Arts building and had sneaked up from a direction he hadn't expected. Immediately, he whirled to face her, throwing his arms up in an exaggerated gesture of exasperation, raising his eyes to the sky, asking, "Why? Why me?" Grinning, he put his arm around her shoulder conspiratorially and confessed in her ear that the kids at the Boys' Home had been giving him a rough time all semester about his "collegiate" look. He glanced furtively around the quad, then whispered, "They nicknamed me Biff."

"Biff?"

"Shush!"

She shook her head, laughter like liquid, inside her throat, her chest. "Oh, no, I'll remember that one."

Had there been sparks?

God, yes.

She remembered how conscious of his touch she was that day— through her blouse and sweater, even her wool coat. "The Princess and the Pea," she confessed to him later—she could have been wearing twenty coats, and she would have felt the negligible weight of his arm on her shoulder, his hand on her back.

Later that afternoon, alone in her office, she had watched from the third-floor window a boy and a long-haired Asian girl roughhousing with each other, he trying to swing her to the tree-shadowed lawn, her hair flying out behind her like a long scarf. She had wondered then, for the first time, what it would be like to make love with Will Sullivan. She sensed that with Will, it would be good in ways she hadn't known that lovemaking could be, and she thought again of when Will had lightly draped his arm around her shoulder that afternoon, for how long—ten seconds? fifteen? Annie had felt that touch like a sudden blast of freezing water.

Sparks.

Fireworks.

Last night as she lay in bed, listening to his bike tape from the next room, she had been afraid: If Will left her, would she ever again feel the kind of passion they shared? It wasn't the most important part of them, or him, or what he meant in her life, but it mattered. It mattered a lot. Was that so wrong? So many women seemed to think it was; before knowing Will, perhaps she had been one of them. The afternoon she told her parents about Will, her mother had shaken her head at Annie across the kitchen table and said in disgust, "Who do you think you are? You don't build a relationship on passion; you build it on trust, Annie, on commitment, on shared goals and loyalty." As if Annie didn't know any better, as if she were still thirteen years old. "Passion. That'll be gone in about two years and so will he," her mother said. "And I will not feel sorry for you."

If Will left, she would get over him eventually, because people simply did, and because as clichéd as it was, life went on. And she would probably be loved again, would probably fall in love with a good person, a kind person, a person like Joe, maybe. But would she cling to him when he made love to her, pulling at his thighs because no matter how close he was, she wanted him closer? Would she plead and whimper when he circled her breasts with his thumb because it wasn't enough? Would she ever be able to let go as much as she had with Will? Ever trust someone so completely? Would there be sparks? Fireworks? And if there weren't, would that really be okay, as her mother seemed to suggest?

No.

"I don't know, Lois," she said finally. "Just holding hands with Will, from day one, was always so intense. I used to shake just being near him." She smiled sadly.

Lois nodded. "I don't know why I asked. I knew right away with

Eric, too." She glanced at her watch. "Damn, I've got to go in a minute, and I haven't even asked about you. Was last night horrible? Were you okay? I think I've been afraid to ask."

At least you did, Annie thought. "Last night was fine," she said.

Lois raised her eyebrows. *"Fine?* Come on, Annie. *Fine* is like *interesting.* You know, what you say when you *don't* want to tell the truth. My, that's an interesting haircut. Hmmm, this is an interesting meal. Yes, last night was fine. Fine, my ass."

Annie smiled. "You're worse than my mother." She stared past Lois at the half-deflated balloons shirking against the back wall. "I just don't know what to say." She spoke slowly because if she didn't, the words would bleed into one another. "Nothing happened. I didn't fall apart or anything."

"Nothing." Lois nodded. "That's what Jilly said the other day when she didn't make the swim team. I asked what was wrong and she just said 'nothing' and stomped off to her room, where I found her, not two minutes later, in the closet, sobbing into a pile of shorts and summer T-shirts." Lois rolled her eyes. "I didn't know whether to yell at her because I'd just washed those damn clothes and they were all ready to get packed way for the winter, or whether to sit and cry with her." She paused, scrutinizing Annie, her eyes dark with concern. "So anyway, save me some time. Where will I find you? Hiding in your office with the cigarettes you think no one knows you're smoking? Crying in the ladies' room?"

"How do you do this?" Annie shook her head in amazement. "It's almost frightening." *And if she can so easily see it, why can't Will?* But you see what you want to. Isn't that always the case? Isn't that what allowed people to have affairs and fight wars and get married to begin with? You close your eyes to the stuff you can't handle and you keep going and you keep believing that somehow it will all work out. You pray or you take alternative vitamins or you collect lucky coins or make wishes on birthday candles and falling stars. Absently, Annie lifted her empty coffee cup, turned it, set it down. The cup thunked hollowly against the plastic table. The sound seemed to come from inside her chest. She said, "Will didn't get home until after eleven. He slept on the couch last night."

"And?"

Annie glanced sharply at Lois. "And what? You don't think that's enough? He knows Halloween is painful for me; he knows I'm insecure about Kayla." He should have known that she needed to be held and reassured. Five minutes of his time. And if he hadn't known? Well, that hurt, too. That was probably worse.

"She's his ex-wife, Anne, and she's got custody of Brooke. Trust me, nothing happened. They probably had a dozen things to talk about. Come on, you don't honestly think something happened, do you?"

"I think he thought about it." It. Another pronoun because *it* was easier than all the possibilities of what *it* meant. It, as in making love to her, or it, as in going back to her. Or it: simply watching her in the coppery porch light as she hugged her thin runner's legs against the cold, and missing her. Across the Commons, another balloon popped. A talk show was on the TV now.

"What's it going to take to make you feel secure?" Lois asked. "I mean, he left her for *you*. Maybe he slept on the couch because he didn't feel well or he thought you were asleep and didn't want to wake you, or he needed time to think. It was probably a tough night for him, too."

"Please."

"Please what?" She shook her head. "You're looking for things to be wrong, Annie."

Maybe she was. Cataloging in her heart all the reasons why it wouldn't work, as if this could prepare her when finally he said what she'd already rehearsed in her mind a dozen times. Like falling asleep to a foreign language tape, hoping that the sounds will somehow grow familiar. None of it had worked, though. When he didn't come to bed last night or even ask how she was, but stood there on the other side of the bedroom doorway, his sadness like a too-strong cologne, she had felt something crack open inside her, and she had known that nothing could ever prepare her for the time when he said he needed to leave.

"I mean, he doesn't live with his own child anymore because he wanted to be with *you*. *You*, not Kayla. You're going to lose him if you don't stop this."

"Thanks, Lois." Annie jerked her gaze away. "That really makes me feel better." She didn't know who she was more upset with—herself, because Lois was right and she *was* wallowing, or Lois, because she wouldn't give Annie a goddamn break, or Will, for assuming that just because she wasn't falling apart she was okay. All of the above? None of the above? A and B but not C? B and C but not A? "Fine," she said. "What do you propose, then? That I *fight* for my man?"

"You act like there's something wrong with that."

"Isn't there?"

"I don't know, Annie. You tell me. You certainly fought for him before."

"Is this even about me?" Annie asked after a moment. "Because I can't do it today, all right, Lois? I'm not your personal punching bag."

"No, you're not." Lois tossed her keys into her purse, hands shaking. "You're absolutely right. I'm not being fair, I'm attacking you, I'm a lousy friend." Her chin quivered. "I guess I'm just having a hard time forgetting that my life was ripped to shreds because of a situation like yours—"

"I know—"

"No, you don't, okay? You don't, and I don't hold that against you because the truth is that I can't really understand what you're going through, either. It's just that you won, you know? You won. And now, what? After all the grief you caused, and I'm not just talking about Carter and Kayla, Annie, I'm talking about what this has done to you— you're just giving up." She stood to go, crying softly. "I know I'm probably jealous," she said. "It's just that I would have given anything, *anything,* to have had one *fair* chance to work it out with Eric. . . ."

Annie thought about it later, walking home along Monument Avenue past its bronze and granite tributes to great Civil War heroes. Lois was right, Annie thought as she passed the statue of Robert E. Lee, his back facing north. When had she *not* had to compete with Kayla? Hadn't it always been about how Kayla didn't understand Will and Annie did, or he couldn't talk to Kayla, but he could to Annie, or lovemaking with Kayla was perfunctory or Kayla wasn't in the mood, and of course, Annie always was—or at least she'd let him think that, hadn't she? Even when she was worried about her job, even when she just wanted to lay with him in the hotel room and watch TV. Competition had always been a part of her and Will, because someone had to win and someone had to lose, and maybe the most unfair part of adultery wasn't the lies so much as it was that the other player never knew that the rules had changed. Like playing what you think is a friendly game of poker and only discovering after you had lost that you had gambled away your home.

Carter had shouted this at her a few nights after she told him about Will. "You never gave me a chance," he said. "I would have courted you if I knew, if I just *knew*, that this was what you needed. I would have rented the hotel rooms," he said. "Or met you for romantic lunches or sent flowers or cards or phoned you sixteen times a day or sixty or six hundred if that's what it would have taken. I would have done anything; I still would."

"But you didn't," she said. "Don't you see that, Carter? We both stopped doing all those things for each other. I should have been doing them for you all along and vice versa, and neither one of us should have had to ask." They passed the Strawberry Street Cafe, a neon strawberry glowing in the darkened window. It looked like a heart.

"Look," he sighed. "When your students are screwing up and are about to fail, do you just let it happen?"

"Come on, Carter, you wanted me to send you a written warning?"

"Yes! Yes! Anything!" He'd slammed his fist into the steering wheel. *"I didn't know,"* he said again. "I didn't goddamn know," and he started to cry, huge racking sobs that she had heard only once before. After the first miscarriage. She'd woken and he hadn't been in bed, and when she finally found him, he was sitting in the parked car, sobbing against the steering wheel, his sounds coming through the glass as if from underwater.

She wondered what would have happened had she and Carter had the baby they had wanted. She knew that Will thought she never would have left Carter if they'd had a child, and a part of her wanted to believe this was true, that she would have put her child first, that she would have been *that* unselfish. But this also terrified her because it suggested that maybe she didn't really need Will as much as she thought. Maybe what she felt for him was just the passion of wanting desperately what she couldn't have. A child. Or another woman's husband.

She heard her grandmother telling her ages ago, though she couldn't remember the why or the when of it, "Be careful of what you wish for—you just might get it."

Dark now, the sky quilted over with clouds. A low fog looped through the dark branches of the streets. She stopped at the gourmet market on Lombard Street for a bottle of wine and ended up getting a loaf of French bread and a jar of Greek olives. She'd make bruschetta tonight. Will loved bruschetta. Spontaneously, she grabbed an expensive Swiss candy bar, dark chocolate with hazelnuts, a bouquet of grocery-store red and yellow carnations. Not until she was standing in line at the checkout did she realize what she was doing—the one thing she had promised herself she never would. She was fighting for him. And she didn't know, as she walked the last few blocks home, as she stared into the lighted windows of the homes and tried to imagine the families who lived inside, tried to see herself and Will as one of those families, if what she felt was desperation or hope. She'd learned in a French class long ago that they came from the same root, *esperer*. She wanted to believe that they were reversible, that what began as desperation could as easily evolve into hope as hope could evolve into its opposite. But the *de* of desperation meant "away from" or "following from." It suggested that the hope came first, and then the despair.

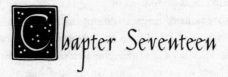

Chapter Seventeen

On Thanksgiving morning the interstates and airports were crowded with traffic. Decades before, when the highway system was first conceived, engineers divided the country into a grid, then drew "desire lines," joining the places people most wanted to be. Years later, airline planners did the same, a map of the sky becoming a diagram of longing. Carter had read this once and had forgotten it until now as he followed the trail of taillights, pulling him north up I-95. He had left for New Jersey at four in the morning, as he and Annie had for the past nine years.

In Richmond, Annie woke at six, though the alarm wasn't set. She pictured Carter alone in the car passing through D.C. by now, the Washington Memorial barely visible to his left as he crossed the Potomac and headed toward Baltimore. If he stayed the speed limit, and she knew he would, he'd be in New Jersey by nine. Exit four off of the turnpike. The blinking signs of motels and gas stations along Route 73. The Super 8 Movie Theater and Olga's Diner, where they'd gone after parties and the senior prom, where they still met former high school classmates when they were back in town. He would stop there to pick up a lemon meringue pie, not pecan, not pumpkin or apple, but lemon meringue, *her* mother's favorite. It was as much a tradition as the day-after touch football game at Memorial Field they always had with old friends.

Another thing he'd do now alone.

Carter was thinking of Annie as he stopped for gas just past the Fort McHenry Tunnel on I-95. Across the interstate he could see the harbor, where an enormous hospital ship was docked, a Red Cross emblem painted on its white bridge. It seemed like something from another century. How odd to see such a ship in a modern city like Baltimore, he thought, where the wounded and sick went to state-of-the-art medical facilities. He closed his eyes and wondered how the hell he was going to do this, how he was going to get through the holiday, how he was going to function, talk, move, smile, eat. Verbs. She had been wrong, he thought, when she told her students that nouns were most important. You could live your entire life with nothing but verbs. *Love, marry, hate, hurt.*

He stared again at the traffic, the steady movement of cars. Families. Couples. And looking back at the water, he thought of Francis Scott Key. He had composed the national anthem not far from here. *"Oh, say can you see, by the dawn's early light."* The words rose and echoed in his mind. They were words he associated with the start of professional baseball games, the Phillies when he was younger, later the Red Sox.

He had loved American history since writing a report on Lincoln in the fifth grade. The paper turned into sixty pages by the time he was done. All the details that compose a life—like the fact that Lincoln was the one who'd declared Thanksgiving a national holiday in 1863. How many people knew that? Or cared? Not many. And it bothered him, because to forget was to suggest that it didn't really matter what one man did.

Chapter Eighteen

The morning after Kayla invited Sungae and Keehwan to her house for Thanksgiving dinner, Sungae rode the bus to school instead of walking, even though she hated buses. She did this so that she could stop by Yong-sun Lee's dry cleaners on the way. Mrs. Lee went to Sungae and Keehwan's church, and everyone knew she did the best alterations for the cheapest. Sungae needed her to let out the waist of the *chorgori,* the shirt part of her *han-bok,* which she planned to wear for the holiday. "I gain freshman five," she giggled as she turned on the dressmaker's platform in the rear of the shop where the air was tropical and damp from the steam irons. Yong-sun Lee only humphed, her mouth full of pins. Later, though, she told Sungae that she was becoming "Twinkie," yellow on the outside, white in the middle. It bothered Sungae all day, not because she didn't understand her friend's words, but because she did.

Sungae had felt it, too, the difference growing inside her like a child. And this difference wasn't as simple as going to the university or learning English; it wasn't even that Sungae was painting the beautiful canvases that Dr. Jacks, head of the fine arts department, wanted to put in a show. The difference was that for the first time in seventeen years, Sungae wanted things she couldn't possibly have. Was this what Yong-sun meant by "becoming like the American"? Did she suspect that Sungae had started to value her future more than her past? After all, the history of Korea is one of endurance, of waiting for hardship to end, while the history of America is one of hope, of waiting for the next experience to begin. Koreans honored their ancestors; Americans honored their children.

Sungae leaned into the mirror to draw a thin line of kohl along her eyelids. In the living room, she heard Keehwan turn the TV back on, then the squeak of leather as he sat in his recliner. The booming of drums and marching band and the cheering crowd: Macy's Thanksgiving Day Parade in New York. She had watched part of it with him earlier, laughing when the big balloon of Mickey Mouse tipped over and floated down the street for two blocks on its back, bumping into lampposts and buildings, the crowd screaming and running away from it. "Afraid of a balloon?" Keehwan had laughed. "Why?"

Americans. Like big children.

In the mirror, Sungae smiled and shook her head, conscious of the tightness in her neck. Mrs. Kim, also from the church, had set Sungae's hair yesterday, and all night she'd slept with the stiff posture, like a corpse, so she wouldn't mess it up. She wanted to look right for her first *real* American Thanksgiving.

Of course, the Korean church hosted a Thanksgiving dinner every year, but eating kimchi and turkey on cafeteria tables covered with paper tablecloths and fold-out pilgrim decorations wasn't the same as real dinner with a real American family.

Outside, it began snowing, just like the pictures on the Thanksgiving cards in the University Bookstore, Sungae thought. Two days ago she had gone there for a tube of Windsor and Newton cadmium yellow, which she never bought. Instead, she stood for nearly an hour in front of the rack of Thanksgiving cards: "Thinking of You across the Miles" with a picture of a mailbox in the snow; "For My Daughter at Thanksgiving," an American mother and daughter laughing in the kitchen together. It was the first year Sungae had been able to read the words in English, the word *daughter* like the sheen of ice on a black road, catching her off guard.

She opened her eyes, glaring at herself in the mirror as if to frighten away her own thoughts. But she could still see the words in bright orange script across the picture of a house in the snow: "Thinking of You at Thanksgiving." Later, sitting in the University Commons, she opened the card, the white halves like the hollow inside a shell, and wrote the word *ttal,* daughter, at the top of the page. Her hand had been shaking, for what else could she say? She had wanted to write it a hundred times, the two handle-shaped strokes of the character above a zagging line, like a bent woman kneeling. Again and again. Daughter. Were there any words more important than this? Only the ones she couldn't write, *omoni,* mother, and *mianhamnoda,* I am sorry. But what good was sorry after seventeen years?

Still, the card was in her book bag right there next to the magazine rack with Keehwan's *TV Guide* and *Newsweek*, and though Sungae knew she wouldn't mail this one, she suspected that she might send the next. Maybe the Christmas card, or the New Year's. She thought of how every year in Seoul, on the last day of the lunar year, relatives and friends went to Seoul Grand Park and flew the kites on which they had written their fears and worries, and they would release the kites so that all these terrible things might be carried away from their lives. But Americans did the opposite, Sungae knew. They wrote wishes on postcards, as Brooke's kindergarten class had done last week, then attached those wishes to helium balloons. They let them go all at once over their school playground, the sky filled with bright circles of color. It made sense to Sungae. Hadn't she learned long ago that what was most dangerous in a person's life wasn't what she feared but what she desired? Lately, Sungae had been desiring to see her daughter again.

Chongmin would be seventeen now. Every day Sungae sat in the Commons or, if it was nice outside, in the sculpture garden of the Fine Arts building, sipping *yulmu ch'a,* Job's tears tea, from a thermos and watching the college girls in university sweatshirts and blue jeans smoking or reading, and she'd think of her daughter. Did Chongmin have a best friend? A boyfriend? Was she a dutiful daughter, waking early in the morning to serve *naeng myun,* cold noodles, to her father? On New Year's Day, did she perform *sae bae,* bowing respectfully to her grandparents? Was she preparing to go to university? What did she want to be? On *paik-il,* her One-Hundred-Day Celebration, had Hwang's family placed the objects around Chongmin to see what destiny she would choose? Did she reach for the book to become the great scholar? The thread to have the long life? The feather to fly far from home? Did she ever stare across the Yellow Sea to the west and wonder about her mother? Of course not. She would have been told Sungae was dead. And all these years, as if to make up for the terrible wrong she had done to Chongmin by bringing her into the world without an honorable mother, Sungae had tried to be dead.

But what if . . . The phrase pushed against the bones of her ribs. Perhaps the *han-bok* was too tight still, squeezing on her heart. She held her palm flat against her stomach and turned sideways to scrutinize herself in the glass. A memory swiveled inside her: another time when she had been standing sideways before a mirror, hand against the newly rounded curve of her belly. Outside, the clicking of bicycle gears on the street out front, the constant ping of bells, the clacking of the trash-metal collector's shears. The word *pregnant, im-shim-han,* like a white crane spreading its wings inside her, lifting off, its whooping echoing across her life, like the sound of her own frightened sobs.

What if she had not gotten pregnant? Never met Hwang? What if, all those years ago when she and Keehwan chose to have the *yon-ae,* love marriage, instead of one arranged by the matchmaker—what if she had heeded the matchmaker's advice? That it was never good for someone born in the year of the sheep, as Sungae was, to marry someone born in the year of the ox, as Keehwan was. "The sheep would only bring trouble," the matchmaker predicted, something Keehwan and Sungae had joked about in the early years of their marriage "You see? I should have married the snake or the rabbit," he would tease when she burned edges of *bin-dae-ttok,* Korean pancake, or let the tea grow cold. "Sheep only brings me misfortune." Later, though, after Sungae returned from the months of living with Hwang, born in the year of the boar—a perfect partner for Sungae—she and Keehwan never again joked about the matchmaker's prediction.

The snow was wet, plopping thickly against the windowpanes, then sliding down the glass in small silvery streaks. Sungae felt a thin gray shadow move across her heart. *What if . . . If only . . . If I could have, I would have . . .* The phrases circled in her chest like vultures, waiting. They had been learning "conditional phrases" in class. Two days ago, they pushed their desks into a circle and had taken turns telling each other about things they wished they had done in the past—the "unreal condition," Annie explained, because it had not happened. Annie had gone first. "I wish I had learned another language," she told them. "If I had, I would have understood my students more."

Ahmad who was sitting next to her, went next: "I wish I had learned to shoot the gun. If I had, I would have killed the soldiers who murdered my best friend."

Sacide said, "I wish we had not come to this country. If we had stayed in Turkey with our child, we would not be so unhappy." Sacide had looked at her husband when she said this, but he was staring outside at the bare tree branches. Sacide had come into class weeping quietly that morning, clutching a crumpled piece of paper that she rushed to show Annie the minute Annie arrived. "Why?" she had sobbed, shoulders heaving. "Why do they do this to me?" It was her phone bill—six hundred dollars—all the calls to Ankara to speak to her son.

When it was Sungae's turn to make a wish, she told Annie, "I don't wish anything."

"Nothing?" Annie smiled too brightly. "It doesn't have to be serious, Sungae—or even true."

Sungae shook her head, unable to meet Annie's eyes. What was the point of such sentences? she wanted to demand. *Why you always teach us these regretful thoughts?* For a moment there had been an awkward silence as Annie waited, and then Yukihiko said something about wishing he had been an actor on the TV show, *Baywatch,* and everyone laughed.

After class, Annie told Sungae, "I'm sorry if I made you uncomfortable. I didn't expect that some of the students would say such serious things. I understand why you felt uneasy."

Sungae nodded. What was she supposed to say? Annie was just standing there with the strange expression on her face, wanting something, Sungae could tell. Finally, she said, "Why do you teach students words which you do not believe are serious? Words are like the gold coins. They should be saved until you can spend wisely."

Annie glanced at Sungae quizzically, and then crossed her arms over her chest as if to hug herself against the cold. "I never thought of language like that," she said. Outside, a red leaf, shaped like a child's mitten, blew against the window. "I've always wanted my students to have fun with the language, to play with it, enjoy it . . ."

Sungae had shrugged uncomfortably. "Wishes are not for playing," she said finally. "Wishes are the same as prayers."

Sungae flicked off the bathroom light and padded across the bare floor to the bed. She sat gingerly, careful not to wrinkle her dress, and stared out the window. Snow already clung to the bent branches of the pine trees and the roof of her studio. On the TV she heard, "From our family at Channel Eight to yours, we wish you a Happy Thanksgiving." In the oval mirror over the bureau, she eyed herself suspiciously, as if she didn't recognize herself—a woman in a pale green *han-bok* with the pattern of pink chrysanthemums. She shook her head in irritation. The *han-bok* seemed all wrong suddenly. Maybe a sweater and skirt? Red church dress? What would the characters on *All My Children* do? Sungae smiled at the thought and tried to imagine how she would dress if she were on the soap. *What if* she wore the high heels and sexy black party dress like Erica? *What if* she wore the big-leg pantsuit with a blouse like Dixie? Low-cut halter dress like Maria? She giggled, holding her palm across her lips in the traditional Korean manner, as if to keep this happiness inside.

Ever since starting school, she had been watching the daytime soap opera less and less, and sometimes on Tuesdays and Thursdays when she was home early, drinking a bowl of *dag-go-gi-guk,* chicken soup, and watching TV, she'd leave the room in the middle of the program, and she'd wander out to the kitchen table to practice subordinate clauses or do a quick sketch for another painting. Before she knew it, music for *One Life to Live* was coming on, and Sungae never did find out if the wedding was ruined or what Edmund was going to do about the child that wasn't his. More and more, Sungae didn't care. For the first time in seventeen years, she was tired of the show. She wanted things to end, for the past to remain quiet, for characters to stop returning from the dead or showing up as the evil double. Even in Korea, it had occurred to her one afternoon, it was only those souls who had not resolved their conflicts, or who had not been mourned properly or who had been forgotten too soon, that would linger in this world rather than move on to the next. And it occurred to her then that maybe *this* was the reason why the memories of Chongmin and Hwang had come back after all of these years. *What if* all she had to do to relinquish the past was to first remember it?

What if? What if Annie was right and wishes didn't have to be so serious? "What if I paint the sky bright purple and the snow green and bare tree trunks cadmium yellow?" she wondered out loud. She glanced at herself again in the mirror, surprised by the thought. What if she sent the Thanksgiving card to Chongmin? The thought fluttered impatiently in her chest. Or what if Keehwan found the paintings? She held the idea inside her like a breath, like a small impossible secret.

In the mirror, her dark eyes looked big and round and hopeful today. Almost like an American's. What if, after all these years, Keehwan could finally understand?

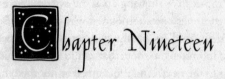

Chapter Nineteen

Except for Kayla's sister Abby, everyone congregated in the kitchen, cooking different things, asking each other, "What do you think? More salt?" or offering opinions about the turkey and how much longer until it was ready. The kitchen smelled of butter and sage, and the windows were steamed with condensation from the heat. Already the sink was piled with dirty dishes, and on the butcher block were plates of cheese and crackers and small bowls of salted nuts, which they kept reaching around one another to grab. It was just like *Chusok,* the Harvest Moon festival, Sungae thought, as she rolled biscuit dough across the flour-covered counter. All the shops and stores would shut down for three days so the family members could travel to the house of the oldest son. The women, wearing their *han-bok*s, would gather in the kitchen to prepare the cold feast, which the men would place on the graves of the ancestors. Later, they would have a big feast at home and at night they would walk to the nearest hill to honor the *Chusok* moon, the most beautiful of the year.

"Do you think it is true that the moon in America is bigger and brighter than the moon in the Korea?" Hwang had asked her on her last *Chusok* in Korea.

"Not possible." Sungae touched Hwang's cheek with her palm, as if he were her child. She knew that what he was really asking was, "Will you forget me once you are in America?"

"Six weeks for maternity leave is not enough time," Zach was saying. They were talking about his and Abby's new baby, Sam, who was three weeks old.

Sungae knew that *maternity* was connected to mother and she understood *leave,* but what was the meaning of the two words pushed against one another like that? Was "maternity leaving" what she had done seventeen years ago? Her throat felt dry, and nervously, she sipped her white wine. Very bitter. Not sweet like traditional Korean wine.

"Six *months* isn't enough time for maternity leave," Kayla laughed as she pushed the turkey back into the oven, juice sizzling against the roasting pan. "Six *years* isn't."

"Oh, I don't know," Emily, Kayla's mother, said. She was the most beautiful American woman Sungae had ever seen. Thick white hair, like a fox, and sharp blue eyes. "I think Abby would go crazy if she was home for six months. It can get pretty lonely being with a baby all day."

"Really? because I can stare at him for hours, even if he's asleep," Zach was saying to Emily.

Me, too, Sungae thought, remembering the afternoons near the end of her pregnancy when she stayed in the apartment alone while Hwang was at the store. Sometimes she just lay on her side in bed, watching as her child kicked from inside her. Other times, as she made *song pyon,* sweet rice cakes shaped like the quarter moon, she would talk to her baby in a soft voice so that she might fill her child with gentleness. But she also made sure to speak in a loud tone about how unlucky her child would be to have a *mang halyon,* bad luck woman, for a mother. This way the jealous spirits would know to leave this baby alone even after Sungae was not there to protect her.

"Remember our first Thanksgiving with Brooke, mom?" Kayla said. "I don't think either Dad or Will even glanced at the football game, and we might as well have served them frozen pizzas for all they cared about the food. It was just Brooke this, Brooke that."

"Oh, we were pretty smitten ourselves." Emily scooped a fingerful of potatoes from the mixing bowl Zach held out to her. "Absolutely perfect," she said. She nudged Kayla. "What do you think, honey?"

But the phone rang then, and Kayla stopped to grab it. "Oh, hi," she said quietly, and then moved across the kitchen to stand at the sink, perfectly still, the long phone cord coiled around her. It was Will, Sungae knew, because the same thing happened at the café when he phoned lately. Kayla didn't continue working at the computer or taking inventory of supplies or icing a cake as she usually did, but just stopped, all of her energy focused on being still. And she held on to the phone for a second or two after she'd hung up, as if she didn't want to let go.

"You can't even stop in and say hello?" Sungae heard her ask quietly now. And then, "Okay, fine. Six is good." Slowly, she unwrapped herself from the telephone cord and replaced the receiver back into its cradle. She stood there for a minute, hands on her hips, as if trying to decide something.

Zach glanced at Emily and said, "I'm going to go check on Sam."

"You don't need to go, Zach," Kayla said flatly, but already he'd left.

"You know, honey," Emily said, "you don't have to let Brooke go to his place tonight." She continued stirring the gravy in slow even circles, though her eyes rested on Kayla. "Nobody would blame you."

Kayla shook her head. "I already told Brooke she could."

"Well, it's above and beyond."

Above and beyond what? Sungae pictured the 747 that had taken her from Korea, and felt her heart quicken with grief. She thought of how difficult it was for Kayla to let Brooke go to her father's for one night and of how she had let Chongmin go forever.

"This isn't noble, Mom." Kayla picked up a dirty measuring cup from the counter, set it back down. "I don't know what I'm doing," she said. "Half of me is only letting her go because I'm hoping she'll hate that woman he's with as much as I do, and he'll see how screwed up this whole thing is." She opened the refrigerator to retrieve the bottle of wine and refilled her glass, but just as she was about to take a sip, she started crying instead. "What if Brooke likes Will's girlfriend, Mom? What am I going to do?"

Sungae imagined the woman living with Will was like the evil villains on *All My Children,* wearing big diamond rings and bright lipstick and always trying to steal the other women's husbands. Sungae wished she had the right words to explain to Kayla that even if this was true, she was doing a good thing for Brooke, that daughters needed to be with their fathers as much as sons did.

Emily was hugging Kayla. "Sarah, do you have children?" she asked politely.

Sungae nodded and said, "I have the daughter." The words surprised her.

"You do?" Kayla asked.

Sungae nodded. "She is seventeen years old." Her heart was beating loudly, and she was grateful for the sounds of the marching band coming from the TV in the next room. "In Korea. She is with her father."

Kayla wiped her eyes on the sleeve of her dark dress. "The girl in the painting with the kite? Was that her?"

"Her name is Chongmin." Sungae's voice caught. She had never said it out loud. *Chongmin.* She felt how it lifted away from her like a bird.

"It was the terrible mistake in my life," Sungae told Kayla after she had finished telling the story.

They had finished dinner over an hour before, everybody talking and laughing and saying how delicious the food was and asking Kee-hwan and Sungae about the holidays in Korea. Afterward, Kayla's father put on Emily's apron and pushed all of the women out of the kitchen, saying, "This is men's work now."

"Ahh, good tradition," Sungae told Emily.

"Don't let them fool you," Emily laughed. "If I know Bill, he's already got the back door open, and he's lighting a cigar, probably offering one to your husband at this very moment."

"But you loved Hwang," Kayla said. They were out walking, Brooke and Emily a few houses ahead. The snow had turned to a light mist. "Didn't you ever wonder what it might have been like to stay in Korea with him and your daughter?"

"Not possible." Through lighted windows, they could see families eating dinner or playing games or watching TV.

"Really? Why?"

"It is difficult for Americans to understand," Sungae said, "but all Koreans understand that duty is more important than love. Duty is like an ancient tree which has survived many seasons. Love is only the blossom."

"And your duty was to Keehwan."

Sungae nodded. How could she explain that even when she loved Hwang the most, she had never forgotten this, had never once protested when Hwang told her, *"Nul surang-he, Sungae, hachiman no-e nampyoni telsu opso"—I love you, Sungae, but I cannot become your husband.* Always when he spoke those words, he said them sadly, in a small voice, and always Sungae told him, *"Na ihe,"—I understand,* though at times, the words burned in her throat like spicy red bean paste and tears streamed from her eyes.

"I don't think I'm as strong as you, Sarah," Kayla said after a moment. "I think I'd hate it if Will had stayed with me only out of duty while he still loved her."

"Why you say only?" Sungae asked. A car drove past, leaving two parallel black streaks down the center of the snow-dusted road.

Kayla shrugged. "Maybe I shouldn't, but duty just seems so empty."

"Why empty?" Sungae squinted at her. "Don't Americans give up many things for their children, change their whole lifestyles, give up the career, throw away freedom?"

"But that's out of love."

"Yes, but also duty—cooking good dinner every night, moving to neighborhoods with best schools, not buying new car so they can pay the fee for education. If parents do not follow this duty, it is considered a very shameful act, right?" She didn't wait for Kayla to agree, but continued. "In Korea, it is the same situation, only instead of parents only making sacrifices for the children, children make it for their parents and ancestors, too. My actions brought terrible shame into my family and Keehwan's family. It was my duty to undo this."

"But to give up your child," Kayla said. They could no longer see Brooke and Emily in the snow-filled darkness, though they could hear Brooke's laugh. "I must seem silly to you, falling apart over letting Brooke go for one night." Her eyes filled and she stopped for a moment and stared up at the cloud-filled sky. There was no moon. "I would take Will back," Kayla whispered. She glanced at Sungae. "I feel like you understand it better than my family would."

"Will is *michinon,* crazy man, if he doesn't come back to you," Sungae said. "You watch. Blossom cut from the tree cannot last."

They watched *It's a Wonderful Life,* which Kayla's father explained was one of the most favorite holiday movies. Sungae was shocked. She had never seen this kind of American movie—all about duty and selflessness—exactly what she was explaining to Kayla. It was actually like a Korean movie. The whole story was about the man who stayed in his hometown and ran his family's business after his father died, even though it was his dream to go to college and travel around the world. At the end of the movie, he is filled with bitterness and regret and just as he is about to jump off the bridge, an angel reminds him that because he has fulfilled his *uiri,* he has the Wonderful Life after all.

Chapter Twenty

When Will's mother was alive, they took turns, Will and Jack and herself, naming out loud what they were thankful for. The Thanksgiving before she died, she said that she was grateful for the twenty years of marriage she'd shared with Jack, and then she locked her eyes on Will's and said she was thankful she'd lived long enough to see him grow up to be someone she was proud of. Will was only seventeen and this holiday wasn't the good memory it should have been. Will was furious at her for dying, didn't feel grown-up in the least, couldn't imagine spending holidays in that dark house, alone with his father. It wasn't that he didn't love his father, but that he couldn't imagine what his father would be like without his mother to make him laugh or to cajole him into setting aside whatever book he was reading to watch a movie.

Kayla had flown up from Georgia for that Thanksgiving holiday. It was the first time she would meet his parents—she and Will had become more serious than either had expected since they'd first met the previous summer at a student-government camp in Boulder. Kayla had worn sundresses while the rest of the girls wore khaki shorts and golf shirts. She chewed on a strand of her red-gold hair during the mock-debates, looking almost bored, though she always zeroed in on something or someone by the debate's end. Will noticed her immediately: the confident aloofness, her tanned arms and legs which, he discovered, he'd see if he woke early, when she sprinted by his dorm window, her Walkman so loud he could hear it clearly if he walked a few feet behind her into the breakfast hall. Will found himself following her to breakfast more and more each week. Kayla listened to famous political speeches when she ran: Martin Luther King's "I Have a Dream," JFK's Inauguration Address, Barry Goldwater's "Extremism Is No Vice."

Since that summer, they had racked up astronomical phone bills, and though they'd been planning the Thanksgiving visit since the last night of the camp, once Kayla arrived in Vermont, Will wasn't quite sure what to do with her. She was his first girlfriend—if she was even that. They had never really talked about it, and he hadn't yet kissed her, though he thought about it all the time. But what if this wasn't what she wanted? They were only high school kids, after all, and she lived a thousand miles away in Georgia. Except she was here, and he loved everything about her.

Will had hated his mother that last Thanksgiving because when she looked at him across the table with her you-have-made-my-life-worthwhile gaze he'd felt the tears he'd been holding back burn in his own eyes. And he wouldn't cry because he was seventeen, and because it wasn't cool to cry, and because it definitely wasn't cool to need your mom *this much* even if she was dying, and because it wouldn't alter the fact that the chemotherapy and the radiation hadn't worked.

For all these reasons, or maybe despite them, Will looked at his mother across the table and said, "Jesus, Mom, lighten up, you're not dead yet."

Had he thought it would sound funny somehow? His father looked as if he'd been punched and said, "Get away from this table before I kill you." His mother reached to lay a hand on Jack's arm. And Kayla, poor Kayla, didn't know whether to be upset or worried or pretend it wasn't happening. Will touched her arm on the way out of the dining room to tell *her* he was sorry.

As soon as his mother started crying, he understood that this was what he had wanted. He wanted her dying to hurt her as much as it did him; he wanted her to stop being so strong and so goddamn brave. He needed her to show him how to grieve, but every time he came close to crying, his dad would bark at him to get a grip. "If she can be strong for us when *she's* the one in pain," he'd remind Will, jabbing his index finger into his chest, "then the least you can do is keep your grief to yourself." Sometimes, more gently, he'd add, "Not yet, William. It's just not time yet, okay?" his voice frightened.

That last Thanksgiving with his mom, Will had gone outside without his coat and stood facing Mount Ascutney. His boots crunched over the frozen snow. He cocked his head and stared through the bone-white birches at the setting sun, keeping his eye on it, as if it were God, trying to escape. Which it did, in an instant, so that suddenly the mountain was just a looming darkness, and the air was twenty degrees colder. He stared at his breath against the purple-black sky and felt as if she were dead already, and he wanted her dead, in a way, because he didn't know how much longer he could hold it all inside. After a while, Kayla came out with his coat, and he shivered into it.

"Do you have any eights?" Anne asked.

Brooke giggled. "Go Fish!"

Will smiled, watching them over the top of the mystery he was pretending to read. Anne had been reminding him of his mother lately. Not in anything as obvious as her looks or gestures, but in the determined expression he often saw in her face. It had been there ever since Halloween. She had never asked him what had happened and when he tried to bring it up the next night, she shook her head and told him, "Don't explain. I know there are things you still need to work out."

"Yes, but you're thinking the wrong thing, Anne."

"I'm not thinking anything," she insisted. "I just hate Halloween, and I'm glad it's over. I don't want to talk about it."

She had prepared elaborate meals lately, the apartment was spotless, the bed made. She began suggesting they go to a new Cuban restaurant, the Smithsonian for the day or Virginia Beach for a weekend. And she tucked cards into his briefcase or picked up a quarter-pound of gourmet jelly beans on the way home for him. She woke early and turned off the alarm before it rang, then gently roused him from sleep by nuzzling his neck or stroking his hair away from his face. A thousand times he'd wanted to tell her to stop. She didn't need to prove to him how wonderful she was because he knew, had known that first time they met in the bar with the chili pepper lights. *You don't have to work this hard,* he wanted to tell her. *Just the fact that you love me and that I love you is enough.* But it wasn't, any more than his mother's cheerful determination not to be beaten by the cancer had been enough. All those books stacked on the floor by the hospital bed they'd eventually moved into the dining room. *The Healing Power of Laughter, The Will to Live is Better than a Living Will, A Survivor's Diary.* What his mother hadn't understood, except maybe at the end, was that it had never been up to her.

He glanced at Annie again, stretched out on the carpet playing go fish with Brooke, their pie plates on the floor next to them. When he had picked up Brooke for breakfast last Sunday, Kayla told him that Brooke could come for Thanksgiving dessert. "She can stay the night," Kayla had added. "If you want." And of course, he'd wanted his daughter overnight, but he also hadn't. "Why?" he wanted to ask. "Why now? Why all of a sudden?" But he knew the answer, and so did she. She could afford to be generous now, to let him try to make this relationship with Anne work, because somehow they both knew it wouldn't. Maybe Kayla wanted him to have Brooke so that later, he wouldn't be able to say that she had sabotaged his chances by not allowing him a fair chance at a new life. Maybe she had assumed that Brooke would dislike Anne or that Brooke would be homesick, and Will would have to see that his relationship with Anne couldn't possibly work. Or maybe Will was the one who didn't really want this to work and he was just looking for someone to blame it on besides himself. Maybe Kayla had been right, and he *wasn't* capable of love. All he knew was that after three months he was ruining what he had with Anne in the same way he'd almost ruined it with Kayla. He could see it in Anne's eyes.

And so he would cut his losses—and Anne's—before it was too late. After the holidays were over, he would go home like a good little boy, and for a while he and Kayla would both try. She would listen to him more and ask questions about his day, and he would do whatever was expected of him, whatever it took to win back her trust. And for Will, there wouldn't be all this uncertainty about whether he'd done the right thing. All this guilt. All this regret. Or would there be? Was the biggest mistake in leaving Kayla? Or would it be in returning to her?

His head ached from trying to sort out what he thought he'd settled months ago. He hadn't acted rashly in moving out. He knew he would miss his daughter. And he knew he would feel guilty for leaving both her *and* Kayla. But he had also known that his marriage had been dead for years, and he didn't want this to be his daughter's only example of what marriage was: two people who no longer touched or kissed or said "I love you," two people who never ate dinner together or even laughed much. He had wanted Brooke to know that happiness was worth fighting for, that it wasn't okay to settle for less. What he hadn't expected was how much he would miss Kayla. Or how, in the midst of teaching his daughter to fight for her happiness, he could also teach her what it meant to persevere and to be loyal and honest and fair.

"You want to play one more game?" Brooke was asking, scrambling to her knees, smashing the cards into a big pile, mixing them up.

Anne tossed Brooke a card that had been hiding beneath the couch. "Absolutely. You think I'm going to let you beat me nine times without trying to beat you back?"

"No, *ten* times!"

"Ten!" Anne reached to tickle Brooke, who squealed and squirmed away. They played so naturally together that they could have been mother and daughter—same dark hair, bangs in their eyes.

Brooke looked up at Will and said, "Daddy, I beat her ten times!"

And Anne turned, smiling softly at him. "Your daughter's a card-sharp," she said.

He wanted to cry, but he felt too confused, as if it were Thanksgiving twenty-four years ago. Will was waiting for Kayla to come out with his coat and promise that things would be okay, and he'd nod and follow her inside where it was safe and warm, knowing all the while that nothing would ever be okay again in his life. He felt his dad's finger in his chest, jabbing at him, telling him to get a grip because *he* wasn't the one in pain.

Chapter Twenty-one

Carter sliced open another carton of books. He set the X-Acto knife down on the desk and took a sip of tea. His hands were shaking. *This is how it starts,* he thought as he sorted the hardbacks into stacks of fiction and nonfiction.

He had simply wanted to drive by her apartment. But God, even that. How could he explain it to anyone without sounding crazy? *And what exactly were your intentions, Mr. Garvey, when you went to your estranged wife's home at—what time did you say it was?*

Stop it, he ordered himself. *This is not a detective movie; you didn't do anything wrong.*

He carried a stack of paperbacks to the second level where the memoirs and autobiographies were located. He paused for a moment at the window, staring across Franklin Street at the university offices outlined in white snow, like chalk drawings on a blackboard. The campus was deserted for the Thanksgiving holiday. In the distance a siren wailed, lifting over roads, treetops, buildings. His heart quickened in his chest, and for the first time, he didn't wonder about what had happened to the victims. He wondered about the perpetrators, and he wondered why they had done whatever they had, and he knew the answers were not as simple as he had always believed.

He set down the stack of books, idly glancing at the one on top. The story of that New York State judge who ended up in prison for stalking his ex-mistress. He'd had a wife, kids, a respectable job, friends. Carter ran his hands through his thinning blond hair and stared absently at the titles shelved alphabetically by author. A guy writing about growing up gay; a woman writing about incest; Styron's book about depression. Everybody with their secrets. He had thought he was immune. He'd had a great childhood, attended his first-choice college, married not *a* woman he loved, but *the* woman he loved—and he was successful in his business, he voted, he recycled, went to church on Christmas and Easter.

He was an arsonist.

He'd looked it up as soon as he got into the shop, read and reread the definition: "willful or malicious burning of property especially with criminal or fraudulent intent." But he hadn't *started* the fire, he reasoned, focusing on the words one at a time. Willful. Malicious. If he stared long enough, even they would crumble into an ashy gray. It had been two hours, and still, he couldn't rid those words from his mind. No matter how many times he tried, no matter how many times he told himself that *he* was the one who had called 911 from the pay phone at the Laundromat; no matter how many times he told himself that if it had been serious he *never* would have walked away.

He left the books for Annie's student—Farshad—to shelve in the morning and returned downstairs, his footsteps muffled by the Oriental runner Annie had convinced him to put down a few years ago. It was snowing flurries again and he stood for a minute in the doorway, the CLOSED sign at his chest. He kept trying to understand what had happened, but the truth was simple: It had been a long day, the first major holiday without her, and he had just wanted to be close to her for a minute. So he turned down Park—her street now—instead of Floyd, a difference of one block. One block. Was that so wrong? It hadn't seemed like it.

And then he parked. And that still didn't seem terrible. Annie had come outside onto the porch to smoke, and he was happy because it was like seeing the old Annie. Sitting in his car for those three or four minutes and watching her had been the best part of the whole lousy holiday. And then she finished her cigarette and went inside. He was going to leave, but he saw that she hadn't put the cigarette out. The butt was still burning on the concrete porch steps, and some dried leaves had caught on fire. All he wanted to do was put it out for her. And so he got out of his car and watched the light go out in the bed-room overhead and even then he was okay, he wasn't wondering why she was out smoking at midnight, by herself on Thanksgiving, why she'd started up again, none of that.

But he hadn't put the fire out. He saw Brooke's pink plastic snow boots on the porch, and here was the part he couldn't explain even to himself. Another siren howled in the distance. He knew there were more accidents on holidays and God, he wanted to call this an accident and it would have been if he had stayed in New Jersey as he'd originally planned, if he hadn't driven down her street, hadn't gotten out of the car and walked over to the porch and seen those boots that shouldn't have been there, seen those boots that kicked him in the gut with re-minders of everything he had been willing to give up for *her*, seen those boots and kicked them over to the flames and then stood there and watched while they began to burn.

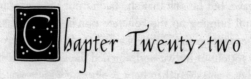

Chapter Twenty-two

The night after the fire they stayed in the Holiday Inn. Annie wondered if this was one of the rooms where they had made love during the two years of their affair. "How many rooms are in this place?" Will had asked her once as they lay across a queen-size bed, the sheets tangled around them, the TV on low.

"Why?" she laughed, but already she knew: He wanted to make love to her in every room. His way of asking for the seasons.

Will had left to pick up takeout Chinese food. Annie lay on the hotel bed, reading a collection of short stories that she'd started over the summer and had forgotten. On the back cover, a Book Cellar price-sticker. Almost every book she owned came from Carter's store. He knew which books she wanted to keep, he always said, because she grew careless with them: a coffee stain or a chocolate fingerprint on the corner of a page, sections underlined in felt-tip.

"Not carelessness. Love," she would chide, reminding him of the children's story, *The Velveteen Rabbit*. The rabbit's nose was no longer pink because the boy kissed him so much, and his fur was shabby from being hugged. Carter just rolled his eyes and left her alone, although once, he crept up behind her when she was reading at the kitchen table, waiting for coffee to brew, and he pressed his thumbprint right in the center of the page.

"There," he said smugly.

"What are you doing?" She grabbed his hand. "What *is* that?"

"I got you a stamp pad," he laughed. "I figured it was more efficient than pizza stains and coffee spills."

She closed her eyes for a minute, as if the memory were outside her, a scene from a movie she didn't have to watch. But it continued to play in her head: the scent of coffee and toast in their tiny kitchen, yellow sunlight splashing over the white tablecloth, Carter standing at the counter, shirtless in a pair of jeans, laughing at her as he poured them each a mug.

Restlessly, Annie turned the book over and stared at the back cover. "Where love has nothing to do with common sense," said the reviewer from the *Washington Post,* ". . . and characters must negotiate the explosive minefield of the human heart." That quote, Annie recalled now, was the reason she had chosen to read this book last spring.

She tilted the book away from the glare of the reading light. The author had old eyes—as if she knew too much. Was it true that in order to write you had to have experienced tragedy? "You gave me a normal childhood for God's sake. How could you?" Carter used to tease his parents. To Annie, also: "Do you have any Russian students? How about some guy named Vronsky? Tall, good-looking, you could fall in love with him, give me some material . . ." Annie wondered if Carter still had the desire to write now that she had given him the tragedy he had lacked.

It hadn't occurred to her until she found the book in one of the still-unpacked boxes in the kitchen, the jacket cover folded in on the last page she'd read—138—that she hadn't read anything other than student essays for four months, she who used to rush headfirst into two or three novels at a time, like waves in the ocean. As a girl, she couldn't get enough of the waves. She'd body surf, jump over them, stand at the breaking point and dare them to tumble her like a bowling pin. As an adult, she did that now with books.

She had sat on the floor this morning in her sweats, absently scratching Ethan's neck as she balanced the open book on her knee. She turned to the page she'd last read, tried to recall the story. A man in his kitchen, making spaghetti with his sons for dinner. A snowstorm; his wife upstairs. She closed her eyes, blocking out the stack of grocery-store boxes, Ethan, who was flopped onto the floor next to her like a throw rug, the drone of the vacuum as Will cleaned the bedroom. It had seemed important, suddenly, that she remember the plot, but all she could see was the fire marshal asking Will if anyone had been smoking on the porch, and Will wordlessly turning to her.

When she opened her eyes, Will was standing across the room, regarding her quizzically. The forgotten plot was her own, she realized.

"You okay?" Will closed the hotel room door behind him. *Stupid question,* he thought. He wasn't surprised when she didn't answer right away.

"I'm fine." She crossed the room to take the paper bags while he struggled out of his coat. "I was watching for you. What'd you get?" He'd woken at four this morning to find her huddled in a blanket at his desk. "Come on, Anne," he had whispered. "Nobody was hurt; it's okay." Brooke hadn't even woken up, and if it hadn't been for someone calling 911 and alerting the fire department, the whole thing would have probably burned out on its own.

She hadn't answered, and he didn't push. He lay on his side in the grayish light, the moon one of those smiling fat happy faces that teachers used to paste at the top of his spelling quizzes. He wished that happiness could somehow be that simple again.

"My god, Will." She pretended to buckle beneath the weight of the food.

He grinned. "I overdid it, huh?"

"What? You?" She started pulling the white containers from the bag. "Egg rolls?" Unfolding the tops, peering in, setting them down. "You got me Szechwan string beans?" He couldn't stand them. "What are you trying to do? Fatten me up for the kill?"

He didn't laugh.

She glanced at him. "Hey, I was kidding."

Will didn't answer because she was right. He was going to leave her. Why else come here? Had he thought he could still pretend that they were only having an affair? That they'd walk out of here after a few hours and resume their real lives? Except his affair with Annie had never been an "only" to him; for two years it had been everything. But already he was using the past tense.

"Will, I was joking," she said again. She stared at him in the reflection of the window. *He's aged somehow,* she thought. He had complained lately about gaining weight and she had refused to see it, but he did look thicker around the waist. It was like she was seeing him for the first time in months. She'd been afraid to look before, afraid that if she saw one change, however slight, she might have to admit to the other differences she had been sensing. He didn't love her as fiercely as he had that night nearly seven months ago when he'd left his family for her. She thought of Sungae and wondered what she had given up in order to come here and understood somehow that it had cost far more than it was worth.

"Are you okay? I mean, *is* this my last meal?" Her voice quavered. "Because if so, there better be some chocolate in here." One last attempt. *Don't do this,* she was thinking.

I don't want to, he thought, and she glanced at him as if she could read his mind. He tried not to think of how he loved that her hair moved like a metronome between her shoulder blades when she wore it in a ponytail, or that he was going to leave her, this woman for whom he'd thought he could change his life. But the knowledge had been there for weeks, and the fire last night had seared it open. He glanced at her and felt the air rush out of his lungs. "We have to talk," he said gently.

Annie set down the container of sweet and sour shrimp she had just opened, and wished that she could hate him right now. A Chinese student had once told her that the only difference between happiness and sorrow was the number of brush strokes needed to write the character. She thought of this as she stared at Will in the dull reflection of the mirror, sitting on the monstrous bed with his head in his hands, as if *he* were the one being hurt.

"Why did we come here?" she asked, turning from the desk to face him directly.

"'Anne, sit with me. This isn't a war." He tossed his boot onto the floor and started yanking at the laces of the other one.

"I don't want to sit, Will. I want to know why we're here."

Through the window, the naked tree branches swayed in the wind. She had told him once about a student from Indonesia, a man in his forties, who was terrified when he first arrived in the States. It was winter and he had never before seen a tree without leaves.

"I don't want to hurt you," Will began.

"Then don't." Her voice was hard. She glanced around the room with its beige textured wallpaper and drapes, its ugly paisley bedspread, the Monet *Water Lilies* print on the wall. She wanted to weep. How could either of them have believed that coming *here* was a good idea?

"Let's just get away for the night, get out of this apartment," he had said. She had believed it really was that simple.

"Can you just listen before you say anything, Anne? Please?" He had tried to imagine a thousand times the words he would use to explain to her that he was unsure. Driving through the reservoir on the way to work in the morning, cycling, feeding Ethan, lying awake at night and watching her sleep. But unsure about what? This was the part he still couldn't fathom because he wasn't unsure about her.

The room was steeped in grayness now, though the sky remained that same frozen white. She had promised herself weeks ago—or was it months?—that she wouldn't cry if and when Will finally found the courage to tell her he needed to go. She had promised herself that she wouldn't make him hurt any more than he already did. He had tried. She knew that. And so what else could she ask of him? But now she wondered how things might have been different if Carter hadn't been so strong the night she told him she needed to leave. What if he had begged her to stay, told her, as she wanted to tell Will, that he couldn't imagine his life without her? Maybe she never would have left if Carter had sat with her on the bed and cried instead of crossing the room to turn off the movie they'd been watching, the muscles in his back taut beneath his faded I READ BANNED BOOKS T-shirt. Maybe she would have stayed if he'd told her he couldn't imagine an entire day without talking to her, without knowing how her classes had gone, without reading her the new *Booklist* reviews over the phone or making a date to go out for Thai food after work. What was the greater act of love? To have let her go, as he had, or to have begged her to stay?

She was crying. She didn't care if it made things harder for Will.

"Please, sweetie, just let me explain—"

"Explain *what*?" she wailed. "How much you miss your daughter and your big house and your *life*. What did you expect?" She was sobbing. "Did you think starting over would be easy?"

"No, I didn't think it would be easy," he snapped. "But I thought I could do it. And you know I wanted to, you *know* I tried—" He glanced up, pleading for her to understand, but she was staring at him, tears coursing down her face. "You *know* that," he insisted, waiting for her to acknowledge him, to nod, to give him this much. When she wouldn't, he continued, speaking quietly. "Lately, it seems that whatever way I turn, I'm not happy. I'm not even sure I can be happy anymore." In the high-rises across the street, windows darkened as people left their offices for the night. "When I'm with you, I miss Brooke, and I'm sorry, Anne—" she glared at him, "but no matter how many times I convince myself that she's fine, I'm not. I don't feel good about myself, and it's killing everything good that I feel about us."

"It?" She shook her head, tears spilling from her eyes. "*It's* not killing anything, Will. You are."

"Why? Why would I do that, Anne? I left my daughter for you."

"And I have no idea how that feels, right?" She was sobbing again. "I don't know how you can be so cruel."

"You're twisting this around—"

"Am I?"

He wanted to tell her yes, but she was right. Again. He was holding it over her, the fact that she hadn't left a child, that she hadn't sacrificed as much as he had. "Would you have?" he asked quietly. "Walked out on your daughter for me?"

"How can I possibly answer that?" Her voice sounded dead, even to her. She felt very far away from him. "And what if I told you yes. Would that really change anything for you now?" When she looked at him, a wave of compassion swelled and then broke inside of her. It shocked her that she could feel this empathy for him, and she realized that this was how Carter must have felt about her the night she told him about Will. "You're like one of those kings in the fairy tales who set up these impossible tests which the suitors must pass in order to win the princess's hand," she told Will. "And of course, they can't." She smiled sadly. "If I thought I was costing you your daughter's love, *I* would leave *you*."

"I know," he said. "And I know you love me, but—"

She turned her back on him and walked to the window. She stared at the huge lighted clock on the Jefferson Hotel, which had once housed alligators in its terraced courtyard and whose grand marble staircase was falsely rumored to have been used in filming *Gone with the Wind*. Annie and Carter had celebrated their first night in Richmond nine years before with glasses of champagne and an outrageously expensive cup of fresh strawberries in that very hotel. She watched the dark minute hand jerk forward, and remembered that in Chinese, the character for *clock* is the same as the character for *death*.

"You want me to be calm and rational," she said softly, still staring outside. "You want me to make everything all right for you by telling you that I understand, but I don't understand at all, Will. I don't." From the hallway outside, she heard the ping of the elevator, and the murmur of conversation as people passed their room. "I think if you really wanted to be with me, you would. I think you'd try harder to figure out whatever it is that's going on with you." She turned to face him, crying again. "And I think you're lying to yourself, because I don't think this has anything to do with Brooke." Outside, dry tree branches squeaked against each other like rusted machinery. "I don't understand why you're doing this," she said when he didn't respond.

"*Why?* Jesus, Anne, you act like this is something I want."

"Isn't it?"

"Yeah, Anne. I turned my whole fucking life upside down ten months ago just so I could do this—"

"I'm not talking about *your* sacrifices!" she cried. "God, Will, why does everything have to be about you? You act like you're the only one with the right to feel pain, and you're blaming me because it's not perfect." She was sobbing. "But don't you think I sometimes miss Carter as much as you miss Kayla and Brooke—and I know, Will, I know, okay? It's not the same, I didn't leave a child." She was trying to catch her breath between words.

"Come on, Anne, don't."

"Don't *what,* Will? Don't tell you the truth? Don't make this difficult? Do you even have any idea how hard Halloween was for *me*—or yesterday, for that matter?"

"Isn't that the point?" He ran his hands through his dark hair. "We didn't go through all the crap we did to end up miserable. Christ, I could have stayed with Kayla for that." He glanced at her. "Look at us," he said softly. "Look at you." But even now, all he could think about was about how beautiful she looked with the city lit up behind her. Miniature white Christmas lights had been strung through the dark trees in front of the James Madison building. They glittered like a whole constellation. It was his mother who had taught him the names for the constellations: the Pleiades, Orion the Hunter, the Big and Little Dipper. He remembered, too, how Anne had told him that the Chinese believe the seven brightest stars of the Big Dipper represent the seven openings of the heart. "I'm tired, Anne. And maybe I'm not as strong as you, or maybe I'm a coward, but I'm tired of having to feel so much all the time. Every conversation, every nuance, is completely loaded."

"It's all about you again, isn't it? Except you're not the victim this time, and I'm not the wife who doesn't understand." She shook her head, and in the mirror he watched the dark line of her ponytail brush against her shoulders. "Do you have any idea what it felt like to watch you mope around yesterday while I entertained *your* daughter?" In her voice rose something ugly he'd never heard before. "Do you have any idea how desperate I was to prove to you that I could make her happy? That she could be okay with us, *us,* Will? And you didn't even try. You weren't even there."

"Goddamn it, Anne!" he bellowed, shocked by the rage in his voice. "Do you have any idea what *I* felt like watching you with my daughter? I was there, all right, I saw how well you got along, and I loved you for that, but it's not just some goddamn fairy tale with a "happily ever after" simply because Brooke liked you. I felt like shit watching the two of you together because I saw how easily *we* could be a family and yeah, it scared me. I felt guilty, okay? I felt bad for Kayla. I felt that Brooke liking you was a greater betrayal to her than the affair had ever been."

Who are you? she wondered. *I don't even know you anymore.* "I can't win," she said. "If Brooke *hadn't* liked me, you would have used that against me."

"Exactly, Anne, I've just been looking for reasons . . ."

"*Why* are you talking to me like this, Will?"

"I don't know, Anne, maybe because everything's starting to make sense. Is this why you started your little fire? To punish me? To get my attention because I *wasn't there*?"

"*What*?"

The warmth was gone from his eyes. "You were pissed? Was that it, Anne?" He didn't believe this for a minute, but he wanted to hurt her, to end this.

She closed her eyes, and in her mind she pictured the news footage she had seen earlier of an imploded apartment complex. The front of the building slid down like a concrete waterfall, and she felt that inside her, her love for him was slipping, too.

The minute he saw her face, he wanted to yank back his words. "Jesus, Anne, I'm sorry. I didn't mean that, I don't—"

"No." She held up her hands as if to ward him off.

"Anne—"

Anne. Why hadn't she ever realized how cold her name sounded when he said it? Anne. Her dad used to call her Annie Rooney, Aspirin Annie, Anna Banana. Nicknames Will had never heard. She looked at him. How could she have been so stupid, so godawful stupid? She moved over to the bed, picked up the book she had been reading, set it in her duffel bag, and walked past him to the bathroom.

"Would you wait?" he asked when she returned, her face splashed with water, but so pale. She had combed her hair, retied her ponytail.

"Why?" She felt strangely detached now as she picked up her coat. *So this is it,* she kept thinking. Everything she had feared.

"I'm sorry," he said. "It was a stupid thing to say, Anne. I'm so sorry."

"You really think I would start a fire?" she asked. "Especially when there was a child in the house?"

"No, my God, no." He looked up at her. He'd fallen in love with her eyes first. And then her mind, her laugh, her body. But right now all he saw was her eyes. They were huge. "Can we please just start this conversation over?"

"Maybe it's better not to." She took a deep breath. She looked so tiny in her black wool coat. "You've been trying to do this for a while, haven't you?"

He nodded, and it caught her off guard, how badly it hurt to hear the truth.

She sank into the hard-backed chair. Neither had turned on any more lights in the room, and Will was suddenly grateful, as if whatever hurt he was about to inflict should happen in near darkness.

He couldn't see her face clearly, just the sheen of wetness on her cheeks, where she'd splashed water. The clock on the nightstand displayed tiny red numbers: 7:28, 7:29. What time had he gotten back from getting the food? It seemed like hours ago; it seemed like ten minutes ago. "I don't know what to tell you," he said after a moment.

Tell me we're going to work this out. Tell me you love me and that you're not going back to Kayla. Tell me that you think I'm a beautiful woman, that you didn't laugh for years until you met me, that you like who you are since I came into your life. . . . She was crying again before she knew it. He got up from the bed and pulled her to him.

"Look," he said, and she could feel how he had to grit his teeth and close his eyes as if it was the hardest thing in the world to say. "I don't want to leave—"

"Then why are you?" she cried.

"Anne, I just need time." He tried to pull back so that he could read her face, her eyes.

"You don't want time," she sobbed. "You want to leave and you've wanted to ever since Halloween, and you don't have the guts to tell me." She pushed his arms away. "You think time will make it easier, Will? You think time will make me hate you less for what you've done, for making *me* say what you should have said months ago?"

"Listen to me, Anne. I don't want to leave you." But he still wasn't saying that he wouldn't.

When he looked at her, she was reminded of how her students often regarded photographs of their native countries, places they would be saying good-bye to for the rest of their lives. She thought of how Shin-pin had slowly traced her fingers over the picture of Shanghai in one of their texts, how Ba had held his postcards of Ho Chi Minh, cupping them gently at the edges, as if they were as fragile as the coconut-husk toy boats he said he'd sailed on the Dong-nai River with his cousins.

She was sobbing again. Weeping. She was losing him, and there was nothing that she could do.

He'd never heard her like this, and it scared him. He wanted to promise her that he'd stay, wanted to promise her that it would be all right, but would it? He felt as if they were drowning. He'd never imagined it like this, never thought she'd fall apart so terribly. Everything he had thought he'd understood these last two months suddenly made no sense. Why would he leave someone who loved him this much? And someone whom *he* loved this fiercely? He heard Anne's sobs and he thought of how his Aunt Debra had collapsed during his mother's funeral. They'd given her a sedative and later, everyone had talked about her "display," but Will had loved his aunt for the vastness of her grief.

"Come here." Gently, he pulled Anne up from the desk chair and onto the bed. He lay back, cradling her against his chest. She still wore her coat. The wool scratched against the skin at his neck. "I'm sorry," he whispered into her hair. It smelled of cigarettes, though he knew she hadn't smoked all day. He squeezed his eyes shut against his own tears. "I'm sorry," he repeated again.

"I don't understand," she said sadly.

"Don't understand what, sweetie?" He spoke into her hair, rocking her.

"How you can speak to me like you did, how you can leave. I don't understand where the love goes."

"Oh, Anne, it doesn't go. You think I'll ever stop loving you? You think I won't miss you every time I see a beautiful woman with dark hair or—" He was crying now. Why was he doing this to them? Why couldn't he be happy with her? "I'm sorry," he said as he held her closer to him.

She pushed herself against his ribs. She felt as if she were lying against the bottom of a flimsy rowboat, rocking, lurching over rough water. So many of her students had escaped their countries this way, terrified against the pitch of water, the wooden ribs of a raft or a boat. Ba had written of it in his telling line on the first day of class.

After that class, Annie remembered, Sungae had asked, "Why you do this? Why you teach us such sorrowful sentence?" and Annie had wondered then if it was true, if the most important things in people's lives were also the most sorrowful, if saying good-bye altered a person in ways that saying "I love you" could not. She didn't want to think so. And yet, Annie knew that if she had asked her mother what her "telling line" was, she wouldn't have said her marriage to Annie's father or the birth of her children, but rather the death of her son. It had changed her. Afterward, she switched from being an oncology nurse to a pediatric nurse. She wanted to be near children. Annie always knew which nights her mother had worked with a teenager who had been in a car accident because when she came home in the morning, she would go straight to her rose garden. Or, in the fall and winter, she'd work in the basement for hours, watering her orchids, rearranging them beneath the grow lights, praying that they would live.

She thought of her own "telling line," *I fell in love with Will,* and realized for the first time that this, too, might be a sentence filled with sorrow.

"Please don't go," she whispered into Will's shirt. It was damp from her tears. He squeezed her tightly. An arm of light from the half-open bathroom door reached across the carpet toward the bed. He kissed her again. The isolated gray strands in her hair seemed almost silvery.

Outside, the *chop* of a police helicopter passed by. He wondered about the kids in the Richmond Boys' Home. Nearly a quarter of them had been granted weekend passes to have Thanksgiving at home with their families, and most of them would return to school worse off. Echoes of "good for nothing" and "stupid," or worse, echoes of silence, of being ignored. Monday, the boys would enter Will's office with an angry strut.

"Please," Annie begged again. Her eyes were swollen, and her head ached from crying. In the odd light of the city, the white sheets became pale blue, the color of new snow. When she first moved in with Will, she had bought white sheets like these. She liked how they always looked crisp and clean, how they didn't fade like the yellow roses of the sheets she'd shared with Carter.

Will didn't answer for a long time. His stomach growled, but he didn't stir, and she didn't want to move from his arms. She wondered if he was asleep. He still hadn't said he would stay. Would she live in the apartment without him? Unpack her boxes still stacked in the kitchen? She tried to picture mornings without Ethan tapping her face with his paw when it was time for her to feed him. She felt herself shudder as a new sob surfaced.

"Shush," he whispered, holding his hand over her face, wiping her cheek with his thumb. His eyes were closed. He thought about the first night they had come to this hotel, how he had assumed she would be shy, that she would want to make love with the lights out. She had surprised him by asking him to leave them on. She wanted to look at him, she said. He remembered her ease, her lack of inhibition, as she walked naked across the room—even when she went to the bathroom, she kept talking with him through the open door. He recalled other nights in this hotel, how she spread the bedspread on the floor once like a picnic blanket and told him, "This is how Arab families eat." They had ordered pizza and she'd brought wine, which they drank from hotel water glasses. Mostly, he remembered how incredibly happy he had been. And he thought then that when people are at their happiest old traumas will resurface, as if the mind knows that it is safe now to dredge up the unhealed wounds. He knew, too, that she was right, and that much of what he was feeling wasn't about her or Brooke but was connected to something far deeper: Why else put himself through this kind of pain unless it was to avoid a far greater one?

The words, *I'll stay,* caught in his throat. He knew if he said them this time, there was no going back. If he said them, he needed to sign the divorce papers and move on. *When does a jump become a fall?* A line from a rap song he'd heard somewhere. His mouth felt dry. "I'll stay," he said hoarsely, and something splintered open inside him, and he was sobbing.

It frightened her. She lifted her head from his chest to look at him. "Will don't. Please, I'm sorry—" His face seemed changed. "I shouldn't have begged you," she was crying more now, too. "If you need to leave, I'll be all right, I promise—" She thought again of Carter telling this to her: *If you need to go, I'll understand,* and she understood anew what those words must have cost him. But Will just kept repeating, "I'm not going to leave, sweetie. I promise." Over and Over. As if saying it enough times would make it come true.

They checked out that night. The clock on the Jefferson Hotel read ten-twenty, although it felt like two or three in the morning. Traffic lights swayed over deserted intersections like Christmas ornaments. Will held Anne's hand as he drove, letting go only to shift gears. He needed to touch her, to hold on. In the morning, he would rework his schedule with Brooke, he would tell Kayla to go ahead with the divorce, get it over with, the sooner the better. At this point it was only a matter of signing the papers. He would figure out what to do about Christmas later.

"You okay?" she asked. Her eyes swollen, her mascara smudged; her hair uncombed, one side pulled free of her ponytail—he had never seen her like this.

"I love you." He was trying not to cry. He'd said that phrase a thousand times. To her, to Kayla, to other women. He wasn't sure what it meant anymore.

Near campus, some of the houses already had Christmas lights up— electric candles glowing in windows, rooftops outlined with red or green or multicolored blinking bulbs. The library was dark, and in the dorms, only a few lights burned. He squeezed her hand, knowing she was thinking of her students, many of whom had had nowhere to go for Thanksgiving. He stared at one of the lighted windows, pictured that student of hers from Indonesia sitting at a desk, staring outside at the starless gray sky and the barren landscape, the trees without leaves.

As he turned onto Grove Avenue, he thought again of the way Anne had sobbed as he held her on the bed, a terrible sound he knew he'd never forget. Something had begun to unravel inside him as he listened to her cry. He didn't know that he could coil it back into the tiny space in which it had been crammed. He stared at the flashing lights of a plane taking off from the Richmond Airport and he wondered if maybe all these years it wasn't love he'd been searching for, but mourning, what Anne had given him tonight.

"What are you thinking?" she asked as they sat at the light at Harrison and Grove Streets.

"I don't know where to start," he said quietly. "I'm thinking about a thousand things at once."

He was thinking that on the left was Carter's bookstore, the only decent one in the city. He used to go there once a week, at least, before he met Anne. It was the one place other than the airport where he could get the Sunday *New York Times* and the *Boston Globe.* Afterward, he'd go to Kayla's Espresso Shop, meet Brooke there, and offer her the comics, or the coupons, which she clipped for her dolls. It was because of this that Kayla got the idea to open a bookstore/café with Carter, which led to the four of them getting together for that fateful dinner. Like one of those connect-the-dot pictures in Brooke's coloring books.

He was thinking, too, of geese migrating thousands of miles to a predestined place, sometimes over miles and miles of dark ocean. They followed the stars or they followed an internal compass sensitive to the earth's magnetic field and, somehow, this kept them from getting lost. He was thinking that for twenty-four years, ever since his mother's death, he, too, had been winging his way through the dark, trying to find a way home. He'd made an entire career out of it, he realized, counseling kids, as if he could give them what he'd somehow lost, as if by healing the wounds in their lives, he might somehow heal the one in his own life. Even all the affairs he'd had, the ending inherent in each, as if he could relive his mother's death, somehow get it right, by loving over and over women he knew he would eventually lose. None of it had worked, though, which tonight had made so painfully clear. And what was the guarantee that with Anne it would? It terrified him, all the ways he might have to change in order to find out who he was and what he wanted. What if, in the end, it wasn't her?

Anne glanced at him, her head resting on the seat back. He saw her as she'd been the first time she had sat in his car like this in the dark, just talking. He'd bumped into her in the Safeway a few weeks after the four of them had met for dinner, and he'd walked with her to the parking lot. It was pouring, so they got into his car since it was parked closer to the entrance and he drove her to hers. How familiar she had seemed, sitting there blowing warmth into her hands. When he got to her car, he hadn't wanted her to get out, so he drove in circles around the parking lot until the torrent subsided. They talked about trivial things: the long checkout lines and the rise in coffee prices. He teased her for reading the *National Enquirer* in the checkout line, told her he was making tacos for dinner, Brooke's second favorite meal after pancakes. Anne made a sad face; she said she wished she were eating dinner at his house.

"Remember that night at the Safeway?" he asked now.

"Every time I went there after that night, I looked for you."

The light changed to green, and he stepped on the gas. "After you got out of my car that night, I couldn't stop thinking about my mother. I never told you that, did I?"

She shook her head.

He turned onto their street. "It's strange. I hadn't thought about it until just now."

"What reminded you?"

"I'm not sure." He slowed down, searching for a parking space. Wordlessly, she pointed one out. "My mother never grieved—or at least not in front of me." He glanced in the rearview mirror. "I never knew if she thought about the fact that she wouldn't see me graduate or get married or have kids or whatever."

"Of course, she thought about it, Will. You don't really question that, do you?"

He waited for a car to pass. The oaks along the curb cast shadows over his face. "Intellectually, I know she missed me," he said, backing the car into the space. "But the way we coped was by acting strong, by not letting each other see how much it hurt, and it seemed to work at the time." He turned off the headlights and ignition. He felt the cold in his fingers. "After she died, though, I wished so much that I had told her how much I loved her. It was the dumb things that hurt the most to remember—how she always made homemade doughnuts for breakfast when it snowed." He smiled. "In Vermont, that meant a lot of doughnuts. Or how she didn't know a thing about hockey, but she'd sit on the couch with us and do needlepoint when dad and I were watching a game, and she'd get all pissed off when whoever we were rooting for lost." He laughed softly. "A thousand things—how she got me through ninth grade algebra. For hours she'd sit at the kitchen table with me and we'd go over and over the lessons, and I'd cry because I didn't get it, and if I didn't pass I couldn't be on the hockey team . . . but I never told her how much I loved her, and she never told me." Without turning, he reached for Anne's hand on the seat and tucked her fingers into his. "Sometimes I think that's what I've been looking for ever since she died—the chance to do it right . . ."

"It?"

"Kayla told me I was incapable of love," he said, "but I think it was grief that I wasn't capable of, maybe until tonight." He turned to face her. "Is that what I sensed that day at the Safeway? That you knew how to grieve?"

Gently, she pulled her hand out of his hand and glanced away. The street was empty. "You ready to go inside?" she asked after a moment.

"Hold on. What just happened here?"

Her eyes were bright again with tears. "I'm starving, and it's cold." They hadn't eaten yet.

"Anne?"

She shook her head sadly. "I begged you tonight, Will, and it wasn't fair—"

"Hey—" He touched her chin, trying to get her to look at him.

"I don't want you to stay with me because I'm sad, or because I remind you of your mother."

"It's not that." He held his fingers lightly to her lips as if to shush her. "That's not what I'm saying, Anne. Don't you see?"

Her mouth trembled. "No."

"I think maybe I really don't know how to love, Anne, because I don't know how to grieve, and I don't mean that to be an excuse." He brushed his thumb over the contour of her cheek. "It's like how, when you close a window so no rain gets in, no air does either. I think that happened to me when she died. Didn't I tell you when I first met you that I couldn't breathe?"

"And now you can?"

"I don't know. I'm scared, Anne. What if it's like those people who are blind or deaf all their lives, and they get the chance to have their sight or hearing restored, and they find once they do, it's too much. Too many colors or sounds and they can't adjust, can't deal with it all? Maybe that's me with emotions." He moved his eyes over her face. "I want to try, though. I want to stop being like this."

Chapter Twenty-three

It was the first time Kayla had chosen a tree without Will. In the past, it had driven her crazy—he'd survey the tree from every angle, squatting down, leaning over, staring up, from ten feet away, from five, then pacing around it, like an Indian chief at a naming ritual. She would sigh dramatically, pointedly. "It's a tree, Will, not a major household appliance." And yet, had it been a washer, a dryer, or a refrigerator, he would have chosen it in a millisecond, not giving a damn. Once, she had loved him for that.

This year she was the one insisting that she and Brooke take a final walk through the lighted aisles of Douglas firs and blue spruces. She wanted Will to like whatever they chose. She wanted him to be proud of her. "You don't think it's too tall, sweetie?" she asked when they had circled back to the spruce Brooke had chosen.

"Even daddy didn't take this long," Brooke complained.

Staticky Christmas carols played through speakers mounted to telephone poles. Bing Crosby. "I'm dreaming of a white Christmas . . ." She exhaled a long breath. . . . "Just like the ones I used to know" . . . and promised herself that she would get through the holiday without Will. She smiled at Brooke. "You're right, honey. I am being picky, aren't I?" She crouched down and aimed her eyes at her daughter's. "Mommy's just a little nervous this year. I never shopped for a tree without your daddy." They were surrounded by families, Norman Rockwell families, she thought. Rosy-cheeked and happy. She wondered if she and Will and Brooke had ever looked like that.

The sadness was mercurial, though; it had been all along. A few hours later, sitting on the couch, the mostly-empty ornament boxes stacked against the basement door for her to take down in the morning, she felt oddly content. "It's the best tree ever!" Brooke had announced jubilantly as she climbed the aluminum ladder, with Kayla's help, to set the angel atop the tree. Later, Brooke turned off the kitchen lights, and her friend, Aisha, got the lamps on either end of the sofa. Kayla waited for the girls to count to three, then plugged in the tree. It blazed to life—three hundred blinking white lights, boxes and boxes of ornaments, the silver rain of tinsel. Kayla looked at the girls and realized that somehow she had managed to make this okay for them. And somehow, once Will came home, she would make it okay again for him, too.

The girls were in bed now, though Kayla could hear them giggling still. She sat in the darkness in front of the lighted tree, sipping a mug of hot chocolate, considering the smell of spruce, which permeated the room. It seemed like an old smell, or perhaps it simply reminded Kayla that she was older. She remembered her mother once unwrapping Christmas decorations and holding up a miniature Scrooge. "Unwrapping ornaments is like unraveling the pieces of my life," she'd said.

"Oh, please," Kayla's younger sister Abby had hooted. "What piece of your life is this?" She held up an old Popsicle-stick manger.

"Kayla made that when she was in elementary school!"

"And these?" Kayla laughed, holding out the box of plain red drugstore ornaments.

"Oh, you girls."

Kayla rested the mug against her breastbone. The heat radiated into her chest. It was the first year she hadn't hung the crystal ornament engraved with their wedding date. Or the ones that had belonged to Will's mother and grandmother. Crocheted, hand beaded, some of them made during World War I when there was a shortage of metal. She had repacked them, along with the racing bike ornament she'd found for him a few years ago. It didn't seem right to hang those without him in the house. Next year, she promised herself.

She glanced again at the tree, at the green Gumby figure one of the girls had found and twisted onto a lower branch. Will had given it to her. She couldn't remember why—something sexual, though, something about her flexibility.

It was before Brooke, when they lived together in the basement apartment in Boulder. No kitchen; they used to wash dishes in the shower. It was always dark so that midafternoon felt like that night.

"Like living in Alaska," he said. "Six months of darkness."

"You think they make love all the time, too?" she laughed.

She set her mug on the coffee table, pried the Gumby from the tree branch and took him back with her to the couch. He was faded, more lime green than his original Kelly green. She rested her feet on the edge of the coffee table and sat the Gumby on her knee, Indian-style. Then yoga position, contemplating the world. She smiled, and felt her eyes fill with tears. She bent one of his arms up, the other down, did the same with his legs. A runner. Will used to do that. Then one leg crossed primly over the other, arms folded across his chest. Proper. She sighed and moved back toward the tree. She straddled Gumby on one of the high branches, near the angel. Watching over her. Even after she turned off the lights and darkness filled the room like murky pond water, she could see him—his square head and rubbery bell-bottom shaped legs.

hapter Twenty-four

Will sat in the kitchen waiting for Kayla to finish tucking Brooke into bed. She'd already begun decorating for Christmas, electric candles glowing in the windows, and a lighted tree in the living room. Empty cardboard boxes that once housed ornaments sat in the foyer to be returned to the basement. "When did you get the tree?" he'd asked as soon as he stepped inside.

"Isn't it great?" She stared at it with him. The miniature white lights softened the angles of her face. "We thought about asking you to join us, but then we figured we'd surprise you."

"I am. Very surprised." He sounded hurt, though he didn't want to be, didn't have a right to be. He saw the Gumby figure sitting atop one of the higher branches and it saddened him.

Now, he fingered the edge of the red-and-green place mats as he listened to Kayla call up to Brooke from the bottom of the stairs. "I promise, sweetie, he'll come up again before he leaves."

And then she was moving around the kitchen, pouring coffee, adding hazelnut creamer to his, wrinkling her nose. "One thing I haven't missed," she teased. "I don't know how you can drink this stuff. Pure corn syrup." She set his mug in front of him, holding hers to the side of her face for warmth. Anne did the same thing, he thought sadly. Kayla was wearing sweats and big socks and an old flannel shirt and she looked beautiful.

"I bought some Bailey's," she said after a minute. "You want some with your coffee?"

He cocked one eyebrow. "You're in the holiday spirit early."

"Well, it's been a hard year. I figured we might as well squeeze every ounce of pleasure from it we can." She nodded toward the ceiling. "I just want Christmas to be okay for her."

"It will be." He hoped.

She didn't answer, but only glanced at him over the rim of her mug as she took a sip.

"So, where's that Bailey's?" He wanted to shift the conversation away from Christmas. Kayla's words seemed to imply that it was up to him to make the holiday okay. How could he? And yet, wasn't this the job of any parent? To give his children the lie of childhood for as long as possible? What was the difference, really, between the illusion of Santa Claus or the tooth fairy and the illusion of a happy family, of parents who loved each other?

While she was getting the Bailey's from the buffet in the dining room, he opened the cabinet over the refrigerator and pulled out two crystal aperitif glasses, thinly coated with dust. The last time they'd used these was the previous Christmas Eve. He hadn't yet told her about Anne, and for a moment, standing at the sink, rinsing the glasses in warm water, a tinsely mix of rain and snow falling across the yard out back, he felt like George Bailey in *It's a Wonderful Life,* realizing that nothing had changed: Bedford Falls was still Bedford Falls and not Pottersville, and he had a wife and child.

"Did you know that they make the boxes for Bailey's in Lockerbie, Scotland? Remember? Where that Pan Am jet was bombed?"

"Where'd you hear that?" He held the glasses for her as she poured.

She shrugged. "The radio, I guess."

"That was our first married Christmas."

She smiled. "It felt wrong to be happy, remember?"

"We were still in that basement apartment. God, no sink. You used to wear a raincoat to do the dishes in the shower."

"I was remembering it the other night when I was going through the ornaments. Did you see the Gumby?"

He nodded, not wanting to remember.

She took her glass and turned to set the bottle on the counter, glancing over her shoulder at him. Light caught in her earring. "You look stricken," she said. "I promise, I'm not trying to seduce you." She slid into her chair, knees resting against the table edge, and laughed, gesturing with her free hand to her clothes. "Jesus, Will, give me a little credit. I could certainly do better than this."

He grinned. "I thought maybe you were going for the subtle approach."

"Well, this is subtle all right." She rolled her eyes, her thick curly hair casting shadows across her pale features.

For a moment, neither said anything. He couldn't look Kayla in the eye. How was he going to tell her? *I'm staying with Anne.* Stay. It had once meant "to be firm or strong," Anne had told him. He was neither.

"Did Brooke tell you wants a NASCAR Barbie?" Kayla asked finally.

"That's my girl."

"I figured you were the instigator, though I suppose it's better than the Debutante Barbie, or—"

"Kayla—"

She glanced at him, then quickly away, toward the stairs. "Did you just hear her? She's been having a lot of bad dreams lately."

"Kayla."

She shook her head. "Don't, Will, okay?" Her voice was icy, though her eyes brimmed with tears. She set the glass of Bailey's down sharply. "I can't believe you."

"What? I haven't said a word."

"I thought maybe, just *maybe,* for once in your life, you'd think about someone besides yourself. You'd see how hard I am trying, and you'd do what was right, at least for her."

He wished he knew what was right. What was that line Anne had quoted to him the other night? Something about how the truth was whatever lie you chose to believe. "I don't know what to say," he said now, "except I'm sorry. I am so sorry." How many times had he said this in the last four days? The last four months? And how many more times would he say it in the next four months?

"Don't even." She pushed her chair back from the table and crossed the room to stand at the sink. Her back was to him as she gazed out the same window she'd stared through the night he left. He pictured Anne standing in the hotel room staring at the clock on the Jefferson, saw his mother looking beyond him toward the mountains the afternoon she told him about the cancer.

"What happened?" Kayla said quietly, still staring outside. "You were thinking of coming back and now . . . what changed?"

"I was confused. I didn't want to make a mistake. I wanted to be sure."

"Well, how nice for you. I'm glad you're *sure* now, Will."

Was he? He stared at the curve of her back. What could he say? What words could possibly make this easier for either of them? He thought of Anne's English as a Second Language conversation texts: lessons on how to greet people, on how to apologize or say good-bye or complain or offer a compliment or an opinion. But nothing about how to hurt someone you once loved and still sometimes did.

In the reflection of the window, he could see the doorway behind them, and the tree with its constellation of lights blinking, on, then off, then on. He could see Kayla's face, the gleam of tears on her cheeks.

"Why?" she asked again.

"I don't know, Kayla."

"Not good enough." She turned to him. "Make something up, Will. Tell me another lie." Her voice was steely.

"What do you want me to say, Kayla? It's not you, it wasn't any-thing—"

"Wrong."

"What do you mean *wrong*?"

"I want the truth, Will."

He spread his hands, palms up, on the table. "Look," he said, "you have every right to be pissed. I hate what I've done to you, I hate the way—"

"Goddamn it, Will."

"What?"

She glanced at him in disgust, but didn't answer. She stared past him. "You owe me more than this pathetic I'm-so-screwed-up-I-didn't-mean-to-hurt-you routine." Her voice broke. "You *are* hurting me, Will. You are, and you have and you're just going to keep on because that's all you know how to do." She sipped her coffee, tears leaking into the mug. "Why?" she continued. "Why does it always, *always* have to be about you? *You're* screwed up, *you're* confused, *you're* not sure. Do you ever, *ever,* think about anyone else?"

Anne had said the same thing. Was he really so selfish? Had he always been?

Kayla's words carried the force of a train, each one a separate car, tugged forward by the word before it and the one before that. He noticed the pale bruise on her wrist, and thought of how she could never account for the plum-colored smudges that would randomly appear on her arms and legs. "I must have bumped into something," she'd shrug, as if she were constantly being hurt by things she didn't see.

"What can I say to you that will make this better?" he asked.

She just glanced at him, crying harder. He wondered if Brooke was awake, listening from her room at the top of the stairs. "Kayla?"

"I deserve . . ." She stopped, closed her eyes, and began again. "I deserve—"

"You deserve better," he said quietly.

"I deserve not to wonder," she said sadly.

"Wonder what?"

"Why you don't want me!" Kayla's sorrow emptied across the kitchen. She set her mug down and turned again to the window.

"Please, don't do this," he said. "Not over me, not after what I've done." He moved around the kitchen, tentatively laying a hand on her shoulder, but she whirled away.

"Don't touch me."

He backed off.

"Do you realize how ridiculous you are?" she sobbed. "You come here and tell me that I'm not worth fighting for, that twenty years are not worth *anything,* and then you dare to think you can offer me some measly-assed touch on the shoulder by way of comfort?"

"I'm sorry. I don't know what to say or do—"

"I'm sorry," she mimicked. "You're like one of Brooke's battery-operated dolls. The same old lines. Why don't you just leave?"

"Shouldn't we talk, Kayla?"

"About what?" She wiped her nose on the sleeve of her shirt. "Save your little conciliatory speech, Will. I've heard it before, remember?"

"You don't even know what—"

"Yes, I do." Her voice was caustic. "I'm a beautiful, intelligent woman, and I'm a great mother to Brooke, but I don't fulfill you; I don't make you happy; you need things that I can't give you. How am I doing so far?"

He didn't say anything. That *was* pretty much the gist of it. Except it wasn't that simple. "You know," he said, still not looking at her, "you're so big on honesty, Kayla, on hearing the truth, but I'm not getting much of it from you. Are you happy with me? Do I give you what *you* need? Because if I do, it's one hell of a surprise. You act like we had this great marriage, but when did you ever make an effort to spend time with me on weekends or at night? We didn't laugh together; we didn't even talk unless it was about Brooke. Can you even remember the last time we had an in-depth conversation about *anything*?" He looked at her. She was staring past him, toward the hallway—the lights from the tree washed forward and back like waves. "We're good parents," he continued. "It's the one thing we do well together and I will always love that part of you and that part of us, but it's not enough, and I think you know this, Kayla. You're just too scared to admit it." He took a long breath, held it inside, his heart pounding.

"Just leave," she said, still staring past him.

"So that's it? You have nothing to say?" He yanked his jacket from the back of the chair. "This is exactly what I'm talking about, Kayla. The minute something goes wrong, you just shut down."

"I know, Will. You've told me this a dozen times." She smirked. "And you like the clingy dependent types who fall apart and beg you to stay, no doubt."

"I'm not going to do this. I know you want a fight, and maybe you deserve to have one, but we're both going to end up saying things we don't mean. I care about you, and I know that sounds ridiculous right now, but there it is. And just for the record, I *don't* feel like we wasted twenty years."

"Yeah, well for the record, and I want to be perfectly clear, Will, this divorce is not my decision. It is not what I want, and I think it's wrong. And to answer your questions, no, I'm not happy with you a lot of the time, and yes, I wish things were different. I wish I was in the mood to make love whenever and wherever. I wish I had time to sit around and watch movies with you or get drunk some Saturday night and argue politics like we used to. But you know what? I can't do that, Will, because I have a child to take care of and a business to run and a house, and as much as I'd love to be twenty-five again and free of responsibilities, I'm not. I grew up. I don't expect passion or perfection or whatever it is you think you've found with her."

She turned around to the sink and began rinsing her mug. Just like the first time he left, he was thinking, but it had been April then and still light outside.

As he was walking to the car, she called to him from the front door. "Are you going to take her to Vermont for New Year's?" Her voice was barely audible over the tapping of sleet against the pavement.

He tried to smile. "Like my father would ever accept anyone but you?"

She nodded, but didn't move to close the door. She looked small. And so skinny. Just elbows and knees, she would say, making fun of herself. She used to be vicious about her body, calling herself a Dalmation because she freckled so easily, or hating her ears, which she had never gotten pierced because in kindergarten some boy whose name she probably couldn't remember had told her that she had pointy elf ears. He didn't know why he was thinking of this now, but for the first time it seemed horribly sad: that she would carry that one comment with her all these years.

"Are you going to marry her?"

Sleet stung his face. "I don't know, Kayla." He shook his head. "I haven't thought that far ahead."

A car passed by, its headlights illuminating her pale face. She was crying. "Please don't take her to Bogart's—" Where they used to go, every Saturday night, for drinks.

"I promise, I won't."

She nodded again and, still crying, closed the door.

Chapter Twenty-five

Yukihiko's arm shot up in the air a split second before Ahmad's. "I know I'm going to regret this," Annie laughed. She had just asked for a volunteer to collect the teacher evaluations and return them to the English department. She eyed Yukihiko. "Come on up."

"It is the unfairness situation!" Ahmad cried.

"Why you pick him?" Sungae complained, arms crossed over her chest.

"You are late again, Ahmad," Ba teased.

Yukihiko swaggered to the front of the room in his unlaced high-tops and Tommy Hilfiger sweatshirt.

As Annie closed the door behind her, she heard Yukihiko mimicking her, saying, "Excuse me, but *I* am talking right now." The class broke into laughter. The sound trailed her down the hallway, empty but for a few students.

It was the final class of the semester. Most of the students would be enrolled in the second half of the course in January. Still, it felt like an ending, perhaps because it was. So much depended on those evaluations. She had tried to be casual about it, but as she explained the process—"Use a number two pencil, don't include your name, print the numerical code for your major in the upper left corner"—she was aware of trying to touch each of them: a smile for Shin-pin, a joke for Yukihiko, a glance to Sungae, who regarded her without blinking, as she had for the past week.

Annie had encountered this coldness before from her students, right about this time, three to five months into the semester. It was the second stage of culture shock, when the euphoria of being in a new country dissolved; when they began hating the difficult language and foreign customs and flawed Americans with their too-big supermarkets and shopping malls and selfish hearts. This was the time when the students learned to speak in negatives, when they used contractions more frequently: *isn't, doesn't, can't, won't.*

Still, of all the students, Sungae was the last person Annie would have expected to become so disillusioned. Especially now, when finally she seemed comfortable: participating in the grammar exercises, joking with Yukihiko and Ahmad, laughing one afternoon in the student commons with Sacide.

The previous week, they had been working on prepositions. Everyone was in a good mood, calling out examples. As always, Farshad, who had become the unofficial class leader, began. "We are *in* the classroom."

"But we want to be outside!" Ahmad yelled.

"No, we want *you* to be outside," Yukihiko laughed.

Annie raised her eyebrows in warning. "Outside is *not* a preposition, you two."

"Your book is *on* the desk." Shin-pin glanced shyly at Yukihiko, who grinned and pointed to Ahmad: "But his book is *under* his bed *at* home." He smiled at Annie. "I recover my mistake: two prepositions in the single sentence!"

"Soon we will get *on* the airplane to Turkey," Sacide said quietly.

"Look!" Ahmad cried. "Snow is falling *from* the sky!"

It wasn't, but everyone, Annie included, turned expectantly to the window, then started laughing.

Except Sungae. Eyes brimming with tears, she glared at Annie and told her, "You don't care about position of things. Preposition is just a waste of time for you."

Annie glanced sharply at her and made a feeble joke about Sungae being right—just look at the jumble of books and papers on her desk, a coffee mug, napkins, her scarf strewn across the chair back—but she felt stung not only by the acerbity in Sungae's words, but by the truth inherent in them. Annie's life *was* out of order.

The students had continued calling out more phrases, competing to see how many prepositions they could pack into one statement. Annie nodded and laughed and moved around the room, trying to catch Sungae's eye, trying to understand what was wrong, what had happened, but Sungae wouldn't look at her.

The hallway was quiet now. Her students would be writing their evaluations. Annie could feel the cold sneak in as she opened the doors.

Why you teach us such sorrowful sentences?

Annie paused, pulling her scarf over her nose and mouth before plunging into the cold. No classes for a month, she told herself. Christmas with Will.

DID YOU GAIN NEW INSIGHTS FROM THIS COURSE?

Sungae didn't know what to do. She stared at the pale blue evaluation sheet in front of her, but all she could think about was that Annie was the woman living with Kayla's husband. She had been at the café, making sugar cookies when Kayla blurted it out last week, the day after Will announced that he was going ahead with the divorce. "I know it's lousy of me to have told you," Kayla said as she pulled open and slammed shut the drawers in the café kitchen. "I know she's your teacher, and you respect her, but—" Kayla held up her hands, like a police officer stopping traffic. "This is wrong. I'm sorry." Then she stormed out the door.

Sungae had wanted to ignore Kayla, but words that are spoken are not like words on the computer screen in Kayla's office. Press delete and they just go away. She hadn't wanted to think about Annie strolling into class with a big smile, teaching students about the "unreal conditions"—*If only I had . . . If I could have I would have . . . If I were you . . .*—when all the while she was living the unreal condition with

Kayla's husband. It was not her right. It was not fair. Sungae had paid for her own similar mistake. How was it that Annie would not pay as well, and that she would have everything Sungae had once wanted?

Sungae thought then of the Korean game, *yon oulligi,* in which boys covered the strings of their kites with *kaemi,* a mixture of glue and crushed glass, then tried to cross strings with other kites, until they cut the others down. Annie had done the same thing to Kayla, Sungae thought. A person's heart is not so different from the paper kite, held up by only the fragile string.

Sungae had been shivering, so she grabbed her cardigan from the butcher's block and wrapped it around her neck like a scarf. She could only remember being this cold once before—a few minutes after Chongmin was born. Her hands and legs were shaking and she couldn't catch her breath. The kitchen—with its sterile white-tiled walls and metal countertops, stainless steel sinks and fluorescent lights—was like the hospital delivery room. So cold. Soon Keehwan would come to take her home.

The butter cookies had another four minutes to go, but she opened the oven door to check on them anyway. Heat fanned her face. The cookies looked pregnant. Swelling. She wanted to smash them, the smell of butter making her nauseated.

She felt that way again now as she began filling out the class evaluation. She thought of Kayla on Thanksgiving night, staring up at the sky and saying in the voice filled with sorrow, "I would take him back, you know."

And then she thought of Annie with her "telling lines" and her insincere voice, telling students the lies: "You can be whatever you want in future tense." Not true. Sungae squeezed her eyes shut, tears spilling from beneath her lashes. For the first time in seventeen years, she didn't try to stop them. They reminded her of the night her water broke, something releasing inside her. She remembered the warm wetness leaking from between her legs, darkening the sheets so that at first, she thought it was blood. Her water smelled almost metallic, like air before rain.

*   *   *

HOW WOULD YOU EVALUATE THIS INSTRUCTOR AGAINST OTHER INSTRUC-
TORS WHOSE CLASSES YOU HAVE TAKEN AT THE UNIVERSITY?

Evaluate: to determine the significance, wealth or value of. Ba just
learned that word this morning on the number seven bus. To get to
school each day from his apartment on the south side of the city, he
took the number seven, then transferred to the number nine, sometimes waiting in the graffiti-covered bus shelter for nearly an hour.
Teenage boys harassed him, calling him "Chink" and complaining that
the shelter stank of soy sauce. Ba simply stared at his *Webster's Pocket
Dictionary,* repeating words over and over in his mind: *evacuate, evict,
exacerbate.* The violence of the English language frightened him.

Fifty words a day. He forced himself to use them in conversations, in
his essays. This morning he discovered *euphony: a harmonious succes-
sion of words having a pleasing sound.* Annie's voice is euphonic, he
thought, and though Vietnamese and English were vastly different, he
imagined that if his mother, whose voice he could no longer recall, had
ever learned this language, she, too, would sound euphonic, her quiet
words flowing one after the other like the glossy pages of a child's picture book.

He told himself that the words he memorized would help him do
well on the MCATs, which he was taking next spring. But in truth, he
combed the dictionary as if it were a sandy beach. Each word was a
seashell, the hollow case spun around a memory, long since dead. In
the word *roll,* the double *l*s pronounced with difficulty as if his mouth
were stuffed with cotton, Ba recalled the cellophane and bamboo
lantern he carried while he paraded through the streets on his father's
shoulder for *Tet Trung Thu,* or Children's Holiday. He held the
rounded spiral of the word *occasion* on his tongue and saw his mother
making *ca nuong troui,* mint fish rolls. Chunks of catfish sizzled in the
wok. The smell of mint. The zipper-sound of his aunt pushing a cu-
cumber back and forth over the grater.

Ba understood now that every word he learned was a key to his life.
This was the insight Annie had taught him. Carefully, he printed on the
blue form: "Thank you."

*   *   *

WHAT PERSONAL QUALITIES DID THIS INSTRUCTOR HAVE WHICH HIN-
DERED HIS/HER TEACHING?

"Annie is the woman living with Kayla's husband," Sungae had
blurted furiously to Keehwan that night when he picked her up from
Kayla's. "Who does she think she is? Double-skinned woman. She think
she is a cat, have the nine lives? How can such a woman be the teacher?"

"You are too hasty," Keehwan said gently. He slowed the car as he
pulled onto their street. Even with only a faint moon, it seemed brighter
than usual, Christmas lights shining from most of the houses, lamplight
shimmering across frozen lawns. Keehwan pointed to the pin oak next
to their driveway, the quarter moon caught in its naked branches like a
wounded bird. "Do you know what that is?" he asked her.

She glared at him. "Why you asking nonsense questions?"

"A tree without the leaves is still a tree, Sungae." *Annie is still your
teacher, and seventeen years ago, you were still my wife,* he was saying.

"Not the same," she whispered, her voice breaking in half like a firecracker.

She had gone to her studio that night and opened a can of Mars
black, climbed the ladder, and began slapping the acrylic onto the canvas, covering everything she had accomplished. *Describe a room using
as many prepositions as possible.* Sungae had painted a sleeping mat
covered only *with* sheets: It had been summer then, the baby just starting to kick, startling her into surprised exclamations; *through* the window, an eyelash-moon blinked *over* the bamboo tree. *Beside* the mat, a
woman's cadmium red silk blouse shone like glossy lips. She painted
the man's laughter green like the grass *in* Seoul Grand Park, painted
the woman's quiet moans the blue-purple *of* water. But the night Kayla
told her about Annie, Sungae blacked out the entire scene, covering
over the colors and shapes of the past that she didn't want to remember; that she never should have painted to begin with.

DID GRADING ACCURATELY REFLECT THE EXPECTATIONS OF THE IN-
STRUCTOR?

After my best friend was shot by the Israeli soldiers I came to
this country to start the new life. Miss Helverson helps us. She

teaches students the most important ingredient in foreign student's education. She teaches us how to laugh. Also the grammar
and American vocabulary. She likes all students very much. I
think she will give to us all the A+!

LIST THE THREE ASSIGNMENTS WHICH YOU FELT WERE MOST HELPFUL TO
YOUR UNDERSTANDING OF SUBJECT MATTER BEING TAUGHT, AND BRIEFLY
EXPLAIN WHY.

Sungae had been making a list for Hwang the night her daughter was
born—things to do for the child she would never see: *Do not let her sit
on rocks or she will become hard-hearted; help her find success in the
world by carrying her up a flight of stairs before you carry her down. . . .*
She made another list now. All the assignments she'd done this semester: the telling line, fifteen adjectives to describe herself; the biography
page using only past tense verbs, a paragraph about current situation
using only present tense, a compare-contrast essay between the old life
and new. She thought about Annie, her name like a too-sweet dessert,
making Sungae's teeth throb. Annie with her secret and her grammar
lessons in which "mistakes are okay." Annie, living with Kayla's husband.

She thought, too, as she often did when Annie made them write, of
Chongmin. It was as if years ago, Sungae had squeezed her memories
from her heart into the tips of her fingers, like icing in a pastry bag, and
now the memories were being pushed onto the page. She thought of
how Hwang hadn't gotten out of the car to walk her to the blue metal
doors of the Women's Maternity Hospital that night, how he made her
walk that gang-plank of sidewalk alone, how a part of her hated him
for that, hate she couldn't afford to feel because there was too much
for everyone else: the doctor who shoved his hands inside her without
ever looking at her face, the nurse who snatched the baby away from
Sungae even though Sungae was crying and pleading to hold her. "One
day, you will be thankful," the nurse told her from the doorway. Her
eyes were like sharp stones over her pale blue surgical mask.

Pale blue. The same color as the evaluation form. "Why does *she*
have the right to take our stories from us?" Sungae wrote. "Stories are

like children. Very fragile. You don't hand them to strangers. What if we are not ready to let them go?"

The baby had been taken from her while the placenta was still inside her, she remembered. Her eyes blurred with tears. She turned the paper over, continued writing on the back.

"You novelist?" Yukihiko joked at Sungae. The radiator clanked in the background.

She ignored him. She hated pale blue. It was the color of American eyes, the color of the divorce papers the lawyer sent Kayla in the mail. The morning they arrived, Kayla had sat at the prep counter where Sungae was decorating gingerbread men, reading the papers over and over. Kayla's eyes were as dark as the raisins Sungae pressed into the dough. When Brooke called to Kayla from the office, where she was coloring at her mom's desk, Kayla never looked up from the blue documents. "Could you help her, Sungae?" she asked.

A few minutes later, when Sungae returned, Kayla held her face in her hands. She didn't make the usual crying sound, just a silent shuddering, each breath like a heavy bundle falling end over end down a flight of stairs.

"She tell her students that mistakes are okay," Sungae wrote. "Not true. Mistakes are knives. Cutting things apart."

Chapter Twenty-six

As soon as Carter saw her car in the parking lot of the Daily Grind, he felt the pressure in his chest subside, as if a terrible storm had blown through him. He realized he had been searching for her car, hoping she would be here. It was her ritual to grade papers somewhere besides home—somewhere with decent coffee and music and other people around for distraction.

"No other instructor is going to allow the students to rewrite infinitely," he used to tell her. "You're not helping them in the long run." He felt they were taking advantage of her good nature, some of the students revising every assignment of the semester four and five times.

"I feel like I'm evaluating their life," she told him once. She was sitting at the kitchen table, her grade book opened in front of her, stacks of essays and assignments in various piles. "It's as if they think I'm the Wizard of Oz, handing out hearts and courage and the ability to start a new life in a foreign country." Though it was early evening, it looked as if she hadn't left the table since breakfast. The nearly empty coffeepot was still on, the toaster hadn't been put away, her hair was uncombed.

"The wizard was just an old man behind a curtain," he said. "Or in this case, an exhausted woman who needs to stop worrying about her students and eat dinner with her husband."

"They're just so desperate to succeed, Carter."

"I know, love, but you're a teacher, not a magician." He stood behind her and gently tugged her hair free of the scrunchy, combing it with his fingers. The ends were still damp from her shower that morning. He inhaled the vanilla scent of her conditioner. "You can only do so much."

She tilted her head back and gazed up at him so that he was cradling her face in his hands. "You don't understand," she said. The dark depressions beneath her eyes made her look gaunt, as if she herself were a refugee. "To give them a B or God forbid, a C would be like firing them from their job."

"Come on, Annie, its *grammar*."

"I wish, Carter, I really do. But it's not. It's their life."

He sat for a moment in his car, the engine still running, the defroster barely keeping the windshield from icing up despite the blinding sun. He pulled in a deep breath, counted to ten and slowly exhaled. Then again. What was he doing here?

He told himself he just wanted to say hello to her, to ask about the semester. They had been friends for nearly thirty years—couldn't they be friends again? Wasn't it better than nothing at all? And he wouldn't ask what her plans for the holiday were, or how her Thanksgiving had gone, if she was happy now that she had what she wanted, if she ever missed him. *If.* He wouldn't tell her that he'd hired her student, Farshad, or that he knew she had taught her students conditional phrases before Thanksgiving, or that the phrase *what if* echoed his entire world now, reverberating back to him across the huge emptiness of his life without her.

What if he'd gone to the video store alone the night she told him of the affair? What if she never had the chance to say that phrase: *I'm in love with Will.* With enough time, couldn't the words have dissolved inside her? What if he had refused to accept the word *affair* when she had told him that night in the rain? What if he'd kept driving, gotten on I-95 and headed south to Saint Augustine, to the hotel where they had honeymooned? *Casa de Sueños.* House of Dreams. They would wake to the clop of horseshoes in the narrow streets; the fan whirring softly overhead, fracturing the sunlight into triangles that washed over their faces intermittently. Palm leaves shadowed on the ceiling. At night, echoes of Latino music from the candlelit courtyard and moonlight falling through the antique lace curtains. What if he had presented the memories to her like evidence in a murder trial? What if he had demanded that she be accountable? Their marriage had been a life.

Or what if they had fought more throughout their marriage? Ugly shouting matches and silences, accusations. They had been so sure of themselves, so sanctimonious: Nothing would ever come between them because *they* wouldn't let it. Like Icarus, the boy with the wax wings who flew too close to the sun, they had believed they were invincible. Annie had written a paper about Brueghel's painting *The Fall of Icarus* in an art history class in college. "How does the world simply go on while a boy falls to his death?" she had written. "How does one life become so insignificant?"

Abruptly, he shut off the engine. He felt as if his heart had just stopped. Plumes of exhaust rose from the cars idling at a nearby red light. He watched as a man wearing a Santa Claus hat carried a box of wine from the liquor store across the street. Eleven more days until Christmas. He swallowed. Maybe when she saw him again, he told himself, maybe then she would realize . . .

She didn't glance up when he entered the café. She was sitting on a stool facing the window, her back to the shop, the sunlight full in her face as she stared intently at a paper. Irish Christmas ballads were playing, and the place was jammed, conversations buzzing around him, extra chairs loaded with holiday shopping bags and coats. He ordered a mocha latte and tried to breathe, inhaling the rich scents of the coffee: Sumatran, Ethiopian, Kenyan. In front of him, a woman squatted before a little girl trying to decide what shape of butter cookie she wanted: a Christmas tree or a snowman. "But they *both* look so good," the girl said. "The woman caught Carter's eye and shook her head. "She's trying to get *both,*" she whispered.

"Smart girl," he answered, smiling. He sounded so normal, and for a moment, he felt a rush of gratitude toward this woman simply for having spoken to him. *I'm fine,* he wanted Annie to know. *I'm okay without you.* His hands shook, though, when the girl making coffee handed him the soup-bowl-size mug topped with whipped cream and chocolate syrup. It looked like a sundae. Walking across the crowded shop, balancing the awkward drink, he nearly tripped on a woman's scarf, which had fallen onto the floor. Two girls started giggling, and his ears burned; he wondered if they were laughing at him.

And then her voice, his name: "Carter?"

"Hey." He smiled sheepishly, still concentrating on not spilling his drink. "Do you mind if I sit with you a minute?" He felt like a teenager, his heart revving up like an old-fashioned arcade game: buzzers, flashing lights, zinging bells. He gestured toward the empty stool beside her.

"I'd love you to sit. I saw you come in, but I wasn't sure . . ."

She had seen him. His heart quieted in his chest. "How are you?" he asked. "You look great." She did.

"I'm okay," she said. "You?"

He nodded, tears swelling in his throat. She was so familiar it hurt. If he leaned closer, would he smell the vanilla scent of her conditioner? *If.* "*If I were a carpenter and you were a lady, would you marry me anyway, would you have my baby?*" Andrew Cordivari had followed her around the recess yard in the fifth grade singing those words to her after they learned about reproduction in their sex education class. Carter grinned, remembering. Nobody else had this history with her.

"What is it?" She was smiling, her chin resting in her palm, fingers curled toward her mouth. The light streaming through the glass seemed to collect in her white shirt.

He shook his head. "It's just good to see you."

She nodded. "It's good to see you, too." She had a smudge of mascara below one eye. She was wearing earrings *he* had given her.

"Nice earrings," he teased. He knew that she never remembered which ones she was wearing and so would reach up to grab one, turning the small pendant slowly between her fingertips. She did. Exactly that. He wanted to cheer. He still knew her. She hadn't changed. Thin bangles shimmied down her arm, collecting at her wrist, at the triangle-shaped scar where she'd burned herself with an iron when she was eleven. He thought of how for over a decade he had known Annie's body better than anyone had: the surprise of pale hair at the nape of her neck; the perfect shape of her knees or the silvery scar across her abdomen from an operation she'd had at three weeks old. But then they'd go home to New Jersey for a holiday or a birthday and his mother or his sister, Molly, would comment about some small change, maybe Annie's ponytail held higher or her bangs cut shorter—and Carter would be astonished because he hadn't noticed, and because they could see her in ways he was never able to.

He glanced at her again. A part of him had hoped that with enough time he would be able to look at her with the same clarity his sister and mother had had, that he would be able to see what must have been invisible to him all those years—a hardness in her eyes or the set of her mouth, some rigidity in her voice or her touch—and he would understand finally what it was that had allowed her to leave. But she looked exactly the same. She hadn't cut off her hair or gained weight or lost weight or painted her fingernails electric blue or pierced her nose. He smiled. She was still the woman he loved.

He lifted the mocha awkwardly in both hands and took a sip. It was awful. Muddy and too sweet, but he didn't care. The haunting sound of a flute rose over the whir of the coffee grinder, the hiss of milk steaming, a man's easy laugh. Snippets of conversation floated around them:

". . . looked everywhere . . ."

"—gets worse every year."

"Try the roasted vegetables."

Annie leaned forward, brows furrowed, to peer more closely at his drink.

"—a Christmas Eve tradition in Iowa."

"—doubt is half of it."

And then she sat back, arms crossed over her chest, detective-like. "Is that *mocha,* Carter? Whipped cream?"

"I confess." He grinned.

"My God, *you*? Eating sugar! *Why*?"

He cocked one eyebrow. "Why not?"

She laughed. "What do you mean, *why not*? The sugar thing was such a big deal with you. For what—fifteen years, *at least*? What happened?"

"Nothing. Honestly." But his voice caught: something tore inside him. How could she ask what had happened? *You left me,* he wanted to remind her. *That's what happened.*

"Nothing?" She squinted suspiciously over the rim of her mug. Her eyes were greener than he remembered. He glanced away, staring into the sunlight the way as a child, he'd once stared into an eclipse after Annie warned him not to, afraid it might blind him.

Eclipse. From the Greek *ekleipsis,* meaning "to abandon" or "to leave." She had told him this, of course. And *happen,* related to the Old Slavic *kobu* or "fate." Is that what her leaving had been? Fate? Destiny? He knew she wanted to believe this, that everything happened for a reason—why else had she met Will? He took another sip of coffee.

"Do you remember how you wouldn't even buy ketchup because it had what—a teaspoon of sugar in it? And, God, remember the cookie episode?"

His face froze. Had he just been a joke to her? Did she make fun of him now with Will? The cookie *episode*? Like the title of a *Seinfeld* rerun. And what would this be, the mocha *episode*? Would she go home tonight and laugh about him with Will? *You should have seen him trying to drink out of that bowl. . . .* He closed his eyes. No. She wasn't like that. She had never been cruel. She didn't mean to be now. Still, he was remembering it—the cookie episode.

She had come home excited because she'd found a new health food grocery store that made sugar-free peanut butter cookies. "I even read the label," she laughed. "No sugar, no butter, no eggs. Voilà!"

But the next week when she asked if she should pick up another package, he told her, "Actually, I still haven't eaten the ones you bought, Annie. They had hydrogenated oil in them."

She'd looked at him quzzically, sadly, then walked out of the room. He found her at the kitchen table, dunking one of the crumbly cookies into a cup of coffee, then wearily eating it. "I guess I'm not healthy enough for you, either," she said. "Now I've got hydrogenated oil in me."

"Why are you taking this personally?" he asked.

She shrugged. "I can't even do things for you. Everything I try is wrong. How else should I take that?"

"Carter?" she asked now. "Did I upset you?"

No, love, he started to say, but stopped himself. He shook his head. "I was just remembering what an idiot I was." *I'm different now,* he thought, taking another sip of the godawful coffee and absently glancing at the student paper atop the stack closest to him: "I will watch my best friend die every night in my dream." The Palestinian kid. Farshad had mentioned him a few times. "Future tense?" Carter asked, gesturing to the sentence. He knew she'd taught it in early November.

"Changing the subject, are we?" She smiled. "But yes, that was future. I taught it earlier than usual. I was hoping to get this kid to stop writing about his best friend's death for a little while."

"I take it, it didn't work?"

She smiled. "Failed miserably."

"Didn't you tell me once that a lot of cultures don't have future tenses?" *I live in that country,* he thought.

She said something, but he didn't hear her.

"Can you believe that sun?" she asked, lifting her chin to the window and squinting into its brightness. "It's hard to believe they're predicting snow by rush hour."

He stared at her. Across the street, a metal EXXON sign clanked against its aluminum pole. How could she talk to him about the weather? *You were my* wife, he wanted to shout; *we were* married. The words boomeranged inside him. And yet, this was what he had wanted, wasn't it? To stop by like it was no big deal and say hello and chat for a minute? To be friends? Buddies? The words burned at the base of his throat. He and Annie used to be able to talk for hours, the architecture of their conversations gothic and wonderful: a castle with turrets and flying buttresses, secret tunnels, trap doors, hidden rooms. They would talk for hours until one of them might look at the other and ask, "How did we get here?"

Behind them, a man and a woman were leaning toward each other across the table, holding hands. He wore a wedding ring; she didn't. The Irish CD had started over.

He took another sip of the coffee, already half cold, then pushed it away dispiritedly and stood, his stool scraping the slate floor.

She glanced up. "What's wrong?"

"I have to go," he said thickly, and drew in a sharp breath as if he could push the sadness down. "I guess I wasn't as ready for this as I thought—" he swallowed and stared outside, focusing on the plastic reindeer on the rooftop of the gas station across the street. He'd stopped believing in Santa when he was eight, a year before she did, and for some reason, he had been desperate that she not find out the truth. He remembered tracing Santa's trajectory around the world for her on the lighted globe in his dad's study, estimating miles and distances, predicting Santa's arrival in the United States. He remembered pointing from his bedroom window to the flashing light on an airplane and telling her it was Rudolph's nose. Now, it occurred to him that maybe he'd spent his entire life desperate for Annie to believe in something that had never really existed: Carter. Who was he without her?

He patted his pockets as if feeling for keys or gloves. "It was good to see you," he said after a moment. A lie. He watched the bangles slide along her wrist as she took a sip of coffee, her eyes focused on him. *"Her face was sad and lovely with bright things in it."* A line from *The Great Gatsby*. He had started reading it again, from the same dog-eared paperback he'd used in college, his handwriting in the margins unfamiliar. "Irony!" he'd scrawled next to underlined sentences. He had thought then that it was a literary term. *Twenty-one, twenty-two years old, you never guess, do you, how ironic your own life will become?*

"If I don't see you before . . ." she glanced down sadly, hands open in her lap. "I'm glad you stopped in, Carter. I really am. I hope you have a great holiday."

A great holiday. The words crashed against the walls of his chest like dark waves onto a beach. He felt them rise in his throat, turn them-

selves inside out and hurl themselves forward. *A great holiday.* He nodded at Annie and pushed himself out into the wind. He was nearly
sputtering with grief and rage. *A great holiday.* Was she kidding? Did
she really not understand the cruelty in those words? Did she not understand that a great holiday was completely beyond the realm of any
possibility he could imagine?

He got into the car and turned on the engine, shivering, cold air
rushing from the heating vents. He glanced at her car sitting next to his
in the parking lot, sun glinting off the taillights, the I DRINK COFFEE FOR
A LIVING bumper sticker. He tasted salt and his own tears. *People split
up everyday,* he kept thinking. *One out of two marriages. A divorce
every 26 seconds.* Why couldn't he get over it? And in the next breath,
he wondered why he should have to.

He wondered, too, as he had every day since she left, what it was that
had allowed her to go, why she, of all people, had been unable to hold
on to him. And yeah, she loved Will; he could accept that. He wasn't
so naïve that he'd never imagined that someone could fall in love with
her. It used to amaze him when people didn't. He could even imagine
her falling for someone else. It had happened to his best friend from
high school seven years into his marriage, and it had happened to his
own father at a time when his parents thought he was too young to understand. But to actually leave? When had Annie learned how? He
kept coming back to the miscarriages. *Once you lose what you want
most in your life, is it easier to relinquish everything else? Is loss just one
more habit, like riding a bike or learning to swim?*

She rapped on his window. "Carter, are you okay?"

What would you do if I said I wasn't, he wanted to ask, but he only
nodded and closed his eyes, resting his forehead against the steering
wheel. The leather was so cold it burned. The air coming out of the
heater was still freezing. He tugged at a thread in his sweater, one she
had bought for him their last Christmas together—not even a year
ago. Sweaters, argyle socks, a brass reading lamp—she was always
worried about his eyes, his penchant for reading in dim light. She had
baked his favorite health food cookies and muffins—no fat, no sugar,
no cholesterol, and filled the freezer. Only later had he understood:

Already she had been preparing for the time, six weeks later, when she would leave.

He had wanted to ask her a thousand questions then. He still did. The last time they went out for Thai food or to a movie, the last time they argued about a book, the last time they made love—did she remember it? Had she known it would be the last time? Because he never had. And so he couldn't recall what she had ordered for dinner or what she wore or where in the restaurant they sat or what they talked about. He didn't know the name of whatever book it was, whatever movie. He didn't remember what she felt like the last time he entered her, if it was morning or night, if he could see her face when she came—if she had even climaxed? Or had that been an act, too, like the holidays?

"Carter?" She knocked again on the window, and he shook his head without lifting it, then listened to the sound of her footsteps growing smaller, retreating. Tears ran down his face into the collar of his coat. He heard the click of something opening and felt more cold blast through him. But it was her, sliding into the passenger seat, reaching forward to turn down the heater, which wasn't yet blowing warm air.

"Get out," he said roughly.

"Let me help, Carter."

"You?" He wanted to laugh. Talk about irony. "You can't."

"I can try."

He shook his head. "Please leave me alone."

"I'm worried about you, Carter."

Laughter pushed into his chest and lungs and throat. What could he say to that? Did she want *him* to reassure *her*? He closed his eyes against the bright sunlight. When he spoke finally, his voice felt like a narrow wire, unable to support the weight of his words. "I was almost okay until you wished me a great holiday." He lifted his head from the steering wheel, amazed at how heavy it felt, at how much effort it seemed to require. "It was as if I were just some stranger."

"I didn't mean it like that."

"No?" He glanced at her, sitting next to him, head bowed like a penitent schoolgirl. In the glaring light, he noticed the start of crow's feet at the corners of her eyes, the beginning of gray in her hair, and he thought, *This is aging her,* and felt a rush of gladness. "Did you even think about what you were saying?" His voice was softer. "Your hello on the phone—one word—is better than that. Honest, at least."

He felt the air around her grow still as the words registered. He expected her to slam out of the car, but he didn't care anymore. What difference could her leaving *now* possibly make? He almost laughed.

When she shifted to face him, her eyes were dark but not angry. "So it *was* you making the calls," she said. She scanned his face. "Will thought it might be, but I . . . it's so unlike you, Carter." She touched his arm. "Why?"

"Why?" he parroted, staring at her hand on his sleeve. When was the last time anyone had touched him other than to hand him a credit card or take a receipt? *I'm only thirty-four,* he wanted to sob. He might as well have been sixty.

"Why?" he repeated again, and without warning, he was laughing. He glanced at her. She was staring at him. "I'm sorry," he said, trying to stop, "I just can't believe you actually asked that." He started laughing again, saying *why* over and over as if it were the funniest word he'd ever heard. "Why?" he gasped. "*Why* do you think?"

"This isn't funny, Carter."

"I know, I know." He held one hand over his eyes, shaking his head, but he couldn't stop. "Why? Why else? You left!" He knew that if he stopped laughing he would shatter. Like being on an amusement park ride, spinning so fast that the centrifugal force pins you into place. His laughter was like that. He was afraid to slow down. "What's really funny," he said, "was that I was just supposed to understand your leaving and move on, and I actually—" He looked at her, trying to be serious, but he couldn't. "I actually thought—" He punched his thigh, trying to catch his breath. "I actually thought that hearing your voice would help." He swiped his hand across his face, his closed eyes, and took a heavy breath as if he'd run a race.

"Carter—"

"No. Wait." He held up his hand, laughing again. "Guess what else I did?"

"I don't want to know. You're scaring me, Carter."

"I hired your student." He doubled over, his ribs aching, tears streaming from his eyes.

"My *student*?" Her face tensed.

"God, who did I think I was? The 'spy who loved you'?"

"Which student?"

She was still touching his arm, not even holding it really, but just resting her palm to his sleeve, a reminder that she was there.

"It was Farshad," he choked, and he was sobbing then, gripping the steering wheel, his chest heaving, feeling as if it would split in two. "Just leave," he cried, but instead she reached to hold him. Her wool coat smelled faintly of perfume and cigarette smoke and coffee, and her hair *did* smell like vanilla, and he felt something release inside him. He felt as if she were physically holding him intact.

"It's okay," she kept whispering over and over, as if he were a child. "It's okay, I'm going to help, Carter, I promise." Her hand moved in gentle figure eights on his back.

Outside, it finally began to snow, the flakes twirling madly in the yellow light.

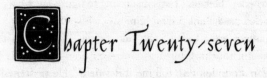

Chapter Twenty-seven

Ever since Anne had come home from the Daily Grind, Will had felt uneasy. She was unnaturally quiet. At first, he assumed she was just worn out from grading. More than once, though, he glanced at her and had the sense that she was about to tell him something, but then stopped herself. "Anne, did something happen with the job?" he finally asked. He couldn't imagine what else it might be.

"I'm just tired," she said. "A little down, I guess."

"Is it the holidays?" Only eleven days away. Their first Christmas together. How many times had they tried to imagine what it would be like? He and Kayla had always opened their presents on Christmas Eve; Anne and Carter on Christmas morning. What would they do now that they were together? And stockings: He and Kayla filled them; she and Carter didn't. A real Christmas tree or fake? The black-and-white or the colorized version of *It's a Wonderful Life*?

Last year, when she went to New Jersey with Carter, he'd been panicked that upon her return she would tell him it was over: She couldn't do it, leave the boy she'd grown up with. He had imagined she and Carter surrounded by his family, opening gifts one at a time, in order from youngest to oldest. It took hours, she had told him, the family going through a couple of pots of coffee, her nephews and nieces filling up on sugar cookies.

Annie leaned against the couch back, idly scraping the polish from her nails. "Are *you* worried about the holidays, Will?"

"No, sweetie," he lied. "I was just trying to figure out what's wrong." What the hell wasn't she telling him?

"I ran into Carter today," she said finally. "He was at the Daily Grind."

"And you were going to tell me this *when*?" He tightened his grip on the beer he was drinking. "What if I hadn't asked?"

Her eyes were bright. "I don't need the interrogation, Will. I'm tired, and seeing him was depressing, and I'm sorry if I didn't tell you the minute I walked in the door. I just wanted to enjoy dinner with you first."

"I'm sorry." He paused, took a swallow of beer. "I just don't trust that guy. So what happened? Did you talk?"

She nodded.

"About?"

"God, Will, I don't know. The weather, the holidays, he was drinking a mocha—"

"Carter?" he hooted. "What? He's trying to impress you?"

"Please don't make fun of him," she said. "If he was trying to impress me, it's all the sadder." She glanced down. "He was my husband, Will. I loved him once, you know? And he wasn't just the pathetic loser that you like to see him as. He's funny and caring and—" Again, she seemed on the verge of saying something, but then she shook her head. "I hurt him *again* today."

"He hurt himself, Anne. He knows you go to the Daily Grind to grade. He's the one who put you both in an awkward position."

"You don't understand. I felt absolutely nothing for him, Will. *Nothing.*" Her eyes filled. "What kind of person am I?"

"You are a wonderful, giving person," he said. "A person that I love more than anything in the world." She nodded, but she wasn't listening. He sighed. This was why he didn't trust Carter, no matter how much Annie claimed he cared about her. Carter was a passive-aggressive martyr who somehow always found a way to make Annie feel lousy about herself.

"You know, sweetie, if you were really the unfeeling monster that you think you are, you wouldn't even be worrying about Carter right now. The way you responded to him was normal."

"*Normal* to be married to someone for nine years and feel nothing?" She looked exhausted, pale and too thin. "I wish *you* felt *nothing* for Kayla," she said bitterly.

He glanced at her. "Is that what this is about?"

"No," she said. "I just hate it when you act like a psychologist with me."

"I don't mean to, sweetie." He didn't know what else to say. She wanted an argument with him for some reason, but why? To punish herself for not feeling anything for Carter? Or to punish him for feeling more than he should for Kayla? "I love you," he said. What else was there?

She shook her head. "Maybe you're just saying my reaction is normal because you're afraid. What if I don't feel anything for *you* five years from now? Will that be normal, too?"

"Come on, Anne."

"I'm serious," she said, her voice forlorn. "How can you be sure that I won't change my mind about us the way I did with Carter?"

"Don't do this," he pleaded. "Don't tear *us* down just because he—"

"At least *you* struggled. *You* had doubts—"

He tried to smile, to get her to smile. "So now that's a good thing?" But she only glanced at him helplessly and walked past him into the bedroom.

"I'm not negating what you're saying," he said from the doorway. "I just don't agree." She didn't answer. Even with the lights out, the room seemed luminescent, like the inside of the snow forts he'd built as a boy. He watched as she peeled off her jeans and sweater and climbed into bed, still wearing the turtleneck she'd had on all day.

"You're worrying me," he told her a few minutes later, sitting on the edge of the bed. He lifted her hair away from her face, surprised as he always was by the weight of it. "I don't know how you can say you didn't struggle," he said. "The entire two years of the affair, you were the one who was so torn apart, much more than I was." Her eyes were closed. Tears caught at the ends of her lashes.

"I loved how you confronted things head-on," he continued, gently combing her bangs from her face. "Even in the beginning, you were the one who really wrestled with what we were doing. I was too much of a coward. I couldn't even begin to do that until after I left."

"But what if it happens again?" she whispered sadly.

"What if *what* happens?"

"I don't want to fall out of love with you, Will."

His heart tightened. "You won't," he promised. I won't let you." But they both knew it wasn't so simple. He leaned down, resting his face against her. Tears leaked from her closed eyes onto his cheek.

"I just want to sleep," she whispered.

He lay awake later, listening to the clink of water in the metal pot in the kitchen—the leaking roof. Even Ethan was restless tonight, prowling about the hallway. Will turned onto his side, staring absently at the shapes and colors emerging from the gelid dimness of the room like the images of a Polaroid. Beside him, Anne stirred, her hand on his arm. Usually, she needed her own space when she slept, and kept a line of white sheet between them, with one foot always protruding from the covers as if she were prepared to get up quickly. He remembered the night he woke to find her sitting at the foot of the bed, whimpering softly. "Sweetie, what is it?" he'd asked in alarm. Her foot was stuck. Twisted in the sheets. He had wanted to laugh as he gently untangled her. She was still half asleep, and so distraught.

Tonight, though, when Will shifted, Anne moved also, keeping close to him, always touching him. Her foot was against his shin; her hand was on his arm.

Ethan stalked into the room and leaped soundlessly onto the bed. Will reached his hand out and the cat crept forward to sniff his fingers. "Why aren't you asleep?" he whispered to the animal, scratching his ears. Ethan purred and plunked down, squinting his eyes in contentment. There were no cars out tonight, no dogs, and no wail of sirens from downtown. Just the clinking of water into the pot in the kitchen.

Will rolled onto his other side and felt Anne follow, her knee resting lightly against the small of his back. He couldn't shake the feeling that no matter how close she stayed, there was a huge distance between them.

Chapter Twenty-eight

Annie woke early. Her first thought was of Carter confessing that it was him making the crank phone calls, that he'd hired Farshad at the bookstore. She lay on her side in the gray darkness, staring at Will as he slept. *Why* hadn't she told him? But Carter had promised he would stop, she told herself, and she hadn't wanted to upset Will or defend Carter's actions. Carefully, she moved from beneath the blankets, gently tucking one of the quilts around Will's shoulder. Squares of lavender and burgundy and periwinkle blue, the colors of the mountains behind Will's childhood home, mountains Annie imagined Will's mother had been thinking of when she sewed that quilt.

Will turned onto his back, mumbling in his sleep, and Annie lay her hand tenderly against his chest as if to steady him. His heartbeat pulsed against her palm. *I just need time,* he had told her that night in the Holiday Inn, but she hadn't been able to hear it, afraid that to let go even a little bit would be to lose him. She shook her head against the thought that had plagued her since yesterday: The night in the Holiday Inn when Will had tried to leave, Annie had done to him exactly what Carter had always done to her, made her feel as if something was wrong with her simply because she wanted her own space. What if that night had been the one moment when Will was strong enough finally to tell Annie the truth? What did it mean that she had refused it?

Would it have made a difference, she wondered now, if Carter had just *once* given Annie this much? Let her disagree with him about something—anything—without getting that wounded look in his eyes? She thought of that summer when they joined the YMCA, and he laminated their membership cards back-to-back because it never occurred to him that she might want to go by herself sometimes. "I thought the whole point of joining was so that we could do something together that didn't involve your students or my work," he had said when she mentioned it.

She recalled, too, the times Carter used to take Annie's male students from warmer climates shopping for winter coats or help them buy a car. By the end of the semester, he knew their stories as well as she did. Or if she raved about a book she was in the middle of, he'd start reading it at work without telling her, and then casually mention it in the midst of a conversation. Drying the wooden salad bowl: "I didn't like how Ondaatje ended Hana's portion of the story." *The English Patient.* Or, "I don't believe that Corelli would return to the island year after year and never tell Pelagia that he was alive." *Corelli's Mandolin.* A ribbon of green appeared as he bent over the trash peeling a Granny Smith.

"Corelli was bitter," she answered before she realized what Carter had done. She swatted his arm. "When did you read it? You are such a sneak!"

But then, and she couldn't remember what had precipitated it, she stopped telling him about the books. "How is it?" he'd ask, and she'd shrug and say, "So-so." She didn't know how to explain to him the discomforting sense that something was taken away from her every time he asked, that nothing was hers alone. Until Will, of course. Will had been the one part of her life Carter couldn't touch. She didn't want this to be the reason she had fallen in love in with Will.

In the kitchen, she measured coffee into the filter, then moved across the cold floor to the window, hugging herself against the chill as she waited for the coffee to brew. The sky was beginning to lighten.

"Dawn begins when you can hold a white thread against the sky and distinguish it from a black thread," one of the students had told her.

A light skein of snow lay across the neighborhood. Annie wondered if Will would end up resenting her the way she had come to resent Carter—perhaps without even realizing it until it was too late. *Han tan,* she thought sadly, leaning her forehead against the windowpane. Unrequited resentment.

I understand resentment, of course, Will had said when he first read her article, *but that it would be unrequited, like love . . . I'm not even sure what that means. . . ."* She suspected, though, that he understood now what he hadn't then. How could he *not* resent Annie for keeping him from his daughter? She had resented Carter for so much less. For what really? Loving her too much? She smiled sadly. She could imagine Sungae scowling at her in frustration: Why you teach us such things? Loving too much? Not possible.

"I'm sorry about last night," Annie told Will when he woke an hour later and walked into the kitchen, wordlessly heading straight for the coffeepot. He looked like an overgrown teenager, his hair tufted in clumps, his face unshaved. "I think I was just overtired."

"There's no need to apologize," he said, taking a sip of coffee. He had draped his mom's quilt over his bare shoulders.

"I shouldn't have taken it out on you." She got up from the table, where she had been grading papers, to kiss him, and he folded her into the quilt, resting his chin atop her head. "You're right about Carter," she said quietly. *He has been making the crank calls. He hired one of my students.* "He does make me feel lousy about myself. He always has. Everyone thinks he's such a great guy, and he *is,* but—"

"But it's hard living with a saint. Believe me, I know." He took a sip of coffee. She closed her eyes against his chest, inhaling the musky odor of his skin. "I wish you could play hooky with me," she murmured. "Or maybe you could come home for lunch?" She lifted her face to him, raising her eyebrows up and down suggestively. She loved him. *I'm not going to you let ruin this for us, Carter,* she thought.

"Do we have to wait that long?" Will asked. Already he was hard, and she shook her head, longing flooding through her. Will swiveled awkwardly in the quilt, still keeping them both wrapped in it, and set his coffee mug on the counter behind him. She arched forward, pressing against him. Through her T-shirt, he rubbed her nipple roughly between his thumb and forefinger, and she moaned, weak-kneed, as he yanked up her shirt, bending his mouth to her breast, her hands in his hair, pulling him closer, his hands fumbling with the drawstring of her sweats, pushing them down over her hips.

They put up the Christmas tree to celebrate. The only room big enough was the bedroom.

"So what was your best Christmas?" she asked. Will was standing on his desk chair putting up the lights. On the stereo, Nat King Cole was singing, "O Tannenbaum."

"The first one with Brooke," he said. "She didn't have a clue what was going on, but I was so goddamn happy." He laughed. "I hung her in a stocking after her bath one night and took a picture." He smiled at her, and in the dim light the long muscles in his forearms moved beneath the surface of his skin. "What about you? What was your best?"

"This one." She didn't even pause to think. "Right now."

"No, before this."

Was there a *before this*? She uncoiled more lights from the cardboard tray and handed them up to him. He reached forward to weave the string of bulbs around the upper branches. She watched his fingers, his skin paler than hers, more blue-toned than yellow. A square of darkness on the back of his hand as if it had been stamped there—the open area his cycling gloves didn't cover, and on his ring finger, the pale indent of the wedding band he had worn for twelve years. Once, physicians had read an entire history in a person's hand. In the strength of a handshake, the texture, color, temperature of the skin. In the scars and calluses, the shape of the fingernails, the size of the knuckles. She stared at her own hands, her unpolished fingernails, the small scar near her wrist from an iron, the imprint of the wedding band *she'd* once worn. She thought, too, of how hands held memory, of how she would often forget Will's work number, though if she held a phone in her hands, her fingers recalled the sequence. Or her students, in the midst of writing an essay in English, would suddenly write a word in their native language without realizing their hands' unconscious desire. *Ma nuoc,* Vietnamese for "water ghost"; *shi-jang,* Korean for "market."

What were Will's hands remembering now, she wondered? The Christmas five yeas earlier when he lifted his infant daughter so that she could see the glittery star he'd set atop the tree?

"Anne?"

She shifted her eyes from his hands to his face, patterned now with light. "Senior year in high school was the best," she said, scanning his eyes with her own. His senior year was the year his mother had died.

"Why senior year? Carter?"

"We were dating then, but no. It was me. I'd gotten into Rutgers. . . ." She stared at the angel already atop the tree. She wondered if Carter was in New Jersey yet, and if he was okay. She kept seeing him as he had been that afternoon at the Daily Grind sobbing in the car. Will was watching her, waiting. Why *had* that Christmas been so good? *Was it Carter?* "That was also the first year since my brother died that we really celebrated. Before, we had just been pretending."

Will smiled, shaking his head. "You at seventeen."

"What?"

"If I had known you then . . ."

"I was a bookworm. You wouldn't have liked me."

"I wouldn't have cared. I would have seen those gorgeous eyes. . . ."

The weeks surrounding the holiday were the happiest Annie could ever recall. A month later, when her world fell apart again, she would look back to those days as if they composed a foreign scene captured in miniature inside a glass ball. The joy of these memories made her wonder if the heart knows what the mind cannot—if somehow, a part of her had known to hold on, to listen carefully, to watch, and to remember. But she also knew that she could not have been as happy as she was for those twelve days of Christmas had she, even for a second, suspected what was to come.

Chapter Twenty-nine

It snowed that New Year's Eve, starting before dawn on the last day of the old year. By noon the supermarkets were almost empty of bread and milk, and the video stores looked as if they'd been ransacked by vandals. The roads were nearly deserted but for the flashing yellow lights of the snowplows. People stayed home from work, lounging about in robes and slippers, making alternative plans for the night. Baby-sitters cancelled, unable to drive in the snow, and couples hosting New Year's Eve parties anxiously phoned their guests, encouraging them simply to bring the kids along. Newscasters urged the public to remain at home because of the inclement weather, and across the bottom of television screens glided public-service announcements that all buses would be free that night.

In this country, the end of the year is a time to resolve to do better in one's life. *I will not phone her again,* a man thinks as he trudges home after closing his bookstore. *I will move on,* he resolves. Icy snow stings his face. Resolve. He holds the word on his tongue. From the Latin, *solvere.* To release, unbind. He looked it up before he left the shop. The streets are quiescent, and even his footsteps are muffled. Like walking on the beach at night.

I will run that marathon, a woman decides as she drifts into sleep. It is not yet midnight. She is grateful that the year is ending. The year of her divorce. In April she will be forty and it frightens her to think that she must start all over again. So many things terrify her: being old and alone, driving in the snow, talking in front of large groups of people, making a fool of herself, saying the wrong thing, not being a good enough mother to her child. She will start the new year by sleeping in and waking up with her daughter.

A few miles away, a woman looks at the TV and asks her husband, "Why they drop ball? What is that ball anyway?" Outside, from a distance, firecrackers explode. Car horns honk like migrating geese. Across the street, the Fitzpatrick children move across the front lawn like winter ghosts in their pale nightgowns, boots and coats. They bang pots and pans, and blow whistles. Koreans do the same thing, making the commotion to frighten away evil spirits. *But the Americans do not know this,* the woman realizes. *They believe that noise is only about celebration. What do they say? Out with the old, in with the new? It is never so simple.*

Perhaps this is why those from other countries are disappointed by the American New Year celebration. Other cultures understand that before you can welcome the future, you must appease the past. You can not simply trade it in like an old car, hoping for a better deal.

Vietnamese living in the United States missed the profusion of flower vendors lining the streets before *Tet,* their New Year. They ached for the smell of fresh paint and floor wax and detergent as women scoured their houses, ridding them of dust and evil spirits and the previous year's happenings. They missed the staccato chop of a woman's voice ordering her sons to rearrange the furniture to confuse those evil ghosts who hadn't been cleansed away. Elaborate metals were prepared for ancestors whose spirits would return to celebrate; children leaped through strings of firecrackers as if they were jump ropes and ate tamarind lollipops coated with sugar. After three days, the streets were carpeted red with "good luck" confetti.

In Taiwan, children stayed awake all night to ensure that their parents would enjoy a long life. In the morning, everyone poured into the street, shouting congratulations because they had survived *Nian,* which means "year" in Chinese, but which is also the name of the great monster who long ago ate people before New Year's dawn. Adults gave the children red envelopes embossed with the God of Fortune character. Inside was money, and if the children did not gamble it away that night, they would receive many riches in the coming year.

In China, the kitchen gods soared to heaven on New Year's Day to report to the Jade Emperor about the family's behavior during the year. The family burned paper boots, courtiers' robes and mandarin caps—clothes for the kitchen god's journey, and they offered sickly sweet New Year's cakes so that the kitchen gods would only report sweet things. Doors of homes and apartments were crowded with New Year's pictures—fat, healthy babies sitting on red carp, many of them upside down, for in Chinese "upside down" and "rich" are homonyms. Groups of teenage boys performed dragon or lion dances in the street, and children ate *yuen-siu,* the round dumplings whose shape symbolized wholeness and unity. Fireworks bloomed and the night expanded with the joyful sound of explosions. Little girls tied red ribbons in their dark hair, women wore red silk dresses and painted their lips bright red; boys donned red jackets or shirts; and men wore red ties. In China, red is the color of celebration. At night, families gathered once more to eat special New Year's soup made with squid and beef and pork, water chestnuts and shiitaki mushrooms, beans, rice noodles—the myriad ingredients a symbol of the rejoining, rejoicing, of the family.

In Iran, on the last Wednesday of the old year, children made wishes, then lingered on street corners and listened to the fragments of strangers' conversations, trying to divine an omen. If they heard a woman complain about the poor quality of the *lavosh* in the bakery that morning, that which they had wished for might also have poor results. The New Year officially began on the first day of spring with the arrival of No-rooz, a tall-as-the-cypress, thin-as-a-puff-of-wind magical figure with a sun-blackened face and boisterous laughter. Iranians believed that the number seven equals good luck, and so once the sun had set and the muezzin had called believers to their evening prayers, they began the celebration by lighting the candles and setting seven objects on a table: a mirror to symbolize a good forecast for the future, an egg to symbolize good reproduction. The children grew quiet. Someone opened the *Qur'an* and began to read: "The Night of Power is better than a thousand months. . . ."

Anne had the flu on New Year's Eve. Will brought her chicken broth and saltines, watching as she lay against the pillows and nibbled on the salty edges with her eyes closed. He licked his index finger, touching it to her collarbone, lifted a crumb, and placed it in his mouth. He lay cool washcloths on her forehead, and her dark eyelashes fringed the white fabric. Mostly, he watched her while she slept. Tenderness, as if she were his child, ignited within him.

"I'm sorry," she said when he hung up the phone after canceling their dinner reservations.

"For what?"

"For ruining our first New Year's."

"Oh, sweetie, I'm just as glad we're staying in. It's a lousy night to be out."

Nearly a foot of snow had fallen, with six to eight more inches predicted by morning. Heat chugged through the old pipes of the apartment: *I think I can. I think I can.* Will tried to recall the last time he had been this content. He couldn't.

As she dreamed, Anne's eyebrows furrowed. She would be chattering with cold, and he'd pile blankets over her, tucking them around her neck. Then he'd return a half hour later to find the covers thrown off, her sweatshirt and socks tossed onto the floor. He loved her.

Chapter Thirty

Farshad, A+. Ba, A+. Sacide, A. Nina, A-. Annie printed the grade beside each name, then blackened in the small circle beneath the appropriate letter with a number two pencil. She skipped over Sungae's name, Shin-pin's. Korkut was an audit, Ahmad a B-, Yukihiko a B. She signed her name in black pen, the gold charm bracelet from Will jingling as she wrote. Three charms to start: a racing bike, a coffee cup, a book. She smiled as she scrawled the date across the bottom of the page. January 7. Yesterday had been the Feast of the Three Kings, which for Annie always signaled the official end of the holiday season.

"It's still hard to believe," Annie had told Will last night. "That we're together like this." How many times had one or the other of them begun this same conversation with these same words? They never grew tired of it: the story of their beginning, of how she had never imagined leaving Carter, of how he had never imagined leaving Kayla. That they had made their love seem all the more miraculous. "I knew I was falling in love with you," she said, "but I thought, especially early on, that if I could just have a small part of your life—coffee on Thursdays—I'd be fine. It seemed like so much then, more than I'd had in years."

They were in bed as they talked. "It wasn't enough for me even in the beginning," he said. "I missed you the most right after I left you, still sitting there with your coffee, already grading." The story had become a ritual, like the ones children ask about the day they were born, wanting to hear it again and again, though they know every detail by heart. He continued. "All I could think about was that there was an entire week between Thursdays."

"So you started phoning in the morning to tell me hello—"

"And then we started meeting after work."

"And after your rides on the weekend."

"The Holiday Inn . . ."

She was lying on his chest. His heartbeat in her ear was like the sound of the ocean in a shell. "I was never greedy until I met you . . ." she began.

But then the phone had rung. A hang-up. Will glanced at her, eyes raised in question. She couldn't look at him. The holidays already seemed blurry and far away.

Why? she wondered now as she sat at her desk. Carter had promised. But she had broken too many promises herself. She thought of his broken laugh that day at the Daily Grind when she had asked him then: "Why?" But *why* was a fraction that could always be divided again.

"*Why? Why do you think?*" His eyes blazing with pain. "*Why did you stop loving me? Why did you leave me?*"

She had slept fitfully last night, afraid. Why hadn't she stopped by the bookstore to say hello? Or phoned to ask about his trip to New Jersey? Why did she feel so little for this man she had loved her entire life? She wondered if it was true what people said about the holidays being the season of suicide? Was Carter capable? She promised herself no, he would *never* do that, and then she got angry at herself for thinking that he'd throw away his entire life just because she left. But who knew what anyone was capable of really? He had never imagined that Annie was capable of leaving him, and she hadn't either until the afternoon she actually did.

She had stopped by the Book Cellar on her way into work. A petite blond girl with close-cropped hair sat at the front desk, reading a novel. Carter was at the bank, the girl informed Annie; he would be back shortly. Annie browsed, retrieving books from the display table or a shelf, drawn by a title, sometimes only a single word: *Unraveling. Hunger.* She read first lines as if entering a house she might buy, stories and chapters becoming rooms into which she imagined her life.

Before Will, books were the only thing in her life she had craved. Not clothes or jewelry or excitement or even certain foods. Just books. A gnawing ache in her stomach sometimes, as if to walk away from a particular sentence or paragraph was to irretrievably lose something she might never again find. But what? And when had it begun? This emptiness she had tried to fill with truths stolen from books.

Light streamed in the high front window, where Carter was display-ing memoirs this month. *Truth Comes in Blows. Journal of Solitude. Do They Hear You When You Cry? Don't Erase Me.* Fear flitted through her. From outside, she heard a car spinning on ice, the hysterical whine of its wheels. A truck backed up, beeping, to the Greek restaurant across the street.

She left after twenty minutes, leaving a note with the girl.

> Sorry I haven't stopped by sooner. Let's get together for lunch or coffee.

After the hang-up last night, Annie had confessed to Will that Carter had admitted to making the calls, that he had hired one of her students to work in his store. "I'm so sorry I didn't tell you sooner," she said. "I really believed that he would stop." She waited for him to say some-thing, but there was only the soft tapping of snow against glass.

"I'm sorry that he's doing this to you," Will said after a moment. She felt panicked suddenly and pushed herself away from him.

He opened his eyes. "What's wrong?"

"Why aren't you angry?"

He sat up, and light slipped over his chest as if he'd just pulled his head through the neck of a shirt. "You *want* me to be angry, Anne?"

"I don't know, Will. All these months, the mere ringing of the phone set you on edge and now it's as if you don't even care." Ethan meowed at the rise in her voice and leaped onto the bed.

"Of course, I care, Anne, and yes, Carter worries me, but I'm probably not as surprised as you were." He moved his eyes over hers. "You trusted Carter, and his actions have to hurt, and you've been carrying this around for—what? Nearly three weeks?" She nodded. "That's what upsets me." He shooed Ethan from the bed and held up his palm for Anne to hold, as if asking for a waltz. She smiled sadly at him in the darkness, and matched her hand to his. Like two halves of a locket. His fingers were the same length as hers, only thicker.

A car crunched over the hard-packed snow of the street out front. "I don't want to lose you, Anne" he said.

The words jolted her. "Why are you even saying that?" She tried to pull her hand from his, but he tightened his grip. "I don't understand where that even came from." Always this threat of loss. Is this how it would always be with them?

"All I'm trying to say is that I understand your not telling me about Carter. I've been the expert at avoiding the truth." In the half darkness, she could see his heartbeat beneath his skin, its steady thud against his chest. Like those transparent rain-forest frogs on the National Geographic Special they'd watched earlier. Skin, lungs, stomach, everything was see-through but their hearts. "It terrifies me to think that I'll start doing that with you, though, Anne. That we'll do it with each other."

"We're going to make mistakes, Will." Her eyes clung to his. She was really asking a question: Can we make mistakes?"

"Not that one, Anne." His voice lowered. "We know this too well, sweetie, that this is how it starts: one lie, even if it's just a lie of omission."

"You make it seem so all-or-nothing."

He stared at her, unblinking. "Isn't it? My God, Anne, we left our families for this."

She swiveled away from her desk to retrieve her book bag from the chair behind her and pulled it onto her lap as if it were a child, heavy and awkward. She dug through the main compartment for the orange she'd packed that morning. What she really wanted was more coffee and a cigarette, though she hadn't smoked since the night of the fire six weeks before. A scroll of white sunlight hung on the beige wall adjacent to the window, spilling over the bookshelves and the right side of Annie's desk. Her eyes wandered to the Xerox copy taped on the wall of Lois's and her daughters' hands, taken years ago when the girls were younger. They'd had off from school and were in the office with Lois that day. Their photocopied hands looked like dark leaves.

The sunlight reached only so far into the narrow room. It didn't fade but just stopped, like a sleeve, a third of the way down Annie's arm. From the hallway she heard the muted voices of other faculty. She glanced again at the grade sheet. Shin-pin. Sungae. The office filled with the scent of orange. They had both averaged Cs and would be devastated. She could see Shin-pin's flushed face and neck, her downcast eyes as Annie returned a homework assignment. Or Sungae, whose papers were so worn by the time she handed them to Annie they were as soft as flannel, and fuzzy with eraser marks. A faint penciled layer of Korean, which she translated phrase by phrase, then overlaid with English.

"I wish I could grade you for trying hard," Annie had told them. "You'd get an A every time. But I can't."

She bit into the orange. The sweetness was so sharp, it seemed to crunch. She stared at the five-by-seven framed newspaper photo of Nixon, which sat on the corner of her desk. It was taken just before he boarded the helicopter that would take him to Andrews Air Force Base on the day he left office. His face was like a glass plate moved too quickly from the hot stove to cold water. How it shatters soundlessly, instantly, but holds its shape.

"Nixon?" Will had asked the first time he came to her office.

"Best president we ever had," Annie said, pretending to sort through a pile of transcripts. If he saw her face, he would see she was lying.

"You're kidding me." He set the picture down and leaned forward to scrutinize her features, peering up at her like a small boy. They had not yet made love. She was still learning his various expressions; he was still learning hers. But he saw her smile and said, "Come on, spill."

She laughed. "It was my brother's. He worshipped Nixon. He was eleven years old during Watergate and watched every second of it on TV. He cried when Nixon resigned." Even after Watergate, though, even after he became a teenager and became interested in football and girls, Patrick kept the picture on his desk, leaning it against an old pencil holder. Annie saved it after he died, not sure why. Some vague notion that who you admire reveals what you long for.

She closed her eyes, resting in the self-imposed darkness. She listened to her own breathing, its steadiness comforting. She had a two o'clock appointment with the dean. What if the evaluations weren't good?

She put a B next to Shin-pin's name. Then Sungae's. She knew the arguments against this: It was a disrespect to the students. It didn't help them in the long run. She wasn't convinced. She thought of Sungae's essays—every time she wrote, it was as if she were excavating, finding shards of something she'd tried to forget. It was not C work no matter how many grammar mistakes she made. It was not average. But was it right or wrong, when the numbers said C, to give her a B? Annie wasn't sure she knew what those words—*right, wrong*—meant anymore. Had it been *wrong* to love Will? Or was it that once you accept that which is *wrong* and begin to call it *right,* you lose the ability to discern the difference between good and bad? She didn't know if she was a good teacher or not anymore, or even a good person. She didn't know what it meant to love Will any more than she understood what it meant to no longer love Carter.

She got up from her desk and stretched, then took her orange over to the window. The sunlight felt like a heat lamp. She closed her eyes and felt the tears well beneath her lids.

"Are you surprised?" the dean asked when Annie finally glanced up from the computerized printout that rated her evaluation scores against the departmental mean and the university average.

"I thought it had been a good semester," Annie said. "I'm happy, obviously." She smiled, holding out her hand in front of her. "My hands are still shaking, though."

"As were mine when I glanced through these earlier. I can't tell you how pleased I was to see such glowing comments from your students again."

Glowing. Not adequate, not good, not satisfactory. *Glowing.* Relief exploded inside Annie like a bright firecracker. Her thoughts careened ahead, disappeared around the curve of afternoon. Her evaluations had been good. No, not good, *glowing!* The word on her tongue dissolving into sweetness. She couldn't wait to tell Will. And Lois. "You can buy me that margarita," she'd laugh, hugging her friend.

The room was a wash of light, a corner office with tall windows on two sides, partially hidden by a curtain of hanging plants. It almost felt as if they were seated on a patio and it was summer. The dean was saying something about the increase in the number of international students . . . an expanded curriculum . . . discussions with various department chairs . . . something about establishing an English as a Second Language program, which was separate form the English Department. She leaned forward, paused dramatically. "Whoever runs this new program . . ." the dean began.

Whoever. The word slammed into Annie—*whoever*—and though she vaguely heard the ones that followed: *director, tenure, salary increase,* she couldn't grasp hold of them. *Whoever* was a dark curtain, obscuring all else. She tried to remember what Lois had said on the phone two days ago about a rumor—"A very good rumor. Trust me, Annie, you won't lose your job." But was this what she had meant? She swallowed, her throat dry, the taste of *glowing* already gone.

"It sounds exciting," she lied, struggling to sound normal, to convince herself that yes, this was the good news that the dean and Lois, and even Will when she told him of it, would want her to see it as. Director of a program, a tenure-track position. If she got the job it would mean more money and more prestige, better pay and benefits. She would be eligible for grants and paid sabbaticals. She could teach English in another country for a year: China or India. Belgium. Will could go with her—they would watch the Tour of Flanders. She felt her mouth arrange itself into a smile, felt the movement of her head as she nodded at whatever the dean was now saying.

". . . As a state-run university, we are obligated to conduct a national search. . . ." the dean's smile flickered uncertainly above the dark green of her suit. "But I am wholeheartedly and enthusiastically encouraging you to apply, Anne." She explained what the job advertisement would say, what the application and interview process entailed: a copy of her curriculum vitae, a presentation to the faculty. "Nothing to worry about."

Annie focused on the rose pattern in the Oriental rug and at the photo on the bookcase of the dean with her husband and daughter at the daughter's graduation. She felt like a schoolgirl around this woman and her perfectly bobbed gray hair and conservative suits, her perfect family, her framed diploma from Duke University (a bachelor of science; from the University of Michigan, a doctorate in biology). She tugged her eyes back to the dean, then to the print just over her shoulder: ochre-tinted, a portrait of biologist Geoffroy Saint-Hilaire, the words ALL ORGANISMS ARE COMPROMISES BETWEEN COMPETING DEMANDS. Was that true? She didn't want it to be. She heard herself telling Will only last night, "You make it seem so all-or-nothing." It, them, their love. And his response: "Isn't it?"

"If I did apply and was not chosen for the position . . ." Annie lowered her eyes, uncertain of what the dean might see in them: resentment, yes, but also anger and confusion. She felt betrayed—by the dean, by Lois, by herself, by Will even, though she didn't know why. How much more was *she* going to have to compromise? And at what point was compromise simply another name for loss?

"I realize it's awkward to be a candidate in the environment where you've worked for years." The dean smiled. "But please don't let it discourage you, Anne. You have single-handedly run our English as a Second Language Program for . . . How many years is it now?"

"Nine." It should have been enough, she thought. Grief flip-flopped inside her. She forced herself to stare into the bright sunlight as if it might burn away the tears now threatening. "Nine years, Annie," Carter had said, looking up from the long table in the lawyer's office. "Don't they count for anything? Don't I?"

"That many?" The dean's voice softened. "I hadn't quite realized . . .

I assure you, though, that this service will weigh heavily in your favor, Anne."

But not heavily enough. Because if the university truly wanted to start at new department and receive funding and apply for grants and attract stronger students, then they would want someone with a doctorate; someone who had published more and had taught abroad, perhaps; someone who knew another language, for God's sake.

"Of course, those years count for something, Carter. This doesn't change what we had; it doesn't alter the memories or the—"

He had stood, tossing the pen down. "You can lie to yourself all you want," he said, "but don't—" His voice was weighted with pain. "This—" He shoved the deposition across the polished oak. The stapled pages fluttered toward her. "This changes everything."

After a moment, the dean asked gently, "Have you ever considered returning to school to complete a Ph.D., Anne? If you were working toward this . . ."

She shook her head, the words plummeting through her. Beyond the window, the trees with their long pale branches encapsulated in ice looked fragile and breakable. The dean was speaking again, but for some reason, it was Will's voice in her head, Will that night in the Holiday Inn asking her if she would have left her child for him. She felt anger simmering so deep within her she could barely feel it. She wasn't even sure it was real.

It seemed impossible that she could even begin to explain to this woman, with her framed diplomas and awards and publications, the choice Annie had made over a decade ago not to get a Ph.D. *I don't care about tenure, about being a director,* she wanted to explain. *I don't even want it.* It had never been the academic *career* that held her. It still wasn't. It was the students, being in the classroom, joking with Yukihiko or getting Ahmad to laugh. It was reading the pages and pages Farshad had written for each assignment, pages and pages she had unfailingly marked, sometimes while standing in line at the Safeway or while sitting on the shaded grass at Byrd Park during Will's Monday night bike races, looking up just as he blurred past. She wanted to tell the dean this—all that Farshad had taught *her:* from February to October a constant northwesterly wind, the *shamal,* blows across the Iranian deserts; even in the summer, *Qolleh-ye Damavand* is covered in snow; there is no month in the Islamic calendar that does not include a day of mourning, there are nearly twenty kinds of roses commonly grown in the Middle East. *I wouldn't have learned this in a doctorate program; I can't put any of it on a curriculum vitae.*

Outside, the wind smudged the dark outline of the trees against the bright sky, and she thought of Sungae's Korean characters, embedded into the white background of paper. The dean stood, offering her hand. "Let me know if there is anything I can do to make the application process easier."

"What happened?" Lois asked. "What's wrong?"

Annie brushed past her, hurrying to the restroom. Once there she turned the faucet on hard, crying now. Lois asked again, "Annie, come on, what did she say?"

"A good rumor?" Annie sobbed. "You really thought I'd be thrilled at the chance to jump through hoops for a position I've had for nine years *without* all of their titles and the benefits?" Her face crumpled. She felt like a fool in the charcoal suit and heels she'd worn for this meeting, as if she'd been trying to impersonate someone else and had been found out. "I shouldn't have to do this," she sobbed, "I shouldn't have to beg for my own job."

Lois swiped a wad of brown paper towels from the dispenser and handed them to Annie. "You're right," she said, "and I'm sorry. I wasn't thinking of it in that way, but you've got to remember that this isn't personal."

"I wish I could just walk away."

"You'd be miserable."

"I can't keep doing this, Lois."

"You don't have a choice." Gently, she dabbed at Annie's face with the paper towels as if Annie were one of her girls, and despite herself, Annie smiled. "Could you also write a note to the dean and tell her to stop picking on me?" She tried to laugh, but then she was sobbing again.

"Annie, what's going on? This isn't just about the job."

"I'm just so tired. I'm so tired of trying to prove to everyone that I'm worth it. I'm tired of having to fight so hard for what I want. I'm not good enough for the dean because I don't have a Ph.D. and I didn't sacrifice as much as Will because *I* didn't leave *my* child, and I didn't love Carter enough—" She took the paper towel from Lois and held it against her cheekbone as if holding ice to a bruise, tears streaming from her eyes. "I know I'm feeling sorry for myself," she said, "but when will it ever be enough?"

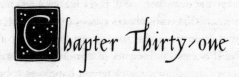

Chapter Thirty-one

Annie liked stepping from a dream as if from an elevator. The promise of coffee, the slant of sunlight across her abdomen as the radio softly sounded its alarm.

In her dream last night, she was teaching. The students were laughing. Students from three years ago, a semester ago, students from this semester—Nina, Farshad—students she hadn't yet met, though she could see their faces clearly.

She woke to the sound of a truck engine idling outside and the scrape of a metal shovel against the sidewalk. *Who would be shoveling at this time of night?* she wondered drowsily. She was curled on her side, away from Will. She hadn't told him yet about her discussion with the dean. He knew only that the evaluations were good, that she hadn't lost her job.

When she had arrived home from the Hacienda, where she and Lois had stopped for a margarita, Brooke was already at the apartment to spend the night. When Annie paused in the kitchen doorway and said, "Hey, you two," Brooke spun around, shouting, "No! Don't come in! You can't look! We're making you a surprise!" Annie blew them both a kiss and lay on the bed, tipsy from the margaritas. She fell asleep, still in her skirt and silk blouse, and woke to them whispering and giggling, carrying in homemade enchiladas, hers with a candle glowing in the middle.

"I love that you're a teacher," Will had told her a few nights ago. "I love that you know that verbs always come at the end of a sentence in Korean, or that there are—what, nearly ten thousand words in Vietnamese?—and that each has dozens of meanings." He was grinning. "What else? That the Chinese character for happiness is based on the idea of a full stomach, that in the Hopi language, the word *heart* is a form of the word *remember* and that—"

"Wait." They were sitting on the floor. He had been cleaning his bike; she was reading *The Skin of the Lion*—"There are long courtships which are performed in absence." "You remember all of that?"

"You're surprised?"

"It's just . . ." She folded the page she'd been reading and closed her book. "Yeah, I am." They weren't even important things. She couldn't recall the context of the conversations in which she'd mentioned them.

"Remember how you told me about that Indonesian writer? The one in prison." He spritzed degreaser on the chain, rubbing with an oily rag. "They wouldn't allow him pencils and paper, you said, and so he told his stories out loud each night, and his fellow inmates memorized them?"

"Promoedya Ananta Toer." He had composed seventeen novels that way.

"Well, you're my story, Anne. The one I memorize." He squatted forward on his toes, not looking at her, just talking. "I want to know, to remember everything about you. Your words, your habits, how you always eat the cheese from your pizza first, how the only time you curse is when you're driving, how when we watched the Tour de France last summer, you kept calling Mario Cipolini, Cipopini."

From outside now, she heard voices. The scraping sound continued. More voices: a police siren blipped on and then abruptly off.

Now, she was fully awake. Will wasn't in bed. She grabbed a flannel shirt from the back of his desk chair and tugged her legs into a pair of sweatpants. Through the dark window she saw the white headlights of a fire truck, the swirling red bulbs, and a silent flashing blue light from atop the police car pulled up behind it. Shadowy men moved across the front lawn, fluorescent yellow stripes on their fireproof jackets. Neighbors stood across the street in pajamas and winter coats. Will was with them.

She heard more shouts from outside then. A man's laugh. Not Will's. He wouldn't be talking with the neighbors if there were any danger, she reminded herself, frantically digging shoes out from the closet. She didn't smell smoke, though she kept pulling in deep breaths, trying to make sure.

In the den, Brooke was still asleep in the pink Barbie tent Annie and Will had given her for Christmas. Annie poked her head inside the opened entrance. Brooke was sound asleep. A pencil-size flashlight drew a white stripe across her face and illuminated the menagerie of stuffed animals lining the walls, their glassy eyes bright in the pink canvas darkness. Annie listened to Brooke as she breathed and watched the steady rise and fall of her chest.

Outside, it took a few minutes to accustom herself to the lights. The porch had been hosed down, and so had the inside hallway and the stairs. Fear opened inside her as she hurried across the lawn, hugging the flannel shirt across her chest.

Will glanced up as she picked her way across the lawn. "Is Brooke okay?" he called. He lifted his arm, and she moved into its circle, fitting the line of her body to his, sealing off any space between them, to maximize warmth. He was still wearing the clothes he'd had on earlier. Annie realized he hadn't been in bed.

"She's still asleep. I'll run back up in a minute. What happened?" Firefighters were pulling the hoses back to the truck. The snow was so hard it sounded like they were dragging them across gravel.

"He lit the goddamn wreath on fire. The door was starting to catch."

"He?"

"I saw him making the call, Anne." He stepped away from her, shrugged out of his jacket, and put it around her shoulders. He handed her his gloves.

"Who? What call?" But she knew.

"*Who?* Who else?" he laughed bitterly. "Carter. He was a block away. At the pay phone."

Another hang-up? Had she slept through that, too? She'd been so tired. She stifled a yawn and glanced back at the door—there was a charred circle in its center.

In the darkness, the red and blue lights continued to swirl.

"I don't understand, Will. Where did you see Carter? You're not suggesting . . ." She squinted up at him, waiting for him to see the fear in her eyes, to laugh and tell her, *No, my God, No. What did you think I was going to tell you?*

"Carter started the fire, Anne."

The sharp air caught in her chest as she gazed over the scene before her, firefighters winding the hoses back onto the trucks, neighbors returning to their homes. When she looked again at Will she thought she saw something gleeful in his expression. A smirk almost, *I told you so,* and for a moment she detested him. How dare he be so righteous, so intact? *If—if—it's even true,* she wanted to scream at him, *we are partly responsible for this.*

He saw it in her face. "What?" he asked. "I'm not the bad guy here."

"Just because you saw him making a call . . ."

"From a block away? His car was sitting right in front of Strawberry Street café."

"Maybe he was having a drink or he had a date or—" But he didn't drink. She felt as if she were caught in one of those dreams where you try to run and your legs won't move.

"Carter?" Will said. "Drinking? Even *you* don't believe that." He looked at her. "Plus his emergency flashers were on. . . ."

"What were *you* doing at Strawberry Street café?"

"I needed a walk."

"Well, maybe Carter needed to get out, too."

"Goddamn it, Anne, are you listening to me? Your ex-husband was a block away from our home. He could have killed us!"

Your ex-husband.

They traveled through the night, she would think in the weeks and months that followed, traveled without stopping, speeding through darkness. There were words that needed to be conquered like distances on a map. After that night, she would retrace that conversation in her mind to try to find the wrong turn, the missed exit, or the detour they might have taken.

But now, still outside, she watched the fire truck grinding away from the curb. The police car remained along with the fire marshal's car.

Will wouldn't look at her. She only had his profile. Half of him. He stood there, stone still, hands in his pockets as if he were a spectator at a soccer game. "Will?" She touched her hand tentatively to his sleeve. She was still wearing his gloves, and its seemed that there were too many layers between them. "You can't say anything to the marshal about Carter." She hesitated, searching his eyes with her own. "At least not until you know for sure."

"You're kidding, right?" He shrugged her hand from his arm.

"Hey." She moved to stand in front of him, reaching her hand up to cup his chin. "Why are you so angry at *me*?"

"I have a *child* up there, Anne."

"And she's safe."

He moved his eyes over her, the anger so intense that she stepped back. His voice was shaking. "I cannot believe you. I cannot believe I could love someone who could allow a child, any child, to be put into the kind of danger he put us all in tonight." He started to turn away, then stopped. "Do you have any idea how I felt when I turnd the corner and saw *our* house, *our* front door, on fire?"

She shook her head. Only yesterday, they had been happy. "I'm not saying we should just forget what he's done."

"Well, what are you saying?" His breath was white against the sky. "Because if you're asking me to feel sorry for him or to feel responsible somehow—" He shook his head. "I can't."

Exhaustion began to set in, as it had in the dean's office and at the hotel after Thanksgiving, when she'd begged Will not to leave her. "This is about me, Will, not Carter. *I* can't deal with his entire life getting ruined over this. Arson is a crime. He'll go to prison."

"He should!" He glanced at her, his eyes hard, but only for a moment before his voice gentled. "I know you don't want to accept this, but at least give me as much credit as you give him. I would never make an accusation like this unless I was sure, and I would never deliberately hurt you."

You accused him of making those phone calls for a month before you were sure, she wanted to say, but it was pointless. Will had been right.

Later, they sat at the kitchen table with the fire marshal. She had already confirmed for him that no, she hadn't heard any sounds around the time that the fire had started, and yes, she had given up smoking since the last occurrence. She made coffee and carried the mugs to the table one at a time, using both hands because she was still trembling from the cold. Will pretended to look at her, to talk to her—"Thanks, sweetie," but his eyes wouldn't meet hers, focusing instead on her chin or her nose.

"What about one of the kids you counsel or have counseled?" the marshal asked Will.

"No way."

The fire marshal raised his eyebrows. "No history of arson?"

"No."

Arson. She felt sick. She had a feeling this was connected to the note she'd left Carter this morning at his bookstore. Why hadn't she stayed, waited for him ten lousy mintues? She glanced at Will, and something tore loose inside her. She hadn't told him about stopping in at the bookstore.

"You sound pretty adamant, Mr. Sullivan," the fire marshal was saying.

"I am." His arms were crossed over his chest.

"Any reason?"

"Those kids don't have any beef with me. They're an easy target, and I understand you're just doing your job by asking, but you're barking up the wrong tree. Believe me, if I had the slightest suspicion, you'd know it."

She'd never seen him like this. Beyond anger or fury. She thought she had known all of his emotions and the whole itinerary of his gestures. She stood on the other side of the room, leaning against the counter, watching him from a distance—his thick boyish hair, his cheekbones windburned from cycling. She still didn't know where he had gone tonight or why he'd been out. When she went to sleep, he said he was going to read for a while. Had he lied? She knew all too well how capable they both were of deceit.

On the counter was bowl of unpeeled half-rotten bananas for banana bread or muffins or pancakes. A Far Side day calendar still on January 4. One clown throwing a pie at another. "Don't do that, Spunky. I have friends in pie places."

Kayla had had a date tonight, which is why they had Brooke. Will had seemed happy at dinner—I'm glad she's getting on with her life—but now Annie wondered. Had he been checking up on Kayla? Was he jealous? She'd read somewhere that you only suspect others of what you yourself might do, which is why Carter had never suspected Annie of having an affair. She had held it against him—*How, how could you not have known something was wrong, was different? For two years, Carter. How can you say you knew me?* But she understood now that he hadn't guessed because it was a betrayal he himself would never commit. All along, though, Will had suspected that Carter was incapable of letting go. Perhaps because he himself was unable to do the same. She stared at him across the room, her heart exploding in tiny bursts, and realized that she didn't trust him and that he didn't trust her. They were people capable of betraying those they most loved.

After the fire marshal left, they closed the door to the den so that Brooke would not hear them. He sat away from her, in his desk chair.

"Thank you," she said. He hadn't mentioned his suspicions about Carter.

He nodded.

"I love you."

"I love you, too." But his voice still sounded angry.

"Will?"

His eyes landed on her.

"Say something."

"I don't know what to say. You're asking me to choose between you and my child."

"No, Will, you're making it into a choice." She started to get up from the bed, wanting to touch him, but he shook his head. "Don't."

"Why?" But she knew why. She stared at the photos of Brooke on the desk behind him and knew that if she reversed the situation, if Kayla had started the fire, and if Annie's child had been asleep, she couldn't have forgiven Kayla. She would have hated her and would have been devastated if Will defended her. But she also would have understood, wouldn't she have? And she wouldn't have turnd it into an ultimatum.

"You have to make a decision," Will was saying wearily. "I won't mention Carter's name to the police, Anne, but I can't stay with you if that's your choice. I won't be able to live with myself." He paused and then continued. "What if something had happened?"

"It didn't, though. Look at her, Will. She's fine."

"But I'm not."

"And sending Carter to jail will solve that?" He didn't answer. "If it is Carter . . ." She needed to use the conditional. "Doesn't it matter that he's doing this because of us, because of what we did? What *I* did?"

"No."

"You feel no responsibility?"

"Only to her." He nodded toward the closed door where his daughter was sleeping.

"Not to me."

"Oh, Anne." He shook his head, the movement altering the shadows on the wall behind him. "I feel enormous responsibility to you. You know that."

Did she? She wanted to hurt him, tell him, *No, I don't know that at all, Will.* But she only nodded. It didn't matter whether or not he felt responsibility toward her. She didn't want him staying because of that, and she'd already begged him to stay once before.

His face was camouflaged by darkness now.

"You know what I love about us?" she had asked him once.

"Our wild and passionate lovemaking?"

She laughed. "Well, that too. But I love that nothing holds us together except us. No house or car or children or family. Nothing, Will." They were sitting in his car in the parking lot of the 7-Eleven.

"We're both exhausted right now and the only reason we're here is that we need to see each other for five minutes. I like that. I hope that's always our reason for being together—because we need to be."

"I adore you, Anne." He had turned to her, brushing her hair away from her face. "You always see what we have instead of what we don't."

"I know you think I'm being a jerk," he said.

"No."

"But I swear, Anne, this is not an excuse to run from you."

"Then what?"

"How many times am I going to have to choose between you and my daughter and *not* choose her? There's going to be a cost for that."

"You don't know—"

"I do!" he cried. "Every day at work, I see what happens when parents fail their kids again and again." He stared at her. "How am I different, Anne, if I keep putting her needs and her wants, and now her safety, second to my own desires?"

"You're a great father, and I love that about you. I've always loved that. And Brooke knows that, Will. She feels it." She stared down, absently combing the weave in the cotton blanket. "She doesn't even know what happened. You're the one making this into a bigger issue than it needs to be." She felt his eyes on her. "I'm sorry." She spoke softly. "I just don't believe that this is really about her."

He regarded her somberly. Outside, pine branches shushed against the side of the house. "That's what I told myself, too," he said quietly. "Every time I lied to Kayla to be with you, I convinced myself that it had nothing to do with my daughter."

My daughter. *Your* ex-husband. Words like boundaries on a map.

"I told myself this same thing the night I left—it's not about her—and God knows, I probably believed it, but now this—" He moved his arm toward the window, gesturing toward the lawn, the street where the fire trucks had stood, and the burned door below. She wanted to reach for his hand across the dark space that separated the bed from his chair, as if she could save him. "You know what?" he continued. "I love you so much that a part of me wants to believe it again, that this has nothing to do with her." His voice was hoarse. "But she could have been hurt tonight, and I'm her father, Anne. It's *my job* to take care of her."

She still couldn't see his face clearly.

"This is why, before you, whenever I started to love, to think about a life away from Kayla, a life with someone else, I just ended it. That was my rule and then, I don't know. I met you, Anne, and—"

Before you.

Whenever I started to love.

I just ended it.

She didn't hear whatever he said next. It didn't matter. *He lied to me,* she thought. *He lied. There were others.* She felt as she had during each miscarriage. Not before it actually happened when she was panicked and scared, staring at the ceiling and trying to be calm, and not after, when she was so empty she couldn't even cry, but during, when she was actually losing the child, her body betraying her, and there was nothing she could do because by the time the pain really hit, the doctors had told her after the first one, the child—the fetus—was already dead.

So it was with love.

I don't want to lose you, he'd said only last night when she told him about Carter. *No more secrets.*

She was crying.

"What?" he asked. "What did I—?" And then he realized what he had inadvertently told her. "Anne, it's not—" He closed his eyes. "Look, I wanted to tell you. I'm sorry. It was way before I ever met you, but still . . ."

"How could you lie to me?" she sobbed quietly. "For three years, Will. How could you let me leave a marriage for—for *what?*"

"What else could I have said, Anne? It was the first night we went out, and you were already so frightened and I knew—and you know I'm right about this—that had I told you the truth, you would have been out of there in a heartbeat."

"Would that really have been so bad?" she cried. Maybe she wouldn't have ever begun the affair if she had known the truth. And even if she had, maybe she wouldn't have left Carter, knowing that affairs were a pattern with Will. There wouldn't have been a fire; there wouldn't have been all this pain.

"How can you say that? You're the love of my life, Anne."

Good, she'd hurt him. *Even a voice can be wounded,* she thought. But she couldn't stop crying. "Where were you tonight?"

"I told you, Anne, I was taking a walk."

"I don't believe you."

His face paled. "I didn't want to wake you by turning on the light and Brooke was in the den, and I just, I don't know, I was restless." He leaned forward, the chair creaking. "You know what I was thinking about when I was out there? I was thinking about how this place is too small when Brooke's here and how I want a house—for *us,* Anne."

She turned away, burying her face in the pillow she was cradling, trying to muffle her sobbing. She felt the bed sag as he sat next to her, felt his hand on her back, gently patting her, but still, she couldn't stop crying. She realized that he knew how to leave. He'd done it before, many times perhaps. He knew he'd be okay eventually. He knew he'd fall in love again. And she knew, too, that this was why he could never understand or forgive Carter. He couldn't understand that sometimes people don't get over the loss of love. Sometimes they can't.

Around five, Will got up to feed Ethan. The sky was still dark. When he returned, he had an orange, and she watched his fingers as he peeled it and pried it into sections. After this night, she would always associate oranges with loss. And Will? If they untangled themselves from each other's lives, what would he remember of her? Of this night? Who would she become in his mind? The woman with the crazy ex-husband? Another wave of grief crashed over her. At least Carter had been loyal, she thought, at least he'd fought for them, for love. At least he'd believed in it.

She wanted to hate Will, but there was no room for anything but sadness. He sat next to her on the bed and offered her a segment of orange. She touched his arm. He had taken off his sweater earlier and was wearing only a T-shirt. "I love your arms," she said quietly, and he put them around her. She traced the line of muscles with her eyes. Most people didn't realize how much cyclists use their arms.

"Please don't choose him," he said into her hair.

"I have to." She whispered it into his chest. Injecting their words directly into each other's skin, like vaccinations against what was to come.

"Why?" he asked.

She didn't answer.

At six, Annie made coffee while he showered and got dressed for work. He'd drop off Brooke at Kayla's on the way. When it was her turn to shower, she turned on the water as hard as she could and cried. She wanted the hot needles of water to drive out the images that kept circling in her mind: Will with another woman; Will tunneling his head beneath the blankets, his tongue on another woman's breasts, and rib cage, the hollow of her stomach; Will laughing at something that other woman had said. These images hurt far worse than the ones Annie had once had of Will and Kayla—ordinary pictures of the two of them watching TV in bed at night or trick-or-treating with Brooke—because these images of the other women were reminders of all the things that until now Annie had believed were hers and Will's alone.

After he left, she sat at the kitchen table for most of the morning and watched the sun rise over the tops of the bare trees. The neighborhood was a fairy-tale world, all white-icing houses and perfect spirals of chimney smoke. Brooke had gotten a set of Disney videos for Christmas and the three of them had watched *The Little Mermaid* last night, *Hercules* the week before. Annie had promised her *Beauty and the Beast* next time, then *Aladdin*. No matter what the story, though, the characters in love always came from separate worlds, and happiness meant that one of them must sacrifice forever the world he or she had always known. Always there was a choice. Her own seemed impossible.

As she paced across the kitchen to make another pot of coffee, she was aware of the cold linoleum on the balls of her feet and her toes. The ache in her back as she bent to retrieve the coffee from the refrigerator. The fingers of her right hand were sore from holding a pen to grade for so many hours. She had felt like this before, after each of the miscarriages, defined by absence. Like a Japanese painting, a mountain range represented by a single line. *Shibumi,* the value of empty space.

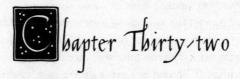

Chapter Thirty-two

They say that your life flashes before your eyes when you are about to die, and Will wondered if it was the same when a relationship ends.

He stared again at the yellow square of paper in his hands. "Anne. 12:48. Please call." He'd been in session with Raphael when she phoned. He shifted a few files around on his desk, stalling. He didn't want to hear her say what he knew she would.

He wished he could ride, to disperse this energy throughout his body, pushing it from his chest into the muscles of his arms and legs. It would be a week, maybe two, he figured, before the roads would be dry. He exhaled sharply and lifted the receiver, and when she picked up on the first ring, he smiled, despite himself. She once joked that there were skid marks on the floor from her racing down the long hallway from the kitchen to the bedroom to grab the phone before the machine picked up. "Hi." He laughed. "Was that the screeching of your heels on the wood that I just heard?"

She sounded relieved. "I think I set a record. Anyway, thank you."

"For what?"

"For calling back. I was afraid you might not." She exhaled slowly. "Or maybe I was afraid I wouldn't pick up. I don't know. I'm confused."

"I know. Me, too."

"I wish I could hate you for what you told me last night."

"It'd make it easier, wouldn't it?"

"Is that what you wanted, Will?"

He'd asked himself the same thing over and over. Had he been trying to protect himself by pushing her away? "No." Not this time.

"I went to the bookstore this morning," she said. "Carter knows you saw him last night, Will, and he's getting professional help. I watched him make the phone call." He pictured her pacing about with the cordless phone, back and forth across the bedroom, sunlight puddled on the unmade sheets, or in the kitchen, wiping the counters as she talked, rinsing out her coffee mug.

"I don't want to lose you," he had told her only two nights ago. It had been a remote possibility then, but no more. All morning this fear had been inside him like the beginning of a flu, like the stillness of the sky before snow. He'd known it during his sessions with Cole, Dameon, Raphael, and later, as he stood in the faculty lounge talking to the other counselors, holding a Boston cream doughnut, stirring his coffee.

He leaned forward over his desk, rubbing his temples. "That's good," he lied. He tried to remember Carter from that first night—if he'd liked him, and what they had talked about when Annie and Kayla disappeared to the ladies' room, complimenting each other's dress and hair like teenage girls eager to become friends. He had thought that Carter wasn't good-looking enough to be with Anne—not that he himself was. He remembered that Carter constantly followed Anne with his eyes when she spoke, and even when Carter was talking business with Kayla, and Anne and Will were talking about who-knows-what, Carter had been aware of what she was saying, and had been in both conversations at once. He drank O'Doul's nonalcoholic beer and didn't eat dessert. "He's a voyeur," Annie had teased, placing her hand on Carter's arm. "He likes to watch me." Will thought Carter was a nerd, a nice guy, but nothing exciting. Passionless. But Annie had loved him.

"I told him I would go with him to the psychiatrist's." For a moment, there was silence. "I think we need counseling, too." Her voice trailed off. "Will?"

"Anne, I thought I . . ." He moved the pencils on his desk. "You haven't made a decision—"

"What do you mean? He's got an appointment with the psychiatrist for this afternoon. He's taking responsibility. I thought that's what you wanted."

What he wanted. A lot of things: her, of course, and to be a good father to Brooke. To be able to cycle soon, go to Ireland someday, see the Tour de France in person, grow old with someone he loved, with Anne. But so what? People wanted all the time, and what they wanted wasn't necessarily right or wrong or good or bad, it just *was*. He bounced a pencil on its eraser point, caught it, and bounced it again. She wanted so desperately for things to be okay and they weren't. Carter's promises and good intentions weren't enough, no matter how much she wanted them to be.

"Will?"

"I'm here, sweetie."

She didn't say anything for a moment. When she did, he could tell she was trying not to cry. "What do you want from him?"

He felt like a jerk. He knew he was asking for the impossible, and yet to close his eyes to what Carter had done, tried to do, last night— how could he? He didn't know what he owed her ex-husband. He knew it was something, but not his daughter's safety. What if this was all a ploy to get Anne back? Already it was working; already she was going to the psychiatrist's with him.

She was crying. "I don't understand what you want, Will. If you don't think I should go with him, I won't. I just thought—"

"No, Anne, I admire you for helping him." And he did—sort of— though he was also angry. "Carter's seeking help doesn't change things for me." He spoke slowly. "I see this all the time, Anne, and the one thing I know is that he's going to get a lot angrier before he even begins to deal with whatever's going on. You can't promise me there won't be a next time, another fire, maybe a bigger one. You can't even promise that he'll get better."

Her voice was quiet. "So, you want me to forgive you, but you can't do that for anyone else?"

"That's not fair," he said. "You can hardly compare what I did—"

"What you did is worse." She paused. "You must think I'm an idiot." Her words were edged with pain. "You don't want me, Will. You haven't for months. How many ways do you have to tell me before I get the hint?"

He shook his head. How many times and in how many ways would he have to prove that he loved her before she believed it? "Don't, Anne, come on."

She laughed sadly. "I'm no different than Carter, am I? I just don't get it." Her voice grew distant. "I can't believe I'm still trying."

He sighed. "I love how much you try." She used to joke that she was a barnacle—attached to him for life.

Silence. He could not even hear her breathing, or her crying, as if she were holding the phone away from her mouth. He waited, gazing at the framed photo on the opposite wall. The Rocky Mountains. One of Kayla's photographs.

"Anne?" He spoke gently, as if waking her from sleep.

"I'll see you when you get home," she said coldly. "I need to go to that appointment."

He sat still for what seemed a long time, but probably wasn't. In the bottom drawer of his desk, beneath old file folders and evaluation sheets and a pocket dictionary, was the composition notebook he'd bought over two years ago in which to record his thoughts of her. He leafed through it, not pausing on any one page, not stopping long enough for a word, a date, or her name. He noticed the variations in his handwriting, in the darkness of the ink. The carefully scribed entries, details as precise as thumbprints. Or hurried and scribbled, the letters like panicked animals stampeding across the page. This was all he had, he realized. This, the Christmas gifts, and some cards. Souvenirs. Once, when she had to travel to a conference in Miami, she used her phone card to call him at work and later saved the bill. Evidence, she said, that they existed.

Chapter Thirty-three

Annie didn't see Carter's car in the parking lot of the medical center, and so she waited, running the heater on high and listening to National Public Radio interview a biologist about the chemistry of love. "True attachment between individuals involves the limbic system, the hypothalamus . . ." She only half listened, thinking instead of all the times these past few years she'd sat in the car in some parking lot, waiting for Will. Waiting half an hour at Dunkin' Donuts just to see him for five minutes at the end of the day. Waiting in the parking lot of the Italian restaurant on Sunday mornings. *How was your night?* Saturday—date night—he always went out with Kayla, she with Carter. The unspoken question lay heavily between them. *Did you make love to her? To him?* And Thursday nights, they met in the parking lot of the Catholic church near the Holiday Inn. Applying lipstick, dabbing her wrists with perfume, fussing with her earrings or her hair. She was always nervous, even after two years, worried that something had happened, and that he wouldn't show up. He was the same way. "Now I can breathe again," he'd say when he finally saw her.

"Attachment is a chemical as well as an emotional process which takes about four years to complete . . ." Four years. They'd known each other less than three. *It's not enough time,* she thought, panic rising in her lungs. She didn't want to think about it, though, didn't want to wonder if this would make it easier for them to leave each other, didn't want to believe that their lives—Kayla's and Carter's included—had been ruled by something as scientific as hormones or chemicals.

Only yesterday she'd been sitting in the dean's office. Only yesterday. She kept repeating the words in her mind, as if somehow the mere fact that it was *only yesterday* could minimize all that had happened. Numbly, she watched cars pull into the parking lot and people hurry toward the glass entrance of the three-story brick building. A discreet wooden sign stood out front: FAMILY COUNSELING AND PSYCHIATRY.

Annie thought of Will's words: *"I admire you for helping him."* Admire? She'd wanted to laugh. *Why? I'm not doing it for him. I'm not doing it for the right reasons or because I'm a good person.* She leaned her head against the seat rest. Yes, she thought, she was worried about Carter and yes, she wanted him to get help, and a part of her still loved him and felt responsible. But mostly, she was here because she was selfish and because she would do whatever she had to, to keep Will in her life. And she had thought this would help. A part of her still hoped that it would. Will wasn't a vengeful person, she tried to convince herself, and this desire to punish Carter was really about something else.

"Levels of oxytocin, the molecule responsible for attachment, will rise if someone holds your hand, or simply touches you. Consequently, frequent contact with that individual may result in a chemical dependency—an addiction—not to the person, though this is what we believe, but to the increased levels of oxytocin."

She turned the radio off and set her sunglasses on the seat beside her. Letting go of Will—was it really just a matter of weaning herself from his touch? From him? Like giving up chocolate or alcohol or cigarettes? She wanted love to be more. She kept remembering him last night, telling her, "Yes, there were others, Anne." *Others.* "I'm sorry. I am so sorry for lying to you. I never—"

"How many?" she had asked, but he only shook his head and told her, "Don't."

She had felt stupid. She had destroyed her marriage for nothing? Two years from now, or five, would there be another woman to replace her, another woman that he would love, and one day would he tell her, too, that yes, there had been *others*?

"Did you love them?" she had asked.

He looked stricken. "My God, no, not like you, Anne. No."

"But you did love them."

And he had nodded.

She traced her fingers over the weave of the blanket. "So I'm just part of a pattern." It wasn't a question, though he took it that way.

"You know better," he said.

She was crying. "Do I?"

Once Carter arrived, the psychiatrist led Annie and Carter into his office.

"We've been repainting the walls in the offices," he explained, reaching to light the peach-colored candle on the end table next to him. "You can call me Dan, and let me know if this scent is too strong. It's been a losing battle, trying to mask one obnoxious smell with another."

Annie smiled. She liked his voice—gentle, but not condescending.

"I have in my notes that you felt this was an emergency." He addressed himself to Carter. "I have some of the details here—" he glanced at the file folder lying unopened on the love seat next to him, "—but maybe you could tell me a little about what's been going on prior to last night?"

Carter nodded but didn't say anything, rubbing his thumb back and forth over the wooden armrest of his chair. He'd kept his baseball cap on, and the brim hid his eyes, though she could see his eyelashes were wet with tears. *I'm sorry,* Annie wanted to tell him. Had she ever? Had she ever said just that, *I'm sorry,* without connecting it to her own defense—but *I never meant . . . I didn't plan . . .* Just *I'm sorry.*

She never had.

Dan leaned forward, elbows on his knees, trying to meet Carter's downward stare. He was in his fifties and overweight, with thick white hair. "Okay, Carter, we're going to take this real slow," he said. "I'm going to ask some basic questions and we'll go from there." And then he backtracked, asking Carter his age, what he did for a living, and were both parents alive and how often did he see them? Any siblings? How about a history of drugs? Alcohol?

After some one- or two-word answers, Carter's voice grew stronger and his posture relaxed. Then he started talking: "My ex-wife, six months ago . . ." He stopped and started over. "No, let me be exact. Six months and eight days. I'll give you hours and minutes, if you want. That's how I live now." His words seemed to slam into the room. Annie wasn't ready for this. That morning, he'd been apologizing and asking her to help. But now . . . "I've been—what would you call it? Stalking? Is that the correct word, Annie, or, excuse me, it's *Anne,* right?"

She started to answer, but Dan held up one finger. "Hold on." He stared at Carter. "You *don't* call what you've been doing—the phone calls, hiring her student, the fire—stalking?" he asked.

"I call it grief."

"Annie?" Dan said.

"I think it's more like punishment," she said quietly. "Or revenge. And I understand to a certain extent—"

"Look, *Anne,* I know you mean well, but I don't want your understanding, okay?" Carter glanced at her.

"What's wrong with Annie's understanding?" Dan asked Carter.

"It's insulting."

She didn't look at Carter, because she was afraid she'd start crying. He was probably right, it was insulting. She wasn't sure why she was here anymore. How was this helping? *Who* was it helping? Had she thought that coming here would be a kind of penance? Three Hail Marys and two therapy sessions and all your sins are forgiven? Her hair fell forward, still smelling heavily of smoke. This morning that smell had been in their sheets and pillowcases, even on Will's skin. And now the peach scent of the candle, which she would carry home with her tonight. It would mingle with the smell of the burnt wood and carpet.

"This morning, you wanted me to be here," Annie said finally, "and I am, Carter, but—"

"But what? You want thanks, is that it, Annie?"

"Why am I here, Carter, if you're going to be like this?"

"Maybe that's not such a bad place to begin," Dan said quietly. "Why did you want Annie here, Carter?"

She looked at him finally. Her best friend, the teenage boy in flared jeans who used to sit for hours with her on her front porch, bored and restless, complaining about their parents and teachers, her older brother, his older sister. He was the boy, later the man, who bought her five-pound bags of Gummi bears and joked about how the Gummi police had almost busted him this time for trying to pick out all the red ones, her favorite. He was the man who rocked in his sleep some nights, as if trying to comfort himself, until she touched his shoulder to calm him.

"I don't know why I wanted her here," he said. "Maybe it's just an excuse to be near her, maybe that's what the whole goddamn mess is about, the fires, the phone calls. I don't know." He pulled his cap off, ran his fingers through his hair. "I wasn't trying to hurt you," he said quietly, meeting her eyes. "You know I wouldn't do that."

"I know—"

He turned to Dan. "She'll tell you, I can't kill a mouse, I won't watch a violent movie—"

"Okay, so let's say you did simply need the attention from Annie, some sort of recognition. Why not just phone her and tell her you wanted to talk? Ask her to meet you for a cup of coffee?"

"She knew." He leveled his eyes at hers. His beautiful long-lashed eyes. *If we ever have a daughter, I hope she has your eyelashes,* she used to tell him.

Dan turned to her, eyebrows raised in question. "Annie?"

"We ran into each other before the holidays, and I knew he was having a hard time. . . ." She turned to Carter. "I'm sorry. I wasn't sure what you wanted. You had said you weren't ready." She stared at the play of light cast by the candle—*we'll have to make jack-o'-lanterns soon*—and closed her eyes, not wanting to remember. "It just seemed that stopping by would only drag out the pain more."

"For who?" Carter asked. "For you, Annie?" And she knew he wanted her to say yes, and she knew she couldn't because she hadn't been in pain. Not the way he wanted, not the way he had been. She shook her head.

He turned away as if she'd slapped him.

"It's not as simple as you think," she said. "It's not that I wasn't in pain, Carter, or that leaving you was ever easy." *I missed you on the first day of class,* she wanted to tell him. *I missed you on the days things went well. I wanted to call and tell you—you'll never believe what Sungae did—only you didn't know who Sungae was. I wanted to talk to you yesterday after the dean. . . . And even now, brushing my hair or grading a paper I'll realize my ring is missing and there's a second, maybe half a second, where I panic. I can't remember how I lost it. Or how I lost you.* "I dropped by the store yesterday," she said feebly. It had been too little too late. She knew that. "Didn't you get my note?"

He cocked his head sideways, looking at her. "Who do you think you're fooling, *Anne*? If you really gave a damn, you would have waited ten lousy minutes for me to get back. You were there because you felt guilty. You were there for *you*—" His voice broke. "That's what I regret the most," he said, speaking now to Dan.

"Don't tell me, tell Annie," Dan said. "Look at her." And for a moment they almost smiled. How many times as kids had they fought about something stupid and been forced to make up by their parents? "He called me ugly." "She took my coloring book." "He stepped on my sand castle." And their mothers would pull them by the wrist and make them look at each other and apologize.

Carter glanced at her tentatively. It hurt to look at him, to really look. When was the last time she had? Long before the separation and divorce, she thought. Before Will. Before the third miscarriage, maybe before the second. A long time ago. *I don't know you,* she realized. But when did the not knowing begin?

"What I regret about the fire, and even the phone calls, is that I gave you a reason to dismiss me," he said slowly, eyes brimming. "I'm the bad guy now. I'm the screwup. Now you don't have to feel guilty for what you did. You don't have to think about how I didn't deserve what you, *you*, my best-goddamned-friend—" He clenched his jaws, speaking through his teeth. "I wasn't worth fighting for."

The same thing she'd said to Will, Anne thought, filled with grief.

"Nine years of marriage," Carter was saying. "a thirty-year friendship." He snapped his fingers. "Gone. There's no reason, and there's no way I can understand." He was crying. Tears spilled down his unshaved face. He turned back to her. "I loved you," he said. "I wasn't perfect, but I loved you."

"Please, Carter, let's not—"

"No, Annie. Let's."

"This isn't fair, Carter; this isn't why I came here. I told you this morning that I wasn't going to rehash our marriage."

"*Fair?* Do you know that the night you told me you were in love with *him,* all I wanted to do was hold you and tell you it would be okay, that we'd get through it? How could you leave? I kept asking myself, and I'd think of all the good things about us, and I knew, I just knew that if I kept loving you, kept believing in you, we'd be okay—"

"I know I hurt you, Carter, and you're right, you didn't deserve it." She leveled her gaze at him. "I wish I could undo what I've done—" but she faltered then. It wasn't true. Even now.

"You are so full of it, Annie," Carter snapped. "It's almost funny, isn't it? How you only say those words now when the possibility of *undoing* this mess is completely gone."

She looked at Dan. "I don't understand."

"About the only thing I had after you left was the consolation that I tried, that I did everything I could—and now?" He laughed bitterly. "I don't even have that. That's what I regret. Once again, I'm the sucker. I made it easy, didn't I? Carter, the arsonist. Carter, the stalker. Now you've got an excuse. You're off the hook—you don't have to feel guilty anymore. I gave you an out last night."

She felt, rather than heard, the impact of his words, their weight altered by anger. The way a coin or a small stone dropped from atop a high building can pick up enough momentum to kill someone.

"Carter, I don't think Annie needed an excuse to justify her leaving." Dan glanced at her. "I assume she felt the relationship with Will was justification enough."

"That's crap!"

"I'm not saying it was right, Carter. I'm suggesting that maybe the fires were your way of justifying Annie's leaving for yourself. *You've* got a reason now. It makes sense that she would leave someone capable of committing a crime—"

"But the fires were after the fact."

Dan shook his head. "It doesn't matter. You 'fucked up,' as you said. Bingo. There's Annie's reason. Maybe she somehow saw this tendency in you. Maybe she knew you were capable. Either way, isn't it a hell of a lot easier to swallow than the fact that you did your absolute best, everything you possibly could have—and it still wasn't good enough?"

"Why does my leaving have to be about something Carter did wrong?" Annie glanced at Carter. "It wasn't you," she said.

"Please," Carter snapped. "Don't start the 'It's-not-you, it's-me' speech."

"What if it's the truth, Carter? My God, were you always this ego-centric—?"

"Me?" he laughed.

"What do you want me to say? You want me to make up reasons to blame you? Will that stop you from setting my house on fire? Is that—?"

"Hold it," Dan said. "Carter, let's just say that Annie is right—that her leaving wasn't about anything you had done. Can you live with that?"

He glared at her, and again, they both almost smiled, because his expression was so petulant, so purposely boyish. He used to give her that look when they were debating which movie to see or which restaurant to go to and he was trying to get his way.

"I just want to know why you didn't try," he said quietly. "Didn't I deserve that much? I begged you, Annie. You know this. Just go to counseling with me—to give our marriage that, at least. I was willing to close the store for the summer, to go away with you, even to move to another state, for god's sake. Anything, *anything,* to help you find a way back to me."

"Would any of that have worked?" Dan asked her, and for the first time Annie said out loud what she hadn't ever admitted to Carter—or to Will. "Maybe." Maybe it would have worked—counseling, a vacation. Maybe if she'd tried, she and Carter would still be together. Will would be with his daughter. Maybe. Will had asked her this countless times: *If I was wasn't in your life, could you make it okay with him again, Anne?* She had lied, told him no. *Could you really go back to Kayla?* The truth of "maybe" had been unbearable.

Carter's head jerked up. "Maybe? *Maybe?* There was a chance and you wouldn't try, you couldn't give me—Jesus. Jesus." He was sobbing. "*Maybe?* Look, I can't do this—I can't," he said to Dan. He was devastated.

She was crying, too. "I was afraid you would change my mind, Carter. I was afraid you could convince me to stay, and I didn't—I couldn't—"

"*Why?*" He slammed his fist against the chair. "Why is he so important? What is it Annie, what the hell is it that he could give you that I couldn't? A child? Goddamn you, was that it?"

"Carter, this isn't helpful, it's not going to—"

Dan interjected: "He deserves to hear it, Annie."

She stared down, crying, her hair falling in front of her eyes. "I was in love with Will." She spoke softly. It seemed like the worst thing she could possibly tell Carter.

"You were in love with me once, too—" but she was shaking her head, still not looking at him.

"I loved you, Carter, please, *please* believe that, but it was different. I was never *in love* with you."

She waited for Dan and Carter in another office, with the same gray walls and blue carpet. Through a window, the orange sheen of late afternoon light was cast onto the small desk beneath it. She had expected it to be dark outside by now, but the sky was gorgeous—gold, purple, and bright pink. Will would be leaving work soon and driving home the back way, slowing the car as he passed the reservoir to look for the deer that ventured to the forest's edge at dusk to feed. Would she still notice these things without him in her life? A hawk circling overhead as they drove along the James. An osprey. Crayfish in the shallows. Once, during the first spring they were together, as she sat on a nearby rock in her teaching clothes, he showed her how to catch them.

She couldn't stop crying. She had lied to Will in just as devastating a way as he had lied to her. By insisting that she couldn't end the affair and return to her life with Carter, she had altered all of their lives. Was it even true that she had *never* been in love with Carter? She knew only that it was true now, but she could no longer recall when she had first made that distinction. *In* love. Perhaps this was only a myth she had invented after she met Will, a way to give meaning to what she didn't understand, a way to integrate the Annie who loved Carter with the Annie who desired Will.

Dan came in after about ten minutes. He sat on the chair opposite Annie. "Carter's going to check himself into Rosedale for a little while," he said. "He's severely depressed, as I'm sure you know, but you did help him, Annie. I know it probably doesn't feel that way, but he needed to hear the truth."

She shook her head. Will did, too, she realized.

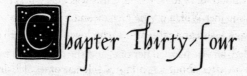

Chapter Thirty-four

Will took the back way home. He stopped at the liquor store for a six-pack of Sam Adams and opened one for the drive, something he hadn't done since before Brooke was born. He didn't realize until he turned onto their street and saw Anne's car parked beneath the streetlight a few doors down how afraid he had been. Nothing had changed since their phone call earlier, or since last night, but the words reverberated through him anyway: *She's here.*

Ethan was meowing at the door before he opened it. The hallway still reeked of wet wood, burned carpet, and the burned plastic berries from the wreath. Brooke's Barbie tent was still up in the den. Anne was in the kitchen, sautéing chicken, her back to him. She hadn't heard him come in, and he paused in the doorway, still wearing his coat, watching her. She had never been much of a cook—most of her recipes originated from the backs of boxes or cans. She rummaged in a silverware drawer. She was wearing the neon-green sweater she'd worn the first time he met her. If he closed his eyes, he thought, he would still see that color against his lids.

"It smells good," he said quietly.

She jumped and a spoon clattered onto the counter. "Darn," she mumbled, swiping at her sweater with a dishrag. She hadn't turned on any lights other than the overhead on the stove. He saw that she'd been crying.

"Sorry."

She shook her head. "Don't be."

"You want a beer?"

She nodded, and he handed her one, and she took it and turned back to the stove without taking a sip. The gas flames glowed blue orange in the dim light. The flame was turned up way too high under the chicken, and any other day he would have said something, maybe snuggled up behind her, planting a kiss on the pulse of her neck as he reached to turn it down. Tonight he just watched, loving her for her excess.

Still facing the stove, she said, "There's something I have to tell you."

"I'm not an idiot, Anne. I know what you have to say."

She glanced at him over her shoulder, then lowered the flame on the stove and turned to face him, leaning against the counter, holding the beer at her chest. "I lied to you, too," she said gently. She was staring at her bare feet. "Not when we first met, but later, when I was still with Carter."

"I don't need to hear this, Anne."

"Maybe not, but I need to say it." She looked at him. "Do you remember how you used to ask me if we ended the affair, could I make my marriage to Carter work?"

His heart lurched in his chest, and he realized he was clenching his fists. She was going back to Carter, was that it? He swallowed a gulp of beer, then another. When he glanced at her, finally, she only stared at him, those gorgeous eyes of hers bright with sadness. "You're going back to him, aren't you?"

"I can't believe you'd even think that. No. I'm only saying that when you asked me that question—if I could make it work again—I lied."

He felt like a jerk—that she felt she even needed to confess this after the lies he'd told her!

"I was so afraid of losing you," she said softly. "I thought that if I said I could make it work with Carter, you'd end the affair." She smiled weakly at him in the dim light. "That was true, wasn't it?"

"I don't know." He felt numb. "Probably."

Her face crumpled. "Anyway, I'm sorry. I just—I just thought you should know. We *both* did what we thought we had to in order to hold on to each other." Crying, she turned back to the stove.

"Anne," he said gently, coming up behind her, leaning his forehead against the back of her head, his lips in her hair.

"Don't," she sobbed. "You're only making this harder."

He stepped back. He felt as if he'd been electrocuted.

After a moment, she drew in a long shaky breath. "I set the table in front of the TV," she said, sniffling. "The salads are ready."

"I'll put Brooke's tent away."

"Dinner won't be long."

It was a formal conversation, as if they were already trying to separate themselves, to circumscribe their relationship by words the way countries are delineated by maps. Distance was inherent in most languages, he knew. In French, the formal *vous,* informal *tu.* In Russian, the formal *vee,* informal *tee.*

He loved her salads—each one a surprise. Red-leaf lettuce, sliced oranges, roasted grapes and macadamia nuts; or watercress, mango, grated carrot, walnuts coated in melted Brie. Salads delighted her. She treated them like Easter baskets, burying treasure: three grilled shrimp beneath a yellow tomato, spicy polenta sprinkled like cheese over spinach. She'd cook dinner in twenty minutes, buy cookbooks titled *Three-Minute Meals,* but spend an hour roasting a handful of grapes.

They ate in front of the TV, sitting on the couch instead of on the floor, picnic-style, as was their custom. They ate the way some people smoke: more to keep their hands busy than because they enjoyed it. Finally, Anne broke the silence. "He's checking himself into a hospital for two weeks. I need to be a part of the therapy at first. I called Lois. I can stay with her." She didn't look at Will.

He swallowed a piece of chicken. "He's good, isn't he?"

"Excuse me?"

"You don't find this the least bit manipulative?"

She looked at him coldly. "I find it sad," she said.

Later, he heard her packing: the zip of a duffel bag, the sliding open of drawers, the door closing on the medicine cabinet. A stack of books sat in a canvas BOOK CELLAR bag near the door.

"This is yours," she said, handing him a SHARE THE ROAD cycling T-shirt, which she liked to wear to bed.

"Keep it," he answered gruffly, wanting to fling it at her.

She stopped in the bathroom doorway, holding her cosmetics in a plastic bag. The light was behind her, and her face was in darkness. "This isn't what I want, you know." Her voice was like perfume, so soft he might miss it if she turned away.

"I'm not the one ending this," he said. "I'm not the one packing my bags." He felt betrayed. Being left again was the one thing he had feared his entire adult life.

"You aren't giving me a choice, Will."

"Choosing an arsonist or me isn't a choice?" His eyes filled. "I gave up everything for you, Anne—"

"And I did for you!"

"A *stalker*?" He turned on his heel and strode into the bedroom, wanting to punch a hole in the wall. "You know what?" he whirled around, pointing his finger at her, not realizing she'd followed him. They nearly collided. She was still wearing the charm bracelet he'd given her for Christmas. "You could have stopped this whole goddamn thing if you'd been honest with me to begin with."

She had pushed past him into the bedroom, but now she wheeled to face him. "Go ahead, Will, say it."

It felt like a game of truth or dare that had gone too far. He didn't want to do this to her. What was the point? It wouldn't change anything. "Never mind." He turned to leave. "Call me when you finish packing. I'm not going to watch this—"

He was halfway down the hall when she called softly, "It's not Carter you care about punishing, is it, Will?" She was standing in the doorway.

"He told you he was making the calls. He told you he'd hired your student. What the hell were you waiting for, Anne?" He threw up his arms in exasperation. "Yeah, I blame you. Is that what you want to hear?"

"I loved him!" she sobbed. "Can you really not understand that?

Can you not, for one minute, put yourself in my shoes and imagine what you would do if this had been Kayla?"

"No, Anne, I can't." His voice was cold. "Because Kayla never would have done something like this."

She looked up, all that dark hair tumbling around her shoulders. He felt as if he were going to be sick.

"If she's so perfect, Will, why did you ever leave her?"

"I don't know."

She started crying again.

"You asked!" he yelled. "Don't you dare turn this around. You wanted to hear it and I told you!" Ethan meowed from the darkened kitchen as if to pull Will away from her. "Shut up," he snapped at the cat. And then to Anne, his voice hoarse, "How dare you put us into the situation you did, and then tell me that I'm not giving *you* a choice! How do I know that you won't keep something like this from me again, Anne?"

"You trust me," she choked.

"Well, I can't. I don't. Not right now."

"Then we're even," she whispered. "I don't trust you, either."

It seemed impossible that after all they'd been through, they could so easily break apart. He would go to work in the morning, and she would drive to Lois's. And when he came home, she would be gone. He glanced around the room and realized that there was nothing from the bedroom that she would take, because nothing here was hers. The photographs were of Brooke; it was his clothing in the closet, his desk, his stacks of books and papers. He felt as if she were already gone.

She had told him once of *talaq,* a kind of divorce still practiced in some Muslim sects, where all a husband has to do is say, "I divorce you," three times to his wife. They had been sitting in Monroe Park. She was on a break between classes. "Sort of like Dorothy in *The Wizard of Oz,* just clicking her heels together three times and repeating, 'There's no place like home,' " he had laughed, reaching to lift a strand of hair that had blown across her mouth. "Abracadabra, and the wife just disappears." He had thought it was absurd, and he didn't give it more than a passing thought.

Now, though, it occurred to him that their own words were just as silly. *Good-bye* was no different from *abracadabra*. How can a word, no matter how many times you repeat it, make the woman you love disappear?

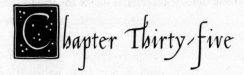

Chapter Thirty-five

Sungae woke to find Keehwan's side of the bed empty. Light from the studio out back shone against the ice embroidered on the windowpane.

"What you doing, old man, silly fool?" she whispered, pushing herself from the bed. But she wasn't surprised, really. This is what she had wanted. For a week now, she had tried to tell Keehwan, "There is something I want—no, *have*—to say to you." She spoke in English, a language where meaning could easily get lost, with the distinction between *want* and *have* embedded in the middle of the sentence, as insignificant as a bookmark holding the place between two pages. In Korean, verbs always came last in a sentence. Their endings were determined not by objects, but by action. In Korean, Keehwan could not have missed the distinction between want, *won-ha da,* and have, *ka-ji-da.* He would have noticed.

She stood in the snow, shivering, and watched him move around the dim cement garage. Her artist's lamp threw his shadow onto the walls, and he became a man on stilts. He was wearing his beaver hat with fur flaps over the ears, and no coat. In his shadow his head seemed too large for his body. Like a Disneyland character. Goofy, Sungae thought, or one of those singing chipmunks Brooke listened to, which drove

Sungae crazy. She felt that way now. Crazy. Why had she done this—taken the most painful experience of her husband's life and painted it on these canvases taller than he? How could she explain to him that the buried past is *always* larger than the present, that memories hidden in darkness continue to expand, like yeast in a cloth-covered bowl.

She had propped the paintings against the cinder-block walls in the order in which they were painted, one atop another. It was as if the walls of the studio had grown closer, the past crowding her out. *Telling Lines* came first, then *Nouns, Subject-Verb Agreement, Adjectives, Simple Past, Present Perfect.* Only *Prepositions,* the canvas she had covered in black the night Kayla told Sungae about Annie, remained unfinished. When she completed that one, there would be seventeen—one for each year of Sungae's life in the United States.

Keehwan shuffled behind the easel, which he had built for her two summers ago. It was more like a skateboard ramp: a ten-by-thirteen sheet of plywood attached to an aluminum extension ladder. He had hammered power outlets along the sides for her to plug in her artist's lamps or the small clip-on electric fans she used in the summer.

Sungae was freezing. She wore only a flimsy robe over her jogging suit and snow boots. She wished she could step into the room and ask, "You mad at me, Keehwan?" But to interrupt a person's thoughts was like removing a cake from the oven before it was ready. There would remain in the center something unformed and raw.

She heard him slide left to stand before the next painting. His shadow loomed over the room. Next to the brightness of the pictures, her husband seemed as transparent as rice paper. She tried to figure out which canvas he was staring at. *Simple Past? Subject-Verb Agreement?* He didn't linger any longer, or any shorter, at this painting than he had at the others. She counted the time by heartbeats, but always it was the same. Each painting was like a station of the cross. *What are you praying for, Keehwan?* she wondered anxiously. *Patience? Forgiveness for a wife who betrayed you a second time?* Maybe he was only counting his own heartbeats, trying to find calmness. She watched his shadow lean away from him, bent backwards at a ninety-degree angle, as if he were made of rubber and had no bones, nothing inside of him to snap or break. She wished this were really true.

She did not need to watch anymore. He stood now in front of *Present Perfect*. The woman and Hwang, the store owner, sit at a low wooden table near a window, which overlooks the Han River. It was the river Keehwan had stared at that night in April when he decided that Sungae could have Hwang's baby—he could have ordered her to abort the child—that she would stay with Hwang, and that when it was over, she would return to Keehwan. In the painting, the sun was setting, and the water was burgundy—black and red, the color of sadness, the color of celebration. On the table was the white envelope that Keehwan had delivered each week. It was the most noticeable part of the painting, and the only white Sungae had allowed. The rectangle seemed torn from the center of the narrative so that no matter what image the viewer regarded—the woman, the man, the teacups on the table between them—always the eye was drawn to that whiteness, that absence at the center of everything else.

The Present Perfect tense is often used to indicate that an action begun in the past is not yet complete, that it continues into the present. . . . Her mind locked on the definition as she trudged over the snow-crusted yard back toward the house, her footsteps thunderous in the gray silence. She wondered if Keehwan would understand. That the envelope was him, that always he had been there between *them,* that he had been, and still was, a part of the narrative, though she had never spoken of it to him until now, never told him the story of those months.

Back in the kitchen, she stood at the sink and ran warm water over her frozen hands. She couldn't stop crying. "Why you do this?" she kept berating herself. But she had done it because she had realized that the paintings were also her *uiri,* her duty. Maybe the word *soul* was really just another name for the word *story,* she had realized. And if this was true, then not telling your story was like murdering your soul. *Silly woman, you watching too much American TV,* she had tried to tell herself, but the more Sungae thought about it, the more she believed it was true.

She pulled bowls and mixing spoons from cabinets and drawers, not caring that they clattered noisily. She stirred ingredients for *yak gwa,* fried honey biscuits, heated the oil in the pan, and slammed the fruit onto the counter to slice: orange, mango, cantaloupe, pineapple. As she sliced into their thick skins, juice ran onto the counter and spilled onto the floor, but she did not notice.

She watched from the window as Keehwan emerged from the studio, his head bowed against the wind. He wove across the backyard carefully to avoid slipping on the ice-sheeted lawn.

"Dr. Jacks think I should have the art show," she had finally told him two nights ago. They had been sitting in the living room, which she and Keehwan had picked out seventeen years ago at Sears. It had been the first display model Sungae saw when Keehwan urged her into the bright crowded store. An ugly low glass coffee table with chrome legs, and matching end tables, the too-fluffy couch and padded chairs. The saleswoman had shown Sungae samples of fabric she could choose, and without hesitating, Sungae had gestured to the white fabric embossed with peach-colored roses. It had reminded her of something—a *han-bok* her mother had once worn? One of the *ibol,* quilts, on Hwang's sleeping mat? She wouldn't allow herself to remember.

"You must not have children," the saleswoman had laughed when Sungae chose the fabric and Sungae, who had only been in the United States for two months then, had somehow understood those words: *You must not have children.* She didn't understand the saleswoman's joke, didn't understand how Americans could look at you and know your greatest sorrow, or how they could be cruel enough to comment, *You must not have children,* but she had never forgotten those words. She thought of them every time she entered that room.

"What did you tell Dr. Jacks?" Keehwan had asked when she told him of the show.

She had shrugged nervously, avoiding his gaze. "Maybe art show is too much work."

Keehwan glanced at her over the top of the newspaper he was reading. "I thought you already finished many paintings."

"But they are so big and heavy; lots of trouble to move them." She hoped he would understand when he saw the paintings. She hadn't been speaking about the canvases but about her memories. She was asking him, was it better to let them be, to leave them where they were?

Her hands had been trembling and she clutched them in her lap. "Maybe you should look at them, make the decision."

He regarded her solemnly and nodded, then returned to his newspaper, though she could tell he did not read the words for a long time.

Now, she watched through the window as he made his way around the side of the house to the driveway to pick up the paper. He was hunched over, and not wearing his back brace or his coat. When he came in the front door, he made a big noise, stamping the snow from his feet, then disappeared to his chair as he did every morning. He did not look at her, though she saw that he was weeping.

Her heart sank. She thought of the Korean proverb that a man cries only three times in his life: when he is born, when he loses his father, and when he loses his country. Were paintings really more sorrowful than that?

Later, they sat wordlessly at the table. The grease from the flower-shaped *yak gwa* soaked into the paper towels beneath them. Instead of coffee, they drank clear beef broth with egg, scallions, and water chestnuts. Keehwan was reading the paper. "Biscuits not bad," he said from behind his wall of words. "Maybe you should make some for Kayla's store."

Sungae shook her head, though he could not see her. "Americans wouldn't like them. Not sweet enough."

"You never know." He put down the paper, though he hadn't finished eating. She started to scold him, *Moko, moko,* "Eat, eat," but saw that he was staring outside toward her studio.

"They are very good," he said after a moment. "You should share your talent." She felt confused. The *yak gwa?* The paintings? Hesitantly, she glanced up and saw the Han River flowing from her husband's eyes.

"*Yongso hecho?*" She whispered.

He nodded. "*Ne, yonso hechulke.*" I forgive you.

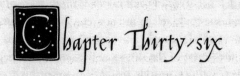

Chapter Thirty-six

Annie tugged the photocopy of Lois's and her daughters' hands from the wall where she had taped it four years earlier. "I'll put this in my new office," she said, scanning the lines of their palms like highways across a road map.

"I could get you a real picture," Lois said.

"No, I like this. Hands are more intimate than faces." Her voice faltered without warning at the word *intimate*.

"Is it Will?" Lois asked gently, wishing Annie would talk. She hadn't spoken his name in over a week.

Instead, Annie laid the Xerox copy between the covers of a hardbound atlas, set it in the half-full box on her desk. "Would you mind packing those?" She nodded to the bookcase beside the door. "Everything on the bottom four shelves. I'll have to go through the top two." Already she was rooting through another drawer, arranging papers into various piles, tossing others into the metal trash can.

Lois didn't know how Annie was still standing. She wasn't eating—only black coffee, cigarettes, and an over-the-counter bronchial medication called Max Alert passed through her mouth.

Lois dragged another carton into the room and began stacking the books, spines up, into the box, absently reading titles and authors' names. *The House of Twilight,* Yun Heung-Gil; *The Gourmet and Other Stories,* Lu Wenfu; *Preface to a Twenty Volume Suicide Note,* Amiri Baraka; *Prison Diary,* Ho Chi Minh; *Childhood in Old Jerusalem,* Ya' akob Yehoshua. They were names Lois could not pronounce, names Annie practiced so that she could say them correctly. Lois remembered the first day of class, five months ago, Annie's voice through the closed door as she learned her students' names.

The dean had reluctantly hired another instructor, a woman who was finishing her Ph.D. in Teaching English as a Second Language, had taught in the Philippines for a year, in Thailand for another year, was writing a dissertation on "Context-restrictive models in ESL writing classes." Lois had no idea what the dissertation was about, but she sensed that Kristina, the new instructor, would do a great job. She was like a younger Annie, full of energy and ideas, eager to please. She'd move her things into the office on Monday. Tomorrow Annie would be gone, a U-Haul trailer hitched to her car as she drove alone to Baltimore, a city where she knew no one, but where she had found a job, tutoring international graduate students.

"You know, you don't have to go," Lois said the night Annie returned from her interview in Baltimore. Annie hadn't even mentioned that she had applied for the position. She simply disappeared one afternoon and returned late, carrying her shoes into Lois's kitchen. Lois shooed the girls out the door and went to stand at the sink where she began placing dishes into cabinets. "I'm sorry, but I don't get it," she said after a moment. "Is quitting your job and moving away from everyone who loves you some kind of penance?"

"Come on, Lois, this is what I need."

"If you tell me you're doing this for Carter, I'll scream. What did that shrink say? That Carter needs 'physical distance' from you in order to face reality? Let him move if that's the case."

"He can't afford to, Lois. He has a business here."

"You can't afford to, either, but you won't accept it."

"I know it seems rash—"

"Seems?" Lois exploded. "It *is.*" She drew in a deep breath. "I know you're hurting," she said. "I'm only angry because I care about you."

"I just feel that if I don't get away, these last few years will all have been for nothing. I'll just slip back into being whoever I was." She stared at her hands, tears sliding down her face. "It's not about Carter anymore or even . . ." She stopped, refusing to say Will's name. "Despite everything that's happened," she said after a moment, "leaving Carter was the right thing for me."

Lois joined her at the table, placing her hand on top of Annie's. "Nobody is debating that."

"I'll never be able to justify what I did to Carter, but when I left him, it was the first time since I was a child, or maybe ever, that I put what I wanted before what everyone else—my parents and Carter and Carter's family—wanted." She paused. "I wish I'd learned to do it years ago. Maybe I wouldn't have caused so much damage." She sighed. "Quitting this job feels like I'm choosing myself again, Lois. I can't explain, I just . . . it feels right."

"Maybe it is. But you didn't even apply for the position here. You know you can stay with us as long as you want. The girls love having you."

Lois's words didn't sink in, though. Annie was just going through the motions.

They worked in silence now. Lois finished the shelves and started wrapping knickknacks into old copies of the student paper. She crumpled the sheets into a tight ball and shoved them inside a blue glass vase. Annie always filled the vase with flowers from Will. Sunflowers, carnations, daisies.

"I don't need that," Annie said without pausing.

"What? You're never going to have flowers again?"

"I'm serious. Take it for your own desk or give it to one of the girls for her room. I don't care. I just don't want it."

"If you didn't care, you wouldn't be making a big deal out of it."

"Look," Annie sighed. "I know you want me to cry and break down or whatever, but I can't afford to right now. I've got to pack, move, and find a new apartment in three days. I've just spent a week listening to Carter convince me of what an awful person I am. The last thing I need is another reminder."

"I'm just worried," Lois said.

"I know, and I appreciate it, really."

"I wish there was something I could do."

"You are."

"I guess you don't want this, either?" She held up the insulated ceramic travel mug Will had given to Annie.

Annie glanced at it, her eyes abruptly filling, spilling over. "Why are you doing this?" she asked quietly.

"Because I'm worried sick. Because I think this move is the last thing you need right now."

"I can't be here, Lois. You know that. Less than a mile from . . ." She shook her head and resumed packing.

"You can't even say his name, Annie."

Annie stopped. "I can say it just fine, okay? *Will.*" She turned away. "Go ahead, Lois, pack the mug, if that's what you want."

Lois glanced at Annie.

She was sorting through a sheaf of different-colored papers now. Writing exercises she'd created over the years, assignments, group activities, conversation topics. "Everything I pick up," Annie said to herself.

"What's wrong?"

She handed Lois the sheet of yellow paper from atop the stack. A conversation lesson. "Saying Good-bye."

Lois glanced at her, then scanned the paper.

If you're hoping to meet someone again soon, you might say:
So long!
See you later!
See you tomorrow (next week, next month).
Take care!

If you want to stay in touch with the person, you might say:
Keep in touch!
Don't forget to write (e-mail, call).
Come back soon.

But if your good-bye will last a long time or is forever, you might say:
Good luck in the future.

I'm so glad I got to know you.
All the best.
I'll always miss you. I'll never forget you.

Annie took the paper from Lois and dropped it with the others into the trash.

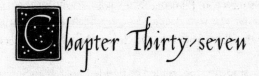

Chapter Thirty-seven

The spring semester began on the first day of February. Already
New Year's resolutions had been forgotten, and SALE signs were
everywhere, as if nothing was worth what it had been only a month
before.

"Hey, Sungae." Yukihiko strutted into the classroom, wearing mir-
rored sunglasses, a dark suit, high-top sneakers. He was munching
Doritos.

"You still here, Marlboro Man?" Sungae teased. "Why you didn't
fail?"

He grinned. "English a slice of cake," he bragged. "No sweat." He
nodded to Ba, held up two fingers in a V to Farshad. Farshad was reading a big picture book about the heart: *The Yale School of Medicine
Heart Book*.

"Why the heart?" Sungae had asked. "Why you not studying the
ear?" He was, after all, a doctor specializing in hearing problems.

"Did you know that women are four times more likely than men to
refuse a heart transplant and twice as likely to die of a heart attack?"
he said, reading out loud. "In an average lifetime, the heart pumps one
million barrels of blood and in one year, it beats three million times."

"*Pshhh,*" Sungae said, shaking her head. She turned back to the door, watching the corridor. As the students trickled into the classroom, Sungae greeted each new arrival: "You have good holiday, Shinpin?" "Good holiday, Keyuri?" She couldn't wait for them to ask her in return: *How was your holiday, Sungae?* Each time she shrugged, trying not to reveal her excitement. "Not so bad, I'm gonna have the art show."

The new students, too, smiled or nodded politely to Sungae as they stopped in the doorway, glancing at their schedules, then the number over the door—310—making sure they had found the correct room. "You foreign student?" Sungae said. "Right place." She lifted her arm expansively like a maître d' in a fine restaurant. She had dressed up for the first day back to school, a bright blue corduroy jumper and white turtleneck. "Sit, sit where you like!" One girl was from Korea and Sungae's face shattered into a smile, like sunlight fracturing water. She patted the desk next to hers. "This is your seat," she announced. The classroom filled with talk and laughter. Finally, Ahmad shuffled in and took his seat.

And then a tall woman swirled into the room. Sungae frowned. "You foreign student?" she demanded. The woman could have been twenty-nine. She looked like an American.

The woman laughed. "It depends," she said. "I've heard some people insist that California is another country—or should be." She walked to the desk, Annie's desk, sweeping off her winter cape like a magician.

The woman set her briefcase on the chair and smiled at Sungae. "I'm sorry, I didn't answer your question, did I? No, I'm not a foreign student. I'm from California. Let me introduce myself." She pivoted to the blackboard and began writing her name in huge sweeping letters. Kristina Wallace.

"Why you not Annie?" Sungae blurted. She had meant to say, *Who are you? Why isn't Annie here?* but the words slipped and got mixed up, like eggs cracked too hurriedly against the side of a mixing bowl.

Again, the woman laughed. "Why am I not Annie?" She tilted her head, pretending to mull it over. Light caught in her gold wedding band and diamond ring. "Well, I'm not Madonna, Hillary Clinton, or the prime minister of England, either. Is that okay?"

Sungae stared defiantly. She crossed her arms across her chest. She didn't nod, didn't say a word. What right did this woman have to make fun of her?

The woman smiled again, then clicked open her briefcase and began rummaging through the papers. Sungae spun around to glance at Farshad, Yukihiko, Ahmad. Ahmad caught Sungae's eye and shrugged uncertainly. Farshad stared straight ahead, hands folded on his desk, his back straight. He looked scared, and for a moment, the image slipped, and Sungae's mind recalled Hwang sitting in that exact position seventeen years earlier. Hwang at the kitchen table while soup ran down the wall like watery paint, and a piece of the shattered bowl spun like a top. But then Ba was standing, raising his hand respectfully, and Sungae felt her breath slide back. She nodded eagerly. *Good job, Ba,* she was thinking. *Good job.*

"Yes?" Kristina Wallace asked.

Ba bowed his head low, a sign of respect. "I hope you will forgive my impertinence," he said softly, "but we were expecting Ms. Helverson to be our instructor." He sat without waiting for an answer.

"I know it's confusing." Kristina spoke gently now. "But Ms. Helverson is no longer with the university."

"Why?" Yukihiko said.

Kristina raised her eyebrows at him. "Ms. Helverson has taken a position elsewhere."

Ahmad asked, "She no longer wishes to teach to us?"

"She sick of students always coming late to the class," Yukihiko said.

Ahmad glared. "Maybe she sick of students always making jokes that are not amusing."

No longer with the university, Sungae kept thinking. *Position elsewhere. Where?* What did that mean? Was Annie still living with Kayla's husband? Sungae hadn't seen Will in weeks. She tried to think, to remember what—if—Brooke had said about Annie lately. Nothing. Just Daddy. "Daddy and me went shopping—"

"Daddy and I," Sungae would correct proudly.

"Okay, Daddy and I went shopping and then Daddy and me went—"

"Daddy and I."

"Why? Why can't I say my own words?"

No mention of Annie.

Kristina was handing out sheets of paper. Syllabus. Policy Statement. Absentee Policy. Definition of Plagiarism. Official words. Now she was writing on the board, pushing so hard on the chalk that it was flaking around her. "Context restrictive," she wrote. "Ethnography. Presupposition." She called out each word as she printed it, like the announcer at the baseball game introducing the players. "Proofs! Knowledge deficit, Structure of interaction!" Sungae felt as if the words were being hurled at her. It was just like the first day of class last semester when everybody was writing and Sungae didn't know what to do. Same thing. They were scrawling the words in their notebooks as quickly as Kristina wrote them. Sungae felt her eyes cloud with tears. *What is ethnography?* She wondered. *Presupposition?* She didn't understand.

When Kristina finished, she was breathing heavily like an aerobics instructor. "This," she said loudly, "is what you will be writing."

Sungae turned in her seat to face the class. Most of the students were looking down uncomfortably, eyes focused on their papers. A few stared blankly toward the front of the room. Yukihiko was whispering to Ahmad. Farshad was still reading, ducking his head to his heart book, lifting words and images like a pelican diving into an ocean for food and carrying them to his mind, repeating phrases and definitions over and over until they were a part of him.

Outside the classroom, Sungae could see the Virginia state flag snap like a kite in the wind.

"So, she wasn't such a bad teacher," Keehwan had said last night as Sungae was packing her supplies: her blue tackle box filled with tubes of paint and brushes.

"What teacher?" Sungae had asked. Her art professors were all men. Dr. Jacks, Dr. Nielsen, Dr. Benson. "You mean *he,* silly man." They were in the studio. Keehwan was measuring the paintings to build frames for her art show.

"No. *She*. Annie," Keehwan said. "Every painting is something she taught you."

"I know these words seem intimidating," Kristina said. "And this is not what you are used to, but my goal for you is not that you write great stories about your past, but that you are prepared for your future." She stood at the podium, gesturing with her arms, like a preacher or a politician. "I read some of the work that you did for Ms. Helverson, and it's excellent. She was a very good teacher." She tried to bribe them with another smile. Sungae glowered. "But as I was reading your past essays, I wondered: How does it help your lives in America to write about your first day in this country or to compare the past and present or to describe each other using as many adjectives as possible?"

"It is the excellent method." Ahmad spoke angrily. "We learn very well in this way. Ms. Helverson, she is the very good teacher."

"Absolutely." Kristina smiled. "But wouldn't it be more beneficial for you to use adjectives to describe, say, tooth decay since you are studying to be a dentist?" He had switched his major at the end of the last semester after failing his Anatomy I class.

Sungae whirled around. How did Kristina know that? She hadn't even called the roll. Despite himself, Ahmad was grinning, beaming sheepishly. Yukihiko punched him in the arm. "She got you, boy!" he said.

Kristina laughed. "This is the context in which I work. The classroom." She backed up until she was at the board and slapped her palm against the chalked phrase: Context restrictive. "The best thing I can do as a teacher is learn everything I can about my audience—you—and what I need to do to reach you. By the same token . . ." She grinned. "If your goal is to become an audiologist, shouldn't you be writing about audiology?" She glanced at Farshad, but he didn't seem to hear. He was staring out the window, jiggling his pencil nervously.

"And let's say you are an artist . . ." Kristina was saying. She watched Sungae from the corner of her eye, but Sungae pretended not to look. "Why not learn to write grant proposals, descriptions of your work?"

Sungae stared at her notebook, at the pale college-ruled lines across the white paper. *Telling lines. The line in a story or novel which hints at what the rest of the narrative will be about.*

"I have the daughter," Sungae had written that first day, the tentative penciled sentence there on the opening page of her notebook. She had used the present tense, and the definite article *the* instead of *a*. *The: indicates a noun that has a specific and unique reference for both the writer and the reader.* Sungae never showed this sentence to Annie, but if she had, Annie would have paused at Sungae's desk and explained quietly that because the reader didn't know who the daughter was or why she was distinguished from all daughters in general, *the* was incorrect. Had Sungae told her, though, that such a rule seemed nonsense to her, for how could someone's daughter *not* be distinguished from every other daughter in the world, Annie wouldn't have forced her to change the article. She would have understood: In any language there is a grammar of the heart, and none of the rules or big vocabulary words—*ethnography, presupposition*—mean anything without that grammar. Like baking a cake with the fancy ingredients but forgetting the tablespoon of baking powder.

Kristina's smile was like a net, swooping them up from dark water like fish. Sungae couldn't breathe. Maybe it was her fault Annie was gone, always giving her a difficult time. "We did this?" she blurted without thinking.

Kristina stopped in the middle of her sentence. "Did what?"

Sungae shook her head. "I'm sorry," she whispered, not sure what to say. She would call Will. Get his phone number from Kayla.

"Context restrictive," Kristina repeated, eyeing Sungae with concern. "We will restrict your assignments to the specific context in which you live. How many of you will need jobs one day? Why not learn to write a résumé?" Except for Farshad, they were all nodding their heads, sitting up straight as if they were at a revival meeting. *What? They think they going to start speaking in the tongues?* Sungae snorted under her breath.

"How many of you rent your home or apartment? Let's learn how to write a letter of complaint to a landlord." Kristina paced up and down the aisles, making eye contact with each of them. Sungae wouldn't look at her. She was like the Wizard of Oz, promising things nobody really needed. Farshad the tin man, thinking he could find a heart in some book. Ba the scarecrow wanting a brain. Sungae the cowardly lion afraid of her own story. Annie had known, though, that what they had needed had been inside all along.

Chapter Thirty-eight

Eleven hours. Will repeated the number, reminding himself that there was an end to this not knowing. Eleven hours. At eight-thirty, Lois would be at work. He would phone and ask her what Kayla, twenty minutes before, had phoned to ask him. "What's going on? Why isn't Anne teaching?"

He had been in the middle of making what most people would call a salad: lettuce, tomatoes, bacon bits, shredded cheese. Most people. Not Anne. Today had been the start of classes for the spring semester, and all morning, and then for a long miserable stretch of afternoon, he'd had to fight the urge to phone her.

"What do you mean 'why isn't she teaching?' " he snapped at Kayla. "And since when do you care about her?"

"Don't be a jerk, Will. I'm at work with Sarah, and she's upset. They had a new instructor in her English class who told them Annie wasn't teaching anymore."

"Sarah? Anne doesn't even know Sarah."

"Sarah was in her class all semester, Will." And there it was—that goddamn gloating tone in Kayla's voice. "You didn't know?"

He set down the salad spinner and paced to the window with the phone. He stared outside at the quarter moon, searching the sky, as he always did, for the Big and Little Dippers. "Look, just put Sarah on," he said wearily.

And then it all made sense. Sarah was Sungae, the Korean woman who Annie had thought disliked her.

Now, he paced around the kitchen, trying to recall Lois's last name so that he could call information and get her number. He'd been to her house with Anne, knew what street she lived on, her address, but information couldn't provide a phone number without a name. "What if this was an emergency?" he had asked the operator, forcing himself to speak slowly. "You might try contacting your local police, sir. Perhaps they can assist you in contacting the party you are trying to reach."

He put the salad stuff away, turned off the water he'd been boiling for spaghetti, slammed a lid on the sauce, turned that off, too, and got out a beer. Two minutes ago, he'd been starving. Now, the last thing he wanted to do was eat. He wanted it to be morning; he wanted to know that she was okay. He hadn't seen her since she moved in with Lois a few days after the fire. She'd come to the apartment while he was at work to pack her things. Each night he'd notice something else missing: the boxes of dishes, her clothes and bureau, the full-length mirror, a photograph that she'd hung in the foyer. She took her books last as if she knew he would miss those the most.

"Bug off," he muttered now to Ethan, who was meowing incessantly. Will didn't know whether he wanted to cry or shout, he was so goddamn angry with himself. For not knowing her best friend's last name. For not realizing that her problem Korean student had been Sarah, Kayla's Sarah, the Sarah he'd known for four and a half years. All semester Anne had talked with him about Sungae, whom she teasingly called Erica, because Sungae often wrote about Erica Kane. Not once, though, *not once,* had it crossed Will's mind that she meant Kayla's Sarah. It should have—if he'd been listening more carefully, if he'd cared more. Because he knew that Sarah, like Sungae, was in her fifties, and she was an artist, and she watched that soap opera with Erica Kane. She used to tell him all the time, "Ahh, you good man, Will, just like Charlie."

"Who the hell is Charlie?" he'd ask, laughing.

"Charlie? You not know Charlie? Charlie on *All My Children*?"

"Why?" Sarah/Sungae kept asking him tonight. "Why she not teach us?" He wanted to weep because there was so much distress in Sarah's voice. Sarah, who Annie had thought hated her. He didn't know what to say. "I'm sorry," was all he came up with. I'm sorry I don't know. I'm sorry she isn't teaching. I'm sorry.

But *why* wasn't she teaching? Was she still at Lois's? He'd spoken to Annie on the phone only twice since she moved out of his apartment, but they hadn't said much beyond asking how the other was. He'd mentioned meeting for coffee the last time, and she asked him what was the point of that, so he let it go.

Now, he pictured her spreading their bedspread on the floor in the Holiday Inn—*this is how Persians eat*—saw her waiting for him at the Daily Grind, bent over her students' essays, underlining in neon green or purple the sentences she loved in their work. Looking up at him, laughing, her eyes invisible behind dark glasses, "A woman with no eyebrows will destroy a man's life," she might say.

"What?"

"It's a Chinese proverb." And then she'd glance at another paper and tell him, "You have to sleep with your forehead uncovered to let the soul return to its destination after the journey of a dream. Tear out one hair and your whole body will suffer."

"Where do those come from?"

"China. I love their history. It's so rich." She had wanted the same thing for them. To have a history.

He got up periodically to get another beer, hoping the alcohol would invite sleep. He would feel like crap in the morning, but he didn't care. Sometime after one o'clock, maybe two, it began to rain, the sound like a heartbeat, steady and comforting. He remembered sitting in the car with her one rainy night in the deserted parking lot of the church where they always met on Thursday nights. It was late. He had driven her back to her car and, as usual, would follow her home to the condo on Grace Street where she had lived with Carter, worried about her safety. Every time, she would urge him to go straight home. "It's out of your way," she would tell him. "You have to get up early. I'll be fine, I promise. It's not like I haven't been out at night by myself before."

"Please, Anne. Don't argue. Just let me do this." She never got it. He didn't do it for her, but for himself.

On the night he was remembering now, silvery beads of water slid down the windshield. It was winter. She told him the Chinese folktale of the cowherd and the Girl Weaver, the stars Altair and Vega, lovers forever separated across the Heavenly River, the Milky Way. Only once a year, on the seventh day of the seventh lunar month, Chinese Valentine's Day, were they allowed to meet. According to legend, it always rained on that night, the Girl Weaver's tears of joy.

He drifted in and out of sleep. If she was sick or in trouble, Lois would have called, he told himself. He felt sure of it. So, where was she? *No longer with the university,* Sarah had said. The words echoed. He remembered that she'd met with the dean the day of the fire, but the evaluations had been good, right? Or had she lied about that, too?

He closed his eyes, trying to recall that night, but the images spun as if he were on a carousel. His memory of the things she'd said, her expressions, things she hadn't said—all seemed blurry.

Somewhere around six, he got angry. "Goddamn you," he said out loud to the ceiling. "You couldn't send me a note, leave a message on my machine to let me know you were okay?"

When he finally phoned Lois at work, she told him that Annie had quit, that she had a new job in Baltimore. "Why?" he asked. "Because of us?"

"She was tired of begging," Lois said coolly. "First you, then the job. And to tell you the truth, Will, I don't blame her."

After Lois hung up, he sat on the edge of the bed, the phone in his lap. He wanted to hurl it across the room. Baltimore, he kept thinking—150 miles away. Two hours. It might as well have been two continents. He could no longer picture her life, where she worked or lived or went for coffee to grade.

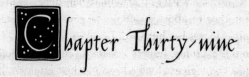

Chapter Thirty-nine

By the end of February, Kayla was running fifty miles a week, train-ing for the marathon in April. The only time to run was at night, after she left the Espresso Shop and fed Brooke. Will baby-sat while Kayla was out. She would watch for his car from the doorway, and as soon as she saw it turn onto their street, she would leave, already run-ning. She didn't want to talk to him, or even look at him. His grief over losing Anne was too painful for her to be near.

On the nights she started late, she'd come home and the house would be dark but for the TV flickering from the family room where Will had fallen asleep on the couch, still in his work clothes, a yellow legal tablet full of notes on the coffee table, or one of his mysteries opened across his chest. She'd turn off the VCR and cover him with an afghan, studying his face. He seemed a stranger to her, this exhausted man who moved more carefully now, as if afraid of breaking some-thing, of getting hurt. Upstairs, she herself moved quietly over the bare floorboards of her room, not wanting to wake him.

A few times, she woke as he was leaving. His careful footsteps through the foyer, the front door quietly tugged closed, his headlights off until he'd pulled the car onto the street. She watched him once from her window, but it made her too sad to see him driving away.

"You're just setting yourself up," everyone told her. "He's using you, Kayla. He's only around because it didn't work out with her. You deserve better." But she wasn't so sure there was better than Will. He'd told her about the fire, about the choice he gave Anne. Despite herself, she loved him. He was her husband. Brooke's father.

And then one morning, he was still there, curled in a fetal position on the couch, the afghan clutched around his shoulders like an old woman's shawl. He was wearing navy sweats and big ski socks, a hole in the toe of one, which somehow made her sad. She hated him, and she felt sorry for him, and she tried to remember why she had fallen in love with him all those years ago, and why, after all he had done to hurt and humiliate her, she loved him still.

He opened his eyes and saw her watching him before she realized he was awake. She blushed when she realized he was watching her, too. "I don't want you staying here again, Will," she said, steeling her voice to compensate for the look of tenderness he must have witnessed.

"Sorry," he said before his eyes closed again. His hair was disheveled, sticking up in tufts, and she smiled despite herself.

"Here," she said a minute later, handing him a mug of coffee the way he liked it, milky and loaded with sugar.

He didn't speak until he'd taken a sip. "Stay a minute," he said drowsily. "Talk to me. I'm not awake," He moved his feet and she snuggled into the cushions at the other end of the couch. It was cold, and he leaned forward to lift the blanket over her knees.

"How's the training going?" he asked after a few sips of coffee.

Wearily, she said, "You don't care how my training's going, Will."

"We can't even have a simple conversation?"

"Why?" She tossed the blanket back to him and stood. "We don't have anything in common, remember? And the last time I checked, we weren't married, we aren't friends, we don't work together." She shrugged. "So what's the point?"

"Forget it." He set down his mug. "Thanks for the coffee. I'll be out of here in five minutes." Already he was reaching beneath the table for his shoes.

She stared past him, focusing on the videos stacked next to the TV: one of his cycling tapes which he had probably fallen asleep to, and *Madeline* and *The Parent Trap*. "Isn't it enough that I feel sorry for you?" she asked quietly.

He glanced up at her. "I'm not asking you for that, Kayla. I know I don't deserve it."

"You're right, you don't." She looked at him for a long moment. "But I know what it feels like to lose someone you love." She walked away then, ending their talk.

Despite that conversation, he did stay over now and then, always sleeping on the couch. He and Kayla moved around each other carefully and politely. On the nights she was doing a long run, he waited up for her. She entered a warm house filled with the smells of tomato sauce, pesto and garlic. The table set. "You're confusing me," she told him once. "This doesn't change anything, Will."

He nodded. "I know, and I'm not trying to confuse you, Kayla. I promise. It's just that we both have to eat, and I don't mind cooking." He glanced at her. "Come on. Go get changed."

She was wired after her runs, high on endorphins and adrenaline. She talked about the café with him, and Brooke, about Sarah and Kee- hwan and Sarah's paintings. She asked about his work, his cycling. They talked about the news, about a cyclist who was organizing a race in Texas to honor both survivors and victims of cancer. "I was thinking of going next year," he said. It would be the twenty-fifty anniversary of his mother's death.

"You should," she said, concentrating on her pasta. She realized that she wanted to go with him.

Another night, setting down her fork abruptly, she asked, "Why didn't we talk like this before?" Her voice sounded plaintive, even to her.

The lease on the apartment he'd shared with Anne was up on the first of April, and he began hunting for something closer to Brooke's school, or at least something on a quieter street. Kayla would find the classifieds by the phone the next morning, the apartment ads circled, an address sometimes written in the margin. Twice, she ran along the street where the apartment was located, hoping, despite herself, to find that it *wasn't* a good street for a child, or that the building was in disrepair. As she ran down the tree-shadowed sidewalks, rectangles of light shimmering from kitchens and bedrooms, she found herself remembering the Italian couple who had lived on the same block as she had growing up. They had been divorced for years, but they shared the house still, he living in the basement, which had its own entrance. The mothers in the neighborhood used to gossip about their situation, shaking their heads and wondering out loud how the wife could bear to live like that. Kayla imagined that maybe she understood.

"How's the apartment search going?" she asked him one Sunday morning as she was on her way out to run. He was sitting on the porch swing, coffee mug next to him, doing the word jumble in the paper, waiting for Brooke.

"After a while, they all look the same," he said. "I've got to decide by the end of the week." His face was windburned, already tanned from cycling.

She hesitated, pretending to fiddle with the Walkman. He was sleeping on the couch most nights now; she had cleared out the coat closet so he wouldn't have to keep packing his clothes in a gym bag. "If you're really not happy with those places, you could stay here until you find something."

He set the paper down and regarded her solemnly. "What are you saying?"

"I'm not sure." She swallowed and looked at him helplessly. "We've been doing pretty well lately, haven't we? And not only with the parent stuff."

He squinted at her to keep the early spring sunlight from his eyes. "Come here. Sit with me. I can barely see you." The swing groaned as he shifted his weight to make room for her.

"I can't," she said, digging at a crack in the cement with the toe of her Nike. A woodpecker chopped at a tree nearby.

"*I* can live with you, but *you* can't sit with me?" He started to laugh, but she stopped him.

"Don't," she pleaded. "I feel like a fool already." She was close to tears, fighting the urge to just turn on the Walkman and run before he could reject her again.

"Hey," he said gently. "Look at me."

She did hesitantly, her heart thundering in her chest.

"I was the fool," he said slowly, enunciating each word. He looked tired and vulnerable, and she understood that rather than asking for her absolution or forgiveness, he was offering her this: a revision of his love for Anne into something less than what it had been, something crazy and impulsive which had temporarily rendered him a fool, as if he'd been cast under some spell and had now woken up. She knew, though, that this had never been the case, knew simply by looking at his eyes that even now he felt he was betraying Anne by saying those words: *I was the fool.* Hurt and love trickled through her, and she wondered if always now it would be like this, the two emotions inseparable.

No one would understand how she could take Will back. Nobody would be happy for her; nobody would think this was a good thing, except Will's dad probably, and Brooke, of course. And what if Anne moved back to Richmond? Or worse, what if she didn't and they still couldn't make it work, Kayla still couldn't make him happy?

"Are you sure about this, Kayla?" Will asked her gently. Shadows moved across his face.

"No, I'm not sure," she snapped. "There's no way I can be, and I'm not asking you to be, either, okay?" She took a deep breath. "I'm sorry. It's just, do you want to be here or not, Will?"

He smiled tenderly at her, his voice soft. "I really do."

She exhaled slowly. "Me, too." She felt exhausted suddenly, as if she'd already run.

He leaned forward and stared down at his hands. "We need to talk about this, though—" He spoke carefully, glancing up at her. "Don't we?"

She felt her neck stiffen. "I don't want to be hurt again," she said, staring past him. Down the street, Mrs. Peterson hobbled down the driveway on her walker to wait for her daughter to pick her up for church. Another person who would be happy if Will moved back, she thought. Her eyes were brimming. "Can you at least promise to be honest with me? Because if you can't do that, Will, then there—"

"Kayla—"

She stopped.

"I want this to work," he said, reaching up from the swing to brush away her tears with his thumb. "I want to try. I want to be the kind of husband you deserve."

Behind them a rustle of branches from the pin oaks along the sidewalk signaled a small breeze and goose bumps formed along her arms. Kayla felt like sobbing, though she didn't know why.

After a moment, he said quietly, "I'm not over her yet, Kayla. You should know that."

"I do." But all she heard was the *yet*.

Chapter Forty

In Baltimore, the cherry blossoms were in full bloom, filling the air with their heavy scent. Annie saved her errands for late afternoon and worked on the papers she needed to review in a nearby café. It was a bright airy place populated with art students and gay couples and people like herself, alone, busy with their studies or work, laptops sometimes on the tables in front of them.

She had been home to New Jersey twice since her move. The trip was easier now, only two hours up I-95. Her mother visited for Annie's thirty-third birthday in late March. They ate lunch in the Baltimore Museum of Art, at a table overlooking the sculpture garden, and struggled to mend all the damage that Annie's leaving Carter had caused. "I knew there was more to it than just this Will person," her mother suggested. "You must have sensed that Carter was becoming ill. Even as a little girl, Annie, you could always tell when something was wrong. Your father would be having a bad day, and you'd crawl into his lap and just pat his face, very gently. Do you remember that?"

Beyond the terraced patio, trees dipped and bowed, leaves flashing silvery and green and white, as if struggling to break free of something. Already the story was being revised, she thought, just as Carter had said it would be, so that he was the bad guy, and Annie the victim. She felt as if she were being revised, too. "I know you want to believe that," she told her mother. "But I left Carter because I loved Will. I still do." It seemed crucial, somehow, that her mother accept this, accept *her*. To succumb to her mother's version of herself was to somehow lose who she was, who she had become in the past two years. She didn't want to let go of her, the woman Will had loved and had taught Annie to love. "I liked who I was with him, Mom." She set down her fork, her eyes blurred with tears. She didn't know how to explain this, even to herself, how it wasn't until she had understood her capacity to cause damage, to be selfish, that she had fully apprehended her capacity for love. Perhaps it was simply that you risk what you value, and with Will, she had risked herself for the first time, believed her happiness was worth more than all the terrible costs.

But her mother needed to see her as the good daughter, perhaps because this was the only means she had of seeing herself as a good mother. "In a way, I suppose it doesn't really matter why you left. You did the right thing in the end, Annie. You stood by Carter."

Annie rode the MARC train to D.C. once, where Carter met her in Union Station and they walked to Chinatown and down to the mall, attempting friendship once again. He was still in counseling with Dan, but less angry now. It had helped him, he confessed, that she had moved from Richmond. "Before, I kept hoping that you'd walk into the bookstore. Every time those bells over the door rang, I'd look to see if it was you. I was afraid to go out in case I missed you, and then that time you came by and I was in the bank . . . I know you left Richmond, in part, for me," he said. "I know what it cost you, Anne."

They were walking along the FDR memorial, a curving tree-lined path through various "rooms" or spaces, each focused on one of the president's four terms. Water sluiced over red granite walls into silvery reflection pools surrounded by shade trees and bronze sculptures. The walls were inscribed with quotes: MORE THAN AN END TO WAR, WE WANT AN END TO THE BEGINNING OF ALL WARS. Tourists snapped pictures, a toddler splashed in one of the tiny pools.

"I didn't move for you, Carter," Annie told him as they continued walking. "I wish I was that selfless." It was important to her that there be no more lies, but Carter wasn't really listening, needing, Annie understood, to believe that she had made this sacrifice for him. His version. Everyone had one.

She wondered often what Will's version was. What, in the end, was the story he would tell himself about their affair, their love? Even the noun he chose would alter what it had been. Her own version, which she told herself often in those first months, was that it didn't matter whether Will had loved her as deeply as she had loved him or whether years from now, he would remember her as only one more in a series of his affairs. What mattered was that she had loved—truly loved—him. This was the story *she* needed to believe.

The news that spring was filled with details of the president's affair with a White House intern. The word *adultery* was everywhere: the headlines of the *New York Times* and the *Washington Post* and in bold black letters on the cover of *Newsweek*. SURVIVING INFIDELITY, in bright red on the cover of *People*: HOW THEY COPE, WHY THEY STAY. Inside, pictures of celebrity wives whose spouses had cheated on them. Everywhere it seemed, politicians and pundits and spin doctors and callers on radio talk shows and students in the café where Annie often graded papers bandied about the words *wrong, immoral, disgusting, abhorrent,* and *sleazy* to speak of the president's actions or the behavior of the woman with whom he had had the affair. The words buzzed around her like angry bees as she sat alone, staring blankly at a dissertation on cancer clusters in third-world countries. She felt stung by the judgments radiating through her. At night, jokes about adultery on Letterman and Leno. Annie didn't laugh.

Instead, she watched the footage on the news of the president, his wife beside him, the president's daughter walking between her parents on the White House lawn, and she thought of Will and Kayla and Brooke and knew that no one, perhaps not even the president himself, really understood what had happened or why. She imagined it was both simpler and more complicated than people wanted it to be.

Lois wrote often. Her letters were breezy and careful. Yukihiko had dropped the writing class after two weeks. Sungae, nearly in tears, had been in to ask about Annie on the first day of the spring semester. Will had called the next day, panicked and then furious: How could Anne not have told him she was leaving? *"He still loves you,"* Lois wrote. In her most recent letter, Lois had enclosed a printed card announcing Sungae's art show. April 23 to May 15. The title of the exhibit was *English Lessons*. "Apparently she did a painting for every writing assignment you gave them," Lois wrote. "Did you have any idea?"

Annie hadn't, and was surprised because she remembered Sungae's evaluation. "Why does she have the right to take our stories from us? What if we are not ready to let them go?" It made Annie smile to think that maybe Sungae had found a way, after all, to tell her story on her own terms, and that in the end maybe Annie's class had helped in some small way. Annie taped the invitation to her refrigerator, hoping that by May she might be ready to return to Richmond for a visit. She would love to see the show, to tell Sungae that she had started a new article and wanted, with Sungae's permission, to name it "Sorrowful Sentences." *I learned a lot from you,* Annie would like to tell her.

Mostly, Annie tried not to think of Will. It was easier here, but still she had phoned Will twice, dialing their old number after rehearsing for over an hour what to say, how to make her voice casual. *Was it all a mistake?* she wanted to ask him. Or was this separation only a plot twist, the requisite complication that every story needs before it can be resolved. Mostly, she wanted to explain why she hadn't told him she was leaving Richmond: *If I had phoned you, if I had heard your voice, I wouldn't have been able to go.* Deep down, though, she knew that she had wanted to punish him, that disappearing from his life was one of the cruelest things she could have done.

The first time she phoned she got the answering machine. The second time the line had been disconnected. She dialed Kayla's number, but hung up when she heard his voice.

She stayed busy with the dissertations she edited: "The Effect of Managed Care on Women Who Seek Abortions in Baltimore." "Understanding the Rise of Depression Among Adolescents in Israel." "Tracking the Rise of Sarcoidosis among Females of Norwegian Descent." She didn't listen to the radio, afraid to hear songs that would remind her of him, and she stayed away from the reservoir where she had gone to walk one morning and saw a group of cyclists. As the days grew longer and warmer and Orioles fans flocked to Camden Yards for opening day and April turned into May, Annie took Sungae's invitation from the refrigerator and tucked it into a drawer. She wasn't ready to go back to Richmond, even for a visit.

Every now and then, a reminder scaled the walls she had erected around herself. Frank Sinatra's "Fly Me to the Moon" leaked from the stereo as she was sitting in the café reading a dissertation on the "Use of Electronic Medical Records in Hospitals in Taiwan." *We'll have to carve jack-o-lanterns soon,* she heard him say. Candles flickered over his face. She felt his thumb against her breast. Another time it was a line in the book she was reading: *And so he became the man who was Thursday to her.* Thursdays in the Commons meeting for coffee. Thursday nights, racing through the mall, meeting him, the Holiday Inn.

The past was like blood, she sometimes thought, seeping through a bandage no matter how tightly you try to wrap the wound.

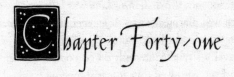

Chapter Forty-one

This is your night," Keehwan told Sungae. "You should enjoy."

"How?" What was she supposed to do? Walk around and look at her own paintings? What would the ladies from the church say? They'd call her a peacock. Vain. She couldn't eat or drink, either— her stomach was too nervous. "Just stand here?" she asked. "How I enjoy that?"

"Like a queen. Do nothing. Everybody admires you tonight."

So she stood near one of the tall windows, coveting the possibility of escape. A breeze moved into the room, carrying the smell of hyacinth and wet earth from the rain they'd had earlier. From outside, she heard laughter, a couple arguing, and the wheeze of a city bus. Her show was being held in the University ballroom, one of the few rooms on campus large enough to hold seventeen paintings the size of conference tables, small movie screens, and billboards. But she felt suffocated by the too-big paintings, larger now that they were framed, and by too many eyes swallowing her up, wondering, "Is she the artist?" She felt unable to breathe in her *han-bok*. And yet she knew that no matter how she felt at this moment, this was her happiest day in over eighteen years.

Because the paintings needed so much wall space, the theater department had erected fake walls in the room's center to hang the smaller works, those that were the size of doors or coffee tables. Consequently, the paintings were hung out of order and were no longer arranged first, second, third. *Telling Line* was followed by *Conditional Phrases,* which was placed next to *Adjectives,* the most peaceful painting, whiteness over everything. Sungae preferred it this way, though, for stories travel a straight line only when complete. Her story never would be. And yet, for all of this, it was somehow finished.

Two nights ago, she had looked it up in the dictionary—the difference between *complete* and *finished.* She looked the words up not in her wallet-size Korean-English dictionary, but in the *Oxford English Dictionary,* as big as a hope chest, the pages like butterfly wings, fluttery and transparent. The librarian showed her the magnifying glass to read the too-small words, millions of words, darting before her eyes like faraway stars until she held the glass to one and it shimmered into focus. *Complete.* From the Latin, *com,* "with,"·and *plere,* "fill." To fill with. Goose bumps had risen along her arms. To fill with. To be filled. *Like being pregnant,* she thought. *I was complete.* And *finish.* From the Latin word for "end" or "limit." She nodded, her breathing shallow, as if to hold these words inside her. She understood now for the first time how it was possible for a story to end without being over. Maybe the most important stories never are. And maybe it's only in the beginning when everything is still possible that any story is ever truly complete.

Outside the university ballroom, trees shivered against the sky, pink now with light. Across the room, Dr. Benson was shepherding guests towards the hors d'oeuvres table. Sungae glanced again at her paintings, all mixed up and out of order. Like her life, she thought. She remembered sitting in a circle in Annie's class once, playing the writing game, everyone laughing, having fun. Annie had written the first line of a story and handed the paper to Ba, who wrote the next line. Ba handed it to Farshad, but first, he folded the paper so that Annie's line was hidden, and Farshad could only see Ba's sentence. Farshad wrote the next line, and handed it to Shin-pin, but he also folded the paper, this time over Ba's line, so that all Shin-pin could read was Farshad's. Each student did the same, telling a story without the privilege of history, of knowing what had come before that single moment. When the paper finally circled the room, and Annie read it out loud, each sentence connected to the previous one, yet the story made no sense. Sungae's own story was like that now, she thought. The plot all crazy and twisted, and her paintings of sadness and happiness all mixed together. And yet it seemed more accurate this way. Her real story never contained a plot, either. One thing happened and she reacted, and then the next, and the next, and each small step seemed logical until the moment that the nurse took her daughter from her, and she saw the whole picture and knew that none of it, ever, would fall into an order that would make sense to her.

Only *Prepositions,* the painting she had covered in black the night Kayla told her about Will and Annie, was in order. She had insisted that it be the last painting. It was the only one not framed, finished but not complete, the only one Keehwan had not yet seen, the only one with the subtitle: *Rooftops,* for this is what the blackness had become, an intricate landscape of roofs, of their various darknesses. The metal glint of a fire escape, the reddish line of a chimney, pools of wetness, rectangles, squares, the triangle of a church steeple, slanted lines of pitched roofs, a blade of shadow, blurry strings of Christmas lights.

As she painted, she had remembered: the first time she saw Keehwan when she was eighteen years old, a student at Ehwa Women's University. She was waiting for the number thirty-two bus to Arongdong station. He was a skinny man with bristly porcupine hair and a leather jacket. She had noticed his hands, scarred and cut, his knuckles bruised, fingernails dirty, and she imagined him in a fight. Only later would she realize the cuts and bruises were from cutting and laying slate roof tiles. She saw him each morning waiting for the bus, sipping the hot tea from a Styrofoam cup, reading *Korean Herald;* later in her art class, it was his hands she kept drawing. And then one afternoon, he was beside her as she was walking home. "You see that?" He pointed to the roof of a house farther down the hill. "An important man lives there. The more tiles in the roof, the greater the prestige." He pointed to another house. Falling sunlight cast multicolored shadows on the curved tiles of the roof so that from above it resembled a bright mosaic. "That family suffered a tragedy," he said. "The weaving pattern of tiles—you see that? They are trying to make whole that which is divided."

He told her that at the end of the Choson dynasty there was an official Tile Bureau. Forty-eight tile experts inspected the materials, and at the end of each year, there was a special ceremony where the workers gathered to smash all the substandard tiles. He laughed—the first time she'd seen his teeth. She still didn't know his name, but already she was falling in love with him.

She had worked on *Prepositions* every day during the winter break, her bones aching with cold, the tiny space heater insufficient against the January bitterness. When she returned to the house in the late afternoon to make dinner, she would feel momentarily disoriented by the sight of Keehwan sleeping in his easy chair with the special pillow against his back, the *TV Guide* on the floor, the kitchen smelling of the bitter gentian-root tea that he drank to unknot his back. *What are you still doing here?* she was tempted to ask, gratitude and grief sliding through her. Gratitude because he had stayed all of these years; grief because he was an old man now, and because she had realized too late that she still loved him.

The ballroom was crowded and noisy. She heard the patter of heels on the polished inlaid wood floor, the tap of loafers, and the rustle of paper as undergraduates from the intro painting classes took notes. So many people: Dr. Jacks and his wife were here, Dr. Benson, the girl with the earring in her nose from art class, and the Japanese man who was new this semester. There were students she didn't know, some of whom just strolled by her paintings as if window-shopping at the mall. Farshad and his wife, Ba, and Cindy Min, the new girl from Korea who was in Sungae's writing class. The ladies from church. Ahmad, Yukihiko, whom she hadn't seen in months. He wore khaki shorts and flip-flops with a ruffled tuxedo shirt and jacket. "Who you think you are?" she laughed when she saw him. "Half-and-half man?"

"Ahh, Sungae, I get dressed up for you. Why you insulting me?" He swiveled around, taking in the room in a glance, then turned back to her. "You gonna be famous, huh? Like Andy Warhol, maybe?"

"*Psshh,* he no artist. Paint big soup can, what kind of art you call that?"

After Yukihiko moved away, she watched faces and studied gestures. Keehwan had wandered over to *Prepositions: Rooftops*. She could not bear to look at him. Would he understand what she was trying to tell him?

Instead of small typed cards describing each painting, Sungae had framed her different assignments with Annie's corrections next to the correlating work. It had been Dr. Nielsen's idea. He suggested it as soon as Sungae told him the title of the show, *English Lessons*. Only *Rooftops,* was different. For this painting, she had written only two sentences. "Korean word for 'write' has the pictograph for 'roof' inside of it. Only when roof is on the house, is the house complete—ready to be 'filled with'; same with words, which are like the beautiful roof tiles: only when they are in proper place, can a story be made whole."

"Not so bad," said Mrs. Kim. She was wearing her best suit, the same one she wore for her second daughter's wedding. She wore white powder on her face and bright lipstick.

"Nah, too big," said Mrs. Lee. Sungae's heart lifted into her throat, and she nodded gratefully to her friends. This was the Korean way to give a compliment: Never say praise outright; never give a person a big head.

Mrs. Park squeezed Sungae's hand. "Not worse thing, I see. Good colors."

Across the room, Will, Kayla, and Brooke came in and glanced around. Kayla spotted Sungae and waved brightly. "It's okay if you don't come," Sungae had told Kayla when she handed her the printed invitation. Kayla's eyes stayed on the title for a long time. When she looked up finally, they had hardened as they did when she dealt with a problem customer or employee, and as they sometimes did even now when she talked to Will. "Don't be silly. Of course we'll come," she said.

Will wasn't looking at the paintings, but at Annie's handwriting, her oddly shaped *f*s, which looked like *j*s. Some of her words were indecipherable. "What's this?" Sungae would ask Annie, unable to read one of her comments, and Annie would lean over the paper, squinting her eyes, and finally say, "Isn't that terrible? I have no idea." Then she'd read the sentence or paragraph again, trying to recall what she must have wanted to say. Sungae wondered if Will missed Annie. Kayla had told Sungae about Annie's husband and the fire and the choices Will and Annie had both made. *You see,* Sungae wanted to tell Kayla, *duty is stronger than love*. But her throat was clogged with the tears that she shed only after Kayla left because Sungae also knew that sometimes to substitute duty for love was like using honey in a recipe that called for sugar. It was too heavy; it would weigh the cake down. Sungae cried, too, because she understood now why Annie was always telling students mistakes are okay. She had needed to believe this. And even though Sungae had always known that "an error the width of a hair leads one a thousand *li* away," a part of her, even after all these years, hadn't wanted it to be true. Yet how could it not be? Seventeen years ago, she had crossed two oceans because of her own mistake, and now Annie lived in another city because of hers. Still, Keehwan was right. Annie had been a good teacher, after all. Sungae hadn't begun a single painting since Kristina started teaching.

Of course, she knew she was learning important subjects from Kristina. They all were. Proposals, documentation of sources, summaries, how to write a research paper, how to analyze a scholarly article. The entire class was immersed in special research projects, lugging books and folders full of articles downloaded from the Internet to class and making notes on index cards.

"Copying," Sungae would complain to Farshad, or Cindy Min, the new girl, during the breaks. "She just teaching us to copy other words, ideas." The assignments seemed empty. Meaningless. Who was she writing to? Who was listening? When Kristina collected their drafts, she simply put a red check mark over anything she liked or that they did well; she wrote "Awk" beside what she didn't understand, and circled grammar, typing, and spelling mistakes. More and more, Sungae missed Annie. She missed writing to her about Korea, using adjectives to describe different kinds of spicy food, or future tense to tell how Koreans believed that *young-sahn,* the spirits of those who died childless, would most likely become violent; and how, if an unmarried son or daughter dies, traditional Koreans would call the shaman to conduct *sahon,* "ghost wedding," uniting the deceased with a "spirit mate." She missed using comparative adjectives to explain how the deeper and longer a person bowed, the stronger the emotion being expressed. Or using as many verbs as possible to portray the chaos of Chagalch'i Fish Market, people selling the cheap souvenirs to tourists, women bargaining for best price, the scent of diesel from the *taekshi,* taxis, mixing with garlic and marinated squid from the street vendors. The odors were like oil and water, she wrote, remaining separate, one atop the other. Mostly, she missed Annie's comments in the margins, "I'd love to hear more about the ghost-weddings, Sungae," or next to a description of Mount Nam Park, "It sounds beautiful!" She missed her sentences highlighted in neon green and fluorescent orange.

One day, maybe tonight after the show, Sungae would write Annie a letter and tell her thank you. "Why you want us to remember our life?" She had asked her on the first day. Now she understood.

"Sungae."

It was Dr. Jacks. He pointed across the room to a woman in a red suit and high heels. "That's Clara Ives. She owns City Gallery. Apparently, she loves your work, and is interested in representing you."

"Very kind," Sungae said uncertainly. What did that mean, she wondered, for someone to represent you? "Why I need that?" she asked Dr. Jacks.

He laughed kindly. "The gallery can do a lot for you, Sungae. Clara thinks she can bring upwards of five thousand on some of these."

"You mean the dollars?" Sungae was incredulous.

Big laugh. "Absolutely."

Kayla hurried across the room now and hugged Sungae. Will lingered in front of *Past Tense.* "I'm so proud of you, Sungae. These are incredible."

"You sorry you came?" Sungae asked.

Kayla smiled, a tiny crooked smile as if her mouth were numb, like after visiting the dentist. She turned toward Will, her eyes finding him immediately. "No," she said, still watching him. "It's good we came."

"But too much sadness."

Kayla shrugged. "He loves her, Sungae. I've known it for a while."

"He loves you, too."

She shook her head. "It's not the same." She paused and said, "The other day when I was running I saw this tree that had been struck by lightning, and it was completely dead, except for this one small branch that was filled with new leaves. And I thought of what you said about love and duty, and I thought about how ninety-nine percent of the time, it's probably right—duty does come first. But not with Will. I realized our marriage is like that tree, Sungae, and there's just that one branch—maybe the love he has for her—that's still alive, and if it stays on the tree, it will die, too." She smiled sadly, then gestured toward Keehwan, who was still standing in front of *Prepositions,* his hands clasped behind his back, a willow tree bent in the wind. "He's been over there a while," Kayla said gently. "Maybe you should go talk to him."

"What do I say?" Sungae asked. But she heeded Kayla's advice, feeling queasy, her *han-bok* damp with sweat. The ballroom was beginning to empty. Beyond the high vaulted windows with their heavy gold drapes pulled back, the lights of the downtown high-rises cast a yellow glow against the inky sky.

"You standing here a long time," Sungae said tentatively.

"*Ch'am ye ppup-ni-da.*" It is very beautiful. In his eyes there was uncertainty, though.

"You wondering why I paint this?" she asked.

"Not why," he said solemnly. "I think I understand why." He glanced at her, then away. "You are grateful to me, I know. Maybe you understand me now. It is true, Sungae, that I wanted to protect you."

She nodded, head bowed.

"But maybe I deceive you," he continued. "You think I am unselfish man because I permit you to have the art show and I make the frames. You think, 'Ahh, Keehwan, good husband,' right? 'So supportive. Modern man'? You do not know that I make the frames because I am afraid. Maybe I want to contain your memories before they grow too big. Not so nice, huh?"

"Not so terrible, either," she said. "Maybe memories need to be contained." They were not so different from dreams, she knew. Both were about loss—we recall what is no longer, we dream of what we do not have. She glanced at the painting, the one she was most proud of, this geography of blackness, which in Korea was the most important color, for without it there could be no light. "When I was painting this, I remembered how, in the church sometimes, I see you leaning back, eyes looking up, and I know you are not praying to God, but studying the structure of the roof. Maybe you are thinking, installation beams not placed close enough. That is why building is so cold. Or you study the water stain, and you think it was too cold to lay the roof and the bitumen was not flexible enough—that is why it cracks, creates the leaks." She paused, her voice thick with tears. "Foolish man, I used to think, wasting time on such thoughts. But then, when I am painting, I suddenly understand: Without the strong roof nothing inside of the church will be protected." She glanced at him, this skinny man in the blue suit, a shiny patch on one sleeve from Mrs. Park's too-hot iron, and felt as if her heart would explode. "Long time ago, you taught me that the roof is the beautiful, complicated structure. You remember? It has to be strong enough to endure all kinds of the weather, you told me, but not so heavy that it will crush what it is trying to protect."

She closed her eyes and swallowed a deep breath. "You are the roof over my heart, Keehwan."

When she looked at him finally, he was smiling. "*Kam-sa-ham-ni-da,*" he said quietly. "Thank you."

After most of the guests had gone, and Keehwan and Dr. Benson and Dr. Nielsen and the student helpers were packing away the food and plastic cups and wine, Sungae walked alone around the room, staring at her paintings. The room was quiet now, and churchlike. Her daughter seemed close to her here. Sungae knew now that she would not try to contact Chongmin. She owed Keehwan that much, not out of duty this time, but out of love.

She glanced at *Prepositions: Rooftops,* and remembered the night she had filled out the birth certificate. She had insisted on filling it out, though she and Hwang had never discussed this. Chongmin. A proper noun. A specific person. Her daughter.

The paintings were simply another way of giving language to what mattered, she realized, a way to remember what was important. Annie once told them a story about the culture of Greenland, where people thought the dead could not sleep in peace until a child was named after them. Maybe memories are the same, Sungae thought, shifting her gaze across the room to the pregnant woman in *Telling Line* and the girl flying a kite in the window. Perhaps memories do not rest until you give them a name, either.

Chapter Forty-two

On the drive home, they talked about Sungae's paintings and Kayla asked Will and Brooke which they liked best. All three of them chose *Telling Line,* Brooke because of all the hidden objects. It was like a game in one of her coloring-activity books. Kayla didn't ask Will why he chose it, and he didn't ask her.

In the bedroom, they undressed silently, moving carefully about one another in the bathroom. After he joined her in bed, she lay for a moment on her side, then took her pillow and held it to her chest.

"What's wrong?" he asked.

"I'm going to sleep on the couch until we figure things out," she said quietly. She couldn't bear to sleep beside him, to be that close, knowing he was leaving again.

"Oh, Kayla—"

The minute he said that, just her name, she knew she was right.

"I don't know what I feel right now," he said. But he had spent a long time with the paintings, hearing Annie's voice in his mind, her laughter, things she had said. A hundred fragments highlighted in bright fluorescent colors in his heart: *It's not Carter you really care about punishing, is it Will? . . . Beautiful's the wrong word. Try happy . . . I've never made a jack-o'-lantern. . . . You're like one of those kings in*

*fairy tales, who set up these impossible tests which the suitors must pass
in order to win the princess's hand. . . . I don't want to fall out of love
with you. . . . You think time will make me hate you less for what you've
done . . . I wish you could play hooky with me. . . . When Brooke's older,
she'll remember. How you called her every night, how you never missed
a single day . . . I'm being greedy aren't I? It's only February and already
I'm talking about April. . . .*

"Will?"

He glanced up. How could he do this to Kayla again? "I do miss
her," he said. "I feel like I probably need to see her—"

"Need?"

"Okay, *want*. But Kayla, I didn't know it until tonight, I swear to
you. I don't even know what I'm saying, this is just—" He ran a hand
through his hair. "I wish I hadn't gone to Sarah's damn show. I wish I'd
just stayed home."

"It would have happened eventually," she said. She sat on the edge
of the bed, feeling crumpled inside, like a car after a terrible accident.
She forced herself to look at him. "I've known for a while."

"Hold it—" His voice was angry, scared, wanting to stop her. "*I*
didn't even know—"

She held up her hand to stop him. She stared at her fingers. Neither
of them had resumed wearing their wedding rings. "I'm going to be
honest with you, too, Will," she said. "Later, I think I'll be too angry.
I'll probably need to hate you for a while, maybe a long while. But right
now I don't. Right now all I see is that you're dead inside. You're not
excited about your cycling or your work, you're drinking to fall asleep
at night—" She looked up at him and smiled sadly. "Yes, sweetie, I do
notice even if I don't say anything." She squeezed the pillow against
her chest. "You're short with Brooke lately, and even with me, and
when we make love—" She squeezed harder, her voice no more than a
squeak. "You just aren't there." She was crying now.

"I wanted to be there," he said.

"I know, but you aren't and the truth is that I'm dead, too. I'm tired
of trying to make you happy and trying to be happy." She glanced at
him. "I've never been more tired in my life, Will."

"Not even after the marathon?" he tried to joke.

He'd been there for her, showing up all over the course, wherever he could. Brooke waved signs that said, GO MOMMY! and the two of them sprayed her with water from plastic water guns they'd bought and told her she was gorgeous and "the best."

"Do you remember when you told me I wasn't capable of love?" he asked now.

"I was angry, Will."

"Do you think it's true?"

She looked at him. He'd lost weight. She noticed it in his shoulders, which seemed narrow—boyish and very old all at once. "I don't know," she said after a moment. "That's what you're going Baltimore to find out, isn't it?"

"You've always been so strong," he said. "I wish I had as much strength, Kayla. I wish I could have been better for you."

"Strength?" she laughed. "This isn't about strength. I'm giving up, Will, I'm quitting, for good this time. I'm not being kind or noble or understanding or any of that." She glanced at him bitterly and then turned away again. "Remember that final scene in *Titanic* where all those people are holding on to the bits and pieces of debris, trying to stay alive until help comes?"

They'd rented the movie a few nights ago. He'd thought of Anne then, too. About how he'd let her go. How he hadn't held on tight enough. "Yeah, I remember."

"Well, that's how I feel, Will. That's me. I've been clinging to this marriage for dear life, but the truth is that I'm already dead." Wearily, she stood, still hugging the pillow to her chest.

"I love you," he whispered.

"Will—" She shook her head in frustration. "You hand out those words like they're lollipops at the doctor's office. They don't make the hurt go away."

His shoulders slumped. "I know."

"Do you?"

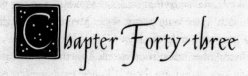

Chapter Forty-three

"**W**hy?" Sungae pointed to Cindy's pink silk *han-bok,* a pattern of white cranes along the hem. It was the first time she had seen Cindy in traditional Korean clothes, and her heart caught, snagged not by memory but by possibility. She was so beautiful. Is this how Chongmin would look in the *han-bok?*

"I'm giving a very important presentation today." Cindy sat in the seat next to Sungae's, eyes cast down. A respectful girl who always spoke in a proper tone.

"You nervous?" Sungae still hadn't settled down from her opening the previous night. She had barely slept and had kept nudging Kee-hwan awake and asking, "You believe? Five thousand dollar people might pay? For *one* painting."

"Not going to sell the paintings, why do you care?" he grumbled.

"We could buy a new car," she said. "What kind you want? BMW? Mercedes? Maybe, Ford Bronco!" She laughed, thinking up names from TV commercials.

"Nah, I want a motorcycle," he teased. "Jay Leno has a motorcycle."

"You think you funny, Keehwan?"

She had been up before the alarm, writing to Annie. Light fell over her shoulders and spilled onto the table. She crossed out, wrote again, and then started over. All these years she had believed her memories were like children: You must hold on tight to them and protect them. She had hated Annie for trying to take them away. But Sungae realized now that she had been only partly right. Memories *are* like children, but eventually you must let them go. How else would they live? "All these years I steal memories from myself, hide them away in bottom of heart, nobody knows they are there," Sungae explained to Annie. "But now I give them back, let them go. You help me. Teach telling line, past tense. Good job."

She had arrived to class early today, excited and anticipating her classmates' congratulations for her show. But Farshad was busy reading his book about the heart, and Ba was studying his vocabulary words. Ahmad was late again.

"Would you accompany me to the Commons to buy the tea during break?" Cindy whispered when Kristina wasn't looking. "I am very nervous about the presentation. I would like to purchase the tea. For settling my nervousness."

Sungae nodded eagerly. "I will buy it for you. Treat you. No problem."

But the break never seemed to come. Usually Kristina stopped the class halfway through. Today, though, she droned on and on, explaining the comma splice, which meant joining two sentences with a comma. She said it was a big mistake.

"Why?" Sungae asked. "Sentences go together maybe." Like her paintings she was thinking. Like her memories. "Sometimes it's not so easy to separate." But Kristina just repeated, "This time no exceptions, Sungae." Kristina smiled. "I thought that's what you wanted."

It was true. It was another reason why Sungae had hated learning English: for every rule there was always an exception: add *ed* to change the verb from present to past, except for *begin, feel, forgive*; except for *hear, lie, teach*; except for *weep*; except for *write*. Or add an *s* to make a noun plural. Except for *child* which becomes *children*; except for *wife* which becomes *wives*. And then there are nouns you cannot count at all, nouns that will never be plural, never have an s: *happiness, grief, sand, water*. Lately, though, these exceptions were what Sungae loved.

Learning English was like painting, she thought. Words are like colors which when added together become something new. Yellow and white become the color of dry rice, of sunlight on the dusty windowpane, of the low morning fog over the mountains near Seoul. The verb *have* and the noun *daughter* become an entire story. If you add another word, like *lost* the color changes, the story grows sad.

She understood, too, that exceptions, these moments in grammar or life, when the rules were altered or broken, were somehow important. If someone said, for example, "She had dark long hair," instead of the *correct* way, "She had long dark hair," you would know that it was because the darkness was what that person wanted to emphasize. You would wonder why, and in that "misplaced" word, you would find an entire history instead of a mistake. Maybe it was like that with comma splices, she thought—two sentences incorrectly joined together like Siamese twins. Sometimes if you separate them, one will die. *I left my home, my country, my parents, my daughter, I will start my life over.* If these sentences were not connected, how could anyone comprehend that the second sentence was far more devastating than the first? The connection of these sentences was like a horrible automobile crash—two things that should never have come together, but did.

When Cindy and Sungae returned from the Commons, the classroom door was shut. "Why? Are we late already?" Sungae asked. The hallway was empty. Through the thin rectangular window she could only see the front of the room, and something written on the board, which she could not read. Kristina obscured her view, standing off to the right, her arms folded across her chest in the pose she adopted when the students did in-class writing.

"Maybe it was the shorter recess today," Cindy whispered.

Sungae pushed open the door. Why hadn't anyone said the break would be short? She didn't look at Kristina, just barreled into the room as if pushing her way through a market and sat down at her desk. Suddenly they were all standing, yelling "Surprise!" and Cindy was laughing, saying, "You weren't supposed to sit down!"

"Why?" Sungae asked, "What are you doing? Give me heart attack!"

"We didn't mean to startle you," Kristina said. Her desk was covered with a paper tablecloth, bottles of soda, popcorn, bags of potato chips, and M&M's in plastic cups. Taped to the blackboards was a Xerox copy of Sungae's invitation, blown up, and the words, *Congratulations, Sungae!* Streamers were looped around desks and chair backs, the coat rack, and the windows. And on Kristina's desk was a white sheet cake, decorated to look like a framed painting.

Sungae glanced at Kristina quizzically, then at the sign over the blackboard closest to the door: *No Food in Classrooms.* She grinned. "You break the rules?" she asked. "Not so bad."

"Always the exception," Cindy teased.

"Except the comma splicing!" Ahmad said.

"Comma splice." Sungae swiveled in her seat to face him. They were all standing up and began to clap when she turned around. Ba, Farshad, Shin-pin, Keyuri, Daisuke, the new boy, Nina, On-Aree. Ahmad stepped forward, head down, shy. He held a Garfield card, which was as big as a poster.

"We are very sorry about the situation. This card, it is not large enough."

"Why?" Sungae glanced at Cindy. "What's he talking about?"

Everyone laughed.

"No, no, it is the serious situation. We search everywhere, all over the mall to find the card big enough to match the paintings."

"You being a wise guy, Ahmad?"

"Why does littlest woman paint biggest pictures?" Ba teased.

More laughter, which she felt in her eyes, stinging them and making her cry. Keyuri began cutting the cake. Shin-pin poured Cokes into the plastic cups. They toasted her. "Why? Why you doing this?" Sungae kept asking, but she was smiling, her eyes filled with tears. She glanced away for a moment, outside. It was so bright out there. Students on the quad were in shorts and T-shirts. The windows were open. Her entire life felt like a surprise party: the art show, Keehwan making the frames for the paintings about Chongmin, and all these friends.

When she turned back to the classroom, Cindy was kneeling before her with a bouquet of flowers. Chrysanthemums. Cindy put her palms on the floor and bent forward, her head bowed to the ground. "No—"

Sungae felt her breath catch in her throat. No one had ever performed the special bow, *sae bae,* for her. Korean children did this for their parents and for their ancestors on special occasions. Chongmin would have done it for her on New Year's Day. "This?" Sungae whispered. "*This* was your presentation?"

"*Ye,*" Cindy answered. She spoke in Korean, eyes lowered, her head bowed thirty degrees. "We, your family in America, we are honored to know the beautiful artist, *hwa-ga.*"

Farshad handed her a box wrapped in pale blue paper.

"We all chipped into it!" Ahmad said.

"Chipped *in,*" Kristina laughed.

Inside was a pair of earrings. One was a silver paintbrush, the other a pallet. Sungae was laughing and crying all at once, a single word, *Why?* falling through her tears, asking a thousand questions.

Chapter Forty-four

He cycled thirty-six miles one afternoon, part of it through Richmond National Battlefield Park, as if this would help him to understand what happens *after* a battle ends. He rode into a headwind, his eyes focused on the thin asphalt road, which looped along an empty field. Bronze plaques were set into the ground, and there was a single cannon on a small hill. Across the street from the park were a row of aluminum-sided ranch houses with manicured lawns. A gray-haired woman washed her car in the driveway. Is this what they had fought for all those years ago, the nineteen-year-old boys who had died? For this? Will wondered. The right to mortgage payments, two cars, swing sets in the backyard? Is this what he was fighting for?

He shifted to the smaller ring, a bigger gear, and coasted now, sweat running along the side of his face and stinging his eyes. By the time he finished, he'd have traces of dry salt like talcum powder along his neck. Once, when he met Anne after a ride, she had touched her tongue to his throat to taste him.

He glanced back at the cannon. The neighborhood kids probably played on it now, pretending it was a horse or a spaceship. You give your cause a name, he thought, something huge and abstract, like *freedom,* or *love,* and this, *this,* was all it turned out to be. He wanted there to be more. A better reason for people to have died, a better reason for him to have hurt, *twice,* the woman he had spent half of his life with, a better reason not to be living in the same house with his daughter, to *never* again live in the same house with her. He would become a week-end father, a Sunday dad. Oh, he'd see her in the afternoons before Kayla came home, but they'd both decided she would have full custody. They didn't want their daughter traveling between two homes, two sets of rules, two different lives. Will, especially, knew that even this carried a cost.

Sometimes it seemed that if he cycled enough, he could ride it out of himself—the desire, the longing, the regret, and the guilt. Even on the hills, he used the larger gears, forcing himself to work harder. He felt like he was clutching air and pulling himself up with his arms, which ached after some rides more than his legs did. Now that the weather was nice, he rode to and from work—twenty-one miles each way. Hours needing to be filled with something, anything—like the buckets of sand his dad used to keep in the back of his pickup during the winter. He needed the weight, the ballast.

He thought of Anne more than ever. And it wasn't the grand abstraction he was after—happiness, joy, passion, love. It was just her, with her crumbs in bed and her gourmet salads, her that he wanted, with that godawful chicken Velveeta she'd cooked once, or Rice-a-Roni, which he kept trying to convince her wasn't really rice. Her, with her dog-eared, coffee-stained, spine-broken books always on the floor by the bed. And her eyes, green or gray depending on her mood and whether they'd made love.

He crossed the train tracks, which were orange in the afternoon light. He concentrated now, swerving to avoid potholes, a crushed soda can, and loose gravel where the road shifted down and ran along the James. A few years ago an acquaintance of his had hit a pothole and was bucked headfirst off his bike as if it were a bull. He was a quadriplegic now. Will thought of him every time he cycled.

He swerved left to avoid some broken glass, then leaned forward, resting his gloved hand on the front tire, making sure there were no fragments. Then the back tire. He grabbed the water bottle from its cage, took a swallow, and put it back. There was a strong crosswind now, which he loved. It was like sailing, with the bike tilted sideways thirty degrees, the wind pushing at him and holding him up. He saw Anne sprawled on her stomach on the floor, playing go fish with Brooke on Thanksgiving night, laughing and rolling over to tell him, "Your daughter is a cardsharp, Will!" All he needed to do was check out those dark greens, and everything she wasn't saying was there. She entered, exited conversations with her eyes as people did rooms. Grand entrances with just a look.

He tried to imagine what those eyes would register if he were to appear outside her apartment—10 West Madison Street, #3. Her work—5109 Roland Avenue. Addresses he knew by heart. Places that had become familiar in his mind. He pictured her apartment: the brightness and small surprises of colors. In the bathroom would be her towels, yellow and white, rolled into tubes and stacked liked loaves of bread in a huge wicker basket. The origami bird mobile from a Japanese student near a window, the birds dipping and soaring. The dishes she'd never unpacked when she lived with him, bright yellow coffee mugs and orange dessert plates. On the coffee table would be one of the turquoise place mats, a white bowl filled with red apples. Her bookshelves would be partially organized: fiction, teaching texts, poetry, biography, reference. There'd be more books on the windowsill, the kitchen table, and the bed.

He'd bought a city map of Baltimore and traveled with his index finger the route he imagined she would follow to work. She would pass the art museum, perhaps stopping there some afternoons to sit in the café and grade papers. The Inner Harbor was only a mile from where she lived, and he pictured her walking there as the weather grew warmer, people-watching. She used to play a game when they went out to eat or sat in the Commons or walked to the yogurt shop up in Carytown. She'd see a couple and try to guess how long they'd been together. Were they wearing rings? Did they touch? How were they dressed? Who paid for the meal?

"Did you know that the longer people are together, the less eye contact they have?" she had told him once. And another time, "Look at us, leaning forward, practically cooing at each other."

"I do not coo!" he protested.

"You coo great," she would say. "I love it when you coo."

"Do you think people can tell that we're in love, that I adore you?"

"My God, Will, it's like we're under a spotlight."

The main branch of the city library was only three blocks south of her street. He pictured her coming home with a stack of books cradled like a sleeping child in her arms. He would surprise her by offering to help. "Can I carry your books?" What would her eyes say? This was the part he couldn't see.

Leaving his own office for the day or coasting by the apartment he'd shared with her, the burned circle of wood on the front of the door a reminder of all that had gone wrong, he tried to reverse the situation in his head and picture her waiting for him. Surprising him. Three months ago, had she done this, unexpectedly showing up in the parking lot by his car after work or sitting on the steps of their apartment when he came home one afternoon, would he have been glad? He tried to tell himself no. Not then. Not when he had just moved home, not when the three of them were eating dinner together at night and Kayla was making an effort to get home earlier so that he could ride, something she had never done before. No, not when he was determined to make it work, when he and Kayla were still talking in the kitchen after her training runs, remembering all the things they'd done well together. And not when he and Kayla were making love again—tentatively, carefully. They were like thin, crystal wineglasses that might shatter if they knocked against each other too roughly. They touched through layers of protective padding: her distrust and fear, anger and wariness. His guilt, numbness, and grief over losing Anne. No, not then. If Anne had shown up, surprising him, he would have been guarded, distant, and unwilling to hurt Kayla. And yet his heart would have been ricocheting against his ribs. *She still loves you. She came back.* He'd willed it a hundred times. *Let her be out there,* he'd pray as he stood in his locked office at the end of the day, changing into his cycling shorts and jersey. *Let me see her car.* He'd ridden by Lois's and the university. He'd sent her silent messages, *I love you,* believing in telepathy.

He imagined finding a café near her home. Surely she would go there to grade, and he would watch her from behind a newspaper, wait for her to glance up. But what if she wasn't alone? Or what if she was and kept watching the door as she used to for him, glancing up every time it opened, something tight and anxious around her eyes? Those minutes like the steel tracks of a roller coaster, she told him once—that steady horrible uphill climb. And then, he would walk in, she said, his eyes on hers, and it was that exhilarating plummet down, then abrupt leveling out. What if he saw that, and it wasn't him she waited for? Or even if it was just a friend, another woman, a colleague, and she was laughing, happy. Would he have the guts to intrude on them? Would he have the right?

He finally decided to drive to Baltimore, but to phone her first and ask her to meet him. He knew she deserved that much—the chance to say no. It was less dramatic, more fair, and more real. And this is what he wanted with Anne. Real.

Pacing about the hotel room, three blocks from where she lived, he tried to prepare himself. He told himself that if Anne didn't answer the phone or if she was out, it didn't necessarily mean a date. It could be work or coffee with a friend. She might be out getting dinner. He played with her earring, the one he'd found in the couch cushions after she left, and caressed it between his thumb and index finger like a good luck charm. And then he was dialing the phone and counting the rings.

His heart stopped when the phone picked up: "Hi, this is four-one-zero . . . ," then began beating again, plodding forward like a disheartened soldier when he realized it was her machine. "I'm not home right now, but if you'll leave a message . . ."

It doesn't mean anything, he told himself. *Just talk to her.* But his voice was uneven and dull. "Hi," he said. "It's me, Anne. It's Will," as if she might not recognize his voice. He waited a moment, no longer sure of what to say. And then he said, "I love you," because what else was there? Never had those words seemed so insignificant. How could she understand what they meant? How could his feelings possibly be conveyed in those eight letters? They were not substantial enough, those two pronouns and a verb.

And then he heard her pick up. "Hold on, Will, I'm here. This stupid machine. I don't know how to turn it off."

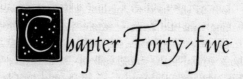

Chapter Forty-five

The answering machine was in the bedroom, and when she heard
Will's voice she didn't move from the table where she had been
eating dinner and reading. A rocket of happiness launched within her,
then exploded into fear. Was Brooke okay? Was he? Ethan? Either
way, he was phoning her. *It's me, Anne. It's Will.* As if he needed to
identify himself. As if she didn't know his voice better than her own.

Slowly, holding her breath, she set down her fork and moved quietly
to stand in the bedroom doorway. She had always loved his voice.
There had been days when she spoke to him on the phone ten or fifteen times. *I've only got a second. I just wanted to say hi.*

Grief ran through her. *Why are you doing this?* she thought. *Why
now, why, when I'm finally okay, when there are entire hours where I
don't think about you?* But already she was crossing the room, desperate to get to the phone before he hung up.

"Thank you," he said. "I wasn't sure if you'd even want to speak to
me." She heard relief in his voice, and hesitation. "Thank you" not
"Thanks."

"I'm not sure I do want to talk to you," she said, but her tone was
gentle. She moved from the bed to the window. The city was streaked
with early evening sunlight, and the brick buildings were more orange

than red. Cars raced past. She moved back to the closet and was surprised by her face in the mirror on the door and the happiness suffusing her eyes. Her hair was still in a ponytail from work, though she'd changed into a faded purple T-shirt and jeans. When she saw herself in the mirror, she didn't see a divorced woman or an adulteress or someone who had lost her job or had three miscarriages. She still saw herself at seventeen or twenty-two, full of hope and energy and plans. Sometimes she didn't understand how she had ended up here, renting a barely furnished apartment in a strange city, eating dinner alone with no husband or children.

She walked back to the window. *Are you still with Kayla?* she wondered. *What happened? How did you get my number?* It was unlisted. She'd asked Lois not to give it to him. *How long have you had it? Why, why, didn't you call before?*

"Can I see you?" Will asked. "I'm in Baltimore, at the Days Inn."

She paused midstep at the window and felt as if her heart were detaching itself from her chest. The last bit of sunlight flashed on storefront windows. It was as if he were calling from another continent, and there was a time delay before the words would register. The Days Inn was only three blocks away, across the street from the library. He was that close.

"Anne?"

"I don't know what to say."

"How about yes?"

Yes. She thought of all the times she had said that word to him. Each yes had been like another link in a colorful paper chain. *Yes, I'd love to have coffee with you, and Yes, Thursday would be great, and Yes, we'll have to do this again, it was fun, and Yes, I'll meet you at the Angel's Grotto Bar, I'll lie to my husband, you will lie to your wife, because Yes, I want to make love to you, even though it's wrong, even though Carter doesn't deserve this, and Yes, I love you Will Sullivan, Yes I want to live with you, sleep next to you, eat pizza in bed with you, and Yes, it's worth all the pain and all the damage.* She pictured him standing in the doorway of her office with his offering of coffee: "I don't know what I'm doing here, Anne." She saw him crossing the finish line in one of his bike races, that moment when he took his hands from the handle bars and sat up, head tilted back as he gulped water, spilling it on his chin and neck. Gliding down the hill, grinning at her as he passed. *Yes.*

"It's not that simple, Will."

No matter how much she loved him, no matter how much she ached to see him, she could no longer think of him—of them—without thinking of all the affairs he'd had before, of how quickly he'd run back to Kayla. How much clearer did it need to be? Will wanted what he couldn't have.

She closed her eyes and sat on the edge of the bed, facing the window. The fading light warmed her face. How could Will comprehend what his confession had done to her? The knowledge was like snow, blanketing the landscape of her memories. Every time she recalled a good moment with him—that afternoon at Pocahontas State Park, the early evening drives, or the winter nights of racing across town to meet him for five or ten minutes at the end of the day, she would wonder if he'd once done this with other women. While she and Carter were visiting infertility specialists or sitting on the deck picking out baby names, had Will been meeting some other woman after work in the parking lot of the 7-Eleven or the Dunkin' Donuts? And had she, that other woman, left work early or lied to her husband, perhaps, to sit in his car, holding his hand and asking about his day? Had Will baked her cookies or pizza and urged her to eat, worrying, as he sometimes had with Annie, that she was too thin? While Annie was at home reading in bed with Carter, had some other woman sat in Byrd Park and watched Will cycle? Had she made love to him in the Holiday Inn, maybe in the same room where he would one day make love to Annie? Perhaps he'd even said it before to *her,* whoever she was: *I want to make love to you in every room.* Had he also told *her* that she was beautiful? And had she believed him, and been willing to risk her marriage and her job for him? *You have the most gorgeous eyes. Don't ever cut your hair.*

Even now, Annie felt humiliated. Not once in their three years together had she ever asked Will, "Why didn't you have an affair before if you were unhappy all these years? What was so different about the autumn you met me?" No. She'd assumed that *she* was the difference, that he'd never had an affair because he hadn't ever met anyone worth the risk. She had assumed that she was the exception in Will's life, not simply a part of a pattern.

"You shouldn't have come," she said quietly. "I don't want to see you, Will." For a second, it was almost true. *You've done this to me,* she wanted to tell him. *I wasn't like this before, this unforgiving.*

"I'm not trying to mess things up for you—"

You already have, she protested silently, tears springing to her eyes. She stared at a woman in a navy suit standing at the pay phone on the corner. Before Will, Annie had never noticed how many pay phones there were. After Will, she knew where they were—on what corners in Richmond, in which restaurants, in the Safeway, and the Daily Grind. Until she began her affair with Will, she'd never noticed the one in front of the post office or near the tennis courts at Byrd Park. Before Will, other than her first year of teaching, when she used to hide in the phone booth in the library basement and call Carter to tell him how her classes had gone, she had used a pay phone maybe a dozen times in her life, mostly in connection to emergencies. Running out of gas or getting lost. She understood now, though, that having an affair is a kind of emergency, too—a sudden loss of direction. How else could she have wrecked so much for so little? For something he could toss away, and for something she would eventually get over? Sometimes she hated Will even for this—the knowledge that she would be okay again. It seemed a terrible thing to learn. If the loss of love didn't devastate a person, what possibly could?

"There's a lot I need to say to you, Anne. I'd like to say it in person."

"There's no point," she said. And there wasn't. She no longer trusted him.

"You can't even hear me out?"

"No."

"That's it? No?" He sounded angry. *Good,* she thought. *It will be easier this way.*

"Where were you these last four months when I had things I needed to say?" Her voice jerked, as something wrenched inside her. He had gone back to Kayla. How long after Annie moved out? A month, two at most? She imagined them discussing the affair the way survivors of an accident might talk about the tragedy. Sleeping in the same bed again. Making love. Had he put his wedding band back on? She closed her eyes and shook her head. She was crying.

"Where was *I*?" he asked. "*I* didn't disappear, Anne. *I* didn't move to another city without so much as a word." He paused. "I'm not ignoring the fact that I let you down," he said softly. "But it goes both ways."

"Why did you call?" Her fingers ached from clenching the receiver. The daylight was a dull pink on the walls now. She had planned a nice night for herself, had rented a movie and made a real dinner. She had been trying to get back into the habit of cooking again instead of eating bagel sandwiches or granola and raisins. Dieting books suggested arranging your food on a pretty plate and setting the table with a place mat, a linen napkin, even a candle. Pour your mineral water into a long-stemmed glass. She wasn't on a diet, of course, but getting over love was the same thing in the end, wasn't it? It was about learning to do with less, and letting go of desire.

"I've wanted to phone you for weeks, but I've been afraid that you'd hang up or that you'd tell me you were happy without me. But I was even more afraid that if I didn't call you, I'd regret it for the rest of my life. And I know, *I know* it sounds like a stupid line from a movie, but I mean it, Anne."

She held the receiver away from her mouth so he wouldn't hear her cry. She'd imagined variations of this conversation so many times these past few months, but had never foreseen this: that the words couldn't possibly undo the damage they had done to each other and to themselves.

". . . You were, you *are,* the best thing that ever happened to me, Anne, and I treated you horribly."

She swallowed hard. "I appreciate your saying that, Will." *Will.* His name the future tense. I *will* love, I *will* laugh, I *will* shop, eat, cry, sleep. I *will* forget you. I *will* say good-bye.

He was silent. The formality of *I appreciate* had stung him. *What did you expect?* she wanted to shout at him. Outside, the phone booth was empty. Annie hadn't seen the woman leave. Two men climbed the steps from the basement-level Indian restaurant, laughing.

"Will you just do one thing for me?" he said finally.

Why? she wanted to say. *No. How dare you even ask?* Instead, she nodded wearily, thinking as she always had when he'd asked something of her, *of course*.

"Will you go to Sarah—Sungae's show before it closes?"

"I got an invitation, Will. I don't need one from you. And why does it matter? You don't even know Sungae." She didn't want him interfering in her life. This was what Carter had done.

"Actually I do know her, Anne. She's worked for Kayla for years. They're friends, I guess. I didn't make the connection. She goes by the name Sarah usually."

A bike messenger wove through the traffic below, the reflector lights on his wheels flashing in the darkness. Annie followed him with her eyes. It made sense now, she thought. Sungae's evaluation, her fury the last month of class. *You don't care about position of things.* "Kayla told her about me? She could have cost me my job, Will. But I suppose you overlooked that when you moved back in, didn't you?"

"She blurted it out one day, Anne. It wasn't intentional."

Her throat tightened. Even now, he was defending Kayla.

"Look, I'm not trying to anger you, Anne. It's just that I went to the show with Kayla, and something about it—I realized that it was you I wanted in my life."

"For how long?" she asked, closing her eyes against the tears. She'd finally stopped feeling sick every time she heard a song by the Cranberries, and her heart didn't plummet anymore when she came home and saw there was no letter from him in the mail. She had gone to a movie alone for the first time in her life and learned to put oil in the car. "Please go home, Will. Work it out with Kayla, be with Brooke. It's what you want."

He didn't answer, and for a moment she panicked, afraid she'd gone too far and that he would hang up. *What is the balance between wanting to hurt someone and wanting to love him?*

Outside, the sun had set, though the street was bright with street-lamps and tiny votive candles from the bistro tables in front of the Afghan restaurant. The Peabody Conservatory of Music was only a block away, and strains of someone practicing a violin curled the air into ribbons. Couples were seated at the tables, laughing and drinking cappuccinos and lattes from soup-bowl-size mugs. Coldness seeped into her arms and chest and lungs.

"I love *you*." His voice was sad. "Not Kayla."

"I've heard that before," she said. When he didn't answer, she asked, "What do you think Sungae's show is going to change, Will?" Her voice was soft now. "What do you think is going to happen?" His answer didn't matter. She simply wanted to listen to his voice for a few more minutes before she hung up.

She had received Sungae's letter a few days ago. Annie couldn't completely understand all of the sentences, but the idea that stories were like children saddened her, not only because it was true, but because it seemed that Annie's own story with Will was another miscarriage.

She wrote back to Sungae that she was sorry she couldn't see her show, but that the next time she was in Richmond, she'd like to visit and maybe see Sungae's paintings. She told Sungae about her article and her ideas for the title. "All these years I've been teaching," Annie wrote, "and I never understood until you were in my class, Sungae, that every language is a language of good-bye, because words really are stories and the only way to tell them is to let them go."

On the phone, Will was still talking. "I'm not even certain I understand what all of the paintings are about or what they mean," he was saying, "but looking at them, I was overwhelmed with how much I missed and needed you, and how empty my life is. . . ."

His words were like stars, all the more beautiful from a distance. ". . . my life without you. And I just thought if you went . . ."

"I can't," she said abruptly.

"Why not?"

"I need to hang up now."

"Please, Anne—"

But she set the receiver down, loving and hating him all over again.

She lay on the bed and hugged a pillow to her chest, listening to the sound of the city below. She was no longer crying, but felt numb and empty inside. *This is something else you've taught me,* she thought. *How to walk away from love.*

After a few minutes, the phone started to ring. She turned off the answering machine when she heard his voice: "Sweetie, can you pick up—?" Still, he continued to call. Twenty rings. Thirty-seven. Fifteen. Twenty-five. She thought of him in his hotel room, alone. She wondered if he'd eaten and suspected he hadn't. He had probably hoped they'd get a bite together.

He kept phoning until sometime after midnight. She pulled the phone up on the bed beside her and fell in and out of sleep. The ringing was like a strangely soothing lullaby, or a distant clanging buoy heard through fog. He rang once at two–forty-four. The red numbers on the clock glowed in her dark room. He called again at four-sixteen, and six, six-fifteen, six-thirty.

When she finally picked up, she heard him scrambling on the other end, groggy, half asleep. His voice was scratchy. She smiled, and tears burned her eyes. He hadn't had his coffee yet. "I was about to give up," he said. "Do you want me to hate you, Anne? Is that it?"

"No."

"Do you hate me?"

She closed her eyes. "I wish I could," she choked.

"Please think about going to Sungae's show. If you don't want to see me after that, I'll let you be." He sounded exhausted.

She thought of her students, how they used to laugh when she taught them idioms: "It's raining cats and dogs." "You're in hot water." "I've got cold feet." She knew that her love for Will was a similar kind of idiom because it made no sense.

Quietly, she told him, "I'll take the train to Richmond on Saturday. I'll go to the show, but that's all I can promise."

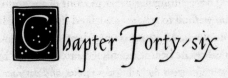

Chapter Forty-six

"Can I drive you back?" Will asked.

"No." Annie was staring out the window, which was streaked with midafternoon sunlight.

"Why not?"

"I don't want to be alone with you for that long." Two and a half hours. What if after fifteen minutes they realized that nothing had changed? She knew that if they rewound their affair back to the night they had first met and searched for the place where they might splice in an alternative plot, a different ending, they would not find it. She would do nothing differently, and neither would he.

She glanced down as she spoke. He wanted to tug gently on her ponytail, whisper, "Hey," and have her turn to him. He wanted to cup his hand to her chin and lift her face to his. *Look at me.* For three hours, ever since she stepped off the train, she had refused to meet his eyes. "Sometimes when you look at me, it's as if we're making love," she had told him once. "You enter me with your eyes."

She was wearing the green sweater she'd worn the first night he met her, and he knew she'd worn it for him. "You dolled," he said when she stepped off the train and she smiled easily and nodded and he loved her for not being coy.

"You, too," she said. He'd chosen her favorite shirt; she'd always told him it made his eyes look bluer.

But now they were sitting in his car in front of the train station and all the things he wanted to tell her remained unspoken. He wanted to tell her how Brooke had a crush on her dentist and she was only six, and God, how would he bear it when she started dating? *You'll have to shoot me with tranquilizers,* he wanted to joke, *and distract me from interrogating her dates like a KGB officer. Asking for the seasons,* he thought. *Will we be together then? When Brooke is sixteen and I'm fifty-two and you're forty-three?* He wanted to tell her that the bike races at Byrd Park had started, but he didn't have the heart for racing, not without her there, and that, no matter how many miles he rode, he felt old for the first time in his life. But he'd said none of this. Instead, they spoke like strangers at a school reunion, connected by a past they didn't want to talk about.

He thought of that night they'd run into each other in the Safeway— only the second time he'd ever spoken to her—of how he drove her to her car in the rain and hadn't wanted her to leave. They'd driven in circles then, talking and laughing like two old friends. He wished it were raining now. "Talk to me, Anne," he said. "What's wrong?"

"Nothing, I just—" She shook her head. "I don't know what you want, Will. I don't know what you expect from me." She sighed, laid her head back against the seat, and closed her eyes. "I guess I don't know what I expect from myself, either."

"Let me drive you home," he said. "It'll give us a chance to talk."

"That's what I'm afraid of."

"Why?"

She smiled softly, her eyes still closed. "Because you'll say all the right things—you always do—"

"And that's a problem?"

She opened her eyes and stared at the hollow beneath his Adam's apple. "You'll make me laugh," she said. "You'll probably put on a Cranberries CD."

"I promise." He smiled, but still she wouldn't look at him. "Scout's honor. No Cranberries."

But she turned abruptly away and crossed her arms over her chest defensively. *Your promises are empty,* she thought.

He sat back against his seat, one arm draped over the steering wheel. "Why don't you just say it, Anne?" His voice was edged with anger.

She regarded him coldly. Oh, but not *him,* of course, not his eyes—the side of his jaw, maybe, or his chin. Why had she come if she couldn't bear to look at him?

"I don't trust you, Will, and I don't know that I can again, or if I even want to."

"I'm not asking you to trust me. I'm asking for a chance." He slapped the visor down against the glare of the sun. "What is it that you're waiting for me to say? What are the magic words that I obviously haven't spoken?"

"Why are you yelling?" she demanded. "I didn't lie *to you* for over two years. I didn't hop in my ex's bed the first time we had an argument."

"No, you just disappeared! The one thing in my life that I was afraid of was that I would lose someone else I loved. We hurt *each other,* Anne. This is not all my doing." He paused. "Look, if you want an apology, I'll give you one. I will tell you I'm sorry every day of my life." His voice broke. "What more can I do? Name it," he pleaded. "And I will try."

"That's exactly what I said to you after we found out about Carter, and you basically told me there was nothing I could do. Why should this be different?"

"Come on, Anne. Haven't we punished each other enough?"

"What if it happens again, Will?"

"You said Carter was doing better."

"And you told me that there weren't any guarantees." She stared past him, her eyes aching in the midafternoon brightness. From behind a copse of trees, a flock of geese lifted up and flew overhead. One of her students who hunted told her that sometimes when they shot one goose in a pair, the other would turn back and fly into the gunshots to be with his mate. She wanted to badly to believe in Will, and to trust him again, but at what cost?

"There are all these things going through my head right now," he said. "I want to promise you everything: that I will never *ever* let you go again, that I will never lie to you—" He stopped. "But I can't because I think of the lie I told you that night in the Angel's Grotto about—" he glanced at her, "about the other women, and all I can think is that I'd do the exact same thing again, knowing everything I do right now—if it was a choice between the truth and not having had the last three years with you."

"Then you're selfish." Her voice was thick. She felt rather than saw him turn away to stare out his window, his fingers gripped tight around the steering wheel. She thought of Sungae's *Adjectives,* her favorite of all the paintings. It was fifteen different shades of white.

An Amtrak train pulled behind the station and she wondered if it was hers. Why was she doing this? She'd chosen to come here; she had dressed for him. She loved him. All the more for saying that given a second chance, he would do the exact same thing. She would have wanted him to. She couldn't even begin to imagine who she would be without having had him in her life. "Will?"

He turned to face her, his eyes bright with tears. "What?"

"I'm afraid to love you again. I don't want to start hoping that this time things will be different—"

"But what if they are?"

"What if they aren't?"

She looked at him then. Those gorgeous eyes, those gorgeous *sad* eyes, and he thought of that first night at dinner, how she had rolled her eyes dramatically as she took a bite of dessert. Or that night at the Angel's Grotto, when her eyes were scared and unsure. The first time he entered her, that afternoon at the Holiday Inn, she never closed her eyes, but stared into his so intensely that *he'd* had to turn away and concentrate on the faux wood on the headboard, the ugly bedspread to keep himself from coming. Her eyes were sexual and sensual, and he'd never had anyone watch him as she had. He'd never felt so caressed by someone's gaze.

"I've missed your eyes," he said.

She glanced down.

"Look, can we just get a cup of coffee somewhere? A late lunch? Early dinner? I promise, I'll put you on the next train out of here." He lowered his voice. "We could even get a pizza."

She smiled reluctantly. "Don't do that."

"What?"

"That. Try to bribe me."

"Is it working?"

Her eyes filled. "Of course it is."

"I love when you smile," he said.

She stared down at her hands. "How do you know that you're not coming to me for the wrong reasons?"

"Look at me."

She did.

"Is loving you the wrong reason, Anne? Because that's why I'm here."

"But how can you be sure? Maybe you just want what you can't have, Will. Maybe you're afraid."

"Of *what*?"

"That Kayla was right about your being incapable of love."

He leaned his head back against the seat. "Is that what you think?"

"I'm not trying to hurt you, Will. I wish more than anything that I could just forget all that's happened and go back to Baltimore with you and go out for dinner and—" she closed her eyes, and when she spoke, her voice was a whisper, "and make love with you . . ."

"But I'm not asking for all of that, Anne. I know you aren't ready. I know that it'll take time for us to work things out. I just want us to talk."

"I can't."

"Fine, then. I'll walk you to your train—" He turned off the ignition and started to open his door.

"Don't you think you need to be alone for a while, Will?"

"It doesn't look like I have much choice," he said coldly.

"You can always have another affair—"

He turned to her, furious. "Wait just a minute—"

"No, you wait!" she cried. "You have never been alone! I'm not even sure you've ever been faithful to anyone! You have always, *always* had a backup—"

"You are so wrong," he said. Abruptly, he turned away from her, his face hard, a tiny muscle clenching and unclenching near his jaw. She stared into the sunshine and at the people walking into the station—a couple wearing backpacks and holding hands, a single man in a baseball cap who reminded her of Carter.

"Would it be so awful if I was right?" she asked quietly.

"Yeah, it would."

"Why?"

"*Why?* You're telling me that I have never loved anyone, including you, and that I've basically just used women as some kind of *backup plan*?"

"I don't think you've just used women, Will." She touched his sleeve. "I *know* you didn't use me. I know you tried."

"Well, you don't get A's for effort, do you?" He turned the ignition back on and reached to turn up the air conditioner. "Twenty-four years, Anne. You'd think I would have learned by now." He turned to her, his eyes brimming. "I really thought I had with you. After that night in the Holiday Inn . . ."

"I know," Annie said gently. "But maybe it's not possible to really love someone until you deal with the fact that you never told your mom how much you loved her. Maybe it's not enough just to grieve. It just seems like you keep saying those words again and again and again, hoping that someone will say them back in such a way that this emptiness in you will disappear."

You hand out those words like they're lollipops at the doctor's office, Kayla had told him. *They don't make the hurt go away.*

He was still leaning back, eyes closed, his breathing heavy, as if he'd run a race. "How do you know all of this?" he said sadly. She watched the rise and fall of his chest. Tears streamed from his eyes. "I don't want to lose you."

"I'm not going anywhere."

"Except to Baltimore."

She nodded. "You realize that once you don't feel so empty, you might not need me."

"I'll still want you."

She nodded again. "Will you call me in a couple of weeks and let me know how you are?"

"Do I have to wait that long?"

She started to answer, but he placed his palm lightly over her mouth. "Don't," he said. "It's okay. I know I've got a lot to take care of, and I will. I want you to be able to trust me again, Anne." He sighed wearily. The afternoon seemed too huge, too empty. "I know I need to set up a real home for myself, which I've never done, and I need to mourn the end of my marriage and I probably need to drive up to Vermont and talk to my dad about a lot of this." He smiled weakly at her, the smile she had always loved. "And I need to stop talking and let you catch your train, don't I?"

Chapter Forty-seven

Carter stood beneath the *Spirit of St. Louis* in the National Air and Space Museum. The huge glass-vaulted room echoed with the voices of tourists, the squeak of stroller wheels, and the rustle of maps. Behind Carter a young father crouched with his son and pointed at the 1903 Wright Flyer, constructed of wood and muslin. "This was the very first airplane," he explained, but the little boy only laughed. "Oh, Dad! It was not!"

Across the room, Annie stood in line to touch a piece of the moon, a gray lump of basaltic material four million years old. Carter caught her eye and they exchanged a smile. He gestured to the line composed mostly of kids—boys, it seemed—and shook his head at her, teasing. *Only you, Annie.* She grinned and waved him on. He turned back to the *Spirit of St. Louis,* looking at the black N-X211 painted beneath the left wing of Lindbergh's plane and at the tires no bigger than bicycle wheels. Around him was the flashing of lights as people snapped photos. August sunlight played against the glass ceiling. After all these months, it still pained and thrilled and confused him that he and Annie could do this—laugh, talk, visit museums together, and smile.

He told himself this was enough. The friendship they had stepped so hesitantly into was almost like a museum itself. They met here, in D.C., once a month now, visiting the museums, going to art exhibits, talking about books, and eating at their favorite West African restaurant in Adams Morgan. Riding the metro over, they'd tell each other that maybe they should try another place, but they never did. The last time they were there, she had mentioned that Will didn't like this kind of food and Carter had felt his stomach seize in grief. *Did you bring him here?* he had wanted to ask, but the words were stuck, lodged painfully in his chest. He still thought of it as *their* place. At the same time, though, his heart had soared to know that Will didn't like West African food. At least there remained something that Carter alone could share with Annie.

Behind him was the *Apollo 11* Command Module, which carried the first men to the moon, and the *Friendship 7* module in which John Glenn orbited the earth alone. Carter wondered what he'd thought about during all those nights, cast off into space, and imagined it was similar to how he felt, circling his own world from a distance, afraid he might never get back. He'd begun a novel, had already written the first three chapters, had started dating again, and at Dan's suggestion, had placed an ad in the personals. He had been surprised by how many intelligent and beautiful women there were who seemed to genuinely like him, who asked smart questions and who made him laugh. But it all felt wrong, he'd complained to Dan. These women were witty and fun, but to him, it felt like too much work.

Carter understood now, with Dan's help, that he and Annie hadn't become close until after her brother died in Annie's junior year and that Carter had, in some ways, become a replacement for Patrick. That was why she loved him, why she had always been terrified of losing him, and why, perhaps, she couldn't ever really be *in love* with him. Carter accepted this in his head. But every time he saw her, he wanted to ask: *Was it always like that? Always? Wasn't there ever a moment when it was just me? What about our wedding? Or all those months of trying to conceive a child? What about our first summer as a married couple? What about then? How could we not have been* in love *that summer?*

He knew Annie was back with Will again, and that every weekend, either Will took the train up to Baltimore, or she went down to Richmond. He forced himself to ask in a casual voice, "Are things okay with you guys? You think you'll move back?"

She was always vague and noncommittal, and glanced away when she answered, fiddling with her drink. "It's hard," she'd tell him. "You know how it is." She knew he was dating. "What about you?" she'd ask. Earlier, walking through the Ice Age with him in the Museum of Natural History, she had paused, looked at him directly, and said, "Are there things in your life that are better without me?"

They were standing in front of a display of extinct animals. Cold air gushed through the vents, and he saw how desperately she wanted him to tell her that yes, some things were better, but he didn't. He told her the truth: No.

Chapter Forty-eight

When she pictured their beginning, those first autumn months of living together, she saw it as a circle of orange, as if they had inhabited the insides of a lighted jack-o'-lantern. How unaware they were of the blackness surrounding them, and how naïve not to know that it was this very blackness that allowed the jack-o'-lantern to appear, in comparison, so beautifully awash with light.

Now, a year later, she set the papers she had been editing on her lap and leaned her head back against the couch. From the windowsill, two pumpkin faces glowed, one with a smile in the shape of a canoe; another with a lascivious leer, stern eyebrows. Across the room, on the kitchen table, was a small one with heart-shaped eyes. The edges were curled in and burned, as if it were weeping brown tears. Annie's favorite pumpkin was the oval-shaped face. His mouth an elaborate swirl, curlicued—spiraled eyes, ornate brows, swooping down and then up again, like wings.

"Is he laughing or crying?" she had asked when Will finally spun this one around. They'd been sitting on the floor. Three days ago. The coffee table was covered with newspaper and pencils, carving knives, a mixing bowl of pulp and seeds which they had pulled from the pumpkins' interiors.

"He's hysterical," Will said. "Crazy. Out of his mind." He lowered the lighted candle into the pumpkin's center. Flames whirled eerily from the spiraled eyes.

"He's crying now. It must be grief." Her own jack-o'-lantern was traditional, with triangle eyes and a gap-toothed mouth.

"Happiness will do that, too, won't it?" he asked.

"Make people crazy? Is that what we are? Out of our minds? Bonkers?"

"Absolutely nuts. Two sandwiches short of a picnic." When he spun the oval face back around, light traveled over the walls. "So what do you think?" Surveying the room. "Will these keep you company?"

With papers still on her lap, she reached up to turn off the lamp behind her. The entire room was flickering. She felt as if she were in a boat, on a lake of shadows and light. He was in Richmond, of course. Trick-or-treating with Brooke and Kayla. He'd called twice already—to tell her he loved her, and to make sure she was all right.

She had bought a bag of candy just in case, but she didn't really expect any children here in the city. Despite some of the signs in store windows, TRICK OR TREATERS WELCOME, she knew most of the kids who lived in the nearby apartments or public housing would go to the suburbs or to the mall a few miles north. The room smelled of burnt pumpkin and broiled lamb from the Afghan restaurant next door.

Abruptly, she flicked on the lamp again. She sensed her mood sliding, a dark wave washing higher up on the beach. She stared at the dissertation in her lap: "Physical Manifestations of Homesickness in Foreign Students." One of the studies showed that within three to five years, Americanized Russian Jews had adopted a more stooped posture. "It is as if they are caving in on themselves," the student wrote, "something hollow in their centers." If they did not become Americanized, however, and retained their culture, traditions, and language, they did not get this bowed posture. In another section of her paper, the student had written about SUDS, Sudden Unexpected Death Syndrome, a catastrophe affecting young men who had moved from their native country to live in another. They died in their sleep without apparent cause. The only consistent pattern was that their hearts weighed more than an average heart should. The Japanese called it *pokkuri,* the

Filipinos, *bangungut*. "In every instance, the deaths occur in countries where there exists no word for homesickness," the student had written, "As if the language itself were unwilling to accommodate this malady, the way some cultures once refused to acknowledge AIDS."

Annie thought of the time in class when her students all sat in a circle and used comparative and superlative forms of adjectives to describe each other. Sacide had described herself: "I am the homesickest; I am more homesick than Ba, Nina, Farshad, Ahmad, Sungae—" she glared at her husband, her eyes dark with tears. "I am more homesick than him." The lighthearted mood of the class had abruptly shattered.

"Homesickness is one of the illnesses doctors don't know how to cure," Annie said softly. "Isn't that right, Farshad?"

He had nodded. "Like asthma, it is a chronic condition. Sometimes for no reason, we remember something from our countries or our homes—" he paused. "And for a while, it hurts to breathe."

"While many doctors have proposed that the enlarged heart results from too little thiamin," the dissertation continued, "other physicians and psychiatrists suggest that the heart is swollen with despair, weighted with memories of home."

Annie got up from the couch. *Not tonight, not this dissertation,* she thought, setting her pen on the coffee table. She leaned over the pumpkins, one at a time, and blew out their candles. Like tucking children into bed. She was tired and she missed him. Her own heart felt heavy. It always would when he was with Kayla.

She did not blow out the candle in the oval-faced pumpkin, but picked it up and took it with her into the bedroom. Orange light spilled onto her arms and hands, as if it were a bowl full of punch. She thought of her students in Richmond, who would have started another semester. Ba had taken his MCATs and been accepted into medical school, Lois wrote. Sungae was still taking English classes and constantly complained about Kristina. Yukihiko was back in the program. Ahmad was thinking of switching his major to digital arts—he and Yukihiko wanted to design computer games. Shin-pin had gone back to Taiwan for the summer and decided not to return. Farshad had left the United States in early August to live in London. A third of all people who study or work in a foreign country leave early, Annie knew. First, Korkut and Sacide. Then Shin-pin, Farshad. They can't adapt, and are not prepared for the anger and the loss. It was the second stage of culture shock, and it usually occurred after four to six months. Some travel though it quickly, but others never find a way out.

She fell asleep, waking a little after one in the morning to find the room awash with light from the jack-o'-lantern. Will was sitting on the edge of the bed, taking off his shoes. "You drove all the way back tonight?" she asked. He had to work tomorrow. She hadn't expected to see him until the weekend.

"I missed you," he said.

"Are you okay?"

He nodded. "I kept thinking about last Halloween, and all night I just had this urge to be here." He stood, orange light sliding over him.

She watched as he climbed out of his jeans, then lifted his turtleneck over his head and crawled beneath the sheets. He was freezing. She lay on top of him, trying to press her warmth into his skin. "I love you," she whispered, tears scratching her throat. She kissed his neck. He hugged her tightly, then rolled her slowly onto her back. Outside there was the rumble of buses and cars. He was inside her now, watching her. The jack-o'-lanterns were grinning, *crazy in love*. The homeless woman whom Annie sometimes found sleeping against the brick wall of the parking lot out back was crazily singing "Jingle Bell Rock" as if she had gotten the seasons confused.

One of each, Annie thought, as she pulled the blankets over Will's shoulders. She began to rock with him, flames of light flickering within her. It had seemed romantic at the time to ask Will for this—a winter and spring, a summer, an autumn, but she saw now that it had also been practical, for love, like language, is not a thing, but a place—a world that you learn to inhabit slowly. And in a new love, as with a new language, there are four stages of culture shock. You must travel through each: infatuation, grief, acceptance, and joy. Language experts say it takes nearly fifteen months. At least four seasons.

Some Things That Stay
Sarah Willis

*If Brenda passes her maths test, it will definitely be a miracle.
On the scale of one to ten, I'll give it an eight. I'm going to add
them all up. When they hit a hundred, I'll believe in God. But
I'm going to deduct some points for making my mom sick. I figure if there is a god, He'll prove himself, even if I stack the
deck'*

Tamara Anderson's father is a landscape artist who quickly tires
of the scenery, so every year her family seeks out new locations
for his inspiration. But when the Andersons move to a farm-
house in Mayville, New York, in the spring of 1954, it begins to
work a strange magic on fifteen-year-old Tamara. And while
the girl-next-door tries to introduce the Anderson children to
religion, the boy-next-door is equally keen to introduce Tamara
to sex.

But then her mother is diagnosed with tuberculosis. Tamara
has to struggle with her fear of losing her and her anger at being
left in charge of two younger siblings, while her father becomes
increasingly distant, escaping into the world of his art.

**A deeply moving story, with a profound understanding of
family dynamics and adolescent anguish.**

'Convincing, memorable . . . quietly defiant'
New York Times Book Review

'A luminous, impressive debut'   *Publishers Weekly*

'Quirky and believable . . . consistently compelling'
Los Angeles Times

Remember Me
Laura Hendrie

Rose Devonic is an unorthodox, ferociously determined twenty-nine-year-old living in the tiny mountain town of Queduro, New Mexico. In winter she sleeps in a mostly abandoned motel, and in summer lives out of her car. A tragedy in Rose's past has made her an outcast who trusts nothing except her own ability to survive.

But now, after another failed love affair, Rose is returning for the winter to pick up the pieces of her life. She finds a less than warm welcome in store for her. *Remember Me* is the captivating story of Rose's battle to win the hearts and – minds of her lifelong neighbours – or at least a little respect from a town that has treated her with brutal indifference. Along the way, she comes to understand that only by facing her ghosts will she be a███████████ ultimately liberating challenges of be█████████████, and love.

'graceful, natural writing, deftly dra███████████ a compelling story. Laura Hendrie has s███████████ all of those elements, it is hard to belie██ this ██ ██ st novel. Vividly written, full of hu████ ████ ██ █. *Remember Me* is a book with heart' ███████ *USA Today*

A SELECTION OF NOVELS AVAILABLE
FROM JUDY PIATKUS (PUBLISHERS) LIMITED

THE PRICES BELOW WERE CORRECT AT THE TIME OF GOING TO PRESS. HOWEVER JUDY PIATKUS (PUBLISHERS) LIMITED RESERVE THE RIGHT TO SHOW NEW RETAIL PRICES ON COVERS WHICH MAY DIFFER FROM THOSE PREVIOUSLY ADVERTISED IN THE TEXT OR ELSEWHERE.

0 7499 3257 0	**Some Things That Stay**	*Sarah Willis*	£6.99
0 7499 3247 3	**Remember Me**	*Laura Hendrie*	£6.99
0 7499 3253 8	**Maternal Instinct**	*Caroline Leavitt*	£6.99
0 7499 3200 7	**Three Women**	*Marge Piercy*	£6.99
0 7499 3160 4	**Four Mothers**	*Shifra Horn*	£6.99

All Piatkus titles are available from:

www.piatkus.co.uk

or by contacting our sales department on

0800 454816

Free postage and packing in the UK

(on orders of two books or more)